MW00396117

The Benefactress

by Elizabeth von Arnim

Originally published in 1901.

Man bedarf der Leitung

Und der männlichen Begleitung.

Wilhelm Busch.

CHAPTER I

When Anna Estcourt was twenty-five, and had begun to wonder whether the pleasure extractable from life at all counterbalanced the bother of it, a wonderful thing happened.

She was an exceedingly pretty girl, who ought to have been enjoying herself. She had a soft, irregular face, charming eyes, dimples, a pleasant laugh, and limbs that were long and slender. Certainly she ought to have been enjoying herself. Instead, she wasted her time in that foolish pondering over the puzzles of existence, over those unanswerable whys and wherefores, which is as a rule restricted, among women, to the elderly and plain. Many and various are the motives that impel a woman so to ponder; in Anna's case the motive was nothing more exalted than the perpetual presence of a sister-in-law. The sister-in-law was rich—in itself a pleasing circumstance; but the sister-in-law was also frank, and her husband and Anna were entirely dependent on her, and her richness and her frankness combined urged her to make fatiguingly frequent allusions to the Estcourt poverty. Except for their bad taste her husband did not mind these allusions much, for he considered that he had given her a full equivalent for her money in bestowing his name on a person who had practically none: he was Sir Peter Estcourt of the Devonshire Estcourts, and she was a Dobbs of Birmingham. Besides, he was a philosopher, and philosophers never mind anything. But Anna was in a less agreeable situation. She was not a philosopher, she was thin-skinned, she had bestowed nothing and was taking everything, and she was of an independent nature; and an independent nature, where there is no money, is a great nuisance to its possessor.

When she was younger and more high-flown she sometimes talked of sweeping crossings; but her sister-in-law Susie would not hear of crossings, and dressed her beautifully, and took her out, and made her dance and dine and do as other girls did, being of opinion that a rich husband of good position was more satisfactory than crossings, and far more likely to make some return for all the expenses she had had.

At eighteen Anna was so pretty that the perfect husband seemed to be a mere question of days. What could the most desirable of men, thought Susie, considering her, want more than so bewitching a young creature? But he did not come, somehow, that man of Susie's dreams; and after a year or two, when Anna began to understand what all this dressing and dancing really meant, and after she had had offers from people she did not like, and had herself fallen in love with a youth of no means who was prudent enough to marry somebody else with money, she shrank back and grew colder, and objected more and more decidedly to Susie's strenuous private matrimonial urgings, and sometimes made remarks of a cynical nature to her admirers, who took fright at such symptoms of advancing age, and fell off considerably in numbers.

It was at this period, when she was barely twenty-two, that she spoke of crossings. Susie had seriously reproved her for not meeting the advances of an old and rich and single person with more enthusiasm, and had at the same time alluded to the number of pounds she had spent on her every year for the last three years, and the necessity for putting an end, by marrying, to all this outlay; and instead of being

sensible, and talking things over quietly, Anna had poured
out a flood of foolish sentiments about the misery of
knowing that she was expected to be nice to every man
with money, the intolerableness of the life she was leading,
and the superior attractions of crossing-sweeping as a
means of earning a livelihood.

"Why, you haven't enough money for the broom," said
Susie impatiently. "You can't sweep without a broom, you
know. I wish you were a little less silly, Anna, and a little
more grateful. Most girls would jump at the splendid
opportunity you've got now of marrying, and taking up a
position of your own. You talk a great deal of stuff about
being independent, and when you get the chance, and I do
all I can to help you, you fly into a passion and want to
sweep a crossing. Really," added Susie, twitching her
shoulder, "you might remember that it isn't all roses for me
either, trying to get some one else's daughter married."

"Of course it isn't all roses," said Anna, leaning against the
mantelpiece and looking down at her with perplexed
eyebrows. "I am very sorry for you. I wish you weren't so
anxious to get rid of me. I wish I could do something to
help you. But you know, Susie, you haven't taught me a
trade. I can't set up on my own account unless you'll give
me a last present of a broom, and let me try my luck at the
nearest crossing. The one at the end of the street is badly
kept. What do you think if I started there?" What answer
could anyone make to such folly?

By the time she was twenty-four, nearly all the girls who
had come out when she did were married, and she felt as
though she were a ghost haunting the ball-rooms of a
younger generation. Disliking this feeling, she stiffened,
and became more and more unapproachable; and it was at

this period that she invented excuses for missing most of the functions to which she was invited, and began to affect a simplicity of dress and hair arrangement that was severe. Susie's exasperation was now at its height. "I don't know why you should be bent on making the worst of yourself," she said angrily, when Anna absolutely refused to alter her hair.

"I'm tired of being frivolous," said Anna. "Have you an idea how long those waves took to do? And you know how Hilton talks. It all gets whisked up now in two minutes, and I'm spared her conversation."

"But you are quite plain," cried Susie. "You are not like the same girl. The only thing your best friend could say about you now is that you look clean."

"Well, I like to look clean," said Anna, and continued to go about the world with hair tucked neatly behind her ears; her immediate reward being an offer from a clergyman within the next fortnight.

Peter Estcourt was even more surprised than his wife that Anna had not made a good match years before. Of course she had no money, but she was a pretty girl of good family, and it ought to be easy enough for her to find a husband. He wished heartily that she might soon be happily married; for he loved her, and knew that she and Susie could never, with their best endeavours, be great friends. Besides, every woman ought to have a home of her own, and a husband and children. Whenever he thought of Anna, he thought exactly this; and when he had reached the proposition at the end he felt that he could do no more, and began to think of something else.

His marriage with Susie, a person of whom no one had ever heard, had brought out and developed stores of unsuspected philosophy in him. Before that he was quite poor, and very merry; but he loved Estcourt, and could not bear to see it falling into ruin, and he loved his small sister, who was then only ten, and wished to give her a decent education, and what is a man to do? There happened to be no rich American girls about at that time, so he married Miss Dobbs of Birmingham, and became a philosopher.

It was hard on Susie that he should become a philosopher at her expense. She did not like philosophers. She did not understand their silent ways, and their evenness of temper. After she had done all that Peter wanted in regard to the place in Devonshire, and had provided Anna with every luxury in the shape of governesses, and presented her husband with an heir to the retrieved family fortunes, she thought that she had a right to some enjoyment too, to some gratification from her position, and was surprised to find how little was forthcoming. Really no one could do more than she had done, and yet nothing was done for her. Peter fished, and read, and was with difficulty removable from Estcourt. Anna was, of course, too young to be grateful, but there she was, taking everything as a matter of course, her very unconsciousness an irritation. Susie wanted to get on in the world, and nobody helped her. She wanted to bury the Dobbs part of herself, and develop the Estcourt part; but the Dobbs part was natural, and the Estcourt superficial, and the Dobbses were one and all singularly unattractive—a race of eager, restless, wiry little men and women, anxious to get as much as they could, and keep it as long as they could, a family succeeding in gathering a good deal of money together in one place, and failing entirely in the art of making friends. Susie was the best of them, and had been the pretty one at home; yet she was not in the least a success in London. She put it down to Peter's indifference, to his slowness in introducing her to his friends. It was no more Peter's fault than it was her own. It was not her fault that she was not pretty—there never had been a beautiful Dobbs—and it was not her fault that she was so unfortunately frank, and never could and never did conceal her feverish eagerness to make desirable acquaintances, and to get into desirable sets. Until Anna came out she was invited only to the big functions to which the whole world went; and the hours she passed at them were not among the most blissful of her life. The people who were at first inclined to be kind to her for Peter's sake, dropped off when they found how her eagerness to attract the attention of some one mightier made her unable to fix her thoughts on the friendly remarks that they were taking pains to make. In society she was absent-minded, fidgety, obviously on the look-out for a chance of drawing the biggest fish into her little net; but, wealthy as she was, she was not wealthy enough in an age of millionnaires, and not once during the whole of her career was a big fish simple enough to be caught.

After a time her natural shrewdness and common sense made her perceive that her one claim to the scanty attentions she did receive was her money. Her money had bought her Peter, and a pleasant future for her children; it had converted a Dobbs into an Estcourt; it had given her everything she had that was worth anything at all. Once she had thoroughly realised this, she began to attach a tremendous importance to the mere possession of money, and grew very stingy, making difficulties about spending that grieved Peter greatly; not because he ever wanted her money now that Estcourt had been restored to its old splendour and set going again for their boy, but because meanness about money in a woman was something he could not comprehend—something repulsive, unfeminine, contrary to her nature as he had always understood it. He left off making the least suggestion about Anna's education or the household arrangements; everything that was done was done of Susie's own accord; and he spent more and more time in Devonshire, and grew more and more philosophical, and when he did talk to his wife, restricted his conversation to the language of abstract wisdom.

Now this was very hard on Susie, who had no appreciation of abstract wisdom, and who lived as lonely a life as it is possible to imagine. Peter kept out of her way. Anna was subject to prolonged fits of chilly silence. Susie used, at such times, to think regretfully of the cheerful Dobbs days, of their frank and congenial vulgarity.

When Anna was eighteen, Susie's prospects brightened for a time. Doors that had been shut ever since she married, opened before her on her appearing with such a pretty débutante under her wing, and she could enjoy the reflected glory of Anna's little triumphs. And then, without any apparent reason, Anna had altered so strangely, and had disappointed every one's expectations; never encouraging the right man, never ready to do as she was told, exasperatingly careless on all matters of vital importance, and ending by showing symptoms of freezing into something of the same philosophical state as Peter. Their mother had been German——a lady-in-waiting to one of the German princesses; and their father had met her and married her while he was secretary at the English Embassy in St. Petersburg. And Susie, who had heard of German philosophy and German stolidity, and despised them both with all her heart, concluded that the German strain was accountable for everything about Peter and Anna that was beyond her comprehension; and sometimes, when Peter was more than usually wise and unapproachable, would call him Herr Schopenhauer—which had an immediate effect of producing a silence that lasted for weeks; for not only did he like her least when she was playful, but he had, as a matter of fact, read a great deal of Schopenhauer, and was uneasily conscious that it had not been good for him.

While Peter fished, and meditated on the vanity of human wishes at Estcourt, Anna, with rare exceptions, was wherever Susie was, and Susie was wherever it was fashionable to be. For a week or two in the summer, for a day or two at Easter, they went down to Devonshire; and Anna might wander about the old house and grounds as she chose, and feel how much better she had loved it in its tumble-down state, the state she had known as a child, when her mother lived there and was happy. Everything was aggressively spruce now, indoors and out. Susie's money and Susie's taste had rubbed off all the mellowness and all the romance. Anna was glad to leave it again, and be taken to Marienbad, or any place where there was royalty, for Susie loved royalty. But what a life it was, going round year after year with Susie! London, Devonshire, Marienbad, Scotland, London again, following with patient feet wherever the unconscious royalties led, meeting the same people, listening to the same music, talking the same talk, eating the same dinners—would no one ever invent anything new to eat? The inexpressible boredom of riding up and down the Row every morning, the unutterable hours shopping and trying on clothes, the weariness of all the new pictures, and all the concerts, and all the operas, which seemed to grow less pleasing every year, as her eye and ear grew more critical. She knew at last every note of the stock operas and concerts, and every note seemed to have got on to her nerves.

And then the people they knew—the everlasting sameness of them, content to go the same dull round for ever. Driving in the Park with Susie, neither of them speaking a word, she used to watch the faces in the other carriages, nearly all faces of acquaintances, to see whether any of them looked cheerful; and it was the rarest thing to come across any expression but one of blankest boredom. Bored and cross, hardly ever speaking to the person with them, their friends drove up and down every afternoon, and she and Susie did the same, as silent and as bored as any of them. A few unusually beautiful, or unusually witty, or unusually young persons appeared to find life pleasant and looked happy, but they avoided Susie. Her set was made up of the dull and plain; and all the amusing people, and all the interesting people, turned their backs with one accord on her and it.

These were the circumstances that drove Anna to reflect on the problems of life every time she was beyond the sound of Susie's voice.

She passionately resented her position of dependence on Susie, and she passionately resented the fact that the only way to get out of it was to marry. Every time she had an offer, she first of all refused it with an energy that astonished the unhappy suitor, and then spent days and nights of agony because she had refused it, and because Susie wanted her to accept it, and because of an immense pity for Susie that had taken possession of her heart. How could Peter live so placidly at Susie's expense, and treat her with such a complete want of tenderness? Anna's love for her brother diminished considerably directly she began to understand Susie's life. It was such a pitiful little life of cringing, and pushing, and heroically smiling in the face of ill-treatment. No one cared for her in the very least. She had hundreds of acquaintances, who would eat her dinners and go away and poke fun at her, but not a single friend. Her husband lived on her and hardly spoke to her. Her boy at Eton, an amazing prig, looked down on her. Her little daughter never dreamed of obeying her. Anna herself was prevented by some stubborn spirit of fastidiousness, evidently not possessed by any of her contemporaries, from doing the only thing Susie had ever really wanted her to do—marrying, and getting herself out of the way. What if Susie were a vulgar little woman of no education and no family? That did not make it any the more glorious for the Estcourts to take all they could and ignore her existence. It was, after all, Susie who paid the bills. Anna pitied her from the bottom of her heart; such a forlorn little woman, taken out of her proper sphere, and left to shiver all alone, without a shred of love to cover and comfort her.

It was when she was away from Susie that she felt this. When she was with her, she found herself as cold and quiet and contradictory as Peter. She used, whenever she got the chance, to go to afternoon service at St. Paul's. It was the only place and time in which all the bad part of her was soothed into quiet, and the good allowed to prevail in peace. The privacy of the great place, where she never met anyone she knew, the beauty of the music, the stateliness of the service offered every day in equal perfection to any poor wretch choosing to turn his back for an hour on the perplexities of life, all helped to hush her grievances to sleep and fill her heart with tenderness for those who were not happy, and for those who did not know they were unhappy, and for those who wasted their one precious life in being wretched when they might have been happy. How little it would need, she thought (for she was young and imaginative), to turn most people's worries and sadness into joy. Such a little difference in Susie's ways and ideas would make them all so happy; such a little change in Peter's habits would make his wife's life radiant. But they all lived blindly on, each day a day of emptiness, each of those precious days, so crowded with opportunities, and possibilities, and unheeded blessings, and presently life would be behind them, and their chances gone for ever.

"The world is a dreadful place, full of unhappy people," she thought, looking out on to the world with unhappy eyes. "Each one by himself, with no one to comfort him. Each one with more than he can bear, and no one to help him. Oh, if I could, I would help and comfort everyone that is sad, or sick at heart, or sorry—oh, if I could!"

And she dreamed of all that she would do if she were Susie—rich, and free from any sort of interference—to help others, less fortunate, to be happy too. But, since she was the very reverse of rich and free, she shook off these dreams, and made numbers of good resolutions instead— resolutions bearing chiefly on her future behaviour towards Susie. And she would come out of the church filled with the sternest resolves to be ever afterwards kind and loving to her; and the very first words Susie uttered would either irritate her into speeches that made her sorry, or freeze her back into her ordinary state of cold aloofness.

If Susie had had an idea that Anna was pitying her, and making good resolutions of which she was the object at afternoon services, and that in her eyes she had come to be merely a cross which must with heroism be borne, she probably would have been indignant. Pitying people and being pitied oneself are two very different things. The first is soothing and sweet, the second is annoying, or even maddening, according to the temperament of the patient. Susie, however, never suspected that anyone could be sorry for her; and when, after a party, before they went to bed,

Anna would put her arms round her and give her a
disproportionately tender kiss, she would show her surprise
openly. "Why, what's the matter?" she would ask. "Another
mood, Anna?" For she could not know how much Anna felt
the snubs she had seen her receive. How should she? She
was so used to them that she hardly noticed them herself.

It was when Anna was twenty-five, and much vexed in
body by efforts to be and to do as Susie wished, and in soul
by those unanswerable questions as to the why and
wherefore of the aimless, useless existence she was
leading, that the wonderful thing happened that changed
her whole life.

CHAPTER II

There was a German relation of Anna's, her mother's
brother, known to Susie as Uncle Joachim. He had been
twice to England; once during his sister's life, when Anna
was little, and Peter was unmarried, and they were all poor
and happy together at Estcourt; and once after Susie's
introduction into the family, just at that period when Anna
was beginning to stiffen and put her hair behind her ears.

Susie knew all about him, having inquired with her usual
frankness on first hearing of his existence whether he
would be likely to leave Anna anything on his death; and
upon being informed that he had a family of sons, and large

estates and little money, looked upon it as a great hardship to be obliged to have him in her London house. She objected to all Germans, and thought this particular one a dreadful old man, and never wearied of making humorous comments on his clothes and the oddness of his manners at meals. She was vexed that he should be with them in Hill Street, and refused to give dinners while he was there. She also asked him several times if he would not enjoy a stay at Estcourt, and said that the country was now at its best, and the primroses were in full beauty.

"I want not primroses," said Uncle Joachim, who seldom spoke at length; "I live in the country. I will now see London."

So he went about diligently to all the museums and picture-galleries, sometimes alone and sometimes with Anna, who neglected her social duties more than ever in order to be with him, for she loved him.

They talked together chiefly in German, Uncle Joachim carefully correcting her mistakes; and while they went frugally in omnibuses to the different sights, and ate buns in confectioners' shops at lunch-time, and walked long distances where no omnibuses were to be found—for besides having a great fear of hansoms he was very thrifty—he drew her out, saying little himself, and in a very short time knew almost as much about her life and her perplexities as she did.

She was very happy during his visit, and told herself contentedly that blood, after all, was thicker than water. She did not stop to consider what she meant exactly by this, but she had a vague notion that Susie was the water. She felt that Uncle Joachim understood her better than anyone had yet done; and was it not natural that her dear mother's brother should? And it was only after she had taken him to service at St. Paul's that she began to perceive that there might perhaps be points on which their tastes differed. Uncle Joachim had remained seated while other people knelt or stood; but that did not matter in that liberal place, where nobody notices the degree of his neighbour's devoutness. And he had slept during the anthem, one of those unaccompanied anthems that are sung there with what seem of a certainty to be the voices of angels. And on coming out, when a fugue was rolling in glorious confusion down the echoing aisles, and Anna, who preferred her fugues confused, felt that her spirit was being caught up to heaven, he had looked at her rapt face and wet eyelashes, and patted her hand very kindly, and said encouragingly, "In my youth I too cultivated Bach. Now I cultivate pigs. Pigs are better."

Anna's mother had been his only sister, and he had come over, not, as he told Susie, to see London, but to see Susie herself, and to find out how it was that Anna had reached an age that in Germany is the age of old maids without marrying. By the time he had spent two evenings in Hill Street he had formed his opinion of his nephew and his nephew's wife, and they remained fixed until his death. "The good Peter," he said suddenly one day to Anna when they were wandering together in the maze at Hampton Court—for he faithfully went the rounds of sightseeing prescribed by Baedeker, and Anna followed him wherever he went—"the good Peter is but a Quatschkopf."

"A Quatschkopf?" echoed Anna, whose acquaintance with her mother-tongue did not extend to the byways of opprobrium. "What in the world is a Quatschkopf?"

"Quatschkopf is a Duselfritz," explained Uncle Joachim, "and also it is the good Peter."

"I believe you are calling him ugly names," said Anna, slipping her arm through his; by this time, if not kindred spirits, they were the best of friends.

Uncle Joachim did not immediately reply. They had come to the open space in the middle of the maze, and he sat down on the seat to recover his breath, and to wipe his forehead; for though the wind was cold the sun was fierce. "Gott, was man Alles durchmacht auf Reisen!" he sighed. Then he put his handkerchief back into his pocket, looked up at Anna, who was standing in front of him leaning on her sunshade, and said, "A Quatschkopf is a foolish fellow who marries a woman like that."

"Oh, poor Susie!" cried Anna, at once ready to defend her, and full of the kindly feelings absence invariably produced. "Peter did a very sensible thing. But I don't think Susie did, marrying Peter."

"He is a Quatschkopf," said Uncle Joachim, not to be shaken in his opinions, "and the geborene Dobbs is a vulgar woman who is not rich enough."

"Not rich enough? Why, we are all suffocated by her money. We never hear of anything else. It would be dreadful if she had still more."

"Not rich enough," persisted Uncle Joachim, pursing up his lips into an expression of great disapproval, and shaking his head. "Such a woman should be a millionnaire. Not of marks, but of pounds sterling. Short of that, a man of birth does not impose her as a mother on his children. Peter has done it. He is a Quatschkopf."

"It is a great mercy that she isn't a millionnaire," said Anna, appalled by the mere thought. "Things would be just the same, except that there would be all that money more to hear about. I hate the very name of money."

"Nonsense. Money is very good."

"But not somebody else's."

"That is true," said Uncle Joachim approvingly. "One's own is the only money that is truly pleasant." Then he added suddenly, "Tell me, how comes it that you are not married?"

Anna frowned. "Now you are growing like Susie," she said.

"Ach—she asks you that often?"

"Yes—no, not quite like that. She says she knows why I am not married."

"And what knows she?"

"She says that I frighten everybody away," said Anna, digging the point of her sunshade into the ground. Then she looked at Uncle Joachim, and laughed.

"What?" he said incredulously. This pretty creature standing before him, so soft and young—for that she was twenty-four was hardly credible—could not by any possibility be anything but lovable.

"She says that I am disagreeable to people—that I look cross—that I don't encourage them enough. Now isn't it simply terrible to be expected to encourage any wretched man who has money? I don't want anybody to marry me. I don't want to buy my independence that way. Besides, it isn't really independence."

"For a woman it is the one life," said Uncle Joachim with great decision. "Talk not to me of independence. Such words are not for the lips of girls. It is a woman's pride to lean on a good husband. It is her happiness to be shielded and protected by him. Outside the narrow circle of her home, for her happiness is not. The woman who never marries has missed all things."

"I don't believe it," said Anna.

"It is nevertheless true."

"Look at Susie—is she so happy?"

"I said a good husband; not a Duselfritz."

"And as for narrow circles, why, how happy, how gloriously happy, I could be outside them, if only I were independent!"

"Independent—independent," repeated Uncle Joachim testily, "always this same foolish word. What hast thou in thy head, child, thy pretty woman's head, made, if ever head was, to lean on a good man's shoulder?"

"Oh—good men's shoulders," said Anna, shrugging her own, "I don't want to lean on anybody's shoulder. I want to hold my head up straight, all by itself. Do you then admire limp women, dear uncle, whose heads roll about all loose till a good man comes along and props them up?"

"These are English ideas. I like them not," said Uncle Joachim, looking stony.

Anna sat down on the seat by his side, and laid her cheek for a moment against his sleeve. "This is the only good man's shoulder it will ever lean on," she said. "If I were a preacher, do you know what I would preach?"

"Thou art not, and never wilt be, a preacher."

"But if I were? Do you know what I would preach? Early and late? In season and out of it?"

"Much nonsense, I doubt not."

"I would preach independence. Only that. Always that. They would be sermons for women only; and they would be warnings against props."

She sat up and looked at him out of the corners of her eyes, but he continued to stare stonily into space.

"I would thump the cushions, and cry out, 'Be independent, independent, independent! Don't talk so much, and do more. Go your own way, and let your neighbour go his. Don't meddle with other people when you have all your own work cut out for you being good yourself. Shake off all the props——'"

"Anna, thou art talking folly."

"'—shake them off, the props tradition and authority offer you, and go alone—crawl, stumble, stagger, but go alone. You won't learn to walk without tumbles, and knocks, and bruises, but you'll never learn to walk at all so long as there are props.' Oh," she said fervently, casting up her eyes, "there is nothing, nothing like getting rid of one's props!"

"I never yet," observed Uncle Joachim, in his turn casting up his eyes, "saw a girl who so greatly needs the guidance of a good man. Hast thou never loved, then?" he added, turning on her suddenly.

"Yes," replied Anna promptly. If Uncle Joachim chose to ask such direct questions she would give him straight answers.

"But——?"

"He went away and married somebody else. I had no money, and she had a great deal. So you see he was a very sensible young man." And she laughed, for she had long ago ceased to be anything but amused by the remembrance of her one excursion into the rocky regions of love.

"That," said Uncle Joachim, "was not true love."

"Oh, but it was."

"Nay. One does not laugh at love."

"It was all I had, anyhow. There isn't any more left. It was very bad while it lasted, and it took at least two years to get over it. What things I did to please that young man and appear lovely in his eyes! The hours it took to dress, and get my hair done just right. I endured tortures if I didn't look as beautiful as I thought I could look, and was always giving my poor maid notice. And plots—the way I plotted to get taken to the places where he would be! I never was so artful before or since. Poor Susie was quite helpless. It is a mercy it all ended as it did."

"That," repeated Uncle Joachim, "was not true love."

"Yes, it was."

"No, my child."

"Yes, my uncle. I laugh now, but it was very dreadful at the time."

"Thou art but a goose," he said, shrugging his shoulders; but immediately patted her hand lest her feelings should have been hurt. And, declining further argument, he demanded to be taken to the Great Vine.

It was in this fashion, Anna talking and Uncle Joachim making brief comments, that he came to know her as thoroughly as though he had lived with her all his life.

Soon after the excursion to Hampton Court a letter came that hurried his departure, to Susie's ill-concealed relief.

"My swines are ill," he informed her, greatly agitated, his fragile English going altogether to pieces in his perturbation; "my inspector writes they perpetually die. God keep thee, Anna," and he embraced her very tenderly, and bending hastily over Susie's hand muttered some conventionalities, and then disappeared into his four-wheeler and out of their lives.

They never saw him again.

"My swines are ill," mimicked Susie, when Anna, feeling that she had lost her one friend, came slowly back into the room, "my swines perpetually die—"

Anna was obliged to go and pray very hard at St. Paul's before she could forgive her.

CHAPTER III

The old man died at Christmas, and in the following March, when Anna was going about more sad and listless than ever, the news came that, though his inherited estates had gone to his sons, he had bought a little place some years before with the intention of retiring to it in his extreme old age, and this little place he had left to his dear and only niece Anna.

She was alone when the letters bringing the news arrived, sitting in the drawing-room with a book in her hands at which she did not look, feeling utterly downcast, indifferent, too hopeless to want anything or mind anything, accepting her destiny of years of days like this, with herself going through them lonely, useless, and always older, and telling herself that she did not after all care. "What does it matter, so long as I have a comfortable bed, and fires when I am cold, and meals when I am hungry?"

she thought. "Not to have those is the only real misery. All the rest is purest fancy. What right have I to be happier than other people? If they are contented by such things, I can be contented too. And what does a useless being like me deserve, I should like to know? It was detestably ungrateful of me to have been unhappy all this time."

She got up aimlessly, and looked out of the window into the sunny street, where the dust was racing by on the gusty March wind, and the women selling daffodils at the corner were more battered and blown about and red-eyed than ever. She had often, in those moments when her whole body tingled with a wild longing to be up and doing and justifying her existence before it was too late, envied these poor women, because they worked. She wondered vaguely now at her folly. "It is much better to be comfortable," she thought, going back to the fire as aimlessly as she had gone to the window, "and it is sheer idiocy quarrelling with a life that other people would think quite tolerable."

Then the door opened, and the letters were brought in—the wonderful letters that struck the whole world into radiance—lying together with bills and ordinary notes on a salver, carried by an indifferent servant, handed to her as though they were things of naught—the wonderful letters that changed her life.

At first she did not understand what it was that they meant, and pored over the cramped German writing, reading the long sentences over and over again, till something suddenly seemed to clutch at her heart. Was this possible? Was this actual truth? Was Uncle Joachim, who had so much objected to her longing for independence, giving it to her with both hands, and every blessing along with it? She read them through again, very carefully, holding them with shaking hands. Yes, it was true. She began to cry, sobbing over them for very love and tenderness, her whole being melted into gratitude and humbleness, awestruck by a sense of how little she had deserved it, dazzled by the thousand lovely colours life, in the twinkling of an eye, had taken on.

There were two letters—one from Uncle Joachim's lawyer, and one from Uncle Joachim himself, written soon after his return from England, with directions on the envelope that it was to be sent to Anna after his death.

Uncle Joachim was not a man to express sentiment otherwise than by patting those he loved affectionately on the back, and the letter over which Anna hung with such tender gratitude, and such an extravagance of humility, was a mere bald statement of facts. Since Anna, with a perversity that he entirely disapproved, refused to marry, and appeared to be possessed of the obstinacy that had always been a peculiarity of her German forefathers, and which was well enough in a man, but undesirable in a woman, whose calling it was to be gentle and yielding (sanft und nachgiebig), and convinced from what he had seen during his visit to London that she could never by any possibility be happy with her brother and sister-in-law, and moreover considering that it was beneath the dignity of his sister's daughter, a young lady of good family, for ever to roll herself in the feathers with which the middle-class goose-born Dobbs had furnished Peter's otherwise defective nest, he had decided to make her independent altogether of them, numerous though his own sons were, and angry as they no doubt would be, by bestowing on her absolutely after his death the only property he could leave to whomsoever he chose, a small estate near Stralsund, where he hoped to pass his last years. It was in a flourishing condition, easy to manage, bringing in a yearly average of forty thousand marks, and with an experienced inspector whom he earnestly recommended her to keep. He trusted his dear Anna would go and live there, and keep it up to its present state of excellence, and would finally marry a good German gentleman, of whom there were many, and return in this way altogether to the country of her forefathers. The estate was not so far from Stralsund as to make it impossible for her to drive there when she wished to indulge any feminine desire she might have to trim herself (sich putzen), and he recommended her to begin a new life, settling there with some grave and sober female advanced in years as companion and protectress, until such time as she should, by marriage, pass into the care of that natural protector, her husband.

Then followed a short exposition of his views on women, especially those women who go to parties all their lives and talk Klatsch; a spirited comparing of such women with those whose interests keep them busy in their own homes; and a final exhortation to Anna to seize this opportunity of choosing the better life, which was always, he said, a life of simplicity, frugality, and hard work.

Anna wept and laughed together over this letter—the tenderest laughter and the happiest tears. It seemed by turns the wildest improbability that she should be well off, and the most natural thing in the world. Susie was out. Never had her absence been terrible before. Anna could hardly bear the waiting. She walked up and down the room, for sitting still was impossible, holding the precious letters tight in her little cold hands, her cheeks burning, her eyes sparkling, in an agony of impatience and anxiety lest something should have happened to delay Susie at this supreme moment. At the window end of the room she stopped each time she reached it and looked eagerly up and down the street, the flower-women and the blessedness of selling daffodils having within an hour become profoundly indifferent to her. At the other end of the room, where a bureau stood, she came to a standstill too, and snatching up a pen began a letter to Peter in Devonshire; but, hearing wheels, threw it down and flew to the window again. It was not Susie's carriage, and she went back to the letter and wrote another line; then again to the window; then again to the letter; and it was the letter's turn as Susie, fagged from a round of calls, came in.

Susie's afternoon had not been a success. She had made advances to a woman of enviably high position with the intrepidity that characterised all her social movements, and she had been snubbed for her pains with more than usual rudeness. She had had, besides, several minor annoyances. And to come in worn out, and have your sister-in-law, who would hardly speak to you at luncheon, fall on your neck and begin violently to kiss you, is really a little hard on a woman who is already cross.

"Now what in the name of fortune is the matter now?" gasped Susie, breathlessly disengaging herself.

"Oh, Susie! oh, Susie!" cried Anna incoherently, "what ages you have been away—and the letters came directly you had gone—and I've been watching for you ever since, and was so dreadfully afraid something had happened——"

"But what are you talking about, Anna?" interrupted Susie irritably. It was late, and she wanted to rest for a few minutes before dressing to go out again, and here was Anna in a new mood of a violent nature, and she was weary beyond measure of all Anna's moods.

"Oh, such a wonderful thing has happened!" cried Anna; "such a wonderful thing! What will Peter say? And how glad you will be——" And she thrust the letters with trembling fingers into Susie's unresponsive hand.

"What is it?" said Susie, looking at them bewildered.

"Oh, no—I forgot," said Anna, wildly as it seemed to Susie, pulling them out of her hand again. "You can't read German—see here——" And she began to unfold them and smooth out the creases she had made, her hands shaking visibly.

Susie stared. Clearly something extraordinary had happened, for the frosty Anna of the last few months had melted into a radiance of emotion that would only not be ridiculous if it turned out to be justified.

"Two German letters," said Anna, sitting down on the nearest chair, spreading them out on her lap, and talking as though she could hardly get the words out fast enough, "one from Uncle Joachim——"

"Uncle Joachim?" repeated Susie, a disagreeable and creepy doubt as to Anna's sanity coming over her. "You know very well he's dead and can't write letters," she said severely.

"—and one from his lawyer," Anna went on, regardless of everything but what she had to tell. "The lawyer's letter is full of technical words, difficult to understand, but it is only to confirm what Uncle Joachim says, and his is quite plain. He wrote it some time before he died, and left it with his lawyer to send on to me."

Susie was listening now with all her ears. Lawyers, deceased uncles, and Anna's sparkling face could only have one meaning.

"Uncle Joachim was our mother's only brother——"

"I know, I know," interrupted Susie impatiently.

"—and was the dearest and kindest of uncles to me——"

"Never mind what he was," interrupted Susie still more impatiently. "What has he done for you? Tell me that. You always pretended, both of you—Peter too—that he had miles of sandy places somewhere in the desert, and dozens of boys. What could he do for you?"

"Do for me?" Anna rose up with a solemnity worthy of the great news about to be imparted, put both her hands on Susie's little shoulders, and looking down at her with shining eyes, said slowly, "He has left me an estate bringing in forty thousand marks a year."

"Forty thousand!" echoed Susie, completely awestruck.

"Marks," said Anna.

"Oh, marks," said Susie, chilled. "That's francs, isn't it? I really thought for a moment——"

"They're more than francs. It brings in, on an average, two thousand pounds a year. Two—thousand—pounds—a— year," repeated Anna, nodding her head at each word. "Now, Susie, what do you think of that?"

"What do I think of it? Why, that it isn't much. Where would you all have been, I wonder, if I had only had two thousand a year?"

"Oh, congratulate me!" cried Anna, opening her arms. "Kiss me, and tell me you are glad! Don't you see that I am off your hands at last? That we need never think about husbands again? That you will never have to buy me any more clothes, and never tire your poor little self out any more trotting me round? I don't know which of us is to be congratulated most," she added laughing, looking at Susie with her eyes full of tears. Then she insisted on kissing her again, and murmured foolish things in her ear about being so sorry for all her horrid ways, and so grateful to her, and so determined now to be good for ever and ever.

"My dear Anna," remonstrated Susie, who disliked sentiment and never knew how to respond to exhibitions of feeling. "Of course I congratulate you. It almost seems as if throwing away one's chances in the way you have done was the right thing to do, and is being rewarded. Don't let us waste time. You know we go out to dinner. What has he left Peter?"

"Peter?" said Anna wonderingly.

"Yes, Peter. He was his nephew, I suppose, just as much as you were his niece."

"Well, but Susie, Peter is different. He—he doesn't need money as I do; and of course Uncle Joachim knew that."

"Nonsense. He hasn't got a penny. Let me look at the letters."

"They're in German. You won't be able to read them."

"Give them to me. I learned German at school, and got a prize. You're not the only person in the world who can do things."

She took them out of Anna's hand, and began slowly and painfully to read the one from Uncle Joachim, determined to see whether there really was no mention of Peter. Anna looked on, hot and cold by turns with fright lest by some chance her early studies should not after all have been quite forgotten.

"Here's something about Peter—and me," Susie said suddenly. "At least, I suppose he means me. It is something Dobbs. Why does he call me that? It hasn't been my name for fifteen years."

"Oh, it's some silly German way. He says the geborene Dobbs, to distinguish you from other Lady Estcourts."

"But there are no others."

"Oh, well, his sister was one. Give me the letter, Susie—I can tell you what he says much more quickly than you can read it."

"'Unter der Würde einer jünge Dame aus guter Familie,'" read out Susie slowly, not heeding Anna, and with the most excruciating pronunciation that was ever heard, "'sich ewig auf den Federn, mit welchen die bürgerliche Gans geborene Dobbs Peters sonst mangelhaftes Nest ausgestattet hat, zu wälzen.' What stuff he writes. I can hardly understand it. Yet I must have been good at it at school, to get the prize. What is that bit about me and Peter?"

"Which bit?" said Anna, blushing scarlet. "Let me look."
She got the letter back into her possession. "Oh, that's
where he says that—that he doesn't think it fair that I
should be a burden for ever on you and Peter."

"Well, that's sensible enough. The old man had some sense
in him after all, absurd though he was, and vulgar. It isn't
fair, of course. I don't mean to say anything disagreeable, or
throw all I have done for you in your face, but really, Anna,
few mothers would have made the sacrifices I have for you,
and as for sisters-in-law—well, I'd just like to see another."

"Dear Susie," said Anna tenderly, putting her arm round
her, ready to acknowledge all, and more than all, the
benefits she had received, "you have been only too kind
and generous. I know that I owe you everything in the
world, and just think how lovely it is for me to feel that
now I can take my weight off your shoulders! You must
come and live with me now, whenever you are sick of
things, and I'll feel so proud, having you in my house!"

"Live with you?" exclaimed Susie, drawing herself away.
"Where are you going to live?"

"Why, there, I suppose."

"Live there! Is that a condition?"

"No, but Uncle Joachim keeps on saying he hopes I will,
and that I'll settle down and look after the place."

"Look after the place yourself? How silly!"

"Yes, you haven't taught me much about farming, have
you? He wants me to turn quite into a German."

"Good gracious!" cried Susie, genuinely horrified.

"He seems to think that I ought to work, and not spend my life talking Klatsch."

"Talking what?"

"It's what German women apparently talk when they get together. We don't. I'd never do anything with such an ugly name, and I'm positive you wouldn't."

"Where is this place?"

"Near Stralsund."

"And where on earth is that?"

"Ah," said Anna, investigating cobwebby corners of her memory, "that's what I should like to be able to remember. Perhaps," she added honestly, "I never knew. Let me call Letty, and ask her to bring her atlas."

"Letty won't know," said Susie impatiently, "she only knows the things she oughtn't to."

"Oh, she isn't as wise as all that," said Anna, ringing the bell. "Anyhow she has maps, which is more than we have."

A servant was sent to request Miss Letty Estcourt to attend in the drawing-room with her atlas.

"Whatever's in the wind now?" inquired Letty, open-mouthed, of her governess. "They're not going to examine me this time of night, are they, Leechy?" For she suffered greatly from having a brother who was always passing examinations and coming out top, and was consequently subjected herself, by an ambitious mother who was sure that she must be equally clever if she would only let herself go, to every examination that happened to be going for girls of her age; so that she and Miss Leech spent their days either on the defensive, preparing for these unprovoked assaults, or in the state of collapse which followed the regularly recurring defeat, and both found their lives a burden too great to be borne.

There was a preliminary scuffle of washing and brushing, and then Letty marched into the drawing-room, her atlas under her arm and deep suspicion on her face. But no bland and treacherous examiner was visible, covering his preliminary movements with ghastly pleasantries; only her mother and her pretty aunt.

"Where's Stralsund?" they cried together, as she opened the door.

Letty stopped short and stared. "What's that?" she asked.

"It's a place—a place in Germany."

"Letty, do you mean to tell me that you don't know where Stralsund is?" asked Susie, in a voice that would have been of thunder if it had been big enough. "Do you mean to say that after all the money I have spent on your education you don't know that?"

Was this a new form of torture? Was she to find the examining spirit lurking even in the familiar and hitherto harmless forms of her mother and her aunt? She openly showed her disgust. "If it's a place, it's in this atlas," she said, "and if this is going to be an examination, I don't think it's fair; and if it's a game, I don't like it." And she threw her atlas unceremoniously on to the nearest chair; for though her mother could force her to do many things, she could never, somehow, force her to be respectful.

"What a horror the child has of lessons!" cried Susie. "Don't be so silly. We only want to see if you know where Stralsund is, that's all."

"Tell us where it is, Letty," said Anna coaxingly, kneeling down in front of the chair and opening the atlas. "Let us find the map of Germany and look for it. Why, you did Germany for your last exam.—you must have it all at your fingers' ends."

"It didn't stay there, then," said Letty moodily; but she went over to Anna, who was always kind to her, and began to turn over the well-thumbed pages.

Oh, what recollections lurked in those dirty corners! Surely it is hard on a person of fourteen, who is as fond of enjoying herself as anybody else, to be made to wrestle with maps upstairs in a dreary room, when the sun is shining, and the voices of the children passing come up joyously to the prison windows, and all the world is out of doors! Letty thought so, and Miss Leech thought it hard on a person of thirty, and each tried to console the other, but neither knew how, for their case seemed very hopeless. Did not unending vistas of classes and lectures stretch away before and behind them, dotted at intervals, oh, so frequent! with the black spots of examinations? Was not the pavement of Gower Street, and Kensington Square, and of all those districts where girls can be lectured into wisdom, quite worn by their patient feet? And then the accomplishments! Oh, what a life it was! A man came twice a week and insisted on teaching her to fiddle; a highly nervous man, who jerked her elbow and rapped her knuckles with his bow whenever she played out of tune, which was all the time, and made bitter remarks of a killingly sarcastic nature to Miss Leech when she stumbled over the accompaniments. On Wednesdays there was a dancing class, where a pinched young lady played the piano with the energy of despair, and a hot and agile master with unduly turned-out toes taught the girls the Lancers, earning his bread in the sweat of his brow. He also was sarcastic, but he clothed his sarcasms in the garb of kindly fun, laughing gently at them himself, and expecting his pupils to laugh too; which they did uneasily, for the fun was of a personal nature, evoked by the clumsiness or stupidity of one or other of them, and none knew when her own turn might not come. The lesson ended with what he called the March of Grace round the room, each girl by herself, no music to drown the noise her shoes made on the bare boards, the others looking on, and the master making comments. This march was terrible to Letty. All her nightmares were connected with it. She was a podgy, dull-looking girl, fat and pale and awkward, and her mother made her wear cheap shoes that creaked. "Miss Estcourt has new shoes on again," the dancing master would say, gently smiling, when Letty was well on her way round the room, cut off from all human aid, conscious of every inch of her body, desperately trying to be graceful. And everybody tittered except the victim. "You know, Miss Estcourt," he would say at every second lesson, "there is a saying that creaking shoes have not been paid for. I beg your pardon? Did you say they had been paid for? Miss Estcourt says she does not know." And he would turn to his other pupils with a shrug and a gentle smile.

On Saturday afternoons there were the Popular Concerts at St. James's Hall to be gone to—Susie regarded them as educational, and subscribed—and Letty, who always had chilblains on her feet in winter, suffered tortures trying not to rub them; for as surely as she moved one foot and began to rub the other with it, however gently, fierce enthusiasts in the row in front would turn on her—old gentlemen of an otherwise humane appearance, rapt ladies with eyeglasses and loose clothes—and sh-sh her with furious hissings into immobility. "Oh, Letty, try and sit still," Miss Leech, who dreaded publicity, would implore in a whisper; but who that has not had them can know the torture of chilblains inside thick boots, where they cannot be got at? As soon as the chilblains went, the Saturday concerts left off, and it seemed as though Fate had nothing better to do than to be spiteful.

It was indeed a dreadful thing, thought Letty, as she bent over the map of Germany, to be young and to have to be made clever at all costs. Here was her aunt even, her pretty, kind aunt, asking her geography questions at seven o'clock at night, when she thought that she had really done with lessons for one more day, and had been so much enjoying Leechy's description of the only man she ever loved, while she comfortably toasted cheese at the schoolroom fire. Anna, who spent such lofty hours of spiritual exaltation at St. Paul's, and came away with her soul melted into pity for the unhappy, and yearned with her whole being to help them, never thought of Letty as a creature who might perhaps be helped to cheerfulness with a little trouble. Letty was too close at hand; and enthusiastic philanthropists, casting about for objects of charity, seldom see what is at their feet.

It was so difficult to find Stralsund that by the time Letty's wandering finger had paused upon it Susie could only give one glance of horror at its position, and hurry away with Anna to dress. Anna, too, would have preferred it to be farther south, in the Black Forest, or some other romantic region, where it would have amused her to go occasionally, at least, for a few weeks in the summer. But there it was, as far north as it could be, in a part of the world she had hardly heard of, except in connection with dogs.

It did not, however, matter where it was. Uncle Joachim had merely recommended and not enjoined. It would be rather extraordinary for her to go there and set up housekeeping alone. She need not go; she was almost sure she would not go. Anyhow there was no necessity to decide at once. The money was what she wanted, and she could spend it where she chose. Let Uncle Joachim's inspector, of whom he wrote in such praise, go on getting forty thousand marks a year out of the place, and she would be perfectly content.

She ran upstairs to put on her prettiest dress, and to have her hair done in the curls and waves she had so long eschewed. Should she not make herself as charming as possible for this charming world, where everybody was so good and kind, and add her measure of beauty and kindness to the rest? She beamed on Letty as she passed her on the stairs, climbing slowly up with her big atlas, and took it from her and would carry it herself; she beamed on Miss Leech, who was watching for her pupil at the schoolroom door; she beamed on her maid, she beamed on her own reflection in the glass, which indeed at that moment was that of a very beautiful young woman. Oh happy, happy world! What should she do with so much money? She, who had never had a penny in her life, thought it an enormous, an inexhaustible sum. One thing was certain—it was all to be spent in doing good; she would help as many people with it as she possibly could, and never, never, never let them feel that they were under obligations. Did she not know, after fifteen years of dependence on Susie, what it was like to be under obligations? And what was more cruelly sad and crushing and deadening than dependence? She did not yet know what sort of people she would help, or in what way she would help, but oh, she was going to make heaps of people happy forever! While Hilton was curling her hair, she thought of slums; but remembered that they would bring her into contact with the clergy, and most of her offers of late had been from the clergy. Even the vicar who had prepared her for confirmation, his first wife being then alive, and a second having since been mourned, had wanted to marry her. "It's because I am twenty-five and staid that they think me suitable," she thought; but she could not help smiling at the face in the glass.

When she was dressed and ready to go down she was forced to ask herself whether the person that she saw in the glass looked in the least like a person who would ever lead the simple, frugal, hard-working life that Uncle Joachim had called the better life, and in which he seemed to think she would alone find contentment. Certainly she knew him to be very wise. Well, nothing need be decided yet. Perhaps she would go—perhaps she would not. "It's this white dress that makes me look so—so unsuitable," she said to herself, "and Hilton's wonderful waves."

And she went downstairs trying not to sing, the sweetest of feminine creatures, happiness and love and kindness shining in her eyes, a lovely thing saved from the blight of empty years, and brought back to beauty, by Uncle Joachim's timely interference.

Letty and Miss Leech heard the singing, and stopped involuntarily in their conversation. It was a strange sound in that dull and joyless house.

"I don't know what's the matter, Leechy," Letty had said, on her return from the drawing-room, "but mamma and Aunt Anna are too weird to-night for anything. What do you think they had me down for? They didn't know where Stralsund was, and wanted to find out. They pretended they wanted to see if I knew, but I soon saw through that game. And Aunt Anna looks frightfully happy. I believe she's going to be married, and wants to go to Stralsund for the honeymoon."

And Letty took up her toasting fork, while Miss Leech, as in duty bound, refreshed her pupil's memory in regard to Stralsund and Wallenstein and the Hansa cities generally.

CHAPTER IV

Peter, meditating on the banks of the river at Estcourt, came to the conclusion that a journey to London would be made unnecessary by the equal efficacy of a congratulatory letter.

He had been greatly moved by the news of his sister's good fortune, and in the first flush of pleasure and sympathy had ordered his things to be packed in readiness for his departure by the night train. Then he had gone down to the river, and there, thinking the matter over quietly, amid the soothing influences of grey sky, grey water, and green grass, he gradually perceived that a letter would convey all that he felt quite well, perhaps better than any verbal expressions of joy, and as he would in any case only stay a few hours in town the long journey seemed hardly worth while. He sent a letter, therefore, that very evening—a kind, brotherly letter, in which, after heartily congratulating his dear little sister, he said that it would be necessary for her to go over to Germany, see the lawyer, and take possession of her property. When she had done that, and made all arrangements as to the future payment of the income derived from the estate, she would of course come back to them; for Estcourt was always to be her home, and now that she was independent she would no longer be obliged to be wherever Susie was, but would, he hoped, come to him, and they could go fishing together,—"and there's nothing to beat fishing," concluded Peter, "if you want peace."

But Anna did not want peace; at least, not that kind of peace just at that moment. Sitting in a punt was not what she wanted. She was thrilled by the love of her less fortunate fellow-creatures, and the sense of power to help them, and the longing to go and do it. What she really wanted of Peter was that he should take her to Germany and help her through the formalities; for before his letter arrived she too had seen that that was the first thing to be done.

Of this, however, he did not write a word. She thought he must have forgotten, so natural did it appear to her that her brother should go with her; and she wrote him a little note, asking when he would be able to get away. She received a long letter in reply, full of regrets, excuses, and good reasons, which she read wonderingly. Had she been selfish, or was Peter selfish? She thought it all out carefully, and found that it was she who had been selfish to expect Peter, always a hater of business and a lover of quiet, to go all that way and worry himself with tiresome money arrangements. Besides, perhaps he was not feeling well. She knew he suffered from rheumatism; and when you have rheumatism the mere thought of a long journey is appalling.

Susie, whose head was very clear on all matters concerning money, had also recognised the necessity of Anna's going to Germany, and had also regarded Peter as the most natural companion and guide; but she was not surprised when Anna told her that he could not go. "It was too much to expect," apologised Anna. "He often has rheumatism in the spring, and perhaps he has it now."

Susie sniffed.

"The question is," said Anna after a pause, "what am I to do, helpless virgin, in spite of my years,—never able to do a thing for myself?"

"I'll go with you."

"You? But what about your engagements?"

"Oh, I'll throw them over, and take you. Letty can come too. It will do her German good. Herr Schumpf says he's ashamed of her."

Susie had various reasons for offering herself so amiably, one being certainly curiosity. But the chief one was that the same woman who had been so rude to her the day Anna's news came, had sent out invitations to all the world to her daughter's wedding after Easter, and had not sent one to Susie.

This was one of those trials that cannot be faced. If she, being in London at the time, carefully explained to her friends that she was ill that day, and did actually stay in bed and dose herself the days preceding and following, who would believe her? Not if she waved a doctor's certificate in their faces would they believe her. They would know that she had not been invited, and would rejoice. She felt that she could not bear it. An unavoidable business journey to the Continent was exactly what she wanted to help her out of this desperate situation. On her return she would be able to hear the wedding discussed and express her disappointment at having missed it with a serene brow and a quiet mind.

It is doubtful whether she would have gone with Anna, however urgent Anna's need, if she had been included in those invitations. But Anna, who could not know the secret workings of her mind, once more remembered her former treatment of Susie, so kind and willing to do all she could, and hung her head with shame.

They left London a day or two before Easter, Letty and Miss Leech, both of them nearly ill with suppressed delight at the unexpected holiday, going with them. They had announced their coming to Uncle Joachim's lawyer, and asked him to make arrangements for their accommodation at Kleinwalde, Anna's new possession. Susie proposed to stay a day in Berlin, which would give Anna time to talk everything over with the lawyer, and would enable Letty to visit the museums. She had a hopeful idea that Letty would

absorb German at every pore once she was in the country
itself, and that being brought face to face with the statues of
Goethe and Schiller on their native soil would kindle the
sparks of interest in German literature that she supposed
every well-taught child possessed, into the roaring flame of
enthusiasm. She could not believe that Letty had no sparks.
One of her children being so abnormally clever, it must be
sheer obstinacy on the part of the other that prevented it
from acquiring the knowledge offered daily in such
unstinted quantities. She had no illusions in regard to
Letty's person, and felt that as she would never be pretty it
was of importance that she should at least be cultured. She
sat opposite her daughter in the train, and having nothing
better to do during the long hours that they were jolting
across North Germany, looked at her; and the more she
looked the more unreasoningly angry she became that
Peter's sister should be so pretty and Peter's daughter so
plain. And then so fat! What a horrible thing to have to take
a fat daughter about with you in society. Where did she get
it from? She herself and Peter were the leanest of mortals.
It must be that Letty ate too much, which was not only a
disgusting practice but an expensive one, and should be put
down at once with rigour. Susie had not had such an
opportunity of thoroughly inspecting her child for years,
and the result of this prolonged examination of her weak
points was that she would not let any of the party have
anything to eat at all, declaring that it was vulgar to eat in
trains, expressing amazement that people should bring
themselves to touch the horrid-looking food offered, and
turning her back in impatient disgust on two stout German
ladies who had got in at Oberhausen, and who were
enjoying their lunch quite unmoved by her contempt—one
eating a chicken from beginning to end without a fork, and
the other taking repeated sips of an obviously satisfactory

nature from a big wine bottle, which was used, in the intervals, as a support to her back.

By the time Berlin was reached, these ladies, having been properly fed all day, were very cheerful, whereas Susie's party was speechless from exhaustion; especially poor Miss Leech, who was never very strong, and so nearly fainted that Susie was obliged to notice it, and expressed a conviction to Anna in a loud and peevish aside that Miss Leech was going to be a nuisance.

"It is strange," thought Anna, as she crept into bed, "how travelling brings out one's worst passions."

It is indeed strange; for it is certain that nothing equals the expectant enthusiasm and mutual esteem of the start except the cold dislike of the finish. Many are the friendships that have found an unforeseen and sudden end on a journey, and few are those that survive it. But if Horace Walpole and Grey fell out, if Byron and Leigh Hunt were obliged to part, if a host of other personages, endowed with every gift that makes companionship desirable, could not away with each other after a few weeks together abroad, is it to be wondered at that weaker vessels such as Susie and Anna, Letty and Miss Leech, should have found the short journey from London to Berlin sufficient to enable them to see one another's failings with a clearness of vision that was startling?

On the lawyer, a keen-eyed man with a conspicuously fine face, Anna made an entirely favourable impression. When he saw this gracious young lady, so simple and so friendly, and looked into her frank and charming eyes, he perfectly understood that old Joachim should have been bewitched. But after a little conversation, it appeared that she had no present intention of carrying out her uncle's wishes, but, setting them coolly aside, proposed to spend all the good German money she could extract from her property in that replete and bloated land, England.

This annoyed him; first because he hated England and then because his father had managed old Joachim's affairs before he himself had stepped into the paternal shoes, and the feeling of both father and son for the old man had been considerably warmer than is usual between lawyer and client. Still he could not believe, judging after the manner of men, that anything so pretty could also be unkind; and scrutinising Lady Estcourt, because she was unattractive and had a sharp little face and a restless little body, he was convinced that she it was who was the cause of this setting aside of a dead benefactor's wishes. Susie, for her part, patronised him because his collar turned down.

Whenever Letty thought afterwards of Berlin, she thought of it as a place where all the houses are museums, and where you drink so many cups of chocolate with whipped cream on the top that you see things double for the rest of the time.

Anna thought of it as a charming place, where delightful lawyers fill your purse with money.

Susie thought of it with satisfaction as the one place abroad where, by dint of sternest economy, walks from sight to sight in the rain, and promiscuous cakes instead of the more satisfactory but less cheap meals Letty called square, she had successfully defended herself from being, as she put it, fleeced.

To Miss Leech, it was merely a place where your feet get
wet, and your clothes are spoilt.

Early the next morning they started for Kleinwalde.

CHAPTER V

Stralsund is an old town of gabled houses, ancient
churches, and quaint, roughly paved streets, forming an
island, and joined to the mainland by dikes. It looks its best
in the early summer, when the green and marshy plains on
whose edge it stands are strewn with kingcups, and the
little white clouds hang over them almost motionless, and
the cattle are out, and the larks sing, and the orange and red
sails of the fishing-smacks on the narrow belt of sea that
divides the town from the island of Rügen make brilliant
points of contrasting colour between the blue of water and
sky. There is a divine freshness and brightness about the
surrounding stretches of coarse grass and common flowers
at that blest season of the year. The air is full of the smell
of the sea. The sun beats down fiercely on plain and city.
The people come out of the rooms in which most of their
life is spent, and stand in the doorways and remark on the
heat. An occasional heavy cart bumps over the stones,
heard in that sleepy place for several minutes before and
after its passing. There is an honest, tarry, fishy smell
everywhere; and the traveller of poetic temperament in
search of the picturesque, and not too nice about his

comforts, could not fail, visiting it for the first time in the month of June, to be wholly delighted that he had come.

But in winter, and especially in those doubly gloomy days at the end of winter, when spring ought to have shown some signs of its approach and has not done so, those days of howling winds and driving rain and frequent belated snowstorms, this plain is merely a bleak expanse of dreariness, with a forlorn old town huddling in its farthest corner.

It was at its very bleakest and dreariest on the morning that Susie and her three companions travelled across it. "What a place!" exclaimed Susie, as mile after mile was traversed, and there was still the same succession of flat ploughed fields, marshes, and ploughed fields again, with a rare group of furiously swaying pine trees or of silver birches bent double before the wind. "What a part of the world to come and live in! That old uncle of yours was as cracked as he could be to think you'd ever stay here for good. And imagine spending even a single shilling buying land here. I wouldn't take a barrowful at a gift."

"Well, I am taking a great many barrowfuls," said Anna, "and I am sure Uncle Joachim was right to buy a place here—he was always right."

"Oh, of course, it's your duty now to praise him up. Perhaps it gets better farther on, but I don't see how anybody can squeeze two thousand a year out of a desert like this."

The prospect from the railway that day was certainly not attractive; but Anna told herself that any place would look dreary such weather, and was much too happy in the first flush of independence to be depressed by anything

whatever. Had she not that very morning given the
chambermaid at the Berlin hotel so bounteous a reward for
services not rendered that the woman herself had said it
was too much? Thus making amends for those innumerable
departures from hotels when Susie had escaped without
giving anything at all. Had she not also asked, and readily
obtained, permission of Susie at the station in Berlin to pay
for the tickets of the whole party? And had it not been a
delightful and warming feeling, buying those tickets for
other people instead of having tickets bought by other
people for herself? At Pasewalk, a little town half way
between Berlin and Stralsund, where the train stopped ten
minutes, she insisted on getting out, defying the sleet and
the puddles, and went into the refreshment room, and
bought eggs and rolls and cakes,—everything she could
find that was least offensive. Also a guidebook to
Stralsund, though she was not going to stop in Stralsund;
also some postcards with views on them, though she never
used postcards with views on them, and came back loaded
with parcels, her face glowing with childish pleasure at
spending money.

"My dear Anna," said Susie; but she was hungry, and ate a
roll with perfect complacency, allowing Letty to do the
same, although only two days had elapsed since she had so
energetically lectured her on the grossness of eating in
trains.

Susie was in a particularly amiable frame of mind, and in
spite of the weather was looking forward to seeing the
place Uncle Joachim had thought would be a fit home for
his niece; and as she and Anna were sitting together at one
end of the carriage, and Letty and Miss Leech were at the
other, and there was no one else in the compartment, she
was neither upset by the too near contemplation of her

daughter, nor by the aspect of other travellers lunching. Miss Leech, always mindful of her duties, was making the most of her five hours' journey by endeavouring, in a low voice, to clear away the haze that hung in her pupil's mind round the details of her last winter's German studies. "Don't you remember anything of Professor Smith's lectures, Letty?" she inquired. "Why, they were all about just this part of Germany, and it makes it so much more interesting if one knows what happened at the different places. Stralsund, you know, where we shall be presently, has had a most turbulent and interesting past."

"Has it?" said Letty. "Well, I can't help it, Leechy."

"No; but my dear, you should try to recollect something at least of what you heard at the lectures. Have you forgotten the paper you wrote about Wallenstein?"

"I remember I did a paper. Beastly hard it was, too."

"Oh, Letty, don't say beastly—it really isn't a ladylike word."

"Why, mamma's always saying it."

"Oh, well. Don't you know what Wallenstein said when he was besieging Stralsund and found it such a difficult task?"

"I suppose he said too that it was beastly hard."

"Oh, Letty—it was something about chains. Now do you remember?"

"Chains?" repeated Letty, looking bored. "Do you know, Leechy?"

"Yes, I still remember that, though I confess that I have forgotten the greater part of what I heard."

"Then what do you ask me for, when you know I don't know? What did he say about chains?"

"He said that he'd take the city, if it were rivetted to heaven with chains of iron," said Miss Leech dramatically.

"What a goat."

"Oh, hush—don't say those horrible words. Where do you learn them? Not from me, certainly not from me," said Miss Leech, distressed. She had a profound horror of slang, and was bewildered by the way in which these weeds of rhetoric sprang up on all occasions in Letty's speech.

"Well, and was it?"

"Was it what, my dear?"

"Chained to heaven?"

"The city? Why, how can a city be chained to heaven, Letty?"

"Then what did he say it for?"

"He was using a metaphor."

"Oh," said Letty, who did not know what a metaphor was, but supposed it must be something used in sieges, and preferred not to inquire too closely.

"He was obliged to retire," said Miss Leech, "leaving enormous numbers of slain on the field."

"Poor beasts. I say, Leechy," she whispered, "don't let's bother about history now. Go on with Mr. Jessup. You'd got to where he called you Amy for the first time."

Mr. Jessup was the person already alluded to in these pages as the only man Miss Leech had ever loved, and his history was of absorbing interest to Letty, who never tired of hearing his first appearance on Miss Leech's horizon described, with his subsequent advances before the stage of open courting was reached, the courting itself, and its melancholy end; for Mr. Jessup, a clergyman of the Church of England, with a vicarage all ready to receive his wife, had suddenly become a prey to new convictions, and had gone over to the Church of Rome; whereupon Miss Leech's father, also a clergyman of the Church of England, had talked a great deal about the Scarlet Woman of Babylon, and had shut the door in Mr. Jessup's face when next he called to explain. This had happened when Miss Leech was twenty. Now, at thirty, an orphan resigned to the world's buffets, she found a gentle consolation in repeating the story of her ill-starred engagement to her keenly interested friend and pupil; and the oftener she repeated it the less did it grieve her, till at last she came actually to enjoy the remembrance of it, pleased to have played the principal part even in a drama that was hissed off her little stage, glad to find a sympathetic listener, dwelling much and fondly on every incident of that short period of importance and glory.

It is doubtful whether she would ever have extracted the same amount of pleasure from Mr. Jessup had he remained fixed in the faith of his fathers and married her in due season. By his secession he had unconsciously become a sort of providence to Letty and herself, saving them from endless hours of dulness, furnishing their lonely schoolroom life with romance and mystery; and if in Miss Leech's mind he gradually took on the sweet intangibility of a pleasant dream, he was the very pith and marrow of Letty's existence. She glowed and thrilled at the thought that perhaps she too would one day have a Mr. Jessup of her own, who would have convictions, and give up everything, herself included, for what he believed to be right.

As usual, they at once became absorbed in Mr. Jessup, forgetting in the contemplation of his excellencies everything else in the world, till they were roused to realities by their arrival at Stralsund; and Susie, thrusting books and bags and umbrellas into their passive hands, pushed them out of the carriage into the wet.

Hilton, the maid shared by Susie and Anna, had then to be found and urged to clamber down quickly on to the low platform, where she stood helplessly, the picture of injured superiority, hustled by the hurrying porters and passengers, out of whose way she scorned to move, while Anna went to look for the luggage and have it put into the cart that had been sent for it.

This cart was an ordinary farm cart, used for bringing in the hay in June, but also used for carrying out the manure in November; and on a sack of straw lying in the bottom it was expected that Hilton should sit. The farm boy who drove it, and who helped the porter to tie the trunks to its sides lest they should too violently bump against each other and Hilton on the way, said so; the coachman of the carriage waiting for the Herrschaften pointed with his whip

first at Hilton and then at the cart, and said so; the porter,
who seemed to think it quite natural, said so; and
everybody was waiting for Hilton to get in, who, when she
had at length grasped the situation, went to Susie, who was
looking frightened and pretending to be absorbed by the
sky, and with a voice shaken by passion, and a face
changing from white to red, announced her intention of
only going in that cart as a corpse, when they might do with
her as they pleased, but as a living body with breath in it,
never.

Here was a difficulty. And idlers, whose curiosity was not
extinguishable by wind and sleet, began to press round, and
people who had come by the same train stopped on their
way out to listen. The farm boy patted the sack and
declared that it was clean straw, the coachman stood up on
his box and swore that it was a new sack, the porter assured
the Fräulein that it was as comfortable as a feather bed, and
nobody seemed to understand that what she was being
offered was an insult.

Susie was afraid of Hilton, who had been in the service of
duchesses, and who held these duchesses over her
mistress's head whenever her mistress wanted to do
anything that was inconvenient to herself; quoting their
sayings, pointing out how they would have acted in any
given case, and always, it appeared, they had done exactly
what Hilton desired. Susie's admiration for duchesses was
slavish, and Hilton was treated with an indulgent liberality
that was absurd compared to the stinginess displayed
towards everyone else. Hilton was not more horrified than
her mistress when she saw the farm cart, and understood
that it was for the luggage and the maid. It was impossible
to take her with them in what the porter called the
herrschaftliche Wagen, for it was a kind of victoria, and

how to get their four selves into it was a sufficient puzzle. "What shall we do?" said Susie, in despair, to Anna.

"Do? Why, she'll have to go in it. Hilton, don't be a foolish person, and don't keep us here in the wet. This isn't England, and nobody thinks anything here of driving in farm carts. It is patriarchal simplicity, that's all. People are staring at you now because you are making such a fuss. Get in like a good soul, and let us start."

"Only as a corpse, m'm," reiterated Hilton with chattering teeth, "never as a living body."

"Nonsense," said Anna impatiently.

"What shall we do?" repeated Susie. "Poor Hilton—what barbarians they must be here."

"We must send her in a Droschky, then, if it isn't too far, and we can get one to go."

"A Droschky all that distance! It will be ruinous."

"Well, we can't stand here amusing these people for ever."

"Oh, I wish we had never come to this horrible place!" cried Susie, really made miserable by Hilton's rage.

But Anna did not stay to listen either to her laments or to Hilton's monotonous "Only as a corpse, m'lady," and was already arranging with an unwilling driver, who had no desire whatever to drive to Kleinwalde, but consented to do so on being promised twenty marks, a rest and feed of oats for his horses, and any little addition in the shape of refreshment and extra money that might suggest itself to Anna's generosity.

"You know, Anna, you can't expect me to pay for the fly," said Susie uneasily, when the appeased Hilton had been put into it and was out of earshot. "That dreadful cart is your property, I suppose."

"Of course it is," said Anna, smiling, "and of course the fly is my affair. How magnificent I feel, disposing of carts and Droschkies. Now, will you please to get into my carriage? And do you observe the extreme respectfulness of my coachman?"

The coachman, a strange-looking, round-shouldered being, with a long grizzled beard, a dark-blue cloth cap on his head, and a body clothed in a fawn-coloured suit and gaiters, on which a great many tarnished silver buttons adorned with Uncle Joachim's coat of arms were fastened at short intervals, removed his cap while his new mistress and her party were entering the carriage, and did not put it on again till they were ready to start.

"Quite as though we were royalties," said Susie.

"But the rest of him isn't," replied Anna, who was greatly amused by the turn-out. "Do you like my horses, Susie? Or do you suspect them of having been ploughing all the morning? Oh, well," she added quickly, ashamed of laughing at any part of her dear uncle's gift, "I suppose one has to have heavily built horses in this part of the world, where the roads are probably frightfully bad."

"Their tails might be a little shorter," said Susie.

"They might," agreed Anna serenely.

With the aid of the porter, who knew all about Uncle Joachim's will and was deeply interested, they were at last somehow packed into the carriage, and away they rattled over the rough stones, threading the outskirts of the town on the mainland, the hail and wind in their faces, out into the open country, with their horses' heads turned towards the north. The fly containing Hilton followed more leisurely behind, and the farm cart containing the unused sack of straw followed the fly.

"We can't see much of Stralsund," said Anna, trying to peep round the hood at the old town across the lakes separating it from the mainland.

"It's a very historical town," observed Susie, who had happened to notice, as she idly turned over the pages of her Baedeker on the way down, that there was a long description of it with dates. "As of course you know," she added, turning sharply to her daughter.

"Rather," said Letty. "Wallenstein said he'd take it if it were chained to heaven, and when he found it wasn't he was frightfully sick, and went away and left them all in the fields."

Miss Leech, who was on the little seat, struggling to defend herself from the fury of the elements with an umbrella, looked anxious, but Susie only said in a gratified voice, "I'm glad you remember what you've been taught." To which Letty, who was in great spirits, and thought this drive in the wet huge fun, again replied heartily, "Rather," and her mother congratulated herself on having done the right thing in bringing her to Germany, home of erudition and profundity, already evidently beginning to do its work.

The carriage smelt of fish, which presently upset Susie, who, unfortunately for her, had a nose that smelt everything. While they were in the town she thought the smell was in the streets, and bore it; but out in the open, where there was not a house to be seen, she found that it was in the carriage.

She fidgeted, and looked about, feeling with her foot under the opposite seat, expecting to find a basket somewhere, and determined if she found one to push it out quietly and say nothing; for that she should drive for two hours with her handkerchief up to her nose was more than anybody could expect of her. Already she had done more than anybody ought to expect of her, she reflected, in going to the expense of the journey and the inconvenience of the absence from home for Anna's sake, and she hoped that Anna felt grateful. She had never yet shrunk from her duty towards Anna, or indeed from her duty towards anyone, and she was sure she never would; but her duty certainly did not include the passive endurance of offensive smells.

"What are you looking for?" asked Anna.

"Why, the fish."

"Oh, do you smell it too?"

"Smell it? I should think I did. It's killing me."

"Oh, poor Susie!" laughed Anna, who was possessed by an uncontrollable desire to laugh at everything. The conveyance (it could hardly be called a carriage) in which they were seated, and which she supposed was the one destined for her use if she lived at Kleinwalde, was unlike anything she had yet seen. It was very old, with enormous wheels, and bumped dreadfully, and the seat was so constructed that she was continually slipping forward and having to push herself back again. It was lined throughout, including the hood, with a white and black shepherd's plaid in large squares, the white squares mellowed by the stains of use and time to varying shades of brown and yellow; when Miss Leech's umbrella was blown aside by a gust of wind Anna could see her coachman's drab coat, with a little end of white tape that he had forgotten to tie, and whose uses she was unable to guess, fluttering gaily between its tails in the wind; on the left side of the box was a very big and gorgeous coat of arms in green and white, Uncle Joachim's colours; and whichever way she turned her head, there was the overpowering smell of fish. "We must be taking our dinner home with us," she said, "but I don't see it anywhere."

"There isn't anything under the seats. Perhaps the man has got it on the box. Ask him, Anna; I really can't stand it."

Anna did not quite know how to attract his attention. It seemed undignified to poke him, but she did not know his name, and the wind blew her voice back in the direction of Stralsund when she had cleared it, and coughed, and called out rather shyly, "Oh, Kutscher! Kutscher!"

Then she remembered that oh was not German, and that Uncle Joachim had used sonorous achs in its place, and she began again, "Ach, Kutscher! Kutscher!"

Letty giggled. "Go it, Aunt Anna," she said encouragingly, "dig him in the ribs with your umbrella—or I will, if you like."

Her mother, with her handkerchief to her nose, exhorted her not to be vulgar. Letty explained at some length that she was only being nice, and offering assistance.

"I really shall have to poke him," said Anna, her faint cries of Kutscher quite lost in the rattling of the carriage and the howling of the wind. "Or perhaps you would touch his arm, Miss Leech."

Miss Leech turned, and very gingerly touched his sleeve. He at once whistled to his horses, who stopped dead, snatched off his cap, and looking down at Anna inquired her commands.

It was done so quickly that Anna, whose conversational German was exceedingly rusty, was quite unable to remember the word for fish, and sat looking up at him helplessly, while she vainly searched her brains.

"What is fish in German?" she said, appealing to Susie, distressed that the man should be waiting capless in the rain.

"Letty, what's the word for fish?" inquired Susie sternly.

"Fish?" repeated Letty, looking stupid.

"Fish?" echoed Miss Leech, trying to help.

"Fisch?" said the coachman himself, catching at the word.

"Oh, yes; how utterly silly I am," cried Anna blushing and showing her dimples, "it's Fisch, of course. Kutscher, wo ist Fisch?"

The man looked blank; then his face brightened, and pointing with his whip to the rolling sea on their right, visible across the flat intervening fields, he said that there was much fish in it, especially herrings.

"What does he say?" asked Susie from behind her handkerchief.

"He says there are herrings in the sea."

"Is the man a fool?"

Letty laughed uproariously. The coachman, seeing Letty and Anna laugh, thought he must have said the right thing after all, and looked very pleasant.

"Aber im Wagen," persisted Anna, "wo ist Fisch im Wagen?"

The coachman stared. Then he said vaguely, in a soothing voice, not in the least knowing what she meant, "Nein, nein, gnädiges Fräulein," and evidently hoped she would be satisfied.

"Aber es riecht, es riecht!" cried Anna, not satisfied at all, and lifting up her nose in unmistakeable displeasure.

His face brightened again. "Ach so—jawohl, jawohl," he exclaimed cheerfully; and hastened to explain that there were no fish nearer than the sea, but that the grease he had used that morning to make the leather of the hood and apron shine certainly had a fishy smell, as he himself had noticed. "The gracious Miss loves not the smell?" he inquired anxiously; for he had seven children, and was very desirous that his new mistress should be pleased.

Anna laughed and shook her head, and though she said with great emphasis that she did not love it at all, she looked so friendly that he felt reassured.

"What does he say?" asked Susie.

"Why, I'm afraid we shall have it all the way. It's the grease he's been rubbing the leather with."

"Barbarian!" cried Susie angrily, feeling sick already, and certain that she would be quite ill by the end of the drive. "And you laugh at him and encourage him, instead of taking up your position at once and showing him that you won't stand any nonsense. He ought to be—to be unboxed!" she added in great wrath; for she had heard of delinquent clergymen being unfrocked, and why should not delinquent coachmen be unboxed?

Anna laughed again. She tried not to, but she could not help it; and Susie, made still more angry by this childish behaviour, sulked during the rest of the drive.

"Go on—avanti!" said Anna, who knew hardly any Italian, and when she was in Italy and wanted her words never could find them, but had been troubled the last two days by the way in which these words came to her lips every time she opened them to speak German.

The coachman understood her, however, and they went on again along the straight high-road, that stretched away before them to a distant bend. The high-road, or chaussée, was planted on either side with maples, and between the maples big whitewashed stones had been set to mark the way at night, and behind the rows of trees and stones, ditches had been dug parallel with the road as a protection to the crops in summer from the possible wanderings of erring carts. If a cart erred, it tumbled into the ditch. The arrangement was simple and efficacious. On the right, across some marshy land, they could see the sea for a little while, with the flat coast of Rügen opposite; and then some rising ground, bare of trees and brilliantly green with winter corn, hid it from view. On the left was the dreary plain, dotted at long intervals with farms and their little groups of trees, and here and there with windmills working furiously in the gale. The wind was icy, and the December snow still lay in drifts in the ditches. In that leaden landscape, made up of grey and brown and black, the patches of winter rye were quite startling in their greenness.

Susie thought it the most God-forsaken country she had ever seen, and expressed this opinion plainly on her face and in her attitudes without any need for opening her lips, shuddering back ostentatiously into her corner, wrapping herself with elaborate care in her furs, and behaving as slaves to duty sometimes do when the paths they have to tread are rough.

After driving along the chaussée for about an hour, they passed a big house standing among trees back from the road on the right, and a little farther on came to a small village. The carriage, pulled up with a jerk, and looking eagerly round the hood Anna found they had come to a standstill in front of a new red-brick building, whose steps were crowded with children. Two or three men and some women were with the children. Two of the men appeared to be clergymen, and the elder, a middle-aged, mild-faced man, came down the steps, and bowing profoundly proceeded to welcome Anna solemnly, on behalf of those children from Kleinwalde who attended this school, to her new home. He concluded that Anna was the person to be welcomed because he could see nothing of the lady in the other corner but her eyes, and they looked anything but friendly; whereas the young lady on the left was leaning forward and smiling and holding out her hand.

He took it, and shook it slowly up and down, while he begged her to allow the hood of the carriage to be put back, so that the children from her village, who had walked three miles to welcome her, might be able to see her; and on Anna's readily agreeing to this, himself helped the coachman with his own white-gloved hands to put it down. Susie was therefore exposed to the full fury of the blast, and shrank still farther into her corner—an interesting and tantalising object to the school-children, a dark, mysterious combination of fur, cocks' feathers, and black eyebrows.

Then the clergyman, hat in hand, made a speech. He spoke distinctly, as one accustomed to speaking often and long, and Anna understood every word. She was wholly taken aback by these ceremonies, and had no idea of what she should say in reply, but sat smiling vaguely at him, looking very pretty and very shy. She soon found that her smiles were inappropriate, and they died away; for, warming as he proceeded, the parson, it appeared, was taking it for granted that she intended to live on her property, and was eloquently descanting on the comfort she was going to be to the poor, assuring those present that she would be a mother to the sick, nursing them with her tender woman's hands, an angel of mercy to the hungry, feeding them in the hour of their distress, a friend and sister to the little children, succouring them, caring for them, pitiful of their weakness and their sins. His face lit up with enthusiasm as he went on, and Anna was thankful that Susie could not understand. This crowd of children, the women, the young parson, her coachman, were all hearing promises made on her behalf that she had no thought of fulfilling. She looked down, and twisted her fingers about nervously, and felt uncomfortable.

At the end of his speech, the parson, his eyes full of the tears drawn forth by his own eloquence, held up his hand and solemnly blessed her, rounding off his blessing with a loud Amen, after which there was an awkward pause. Susie heard the Amen, and guessed that something in the nature of a blessing was being invoked, and made a movement of impatience. The parson was odious in her eyes, first because he looked like the ministers of the Baptist chapels of her unmarried youth, but principally because he was keeping her there in the gale and prolonging the tortures she was enduring from the smell of fish. Anna did not know what to say after the Amen, and looked up more shyly than ever, and stammered in her confusion Danke sehr, hoping that it was a proper remark to make; whereupon the parson bowed again, as one who should say Pray don't mention it. Then another man, evidently the schoolmaster, took out a tuning-fork, gave out a note, and the children sang a chorale, following it up with other more cheerful songs, in which the words Frühling and Willkommen were repeated a great many times, while the wind howled flattest contradiction.

When this was over, the parson begged leave to introduce the other clerical-looking person, a tall narrow youth, also in white kid gloves, buttoned up tightly in a long coat of broadcloth, with a pallid face and thick, upright flaxen hair.

"Herr Vicar Klutz," said the elder parson, with a wave of the hand; and the Herr Vicar, making his bow, and having his limp hand heartily grasped by that other little hand, and his furtive eyes smiled into by those other friendly eyes, became on the spot desperately enamoured; which was very natural, seeing that he had not spoken to a woman under forty for six months, and was himself twenty and a poet. He spent the rest of the afternoon shut up in his bedroom, where, refusing all nourishment, he composed a poem in which berauschten Sinn was made to rhyme with Engländerin, while the elder parson, in whose house he lived, thought he was writing his Good Friday sermon.

Then the schoolmaster was introduced, and then came the two women—the schoolmaster's wife and the parson's wife; and when Anna had smiled and murmured polite and incoherent little speeches to each in turn, and had nodded and bowed at least a dozen times to each of these ladies, who could by no means have done with their curtseys, and had introduced them to the dumb figure in the corner, during which ceremonies Letty stared round-eyed and open-mouthed at the school-children, and the school-children stared round-eyed and open-mouthed at Letty, and Miss Leech looked demure, and Susie's brows were contracted by suffering, she wondered whether she might not now with propriety continue her journey, and if so whether it were expected that she should give the signal.

Everybody was smiling at everybody else by way of filling up this pause of hesitation, except Susie, who shut her eyes with great dignity, and shivered in so marked a manner that the parson himself came to the rescue, and bade the coachman help him put up the hood again, explaining to Anna as he did so that her Frau Schwester was not used to the climate.

Evidently the moment had come for going on, and the bows that had but just left off began again with renewed vigour. Anna was anxious to say something pleasant at the finish, so she asked the parson's wife, as she bade her good-bye, whether she and her husband would come to Kleinwalde the next day to dinner.

This invitation produced a very deep curtsey and a flush of gratification, but the recipient turned to her lord before accepting it, to inquire his pleasure.

"I fear not to-morrow, gracious Miss," said the parson, "for it is Good Friday."

"Ach ja," stammered Anna, ashamed of herself for having forgotten.

"Ach ja," exclaimed the parson's wife, still more ashamed of herself for having forgotten.

"Perhaps Saturday, then?" suggested Anna.

The parson murmured something about quiet hours preparatory to the Sabbath; but his wife, a person who struck Anna as being quite extraordinarily stout, was burning with curiosity to examine those foreign ladies more conveniently, and especially to see what manner of being would emerge from the pile of fur and feathers in the corner; and she urged him, in a rapid aside, to do for once without quiet hours. Whereupon he patted her on the cheek, smiled indulgently, and said he would make an exception and do himself the honour of appearing.

This being settled, Anna said Gehen Sie to her coachman, who again showed his intelligence by understanding her;

and in a cloud of smiles and bows they drove away, the school-girls making curtseys, the schoolboys taking off their caps, and the parson standing hat in hand with his arm round his wife's waist as serenely as though it had been a summer's day and no one looking.

Anna became used to these displays of conjugal regard in public later on; but this first time she turned to Susie with a laugh, when the hood had hidden the group from view, and asked her if she had seen it. But Susie had seen nothing, for her eyes were shut, and she refused to answer any questions otherwise than by a feeble shake of the head.

On the other side of the village the chaussée came to an end, and two deep, sandy roads took its place. There was a sign-post at their junction, one arm of which, pointing to the right-hand road that ran down close to the sea, had Kleinwalde scrawled on it; and beside this sign-post a man on a horse was waiting for them.

"Good gracious! More rot?" ejaculated Susie as the carriage stopped again, shaken out of the dignity of sulks by these repeated shocks.

"Oberinspector Dellwig," said the man, introducing himself, and sweeping off his hat and bowing lower and more obsequiously than anyone had yet done.

"This must be the inspector Uncle Joachim hoped I'd keep," said Anna in an undertone.

"I don't care who he is, but for heaven's sake don't let him make a speech. I can't stand this sort of thing any longer. You'll have me ill on your hands if you're not careful, and you won't like that, so you had better stop him."

"I can't stop him," said Anna, perplexed. She also had had enough of speeches.

"Gestatten gnädiges Fräulein dass ich meine gehorsamste Ehrerbietung ausspreche," began the glib inspector, bowing at every second word over his horse's ears.

There was no escape, and they had to hear him out. The man had prepared his speech, and say it he would. It was not so long as the parson's, but was quite as flowery in another way, overflowing with respectful allusions to the deceased master, and with expressions of unbounded loyalty, obedience, and devotion to the new mistress.

Susie shut her eyes again when she found he was not to be stopped, and gave herself up for lost. What could Hilton, who must be close behind waiting in the cold, uncomforted by any food since leaving Berlin, think of all this? Susie dreaded the moment when she would have to face her.

The inspector finished all he had intended saying, and then, assuming a more colloquial tone, informed Anna that from the sign-post onward she would be driving through her own property, and asked permission to ride by her side the rest of the way. So they had his company for the last two miles and his conversation, of which there was much; for he had a ready tongue, and explained things to Anna in a very loud voice as they went along, expatiating on the magnificence of the crops the previous summer, and assuring her that the crops of the coming summer would be even more magnificent, for he had invented a combination of manures which would give such results that all Pomerania's breath would be taken away.

The road here was terrible, and the horses could hardly drag the carriage through the sand. It lurched and heaved from side to side, creaking and groaning alarmingly. Miss Leech was in imminent peril. Anna held on with both hands, and hardly had leisure to put in appropriate achs and jas and questions of a becoming intelligence when the inspector paused to take breath. She did not like his looks, and wished that she could follow Susie's example and avoid the necessity of seeing him by the simple expedient of shutting her eyes. But somehow, she did not quite know how, responsibilities and obligations were suddenly pressing heavily upon her. These people had all made up their minds that she was going to be and do certain things; and though she assured herself that it did not in the least matter how they had made up their minds, yet she felt obliged to behave in the way that was expected of her. She did not want to talk to this unpleasant-looking man, and what he told her about the crops and their marvellousness was half unintelligible to her and wholly a bore. Yet she did talk to him, and looked friendly, and affected to understand and be deeply interested in all he said.

They passed through a plantation of young beeches, planted, Dellwig explained, by Uncle Joachim on his last visit; and after a few more yards of lurching in the sand came to some woods and got on to a fair road.

"The park," said Dellwig superbly, with a wave of the hand.

Susie opened her eyes at the word park, and looked about. "It isn't a park," she said peevishly, "it's a forest—a horrid, gloomy, damp wilderness."

"Oh, it's lovely!" cried Letty, giving a jump of delight as she peered down the serried ranks of pine trees.

It was a thick wood of pines and beeches, railed off from the road on either side by wooden rails painted in black and white stripes. Uncle Joachim had been the loyalest of Prussians, and his loyalty overflowed even into his fences. Æsthetic instincts he had none, and if he had been brought to see it, would not have cared at all that the railings made the otherwise beautiful avenue look like the entrance to a restaurant or a railway station. The stripes, renewed every year, and of startling distinctness, were an outward and visible sign of his staunch devotion to the King of Prussia, the very lining of the carriage with its white and black squares was symbolic; and when they came to the gate within which the house itself stood, two Prussian eagles frowned down at them from the gate-posts.

CHAPTER VI

A low, white, two-storied house, separated from the forest only by a circular grass plot and a ditch with half-melted snow in it and muddy water, a house apparently quite by itself among the creaking pines, neither very old nor very new, with a great many windows, and a brown-tiled roof, was the home bestowed by Uncle Joachim on his dear and only niece Anna.

"So this is where I was to lead the better life?" she thought, as the carriage drew up at the door, and the moaning of the uneasy trees, and all the lonely sounds of a storm-beaten forest replaced the rattling of the wheels in her ears. "The better life, then, is a life of utter solitude, Uncle Joachim thought? I wish I knew—I wish I knew———" But what it was she wished she knew was hardly clear in her mind; and her thoughts were interrupted by a very untidy, surprised-looking maid-servant, capless, and in felt slippers, who had darted down the steps and was unfastening the leather apron and pulling out the rugs with hasty, agitated hands, and trying to pull Susie out as well.

The doorway was garlanded with evergreen wreaths, over which a green and white flag flapped; and curtseying and smiling beneath the wreaths stood Dellwig's wife, a short lady with smooth hair, weather-beaten face, and brown silk gloves, who would have been the stoutest person Anna had ever seen if she had not just come from the presence of the parson's wife.

"I never saw so many bows in my life," grumbled Susie, pushing the servant aside, and getting out cautiously, feeling very stiff and cold and miserable. "Letty, you are on my dress—oh, how d'you do—how d'you do," she murmured frostily, as the Frau Inspector seized her hand and began to talk German to her. "Anna, are you coming? This—er—person thinks I'm you, and is making me a speech."

Dellwig, who had sent his horse away in charge of a small boy, rapidly explained to his wife that the young lady now getting out of the carriage was their late master's niece, and that the other one must be the sister-in-law mentioned in the lawyer's letter; upon which Frau Dellwig let Susie go,

and transferred her smiles and welcome to Anna. Susie
went into the house to get out of the cold, only to find
herself in a square hall whose iciness was the intolerable
iciness of a place in which no sun had been allowed to
shine and no windows had been opened for summers
without number. When Uncle Joachim came down he lived
in two rooms at the back of the house, with a door leading
into the garden through which he went to the farm, and the
hall had never been used, and the closed shutters never
opened. There was no fireplace, or stove, or heating
arrangement of any sort. Glass doors divided it from an
inner and still more spacious hall, with a wide wooden
staircase, and doors all round it. The walls in both halls
were painted grass green; and from little chains in the
ceiling stuffed hawks and eagles, shot by Uncle Joachim,
and grown with years very dusty and moth-eaten, hung
swinging in the draught. The floor was boarded, and was
still damp from a recent scrubbing. There was no carpet. A
wooden bracket on the wall, with brass hooks, held a large
assortment of whips and hunting crops; and in one corner
stood an arrangement for coats, with Uncle Joachim's
various waterproofs and head-coverings hanging
monumentally on its pegs.

"Oh, how dreadful!" thought Susie, shivering more
violently than ever. "And what a musty smell—it's damp,
of course, and I shall be laid up. Poor Hilton! What will she
think of this? Oh, how d'you do," she added aloud, as a
female figure in a white apron suddenly emerged from the
gloom and took her hand and kissed it; "Anna, who's this?
Anna! Aren't you coming? Here's somebody kissing my
hand."

"It's the cook," said Anna, coming into the inner hall with
the others, Dellwig and his wife keeping one on either side

of her, and both talking at once in their anxiety to make a good impression.

"The cook? Then tell her to give us some food. I shall die if I don't have something soon. Do you know what time it is? Past four. Can't you get rid of these people? And where's Hilton?"

Susie hardly seemed to see the Dellwigs, and talked to Anna while they were talking to her as though they did not exist. If Anna felt an obligation to be polite to these different persons she felt none at all. They did not understand English, but if they had it would not have mattered to her, and she would have gone on talking about them as though they had not been there.

Both the Dellwigs had very loud voices, so Susie had to raise hers in order to be heard, and there was consequently such a noise in the empty, echoing house, that after looking round bewildered, and trying to answer everybody at once, Anna gave it up, and stood and laughed.

"I don't see anything to laugh at," said Susie crossly, "we are all starving, and these people won't go."

"But how can I make them go?"

"They're your servants, I suppose. I should just say that I'd send for them when I wanted them."

"They'd be very much astonished. The man is so far from being my servant that I believe he means to be my master."

The two Dellwigs, perplexed by Anna's laughter when nobody had said anything amusing, and uneasy lest she should be laughing at something about themselves, looked from her to Susie suspiciously, and for that brief moment were quiet.

"Wir sind hungrig," said Anna to the wife.

"The food comes immediately," she replied; and hastened away with the cook and the other servant through a door evidently leading to the kitchen.

"Und kalt," continued Anna plaintively to the husband, who at once flung open another door, through which they saw a table spread for dinner. "Bitte, bitte," he said, ushering them in as though the place belonged to him.

"Does this person live in the house?" inquired Susie, eying him with little goodwill.

"He told me he lives at the farm. But of course he has always looked after everything here."

When they were all in the dining-room, driven in by Dellwig, as Susie remarked, like a flock of sheep by a shepherd determined to stand no nonsense, he helped them with officious politeness to take off their wraps, and then, bowing almost to the ground, asked permission to withdraw while the Herrschaften ate, a permission that was given with alacrity, Anna's face falling, however, upon his informing her that he would come round later on in order to lay his plans for the summer before her.

"What does he say?" asked Susie, as the door shut behind him.

"He's coming round again later on."

"That man's going to be a nuisance—you see if he isn't," said Susie with conviction.

"I believe he is," agreed Anna, going over to the white porcelain stove to warm her hands.

"He's the limpet, and you're going to be the rock. Don't let him fleece you too much."

"But limpets don't fleece rocks," said Anna.

"He wouldn't be able to fleece me, I know, if I could talk German as well as you do. But you'll be soft and weak and amiable, and he'll do as he likes with you."

"Soft, and weak, and amiable!" repeated Anna, smiling at Susie's adjectives, "why, I thought I was obstinate—you always said I was."

"So you are. But you won't be to that man. He'll get round you."

"Uncle Joachim said he was excellent."

"Oh, I daresay he wasn't bad with a man over him who knew all about farming, but mark my words, you won't get two thousand a year out of the place."

Anna was silent. Susie was invariably shrewd and sensible, if inclined, Anna thought, to be over suspicious, in matters where money was concerned. Dellwig's face was not one to inspire confidence: and his way of shouting when he talked, and of talking incessantly, was already intolerable to her. She was not sure, either, that his wife was any more satisfactory. She too shouted, and Anna detested noise. The wife did not appear again, and had evidently gone home with her husband, for a great silence had fallen upon the house, broken only by the monotonous sighing of the forest, and the pattering of rain against the window.

The dining-room was a long narrow room, with one big window forming its west end looking out on to the grass plot, the ditch, and the gate-posts with the eagles on them. It was a study in chocolate—brown paper, brown carpet, brown rep curtains, brown cane chairs. There were two wooden sideboards painted brown facing each other down at the dark end, with a collection of miscellaneous articles on them: a vinegar cruet that had stood there for years, with remains of vinegar dried up at the bottom; mustard pots containing a dark and wicked mixture that had once been mustard; a broken hand-bell used at long-past dinners, to summon servants long since dead; an old wine register with entries in it of a quarter of a century back; a mouldy bottle of Worcester sauce, still boasting on its label that it would impart a relish to viands otherwise dull; and some charming Dresden china fruit-dishes, adorned with cheerful shepherds and shepherdesses, incurable optimists, persistently pleased with themselves and their surroundings through all the days and nights of all the cold silent years that they had been smiling at each other in the dark. On the round dinner-table was a pot of lilies of the valley, enveloped in crinkly pink tissue paper tied round with pink satin ribbon, with ears of the paper drawn up between the flower-stalks to produce a pleasing contrast of pink and white.

"Well, it's warm enough here, isn't it?" said Susie, going round the room and examining these things with an interest far exceeding that called forth by the art treasures of Berlin.

"Rather," said Letty, answering for everybody, and rubbing her hands. She frolicked about the room, peeping into all the corners, opening the cupboards, trying the sofa, and behaving in so frisky a fashion that her mother, who seldom saw her at home, and knew her only as a naughty gloomy girl, turned once or twice from the interesting sideboards to stare at her inquiringly through her lorgnette.

The servant with the surprised eyebrows, who presently brought in the soup, had put on a pair of white cotton gloves for the ceremony of waiting, but still wore her felt slippers. She put the plates in a pile on the edge of the table, murmured something in German, and ran out again; nor did she come back till she brought the next course, when she behaved in a precisely similar manner, and continued to do so throughout the meal; the diners, having no bell, being obliged to sit patiently during the intervals, until she thought that they might perhaps be ready for some more.

It was an odd meal, and began with cold chocolate soup with frothy white things that tasted of vanilla floating about in it. Susie was so much interested in this soup that she forgot all about Hilton, who had been driven ignominiously to the back door and was left sitting in the kitchen till the two servants should have time to take her upstairs, and was employing the time composing a speech of a spirited nature in which she intended giving her mistress notice the moment she saw her again.

Her mistress meanwhile was meditatively turning over the vanilla balls in her soup. "Well, I don't like it," she said at last, laying down her spoon.

"Oh, it's ripping!" cried her daughter ecstatically. "It's like having one's pudding at the other end."

"How can you look at chocolate after Berlin, greedy girl?" asked her mother, disgusted by her child's obvious tendency towards a too free indulgence in the pleasures of the table. But Letty was feeling so jovial that in the face of this question she boldly asked for more—a request that was refused indignantly and at once.

There was such a long pause after the soup that in their hunger they began to eat the stewed apples and bottled cherries that were on the table. The brown bread, arranged in thin slices on a white crochet mat in a japanned dish, felt so damp and was so full of caraway seeds that it was uneatable. After a while some roach, caught on the estate, and with a strong muddy flavour and bewildering multitudes of bones, was brought in; and after that came cutlets from Anna's pigs; and after that a queer red gelatinous pudding that tasted of physic; and after that, the meal being evidently at an end, Susie, who was very hungry, remarked that if all the food were going to be like those specimens they had better return at once to England, or they would certainly be starved. "It's a good thing you are not going to stay here, Anna," she said, "for you'd have to make a tremendous fuss before you'd get them to leave off treating you like a pig. Look here—teaspoons to eat the pudding with, and the same fork all the way through. It's a beastly hole"—Letty's eyebrows telegraphed triumphantly across to Miss Leech, "Well, did you hear that?"—"and we ought to have stayed in Berlin. There was nothing to be gained at all by coming here."

"Perhaps the dinner to-night will be better," said Anna, trying to comfort her, and little knowing that they had just eaten the dinner; but people who are hungry are surprisingly impervious to the influence of fair words. "It couldn't be worse, anyhow, so it really will probably be better. I'm very glad though that we did come, for I like it."

"Oh, yes, so do I, Aunt Anna!" cried Letty. "It's frightfully nice. It's like a picnic that doesn't leave off. When are we going over the house, and out into the garden? I do so want to go—oh, I do so want to go!" And she jumped up and down impatiently on her chair, till her ardour was partially quenched by her mother's forbidding her to go out of doors in the rain. "Well, let's go over the house, then," said Letty, dying to explore.

"Oh, yes, you may go over the house," said her mother with a shrug of displeasure; though why she should be displeased it would have puzzled anyone who had dined satisfactorily to explain. Then she suddenly remembered Hilton, and with an exclamation started off in search of her.

The others put on their furs before going into the Arctic atmosphere of the hall, and began to explore, spending the next hour very pleasantly rambling all over the house, while Susie, who had found Hilton, remained shut up in the bedroom allotted her till supper time.

The cook showed Anna her bedroom, and when she had gone, Anna gave one look round at the evergreen wreaths with which it was decorated and which filled it with a pungent, baked smell, and then ran out to see what her house was like. Her heart was full of pride and happiness as she wandered about the rooms and passages. The magic word mine rang in her ears, and gave each piece of furniture a charm so ridiculously great that she would not have told any one of it for the world. She took up the different irrelevant ornaments that were scattered through the rooms, collected as such things do collect, nobody knew when or why, and she put them down again somewhere else, only because she had the right to alter things and she loved to remind herself of it. She patted the walls and the tables as she passed; she smoothed down the folds of the curtains with tender touches; she went up to every separate looking-glass and stood in front of it a moment, so that there should be none that had not reflected the image of its mistress. She was so childishly delighted with her scanty possessions that she was thankful Susie remained invisible and did not come out and scoff.

What if it seemed an odd, bare place to eyes used to the superfluity of hangings and stuffings that prevailed at Estcourt? These bare boards, these shabby little mats by the side of the beds, the worn foxes' skins before the writing-tables, the cane or wooden chairs, the white calico curtains with meek cotton fringes, the queer little prints on the walls, the painted wooden bedsteads, seemed to her in their very poorness and unpretentiousness to be emblematical of all the virtues. As she lingered in the quiet rooms, while Letty raced along the passages, Anna said to herself that this Spartan simplicity, this absence of every luxury that could still further soften an already languid and effeminate soul, was beautiful. Here, as in the whitewashed praying-places of the Puritans, if there were any beauty and any glory it must all come from within, be all of the spirit, be only the beauty of a clean life and the glory of kind thoughts. She pictured herself waking up in one of those unadorned beds with the morning sun shining on her face, and rising to go her daily round of usefulness in her quiet house, where there would be no quarrels, and no pitiful ambitions, and none of those many bitter heartaches that need never be. Would they not be happy days, those days of

simple duties? "The better life—the better life," she
repeated musingly, standing in the middle of the big room
through whose tall windows she could see the garden, and
a strip of marshy land, and then the grey sea and the white
of the gulls and the dark line of the Rügen coast over which
the dusk was gathering; and she counted on her fingers
mechanically, "Simplicity, frugality, hard work. Uncle
Joachim said that was the better life, and he was wise—oh,
he was very wise—but still——And he loved me, and
understood me, but still——"

Looking up she caught sight of herself in a long glass
opposite, a slim figure in a fur cloak, with bare head and
pensive eyes, lost in reflection. It reminded her of the day
the letter came, when she stood before the glass in her
London bedroom dressed for dinner, with that same
sentence of his persistently in her ears, and how she had not
been able to imagine herself leading the life it described.
Now, in her travelling dress, pale and tired and subdued
after the long journey, shorn of every grace of clothes and
curls, she criticised her own fatuity in having held herself
to be of too fine a clay, too delicate, too fragile, for a life
that might be rough. "Oh, vain and foolish one!" she said
aloud, apostrophising the figure in the glass with the
familiar Du of the days before her mother died, "Art thou
then so much better than others, that thou must for ever be
only ornamental and an expense? Canst thou not live,
except in luxury? Or walk, except on carpets? Or eat,
except thy soup be not of chocolate? Go to the ants, thou
sluggard; consider their ways, and be wise." And she
wrapped herself in her cloak, and frowned defiance at that
other girl.

She was standing scowling at herself with great disapproval
when the housemaid, who had been searching for her

everywhere, came to tell her that the Herr Oberinspector was downstairs, and had sent up to know if his visit were convenient.

It was not at all convenient; and Anna thought that he might have spared her this first evening at least. But she supposed that she must go down to him, feeling somehow unequal to sending so authoritative a person away.

She found him standing in the inner hall with a portfolio under his arm. He was blowing his nose, making a sound like the blast of a trumpet, and waking the echoes. Not even that could he do quietly, she thought, her new sense of proprietorship oddly irritated by a nose being blown so aggressively in her house. Besides, they were her echoes that he was disturbing. She smiled at her own childishness.

She greeted him kindly, however, in response to his elaborate obeisances, and shook hands on seeing that he expected to be shaken hands with, though she had done so twice already that afternoon; and then she let herself be ushered by him into the drawing-room, a room on the garden side of the house, with French windows, and bookshelves, and a huge round polished table in the middle.

It had been one of the two rooms used by Uncle Joachim, and was full of traces of his visits. She sat down at a big writing-table with a green cloth top, her feet plunged in the long matted hairs of a grey rug, and requested Dellwig to sit down near her, which he did, saying apologetically, "I will be so free."

The servant, Marie, brought in a lamp with a green shade, shut the shutters, and went out again on tiptoe; and Anna settled herself to listen with what patience she could to the loud voice that jarred so on her nerves, fortifying herself with reminders that it was her duty, and really taking pains to understand him. Nor did she say a word, as she had done to the lawyer, that might lead him to suppose she did not intend living there.

But Dellwig's ceaseless flow of talk soon wearied her to such an extent that she found steady attention impossible. To understand the mere words was in itself an effort, and she had not yet learned the German for rye and oats and the rest, and it was of these that he chiefly talked. What was the use of explaining to her in what way he had ploughed and manured and sown certain fields, how they lay, how big they were, and what their soil was, when she had not seen them? Did he imagine that she could keep all these figures and details in her head? "I know nothing of farming," she said at last, "and shall understand your plans better when I have seen the estate."

"Natürlich, natürlich," shouted Dellwig, his voice in strangest contrast to hers, which was particularly sweet and gentle. "Here I have a map—does the gracious Miss permit that I show it?"

The gracious Miss inclined her tired head, and he unrolled it and spread it out on the table, pointing with his fat forefinger as he explained the boundaries, and the divisions into forest, pasture, and arable.

"It seems to be nearly all forest," said Anna.

"Forest! The forest covers two-thirds of the estate. It is the only forest on the entire promontory. Such care as I have bestowed on the forest has seldom been seen. It is grossartig—colossal!" And he lifted his hands the better to express his admiration, and was about to go into lengthy raptures when the map rolled itself up again with loud cracklings, and cut him short. He spread it out once more, and securing its corners began to describe the effects of the various sorts of artificial manure on the different crops, his cleverness in combining them, and his latest triumphant discovery of the superlative mixture that was to strike all Pomerania with awe.

"Ja," said Anna, balancing a paper-knife on one finger, and profoundly bored. "Whose land is that next to mine?" she asked, pointing.

"The land on the north and west belongs to peasants," said Dellwig. "On the east is the sea. On the south it is all Lohm. The gracious one passed through the village of Lohm this afternoon."

"The village where the school is?"

"Quite correct. The pastor, Herr Manske, a worthy man, but, like all pastors, taking ells when he is offered inches, serves both that church and the little one in Kleinwalde village, of which the gracious Miss is patroness. Herr von Lohm, who lives in the house standing back from the road, and perhaps noticed by the gracious Miss, is Amtsvorsteher in both villages."

"What is Amtsvorsteher?" asked Anna, languidly. She was leaning back in her chair, idly balancing the paper-knife, and listening with half an ear only to Dellwig, throwing in questions every now and then when she thought she ought to say something. She did not look at him, preferring much to look at the paper-knife, and he could examine her face at his ease in the shadow of the lamp-shade, her dark eyelashes lowered, her profile only turned to him, with its delicate line of brow and nose, and the soft and gracious curves of the mouth and chin and throat. One hand lay on the table in the circle of light, a slender, beautiful hand, full of character and energy, and the other hung listlessly over the arm of the chair. Anna was very tired, and showed it in every line of her attitude; but Dellwig was not tired at all, was used to talking, enjoyed at all times the sound of his voice, and on this occasion felt it to be his duty to make things clear. So he went into the lengthiest details as to the nature and office of Amtsvorstehers, details that were perfectly incomprehensible and wholly indifferent to Anna, and spared neither himself nor her. While he talked, however, he was criticising her, comparing the laziness of her attitude with the brisk and respectful alertness of other women when he talked. He knew that these other women belonged to a different class; his wife, the parson's wife, the wives of the inspectors on other estates, these were not, of course, in the same sphere as the new mistress of Kleinwalde; but she was only a woman, and dress up a woman as you will, call her by what name you will, she is nothing but a woman, born to help and serve, never by any possibility even equal to a clever man like himself. Old Joachim might have lounged as he chose, and put his feet on the table if it had seemed good to him, and Dellwig would have accepted it with unquestioning respect as an eccentricity of Herrschaften; but a woman had no sort of right, he said to himself, while he so fluently discoursed, to let herself go in the presence of her natural superior. Unfortunately, old Joachim, so level-headed an old gentleman in all other respects, had placed the power over his fortunes in the hands of this weak female leaning back so unbecomingly in her chair, playing with the objects on the table, never raising her eyes to his, and showing indeed, incredible as it seemed, every symptom of thinking of something else. The women of his acquaintance were, he was certain, worth individually fifty such affected, indifferent young ladies. They worked early and late to make their husbands comfortable; they were well practised in every art required of women living in the country; they were models of thrift and diligence; yet, with all their virtues and all their accomplishments, they never dreamed of lounging or not listening when a man was speaking, but sat attentively on the edge of their chairs, straight in the back and seemly, and when he had finished said Jawohl.

Anna certainly did sit very much at her ease, and instead of attending, as she ought to have done, to his description of Amtsvorstehers, was thinking of other things. Dellwig had thick lips that could not be hidden entirely by his grizzled moustache and beard, and he had the sort of eyes known to the inelegant but truthful as fishy, and a big obstinate nose, and a narrow obstinate forehead, and a long body and short legs; and though all this, Anna told herself, was not in the least his fault and should not in any way prejudice her against him, she felt that she was justified in wishing that his manners were less offensive, less boastful and boisterous, and that he did not bite his nails. "I wonder," she thought, her eyes carefully fixed on the paper-knife, but conscious of his every look and movement, "I wonder if he is as artful as he looks. Surely Uncle Joachim must have known what he was like, and would never have told me to keep him if he had not been honest. Perhaps he is perfectly honest, and when I meet him in heaven how ashamed I shall be of myself for having had doubts!" And then she fell to musing on what sort of an appearance a chastened and angelic Dellwig would probably present, and looked up suddenly at him with new interest.

"I trust I have made myself comprehensible?" he was asking, having just come to the end of what he felt was a masterly résumé of Herr von Lohm's duties.

"I beg your pardon?" said Anna, bringing her thoughts back with difficulty from the consideration of nimbuses, "Oh, about Amtsvorstehers—no," she said, shaking her head, "you have not. But that is my fault. I can't understand everything at once. I shall do better later on."

"Natürlich, natürlich," Dellwig vehemently assured her, while he made inward comments on the innate incapacity of all Weiber, as he called them, to grasp the simplest fact connected with law and justice.

"Tell me about the livestock," said Anna, remembering Uncle Joachim's frequent and affectionate allusions to his swine. "Are there many pigs?"

"Pigs?" repeated Dellwig, lifting up his hands as though mere words were insufficient to express his feelings, "such pigs as the gracious Miss now possesses are nowhere else to be found in Pomerania. They are the pride, and at the same time the envy, of the whole province. 'Let my sausages,' said the Herr Landrath last winter, when the time for killing drew near, 'let my sausages consist solely of the pigs reared at Kleinwalde by my friend the Oberinspector Dellwig.' The Frau Landräthin was deeply injured, for she too breeds and fattens pigs, but not like ours—not like ours."

"Who is the Herr Landrath?" asked Anna absently; but immediately remembering the description of the Amtsvorsteher she added quickly, "Never mind—don't explain. I suppose he is some sort of an official, and I shall not be quite clear about these different officials till I have lived here some time."

"Natürlich, natürlich," agreed Dellwig; and leaving the Landrath unexplained he launched forth into a dissertation on Anna's pigs, whose excellencies, it appeared, were wholly due to the unrivalled skill he had for years displayed in their treatment. "I have no children," he said, with a resigned and pious upward glance, "and my wife's maternal instincts find their satisfaction in tending and fattening these fine animals. She cannot listen to their cries the day they are killed, and withdraws into the cellar, where she prepares the stuffing. The gracious Miss ate the cutlets of one this very day. It was killed on purpose."

"Was it? I wish it hadn't been," said Anna, frowning at the remembrance of that meal. "I—I don't want things killed on my account. I—don't like pig."

"Not like pig?" echoed Dellwig, dropping his lower jaw in his amazement. "Did I understand aright that the gracious one does not eat pig's flesh gladly? And my wife and I who thought to prepare a joy for her!" He clasped his hands together and stared at her in dismay. Indeed, he was so much overcome by this extraordinary and wilful spurning of nature's best gifts that for a moment he was silent, and knew not how he should proceed. Were there not concentrated in the body of a single pig a greater diversity of joys than in any other form of pleasure that he could call to mind? Did it not include, besides the profounder delights of its roasted ribs, such solid satisfactions as hams, sausages, and bacon? Did not its liver, discreetly manipulated, rival the livers of Strasburg geese in delicacy? Were not its brains a source of mutual congratulation to an entire family at supper? Did not its very snout, boiled with

peas, make an otherwise inferior soup delicious? The ribs
of this particular pig were reposing at that moment in a
cool place, carefully shielded from harm by his wife,
reserved for the Easter Sunday dinner of their new mistress,
who, having begun at her first meal with the lesser joys of
cutlets, was to be fed with different parts in the order of
their excellence till the climax of rejoicing was reached on
Easter Day in the dish of Schweinebraten, and who was
now declaring, in a die-away, affected sort of voice, that
she did not want to eat pig at all. Where, then, was her
vulnerable point? How would he ever be able to touch her,
to influence her, if she was indifferent to the chief means of
happiness known to the dwellers in those parts? That was
the real aim and end of his labours, of the labours, as far as
he could see, of everyone else—to make as much money as
possible in order to live as well as possible; and what did
living well mean if it did not mean the best food? And what
was the best food if not pig? Not to be killed on her
account! On whose account, then, could they be killed?
With an owner always about the place, and refusing to have
pigs killed, how would he and his wife be able to indulge,
with satisfactory frequency, in their favourite food, or offer
it to their expectant friends on Sundays? He mourned old
Joachim, who so seldom came down, and when he did ate
his share of pork like a man, more sincerely at that moment
than he would have thought possible. "Mein seliger Herr,"
he burst out brokenly, completely upset by the difference
between uncle and niece, "mein seliger Herr——" And
then, unable to go on, fell to blowing his nose with
violence, for there were real tears in his eyes.

Anna looked up, surprised. She thought he had been
speaking of pigs, and here he was on a sudden bewailing
his late master. When she saw the tears she was deeply
touched. "Poor man," she said to herself, "how unjust I

have been. Of course he loved dear Uncle Joachim; and my coming here, an utter stranger, taking possession of everything, must be very dreadful for him." She got up, at once anxious, as she always was, to comfort and soothe anyone who was sad, and put her hand gently on his arm. "I loved him too," she said softly, "and you who knew him so long must feel his death dreadfully. We will try and keep everything just as he would have liked it, won't we? You know what his wishes were, and must help me to carry them out. You cannot have loved him more than I did— dear Uncle Joachim!"

She felt very near tears herself, and condoned the sonorous nose-blowing as the expression of an honourable emotion.

And Dellwig, when he presently reached his home and was met at the door by his wife's eager "Well, how was she?" laconically replied "Mad."

CHAPTER VII

When Anna woke next morning she had a confused idea that something annoying had happened the evening before, but she had slept so heavily that she could not at once recollect what it was. Then, the sun on her face waking her up more thoroughly, she remembered that Susie had stayed upstairs with Hilton till supper time, had then come down, glanced with unutterable disgust at the raw ham, cold sausage, eggs, and tepid coffee of which the evening meal was composed, refused to eat, refused to speak, refused utterly to smile, and afterwards in the drawing-room had announced her fixed intention of returning to England the next day.

Anna had protested and argued in vain; nothing could shake this sudden determination. To all her expostulations and entreaties Susie replied that she had never yet dwelt among savages and she was not going to begin now; so Anna was forced to conclude that Hilton had been making a scene, and knowing the effect of Hilton's scenes she gave up attempting to persuade, but told her with outward firmness and inward quakings that she herself could not possibly go too.

Susie had been very angry at this, and still more angry at the reason Anna gave, which was that, having invited the parson and his wife to dinner on Saturday, she could not break her engagement. Susie told her that as she would never see either of them again—for surely she would never again want to come to this place?—it was absurd to care twopence what they thought of her. What on earth did it matter if two inhabitants of the desert were offended or not offended once she was on the other side of the sea? And what did it matter at all how she treated them? She heaped such epithets as absurd, stupid, and idiotic on Anna's head, but Anna was not to be moved. She threatened to take Miss Leech and Letty away with her, and leave Anna a prey to the criticisms of Mrs. Grundy, and Anna said she could not prevent her doing so if she chose. Susie became more and more excited, more and more Dobbs, goaded by the recollection of what she had gone through with Hilton, and Anna, as usual under such circumstances, grew very silent. Letty sat listening in an agony of fright lest this cup of new experiences were about to be dashed prematurely from her eager lips; and Miss Leech discreetly left the room, though not in the least knowing where to go, finally seeking to drive away the nervous fears that assailed her in her lonely, creaking bedroom, where rats were gnawing at the woodwork, by thinking hard of Mr. Jessup, who on this occasion proved to be but a broken reed, pitted against the stern reality of rats.

The end of it, after Susie had poured out the customary reproaches of gross ingratitude and forgetfulness of all she had done for Anna for fifteen long years, was that Miss Leech and Letty were to stay on as originally intended, and come home with Anna towards the end of the holidays, and Susie would leave with Hilton the very next day.

Anna's attempt to make it up when she said good-night was repulsed with energy. Anna was for ever doing aggravating things, and then wanting to make it up; but makings up without having given in an inch seemed to Susie singularly unsatisfactory ceremonies. Oh, these Estcourts and their obstinacy! She marched off to bed in high indignation, an indignation not by any means allowed to cool by Hilton during the process of undressing; and Anna, worn out, fell asleep the moment she lay down, and woke up, as she had pictured herself doing in that odd wooden bed, with the morning sun shining full on her face.

It was a bright and lovely day, and on the side of the house where she slept she could not hear the wind, which was still blowing from the north-west. She opened one of her three big windows and let the cold air rush into her room, where the curious perfume of the baked evergreen wreaths festooned round the walls and looking-glass and dressing-table, joined to the heat from the stove, produced a heavy atmosphere that made her gasp. Somebody must already have been in her room, for the stove had been lit again, and she could see the peat blazing inside its open door. But outside, what a divine coldness and purity! She leaned out, drinking it in in long breaths, the warm March sun shining on her head. The garden, a mere uncared-for piece of rough grass with big trees, was radiant with rain-drops; the strip of sea was a deep blue now, with crests of foam; the island coast opposite was a shadowy streak stretched across the feet of the sun. Oh, it was beautiful to stand at that open window in the freshness, listening to the robin on the bare lilac bush a few yards away, to the quarrelling of the impudent sparrows on the path below, to the wind in the branches of the trees, to all the happy morning sounds of nature. A joyous feeling took possession of her heart, a sudden overpowering delight in what are called common things—mere earth, sky, sun, and wind. How lovely life was on such a morning, in such a clean, rain-washed, wind-scoured world. The wet smell of the garden came up to her, a whiff of marshy smell from the water, a long breath from the pines in the forest on the other side of the house. How had she ever breathed at Estcourt? How had she escaped suffocation without this life-giving smell of sea and forest? She looked down with delight at the wildness of the garden; after the trim Estcourt lawns, what a relief this was. This was all liberty, freedom from conventionality, absolute privacy; that was an everlasting clipping, and trimming, and raking, a perpetual stumbling upon gardeners at every step, for Susie would not be outdone by her greater neighbours in these matters. What was Hill Street looking like this fine March morning? All the blinds down, all the people in bed—how far away, how shadowy it was; a street inhabited by sleepy ghosts, with phantom milkmen rattling spectral cans beneath their windows. What a dream that life lived up to three days ago seemed in this morning light of reality. White clouds, like the clouds in Raphael's backgrounds, were floating so high overhead that they could not be hurried by the wind; a black cat sat in a patch of sunshine on the path washing itself; somebody opened a lower window, and there was a noise of sweeping, presently made indistinguishable by the chorale sung by the sweeper, no doubt Marie, in a pious, Good Friday mood. "Lob Gott ihr Christen allzugleich," chanted Marie, keeping time with her broom. Her voice was loud and monotonous, but Anna listened with a smile, and would have liked to join in, and so let some of her happiness find its way out.

She dressed quickly. There was no hot water, and no bell to ring for some, and she did not choose to call down from the window and interrupt the hymn, so she used cold water, assuring herself that it was bracing. Then she put on her hat and coat and stole out, afraid of disturbing Susie, who was lying a few yards away filled with smouldering wrath, anxious to have at least one quiet hour before beginning a day that she felt sure was going to be a day of worries. "There will be great peace to-night when she is gone," she thought, and immediately felt ashamed that she should look forward to being without her. "But I have never been without her since I was ten," she explained apologetically to her offended conscience, "and I want to see how I feel."

"Guten Morgen," said Marie, as Anna came into the drawing-room on her way out through its French windows.

"Guten Morgen," said Anna cheerfully.

Marie leaned on her broom and watched her go down the garden, greedily taking in every detail of her clothes, profoundly interested in a being who went out into the mud where nobody could see her with such a dress on, and whose shoes would not have been too big for Marie's small sister aged nine.

The evening before, indeed, Marie had beheld such a vision as she had never yet in her life seen, or so much as imagined; her new mistress had appeared at supper in what was evidently a herrschaftliche Ballkleid, with naked arms and shoulders, and the other ladies were attired in much the same way. The young Fräulein, it is true, showed no bare flesh, but even she was arrayed in white, and her hair magnificently tied up with ribbons. Marie had rushed out to tell the cook, and the cook, refusing to believe it, had carried in a supererogatory dish of compot as an excuse for securing the assurance of her own eyes; and Bertha from the farm, coming round with a message from the Frau Oberinspector, had seen it too through the crack of the kitchen door as the ladies left the dining-room, and had gone off breathlessly to spread the news; and the post cart just leaving with the letters had carried it to Lohm, and every inhabitant of every house between Kleinwalde and Stralsund knew all about it before bedtime. "What did I tell thee, wife?" said Dellwig, who, in spite of his superiority to the sex that served, listened as eagerly as any member of it to gossip; and his wife was only too ready to label Anna mad or eccentric as a slight private consolation for having passed out of the service of a comprehensible German gentleman into that of a woman and a foreigner.

Unconscious of the interest and curiosity she was exciting for miles round, pleased by Marie's artless piety, and filled with kindly feelings towards all her neighbours, Anna stood at the end of the garden looking over the low hedge that divided it from the marsh and the sea, and thought that she had never seen a place where it would be so easy to be

good. Complete freedom from the wearisome obligations of
society, an ideal privacy surrounded by her woods and the
water, a scanty population of simple and devoted people—
did not Dellwig shed tears at the remembrance of his
master?—every day spent here would be a day that made
her better, that would bring her nearer to that heaven in
which all good and simple souls dwelt while still on earth,
the heaven of a serene and quiet mind. Always she had
longed to be good, and to help and befriend those who had
the same longing but in whom it had been partially crushed
by want of opportunity and want of peace. The healthy
goodness that goes hand in hand with happiness was what
she meant; not that tragic and futile goodness that grows
out of grief, that lifts its head miserably in stony places,
that flourishes in sick rooms and among desperate sorrows,
and goes to God only because all else is lost. She went
round the house and crossed the road into the forest. The
fresh wind blew in her face, and shook down the drops
from the branches on her as she passed. The pine needles of
other years made a thick carpet for her feet. The sun
gleamed through the straight trunks and warmed her. The
restless sighing overheard in the tree tops filled her ears
with sweetest music. "I do believe the place is pleased that
I have come!" she thought, with a happy laugh. She came
to a clearing in the trees, opening out towards the north,
and she could see the flat fields and the wide sky and the
sunshine chasing the shadows across the vivid green
patches that she had learned were winter rye. A hole at her
feet, where a tree had been uprooted, still had snow in it;
but the larks were singing above in the blue, as though
from those high places they could see Spring far away in
the south, coming up slowly with the first anemones in her
hands, her face turned at last towards the patient north.

The strangest feeling of being for the first time in her life at home came over Anna. This poor country, how sweet and touching it was. After the English country, with its thickly scattered villages, and gardens, and fields that looked like parks, it did seem very poor and very empty, but intensely lovable. Like the furniture of her house, it struck her as symbolic in its bareness of the sturdier virtues. The people who lived in it must of necessity be frugal and hard-working if they would live at all, wresting by sheer labour their life from the soil, braced by the long winters to endurance and self-denial, their vices and their languors frozen out of them whether they would or no. At least so thought Anna, as she stood gazing out across the clearing at the fields and sky. "Could one not be good here? Could one not be so, so good?" she kept on murmuring. Then she remembered that she had been asking herself vague questions like this ever since her arrival; and with a sudden determination to face what was in her mind and think it out honestly, she sat down on a tree stump, buttoned her coat up tight, for the wind was blowing full on her, and fell to considering what she meant to do.

Susie did not go down to breakfast, but stayed in her bedroom on the sofa drinking a glass of milk into which an egg had been beaten, and listening to Hilton's criticisms of the German nation, delivered with much venom while she packed. But Hilton, though her contempt for German ways was so great as to be almost unutterable, was reconciled to a mistress who had so quickly given in to her wish to be taken back to Hill Street, and the venom was of an abstract nature, containing no personal sting of unfavourable comparisons with duchesses; so that Susie was sipping her milk in a fairly placid frame of mind when there was a knock at the door, and Anna asked if she might come in.

"Oh, yes, come in. Have you looked out the trains?"

"Yes. There's only one decent one, and you'll have to leave directly after luncheon. Won't you stay, Susie? You'll be so tired, going home without resting."

"Can't we leave before luncheon?"

"Yes, of course, if you prefer to lunch at Stralsund."

"Much. Have you ordered the shandrydan?"

"Yes, for half-past one."

"Then order it for half-past twelve. Hilton can drive with me."

"So I thought."

"Has that wretch been rubbing fish oil on it again?"

"I don't think so, after what I said yesterday."

"I shouldn't think what you said yesterday could have frightened him much. You beamed at him as though he were your best friend."

"Did I?"

Anna was looking odd, Susie thought, and answering her remarks with a nervous, abstracted air. She had apparently been out, for her dress was muddy, and she was quite rosy, and her hair was not so neat as usual. She stood about in an undecided sort of way, and glanced several times at Hilton on her knees before a trunk.

"Is that all the breakfast you are going to have?" she asked, becoming aware of the glass of milk.

"What other breakfast is there to have?" snapped Susie, who was hungry, and would have liked a great deal more.

"Well, the eggs and butter are very nice, anyway," said Anna, quite evidently thinking of other things.

"Now what has she got into her head?" Susie asked herself, watching her sister-in-law with misgiving. Anna's new moods were never by any chance of a sort to give Susie pleasure. Aloud she said tartly, "I can't eat eggs and butter by themselves. I shouldn't have had anything at all if it hadn't been for Hilton, who went into the kitchen and made me this herself."

"Excellent Hilton," said Anna absently. "Haven't you done packing yet, Hilton?"

"No, m'm."

Anna sat down on the end of the sofa and began to twist the frills of Susie's dressing-gown round her fingers.

"I haven't closed my eyes all night," said Susie, putting on her martyr look, "nor has Hilton."

"Haven't you? Why not? I slept the sleep of the just—better, indeed, than any just that I ever heard of."

"What, didn't that man go into your room?"

"What man? Oh, yes, Miss Leech was telling me about it. He lit the stoves, didn't he? I never heard a sound."

"You must have slept like a log then. Any one in the least sensitive would have been frightened out of their senses. I was, and so was Hilton. I wouldn't spend another night in this house for anything you could give me."

It appeared that Susie really had just cause for complaint. She had been nervous the night before after Hilton had left her, unable to sleep, and scared by the thought of their defencelessness—six women alone in that wild place. She wished then with all her heart that Dellwig did live in the house. Rats scampering about in the attic above added to her terrors. The wind shook the windows of her room and howled disconsolately up and down. She bore it as long as she could, which was longer than most women would have borne it, and then knocked on the wall dividing her room from Hilton's. But Hilton, with the bedclothes over her head and all the candles she had been able to collect alight, would not have stirred out of her room to save her mistress from dying; and Susie, desperate at the prospect of the awful hours round midnight, made one great effort of courage and sallied out to fetch her. Poor Susie, standing shivering before her maid's bolted door, scantily clothed, anxiously watching the flame of her candle that threatened each second to be blown out, alone on the wide, draughty landing, frightened at the sound of her own calls mingling weirdly with the creakings and hangings of the tempest-shaken house, was an object deserving of pity. It took some minutes to induce Hilton to open the door, and such minutes Susie had not, in the course of an ordered and normal existence, yet passed. They both went into Susie's room, locked themselves in, and Hilton lay down on the sofa; and after a long time they fell into an uneasy sleep. At half-past three Susie started up in bed; some one was trying to open the door and knocking. The candles had burnt themselves out, and she could not tell what time it was, but thought it must be early morning and that the servant wanted to bring her hot water; and she woke Hilton and bade her open the door. Hilton did so, gave a faint scream, and flung herself back on the sofa, where she lay as one dead, her face buried in the pillow. A man with a lantern and no shoes on was at the door, and came in noiselessly. Susie was never nearer fainting in her life. She sat in her bed, her cold hands clasped tightly round her knees, her eyes fixed on this dreadful apparition, unable to speak or move, paralysed by terror. This was the end, then, of all her hopes and ambitions—to come to Pomerania and die like a dog. Then the sickening feeling of fear gave way to one of overwhelming wrath when she found that all the man wanted was to light her stove. On the same principle that a child is shaken who has not after all been lost or run over, she was speechless with rage now that she found that she was not, after all, to be murdered. He was a very old man, and the light from the lantern cast strange reflections on his face and figure as he crouched before the stove. He mumbled as he worked, talking to the fire he was making as though it were a person. "Du willst nicht, brennen, Lump? Was? Na, warte mal!" And when he had finished, crept out again without glancing at the occupants of the room, still mumbling.

"It's the custom of the country, I suppose," said Anna.

"Is it? Well the sooner we get out of such a country the better. You are determined to stay in spite of everything? I can tell you I don't at all like my child being here, but you force me to leave her because you know very well that I can't let you stay here alone."

Anna glanced at Hilton, folding a dress with immense deliberation.

"Oh, Hilton knows what I think," said Susie, with a shrug.

"But she doesn't know what I think," said Anna. "I must talk to you before you leave, so please let her finish packing afterwards. Go and have your breakfast, Hilton."

"Did you say breakfast, m'm?" inquired Hilton with an innocent look.

"Breakfast?" repeated Susie; "poor thing, I'd like to know how and where she is to get any."

"Well, then, go and don't have your breakfast," said Anna impatiently. She had something to tell Susie that must be told soon, and was not in a mood to bear with Hilton's ways.

"How hospitable," remarked Susie as the door closed. "Really you are a delightful hostess."

Anna laughed. "I don't mean to be brutal," she said, "but if we can exist on the food without looking tragic I suppose she can too, especially as it is only for one day."

"My one consolation in leaving Letty here is that she will be dieted in spite of herself. I expect you to bring her back quite thin."

Anna got up restlessly and went to the window.

"And whatever you do, don't forget that the return tickets only last till the 24th. But you'll be sick of it long before then."

Anna turned round and leaned her back against the window. The strong morning light was on her hair, and her face was in shadow, yet Susie had a feeling that she was looking guilty.

"Susie, I've been thinking," she said with an effort.

"Really? How nice."

"Yes, it was, for I found out what it is that I must do if I mean to be happy. But I'm afraid that you won't think it nice, and will scold me. Now don't scold me."

"Well, tell me what it is." Susie lay staring at Anna's form against the light, bracing herself to hear something disagreeable. She knew very well from past experience that Anna's new plan, whatever it was, was certain to be wild and foolish.

"I am going to stay here."

"I know you are, and I know that nothing I can say will make you change your mind. Peter is just like you—the more I show him what a fool he's going to make of himself the more he insists on doing it. He calls it determination. Average people like myself, with smaller and more easily managed brains than you two wonders have got, call it pigheadedness."

"I don't mean only for Letty's holidays; I mean for good."

"For good?" Susie opened her mouth and stared in much the same blank consternation that Dellwig had shown on hearing that she did not like eating pig.

"Don't be angry with me," said Anna, coming over to the sofa and sitting on the floor by Susie's side; and she caught hold of her hand and began to talk fast and eagerly. "I always intended spending this money in helping poor people, but didn't quite know in what way—now I see my way clearly, and I must, must go it. Don't you remember in the catechism there's the duty towards God and the duty towards one's neighbour——"

"Oh, if you're going to talk religion——" said Susie, pulling away her hand in great disgust.

"No, no, do listen," said Anna, catching it again and stroking it while she talked, to Susie's intense irritation, who hated being stroked.

"If you are going into the catechism," she said, "Hilton had better come in again. It might do her good."

"No, no—I only wanted to say that there's another duty not in the catechism, greater than the duty towards one's neighbour——"

"My dear Anna, it isn't likely that you can improve on the catechism. And fancy wanting to, at breakfast time. Don't stroke my hand—it gives me the fidgets."

"But I want to explain things—do listen. The duty the catechism leaves out is the duty towards oneself. You can't get away from your duties, you know, Susie——" And she knit her brows in her effort to follow out her thought.

"My goodness, as though I ever tried! If ever a poor woman did her duty, I'm that woman."

"—and I believe that if I do those two duties, towards my neighbour and myself, I shall be doing my duty towards God."

Susie gave her body an impatient twist. She thought it positively indecent to speak of sacred things so early in the morning in cold blood. "What has this drivel to do with your stopping here?" she asked angrily.

"It has everything to do with it—my duty towards myself is to be as happy and as good as possible, and my duty towards my neighbour——"

"Oh, bother your neighbour and your duty!" cried Susie in exasperation.

"—is to help him to be good and happy too."

"Him? Her, I hope. Don't forget decency, my dear. A girl has no duties whatever towards male neighbours."

"Well, I do mean her," said Anna, looking up and laughing.

"So you think that by living here you'll make yourself happy?"

"Yes, I do—I do think so. Perhaps I am wrong, and shall find out I'm wrong, but I must try."

"You'll leave all your friends and relations and stay in this God-forsaken place where you can't even live like a lady?"

"Uncle Joachim said it was my one chance of leading the better life."

"Unutterable old fool," said Susie with bitterest contempt. "That money, then, is going to be thrown away on Germans? As though there weren't poor people enough in England, if your ambition is to pose as a benefactress!"

"Oh, I don't want to pose as anything—I only want to help unhappy wretches," cried Anna, laying her cheek caressingly on Susie's unwilling hand. "Now don't scold me—forgive me if I'm silly, and be patient with me till I find out that I've made a goose of myself and come creeping back to you and Peter. But I must do it—I must try—I will do what I think is right."

"And who are the wretches, pray, who are to be made happy?"

"Oh, those I am sorriest for—that no one else helps—the genteel ones, if I can only get at them."

"I never heard of genteel wretches," said Susie.

Anna laughed again. "I was thinking it all out in the forest this morning," she said, "and it suddenly flashed across me that this big roomy house was never meant not to be used, and that instead of going to see poor people and giving them money in the ordinary way, it would be so much better to let women of the better classes, who have no money, and who are dependent and miserable, come and live with me and share mine, and have everything that I have—exactly the same, with no difference of any sort. There is room for twelve at least, and wouldn't it be beautiful to make twelve people, who had lost all hope and all courage, happy for the rest of their days?"

"Oh, the girl's mad!" cried Susie, springing up from the sofa, no longer able to bear herself. She began to walk about the room, not knowing what to say or do, absolutely without sympathy for beneficent impulses, at all times possessed of a fine scorn for ideals, feeling that no argument would be of any avail with an Estcourt whose mind was made up, shocked that good money, so hard to get, and so very precious when got, should be thrown away in such a manner, bewildered by the difficulties of the situation, for how could a girl of Anna's age live alone, and direct a house full of objects of charity? Would the objects themselves be a sufficient chaperonage? Would her friends at home think so? Would they not blame her, Susie, for having allowed all this? As though she could prevent it! Or would they expect her to stay with Anna in this place till she should marry? As though anybody would ever marry such a lunatic! "Mad, mad, mad!" cried Susie, wringing her hands.

"I was afraid that you wouldn't like it," said the culprit on the floor, watching her with a distressed face.

"Like it? Oh—mad, mad!" And she continued to walk and wring her hands.

"Well, you'll stay, then," she said, suddenly stopping in front of Anna, "I know you well enough, and shall waste no breath arguing. That infatuated old man's money has turned your head—I didn't know it was so weak. But look into your heart when I am gone—you'll have time enough and quiet enough—and ask yourself honestly whether what you are going to do is a proper way of paying back all I have done for you, and all the expense you have been. You know what my wishes are about you, and you don't care one jot. Gratitude! There isn't a spark of it in your whole body.

Never was there a more selfish creature, and I can't believe that ingratitude and selfishness are the stuff that makes saints. Don't dare to talk any more rot about duty to your neighbour to me. An Englishwoman to come and spend her money on German charities——"

"It's German money," murmured Anna.

"And to live here—to live here—oh, mad, mad!" And Susie's indignation threatening to choke her, she resumed her walk and her gesticulations, her high heels tapping furiously on the bare boards.

She longed to take Letty and Miss Leech away with her that very morning, and punish Anna by leaving her entirely alone; but she did not dare because of Peter. Peter was always on Anna's side when there were differences, and would be sure to do something dreadful when he heard of it—perhaps come and live here too, and never go back to his wife any more. Oh, these half Germans! Why had she married into a family with such a taint in its blood? "You will have to have some one here," she said, turning on Anna, who still sat on the floor by the sofa, a look on her face of apology and penitence mixed with firmness that Susie well knew. "How can you stay here alone? I shall leave Miss Leech with you till the end of the holidays, though I hate to seem to encourage you; but then you see I do my duty and always have, though I don't talk about it. When I get home I shall look for some elderly woman who won't mind coming here and seeing that you don't make yourself too much of a by-word, and the day she comes you are to send me back my child."

"It is good of you to let me keep Letty, dear Susie——"

"Dear Susie!"

"But I don't mean to be a by-word, as you call it,"
continued Anna, the ghost of a smile lurking in her eyes,
"and I don't want an Englishwoman. What use would she
be here? She wouldn't understand if it was a German by-
word that I turned into. I thought about asking the parson
how I had better set about getting a German lady—a grave
and sober female, advanced in years, as Uncle Joachim
wrote."

"Oh, Uncle Joachim——" Susie could hardly endure to
hear the name. It was that odious old man who had filled
Anna's head with these ideas. To leave her money was
admirable, but to influence a weak girl's mind with his
wishy-washy German philosophy about the better life and
such rubbish, as he evidently had done during those
excursions with her, was conduct so shameful that she
found no words strong enough to express her opinion of it.
Everyone would blame her for what had happened,
everyone would jeer at her, and say that the moment an
opportunity of escape had presented itself Anna had seized
it, preferring an existence of loneliness and hardship—any
sort of existence—to all the pleasures of civilised life in
Susie's company. Peter would certainly be very angry with
her, and reproach her with not having made Anna happy
enough. Happy enough! The girl had cost her at least three
hundred a year, what with her expensive education and all
her clothes since she came out; and if three hundred good
pounds spent on a girl could not make her happy, she'd like
to know what could. And no one—not one of those odious
people in London whom she secretly hated—would have a
single word of censure for Anna. No one ever had. All her
vagaries and absurdities during the last few years when she
had been so provoking had been smiled at, had been, Susie

knew, put down to her treatment of her. Treatment of her, indeed! The thought of these things made Susie writhe. She had been looking forward to the next season, to having her pretty sister-in-law with her in the happy mood she had been in since she heard of her good fortune, and had foreseen nothing but advantages to herself from Anna's presence in her house—an Anna spending and not being spent upon, and no doubt to be persuaded to share the expenses of housekeeping. And now she must go home by herself to blame, scoldings, and derision. The prospect was almost more than she could bear. She went to the door, opened it, and turning to Anna fired a parting shot. "Let no one," she said, her voice shaken by deepest disgust, "who wants to be happy, ever spend a penny on her husband's relations."

And then she called Hilton; nor did she leave off calling till Hilton appeared, and so prevented Anna from saying another word.

CHAPTER VIII

But if Susie's rage was such that she refused to say good-bye, and terrified Miss Leech while she was waiting in the hall for the carriage by dark allusions to strait-waistcoats, when the parson was taken into Anna's confidence after dinner on the following night his raptures knew no bounds. "Liebes, edeldenkendes Fräulein!" he burst out, clasping his hands and gazing with a moist, ecstatic eye at this young sprig of piety. He was a good man, not very learned, not very refined, sentimental exceedingly, and much inclined to become tearfully eloquent on such subjects as die liebe kleine Kinder, die herrliche Natur, die Frau als Schutzengel, and the sacredness of das Familienleben.

Anna felt that he was the only person at hand who could perhaps help her to find twelve dejected ladies willing to be made happy, and had unfolded her plan to him as tersely as possible in her stumbling German, with none of those accompanying digressions into the question of feelings that Susie stigmatised as drivel; and she sat uncomfortable enough while he burst forth into praises that would not end of her goodness and nobleness. It is hard to look anything but fatuous when somebody is extolling your virtues to your face, and she could not help both looking and feeling foolish during his extravagant glorification. She did not doubt his sincerity, and indeed he was absolutely sincere, but she wished that he would be less flowery and less long, and would skip the raptures and get on to the main subject, which was practical advice.

She wore the simple white dress that had caused such a sensation in the neighbourhood, a garment that hung in long, soft folds, accentuating her slender length of limb. Her bright hair was parted and tucked behind her ears. Everything about her breathed an absolute want of self-consciousness and vanity, a perfect freedom from the least thought of the impression she might be making; yet she was beautiful, and the good man observing her beauty, and supposing from what she had just told him an equal beauty of character, for ever afterwards when he thought of angels on quiet Sunday evenings in his garden, clothed them as Anna was clothed that night, not even shrinking from the pretty, bare shoulders and scantily sleeved arms, but facing them with a courage worthy of a man, however doubtfully it might become a pastor.

His wife, in her best dress, which was also her tightest, sat on the edge of a chair some way off, marvelling greatly at many things. She could not hear what it was Anna had said to set her husband off exclaiming, because the governess persisted in trying to talk German to her, and would not be satisfied with vague replies. She was disappointed by the sudden disappearance of the sister-in-law, gone before she had shown herself to a single soul; astonished that she had not been requested to sit on the sofa, in which place of honour the young Fräulein sprawled in a way that would certainly ruin her clothes; disgusted that she had not been pressed at table, nay, not even asked, to partake of every dish a second time; indeed, no one had seemed to notice or care whether she ate anything at all. These were strange ways. And where were the Dellwigs, those great people accustomed to patronise her because she was the parson's wife? Was it possible that they had not been invited? Were there then quarrels already? She could not of course dream that Anna would never have thought of asking her inspector and his wife to dinner, and that in her ignorance she regarded the parson as a person on an altogether higher social level than the inspector. These things, joined to conjectures as to the probable price by the yard of Anna's, Letty's, and Miss Leech's clothes, gave Frau Manske more food for reflection than she had had for years; and she sat turning them over slowly in her mind in the intervals between Miss Leech's sentences, while her dress, which was of silk, creaked ominously with every painful breath she drew.

"The best way to act," said the parson, when he had exhausted the greater part of his raptures, "will be to advertise in a newspaper of a Christian character."

"But not in my name," said Anna.

"No, no, we must be discreet—we must be very discreet. The advertisement must be drawn up with skill. I will make, simultaneously, inquiries among my colleagues in the holy office, but there must also be an advertisement. What would the gracious Miss's opinion be of the desirability of referring all applicants, in the first instance, to me?"

"Why, I think it would be an excellent plan, if you do not mind the trouble."

"Trouble! Joy fills me at the thought of taking part in this good work. Little did I think that our poor corner of the fatherland was to become a holy place, a blessed refuge for the world-worn, a nook fragrant with charity——"

"No, not charity," interposed Anna.

"Whose perfume," continued the parson, determined to finish his sentence, "whose perfume will ascend day and night to the attentive heavens. But such are the celestial surprises Providence keeps in reserve and springs upon us when we least expect it."

"Yes," said Anna. "But what shall we put in the advertisement?"

"Ach ja, the advertisement. In the contemplation of this beautiful scheme I forget the advertisement." And again the moisture of ecstasy suffused his eyes, and again he clasped his hands and gazed at her with his head on one side, almost as though the young lady herself were the beautiful scheme.

Anna got up and went to the writing-table to fetch a pencil and a sheet of paper, anxious to keep him to the point; and the parson watching the graceful white figure was more than ever struck by her resemblance to his idea of angels. He did not consider how easy it was to look like a being from another world, a creature purified of every earthly grossness, to eyes accustomed to behold the redundant exuberance of his own excellent wife.

She brought the paper, and sat down again at the table on which the lamp stood. "How does one write any sort of advertisement in German?" she said. "I could not write one for a housemaid. And this one must be done so carefully."

"Very true; for, alas, even ladies are sometimes not all that they profess to be. Sad that in a Christian country there should be impostors. Doubly sad that there should be any of the female sex."

"Very sad," said Anna, smiling. "You must tell me which are the impostors among those that answer."

"Ach, it will not be easy," said the parson, whose experience of ladies was limited, and who began to see that he was taking upon himself responsibilities that threatened to become grave. Suppose he recommended an applicant who afterwards departed with the gracious Miss's spoons in her bag? "Ach, it will not be easy," he said, shaking his head.

"Oh, well," said Anna, "we must risk the impostors. There may not be any at all. How would you begin?"

The parson threw himself back in his chair, folded his hands, cast up his eyes to the ceiling, and meditated. Anna waited, pencil in hand, ready to write at his dictation. Frau Manske at the other end of the room was straining her ears to hear what was going on, but Miss Leech, desirous both of entertaining her and of practising her German, would not cease from her spasmodic talk, even expecting her mistakes to be corrected. And there were no refreshments, no glasses of cooling beer being handed round, no liquid consolation of any sort, not even seltzer water. She regarded her evening as a failure.

"A Christian lady of noble sentiments," dictated the parson, apparently reading the words off the ceiling, "offers a home in her house——"

"Is this the advertisement?" asked Anna.

"——offers a home in her house——"

"I don't quite like the beginning," hesitated Anna. "I would rather leave out about the noble sentiments."

"As the gracious one pleases. Modesty can never be anything but an ornament. 'A Christian lady——'"

"But why a Christian lady? Why not simply a lady? Are there, then, heathen ladies about, that you insist on the Christian?"

"Worse, worse than heathen," replied the parson, sitting up straight, and fixing eyeballs suddenly grown fiery on her;

and his voice fell to a hissing whisper, in strange contrast to his previous honeyed tones. "The heathen live in far-off lands, where they keep quiet till our missionaries gather them into the Church's fold—but here, here in our midst, here everywhere, taking the money from our pockets, nay, the very bread from our mouths, are the Jews."

Impossible to describe the tone of fear and hatred with which this word was pronounced.

Anna gazed at him, mystified. "The Jews?" she echoed. One of her greatest friends at home was a Jew, a delightful person, the mere recollection of whom made her smile, so witty and charming and kind was he. And of Jews in general she could not remember to have heard anything at all.

"But not only money from our pockets and bread from our mouths," continued the parson, leaning forward, his light grey eyes opened to their widest extent, and speaking in a whisper that made her flesh begin the process known as creeping, "but blood—blood from our veins."

"Blood from your veins?" she repeated faintly. It sounded horrid. It offended her ears. It had nothing to do with the advertisement. The strange light in his eyes made her think of fanaticism, cruelty, and the Middle Ages. The mildest of men in general, as she found later on, rabidness seized him at the mere mention of Jews.

"Blood," he hissed, "from the veins of Christians, for the performance of their unholy rites. Did the gracious one never hear of ritual murders?"

"No," said Anna, shrinking back, the nearer he leaned towards her, "never in my life. Don't tell me now, for it—it sounds interesting. I should like to hear about it all another time. 'A Christian lady offers her home,'" she went on quickly, scribbling that much down, and then looking at him inquiringly.

"Ach ja," he said in his natural voice, leaning back in his chair and reducing his eyes to their normal size, "I forgot again the advertisement. 'A Christian lady offers her home to others of her sex and station who are without means——'"

"And without friends, and without hope," added Anna, writing.

"Gut, gut, sehr gut."

"She has room in her house in the country," Anna went on, writing as she spoke, "for twelve such ladies, and will be glad to share with them all that she possesses of fortune and happiness."

"Gut, gut, sehr gut."

"Is the German correct?"

"Quite correct. I would add, 'Strictest inquiries will be made before acceptance of any application by Herr Pastor Manske of Lohm, to whom all letters are to be addressed. Applicants must be ladies of good family, who have fallen on evil days by the will of God.'"

Anna wrote this down as far as "days," after which she put a full stop.

"It pleases me not entirely," said Manske, musing; "the language is not sufficiently noble. Noble schemes should be alluded to in noble words."

"But not in an advertisement."

"Why not? We ought not to hide our good thoughts from our fellows, but rather open our hearts, pour out our feelings, spend freely all that we have in us of virtue and piety, for the edification and exhilaration of others."

"But not in an advertisement. I don't want to exhilarate the public."

"And why not exhilarate the public, dear Miss? Is it not composed of units of like passions to ourselves? Units on the way to heaven, units bowed down by the same sorrows, cheered by the same hopes, torn asunder by the same temptations as the gracious one and myself?" And immediately he launched forth into a flood of eloquence about units; for in Germany sermons are all extempore, and the clergy, from constant practice, acquire a fatal fluency of speech, bursting out in the week on the least provocation into preaching, and not by any known means to be stopped.

"Oh—words, words, words!" thought Anna, waiting till he should have finished. His wife, hearing the well-known rapid speech of his inspired moments, glowed with pride. "My Adolf surpasses himself," she thought; "the Miss must wonder."

The Miss did wonder. She sat and wondered, her elbows on the arms of the chair, her finger tips joined together, and her eyes fixed on her finger tips. She did not like to look at him, because, knowing how different was the effect produced on her to that which he of course imagined, she was sorry for him.

"It is so good of you to help me," she said with gentle irrelevance when the longed-for pause at length came. "There was something else that I wanted to consult you about. I must look for a companion—an elderly German lady, who will help me in the housekeeping."

"Yes, yes, I comprehend. But would not the twelve be sufficient companions, and helps in the housekeeping?"

"No, because I would not like them to think that I want anything done for me in return for their home. I want them to do exactly what makes them happiest. They will all have had sad lives, and must waste no more time in doing things they don't quite like."

"Ah—noble, noble," murmured the parson, quite as unpractical as Anna, and fascinated by the very vagueness of her plan of benevolence.

"The companion I wish to find would be another sort of person, and would help me in return for a salary."

"Certainly, I comprehend."

"I thought perhaps you would tell me how to advertise for such a person?"

"Surely, surely. My wife has a sister——"

He paused. Anna looked up quickly. She had not reckoned with the possibility of his wife's having sisters.

"Lieber Schatz," he called to his wife, "what does thy sister Helena do now?"

Frau Manske got up and came over to them with the alacrity of relief. "What dost thou say, dear Adolf?" she asked, laying her hand on his shoulder. He took it in his, stroked it, kissed it, and finally put his arm round her waist and held it there while he talked; all to the exceeding joy of Letty, to whom such proceedings had the charm of absolute freshness.

"Thy sister Helena—is she at present in the parental house?" he asked, looking up at her fondly, warmed into an affection even greater than ordinary by the circumstance of having spectators.

Frau Manske was not sure. She would write and inquire. Anna proposed that she should sit down, but the parson playfully held her closer. "This is my guardian angel," he explained, smiling beatifically at her, "the faithful mother of my children, now grown up and gone their several ways. Does the gracious Miss remember the immortal lines of Schiller, 'Ehret die Frauen, sie flechten und weben himmlische Rosen in's irdische Leben'? Such has been the occupation of this dear wife, only interrupted by her occasional visits to bathing resorts, since the day, more than twenty-five years ago, when she consented to tread with me the path leading heavenwards. Not a day has there been, except when she was at the seaside, without its roses."

"Oh," said Anna. She felt that the remark was not at the height of the situation, and added, "How—how interesting." This also struck her as inadequate; but all further inspiration failing her, she was reduced to the silent sympathy of smiles.

"Ten children did the Lord bless us with," continued the parson, expanding into confidences, "and six it was His will again to remove."

"The drains——" murmured Frau Manske.

"Yes, truly the drains in the town where we lived then were bad, very bad. But one must not question the wisdom of Providence."

"No, but one might mend——" Anna stopped, feeling that under some circumstances even the mending of drains might be impious. She had heard so much about piety and Providence within the last two hours that she was confused, and was no longer clear as to the exact limit of conduct beyond which a flying in the face of Providence might be said to begin.

But the parson, clasping his wife to his side, paid no heed to anything she might be saying, for he was already well on in a detailed account of the personal appearance, habits, and career of his four remaining children, and dwelt so fondly on each in turn that he forgot sister Helena and the second advertisement; and when he had explained all their numerous excellencies and harmless idiosyncrasies, including their preferences in matters of food and drink, he abruptly quitted this topic, and proceeded to expound Anna's scheme to his wife, who had listened with ill-concealed impatience to the first part of his discourse, consumed as she was with curiosity to hear what it was that Anna had confided to him.

So Anna had to listen to the raptures all over again. The eager interest of the wife disturbed her. She doubted whether Frau Manske had any real sympathy with her plan. Her inquisitiveness was unquestionable; but Anna felt that opening her heart to the parson and opening it to his wife were two different things. Though he was wordy, he was certainly enthusiastic; his wife, on the other hand, appeared to be chiefly interested in the question of cost. "The cost will be colossal," she said, surveying Anna from head to foot. "But the gracious Miss is rich," she added.

Anna began to examine her finger tips again.

On the way home through the dark fields, after having criticised each dish of the dinner and expressed the opinion that the entertainment was not worthy of such a wealthy lady, Frau Manske observed to her husband that it was true, then, what she had always heard of the English, that they were peculiarly liable to prolonged attacks of craziness.

"Craziness! Thou callest this craziness? It is my wife, the wife of a pastor, that I hear applying such a word to so beautiful, so Christian, a scheme?"

"But the good money—to give it all away. Yes, it is very Christian, but it is also crazy."

"Woman, shut thy mouth!" cried the parson, beside himself with indignation at hearing such sentiments from such lips.

Clearly Frau Manske was not at that moment engaged with her roses.

CHAPTER IX

The next morning early, Anna went over to the farm to ask Dellwig to lend her any newspapers he might have. She was anxious to advertise as soon as possible for a companion, and now that she knew of the existence of sister Helena, thought it better to write this advertisement without the parson's aid, copying any other one of the sort that she might see in the papers. Until she had secured the services of a German lady who would tell her how to set about the reforms she intended making in her house, she was perfectly helpless. She wanted to put her home in order quickly, so that the twelve unhappy ones should not be kept waiting; and there were many things to be done. Servants, furniture, everything, was necessary, and she did not know where such things were to be had. She did not even know where washerwomen were obtainable, and Frau Dellwig never seemed to be at home when she sent for her, or went to her seeking information. On Good Friday, after Susie's departure, she had sent a message to the farm desiring the attendance of the inspector's wife, whom she wished to consult about the dinner to be prepared for the Manskes, all provisions apparently passing through Frau Dellwig's hands; and she had been told that the lady was at church. On Saturday morning, disturbed by the emptiness of her larder and the imminence of her guests, she had gone herself to the farm, but was told that the lady was in the cow-sheds—in which cow-shed nobody exactly knew. Anna had been forced to ask Dellwig about the food. On Sunday she took Letty with her, abashed by the whisperings and starings she had had to endure when she went alone. Nor on this occasion did she see the inspector's wife, and she began to wonder what had become of her.

The Dellwigs' wrath and amazement when they found that
the parson and his wife had been invited to dinner and they
themselves left out was indescribable. Never had such an
insult been offered them. They had always been the first
people of their class in the place, always held their heads
up and condescended to the clergy, always been helped
first at table, gone first through doors, sat in the right-hand
corners of sofas. If he was furious, she was still more so,
filled with venom and hatred unutterable for the innocent,
but it must be added overjoyed, Frau Manske; and though
her own interest demanded it, she was altogether unable to
bring herself to meet Anna for the purpose, as she knew, of
being consulted about the menu to be offered to the
wretched upstart. Indeed, Frau Dellwig's position was
similar to that painful one in which Susie found herself
when her influential London acquaintance left her out of
the invitations to the wedding; on which occasion, as we
know, Susie had been constrained to flee to Germany in
order to escape the comments of her friends. Frau Dellwig
could not flee anywhere. She was obliged to stay where she
was and bear it as best she might, humiliated in the eyes of
the whole neighbourhood, an object of derision to her very
milkmaids. Philosophers smile at such trials; but to persons
who are not philosophers, and at Kleinwalde these were in
the majority, they are more difficult to endure than any
family bereavement. There is no dignity about them, and
friends, instead of sympathising, rejoice more or less
openly according to the degree of their civilisation. The
degree of civilisation among Frau Dellwig's friends was not
great, and the rejoicings on the next Sunday when they all
met would be but ill-concealed; there was no escape from
them, they had to be faced, and the malicious condolences
accepted with what countenance she could. Instead of
making sausages, therefore, she shut herself in her bedroom
and wept.

And so it came about that the unconscious Anna, whose one desire was to live at peace with her neighbours, made two enemies within two days. "All women," said Dellwig to his wife, "high and low, are alike. Unless they have a husband to keep them in their right places, they become religious and run after pastors. Manske has wormed himself in very cleverly, truly very cleverly. But we will worm him out again with equal cleverness. As for his wife, what canst thou expect from so great a fool?"

"No, indeed, from her I expect nothing," replied his wife, tossing her head, "but from the niece of our late master I expected the behaviour of a lady." And at that moment, the niece of her late master being announced, she fled into her bedroom.

Anna, friendly as ever, specially kind to Dellwig since his tears on the night of her arrival, came with Letty into the gloomy little office where he was working, with all the morning sunshine in her face. Though she was perplexed by many things, she was intensely happy. The perfect freedom, after her years of servitude, was like heaven. Here she was in her own home, from which nobody could take her, free to arrange her life as she chose. Oh, it was a beautiful world, and this the most beautiful corner of it! She was sure the sky was bluer at Kleinwalde than in other places, and that the larks sang louder. And then was she not on the very verge of realising her dreams of bringing the light of happiness into dark and hopeless lives? Oh, the beautiful, beautiful world! She came into Dellwig's room with the love of it shining in her eyes.

He was as obsequious as ever, for unfortunately his bread and butter depended on this perverse young woman; but he was also graver and less talkative, considering within himself that he could not be expected to pass over such a slight without some alteration in his manner. He ought, he felt, to show that he was pained, and he ought to show it so unmistakably that she would perhaps be led to offer some explanation of her conduct. Accordingly he assumed the subdued behaviour of one whose feelings have been hurt, and Anna thought how greatly he improved on acquaintance.

He would have given much to know why she wanted the papers, for surely it was unusual for women to read newspapers? When there was a murder, or anything of that sort, his wife liked to see them, but not at other times. "Is the gracious Miss interested in politics?" he inquired, as he put several together.

"No, not particularly," said Anna; "at least, not yet in German politics. I must live here a little while first."

"In—in literature, perhaps?"

"No, not particularly. I know so little about German books."

"There are some well-written articles occasionally on the modes in ladies' dresses."

"Really?"

"My wife tells me she often gets hints from them as to what is being worn. Ladies, we know," he added with a superior smile, checked, however, on his remembering that he was pained, "are interested in these matters."

"Yes, they are," agreed Anna, smiling, and holding out her hand for the papers.

"Ah, then, it is that that the gracious Miss wishes to read?" he said quickly.

"No, not particularly," said Anna, who began to see that he too suffered from the prevailing inquisitiveness. Besides, she was too much afraid of his having sisters, or of his wife's having sisters, eager to come and be a blessing to her, to tell him about her advertisement.

On the steps of his house, to which Dellwig accompanied the two girls, stood a man who had just got off his horse. He was pulling off his gloves as he watched it being led away by a boy. He had his back to Anna, and she looked at it interested, for it was unlike any back she had yet seen in Kleinwalde, in that it was the back of a gentleman.

"It is Herr von Lohm," said Dellwig, "who has business here this morning. Some of our people unfortunately drink too much on holidays like Good Friday, and there are quarrels. I explained to the gracious one that he is our Amtsvorsteher."

Herr von Lohm turned at the sound of Dellwig's voice, and took off his hat. "Pray present me to these ladies," he said to Dellwig, and bowed as gravely to Letty as to Anna, to her great satisfaction.

"So this is my neighbour?" thought Anna, looking down at him from the higher step on which she stood with her papers under her arm.

"So this is old Joachim's niece, of whom he was always talking?" thought Lohm, looking up at her. "Wise old man to leave the place to her instead of to those unpleasant sons." And he proceeded to make a few conventional remarks, hoping that she liked her new home and would soon be quite used to the country life. "It is very quiet and lonely for a lady not used to our kind of country, with its big estates and few neighbours," he said in English. "May I talk English to you? It gives me pleasure to do so."

"Please do," said Anna. Here was a person who might be very helpful to her if ever she reached her wits' end; and how nice he looked, how clean, and what a pleasant voice he had, falling so gratefully on ears already aching with Dellwig's shouts and the parson's emphatic oratory.

He was somewhere between thirty and forty, not young at all, she thought, having herself never got out of the habit of feeling very young; and beyond being long and wiry, with not even a tendency to fat, as she noticed with pleasure, there was nothing striking about him. His top boots and his green Norfolk jacket and green felt hat with a little feather stuck in it gave him an air of being a sportsman. It was refreshing to come across him, if only because he did not bow. Also, considering him from the top of the steps, she became suddenly conscious that Dellwig and the parson neglected their persons more than was seemly. They were both no doubt very excellent; but she did like nicely washed men.

Herr von Lohm began to talk about Uncle Joachim, with whom he had been very intimate. Anna came down the steps and he went a few yards with her, leaving Dellwig standing at the door, and followed by the eyes of Dellwig's wife, concealed behind her bedroom curtain.

"I shall be with you in one moment," called Lohm over his shoulder.

"Gut," said Dellwig; and he went in to tell his wife that these English ladies were very free with gentlemen, and to bid her mark his words that Lohm and Kleinwalde would before long be one estate.

"And us? What will become of us?" she asked, eying him anxiously.

"I too would like to know that," replied her husband. "This all comes of leaving land away from the natural heirs." And with great energy he proceeded to curse the memory of his late master.

Lohm's English was so good that it astonished Anna. It was stiff and slow, but he made no mistakes at all. His manner was grave, and looking at him more attentively she saw traces on his face of much hard work and anxiety. He told her that his mother had been a cousin of Uncle Joachim's wife. "So that there is a slight relationship by marriage existing between us," he said.

"Very slight," said Anna, smiling, "faint almost beyond recognition."

"Does your niece stay with you for an indefinite period?" he asked. "I cannot avoid knowing that this young lady is your niece," he added with a smile, "and that she is here with her governess, and that Lady Estcourt left suddenly on Good Friday, because all that concerns you is of the greatest interest to the inhabitants of this quiet place, and they talk of little else."

"How long will it take them to get used to me? I don't like being an object of interest. No, Letty is going home as soon as I have found a companion. That is why I am taking the inspector's newspapers home with me. I can't construct an advertisement out of my stores of German, and am going to see if I can find something that will serve as model."

"Oh, may I help you? What difficulties you must meet with every hour of the day!"

"I do," agreed Anna, thinking of all there was to be done before she could open her doors and her arms to the twelve.

"Any service that I can render to my oldest friend's niece will give me the greatest pleasure. Will you allow me to send the advertisement for you? You can hardly know how or where to send it."

"I don't," said Anna. "It would be very kind—I really would be grateful. It is so important that I should find somebody soon."

"It is of the first importance," said Lohm.

"Has the parson told him of my plans already?" thought Anna. But Lohm had not seen Manske that morning, and was only picturing this little thing to himself, this dainty little lady, used to such a different life, alone in the empty house, struggling with her small supply of German to make the two raw servants understand her ways. Anna was not a little thing at all, and she would have been half-amused and half-indignant if she had known that that was the impression she had made on him.

"My sister, Gräfin Hasdorf," he began—"Heavens," she thought, "has he got an unattached sister?"—"sometimes stays with me with her children, and when she is here will be able to help you in many ways if you will allow her to. She too knew your uncle from her childhood. She will be greatly interested to know that you have had the courage to settle here."

"Courage?" echoed Anna. "Why, I love it. It's the most beautiful place in the world."

Lohm looked doubtfully at her for a moment; but there was no mistaking the sincerity of those eyes. "It is pleasant to hear you say so," he said. "My sister Trudi would scarcely credit her ears if she were present. To her it is a terrible place, and she pities me with all her heart because my lot is cast in it."

Anna laughed. She thought she knew very well what sister Trudis were like. "I do not pity you," she said; "I couldn't pity any being who lived in this air, and under this sky. Look how blue it is—and the geese—did you ever see such white geese?"

A flock of geese were being driven across the sunny yard, dazzling in their whiteness. Anna lifted up her face to the sun and drew in a long breath of the sharp air. She forgot Lohm for a moment—it was such a glorious Easter Sunday, and the world was so full of the abundant gifts of God.

Dellwig, who had been watching them from his wife's window, thought that the brawlers who were going to be fined had been kept waiting long enough, and came out again on to the steps.

Lohm saw him, and felt that he must go. "I must do my business," he said, "but as you have given me permission I will send an advertisement to the papers to-night. Of course you desire to have an elderly lady of good family?"

"Yes, but not too elderly—not so elderly that she won't be able to work. There will be so much to do, so very much to do."

Lohm went away wondering what work there could possibly be, except the agreeable and easy work of seeing that this young lady was properly fed, and properly petted, and in every way taken care of.

CHAPTER X

He sent the advertisement by the evening post to two or three of the best newspapers. He had seen the pastor after morning church, who had at once poured into his ears all about Anna's twelve ladies, garnishing the story with interjections warmly appreciative of the action of Providence in the matter. Lohm had been considerably astonished, but had said little; it was not his way to say much at any time to the parson, and the ecstasies about the new neighbour jarred on him. Miss Estcourt's need of advice must have been desperate for her to have confided in Manske. He appreciated his good qualities, but his family had never been intimate with the parson; perhaps because from time immemorial the Lohms had been chiefly males, and the attitude of male Germans towards parsons is, at its best, one of indulgence. This Lohm restricted his dealings with him, as his father had done before him, to the necessary deliberations on the treatment of the sick and poor, and to official meetings in the schoolhouse. He was invariably kind to him, and lent as willing an ear as his slender purse allowed to applications for assistance; but the idea of discussing spiritual experiences with him, or, in times of personal sorrow, of dwelling conversationally on his griefs, would never have occurred to him. The easy familiarity with which Manske spoke of the Deity offended his taste. These things, these sacred and awful mysteries, were the secrets between the soul and its God. No man, thought Lohm, should dare to touch with profane questioning the veil shrouding his neighbour's inner life. Manske, however, knew no fear and no compunction. He would ask the most tremendous questions between two mouthfuls of pudding, backing himself up with the whole authority of the Lutheran Church, besides the Scriptures; and if the poor people and the partly educated liked it, and were edified, and enjoyed stirring up and talking over their religious emotions almost as much as they did the latest village scandal, Lohm, who had no taste either for scandal or emotions, kept the parson at arm's length.

He thought a good deal about what Manske had told him during the afternoon. She had gone to the parson, then, for help, because there was no one else to go to. Poor little thing. He could imagine the sort of speeches Manske had made her, and the sort of advertisement he would have told her to write. Poor little thing. Well, what he could do was to put her in the way of getting a companion as quickly as possible, and a very sensible, capable woman it ought to be. No wonder she was not to be past hard work. Work there would certainly be, with twelve women in the house undergoing the process of being made happy. Lohm could not help smiling at the plan. He thought of Miss Estcourt courageously trying to demolish the crust of dejection that had formed in the course of years over the hearts of her patients, and he trusted that she would not exhaust her own youth and joyousness in the effort. Perhaps she would succeed. He did not remember having heard of any scheme quite analogous, and possibly she would override all obstacles in triumph, and the patients who entered her home with the burden of their past misery heavy upon them, would develop in the sunshine of her presence into twelve riotously jovial ladies. But would not she herself suffer? Would not her own strength and hopefulness be sapped up by those she benefited? He could not think that it would be to the advantage of the world at large to substitute twelve, nay fifty, nay any number of jolly old ladies, for one girl with such sweet and joyous eyes.

This, of course, was the purely masculine point of view. The women to be benefited—why he thought of them as old is not clear, for you need not be old to be unhappy—would have protested, probably, with indignant cries that individually they were well worth Miss Estcourt, in any case were every bit as good as she was, and collectively—oh, absurd.

He thought of his sister Trudi. Perhaps she knew of some one who would be both kind and clever, and protect Miss Estcourt in some measure from the twelve. Trudi's friends, it is true, were not the sort among whom staid companions are found. Their husbands were chiefly lieutenants, and they spent their time at races. They lived in flats in Hanover, where the regiment was quartered, and flats are easy to manage, and none of these young women would endure, he supposed, to have an elderly companion always hanging round. Still, there was a remote possibility that some one of them might be able to recommend a suitable person. If Trudi were staying with him now she would be a great help; not so much because of what she would do, but because he could go with her to Kleinwalde, and Miss Estcourt could come to his house when she wanted anything, and need not depend solely on the parson. It was his duty, considering old Joachim's unchanging kindness towards him, and the pains the old man had taken to help him in the management of his estate, and to encourage him at a time when he greatly needed help and encouragement, to do all that lay in his power for old Joachim's niece. When he heard that she was coming he had decided that this was his plain duty: that she was so pretty, so adorably pretty and simple and friendly only made it an unusually pleasant one. "I will write to Trudi," he thought, "and ask her to come over for a week or two."

He sat down at his writing-table in the big window overlooking the farmyard, and began the letter. But he felt that it would be absurd to ask her to come on Miss Estcourt's account. Why should she do anything for Miss Estcourt, and why should he want his sister to do anything for her? That would be the first thing that would strike the astute Trudi. So he merely wrote reminding her that she had not stayed with him since the previous summer, and suggested that she should come for a few days with her children, now that the spring was coming and the snow had gone. "The woods will soon be blue with anemones," he wrote, though he well knew that Trudi's attitude towards anemones was cold. Perhaps her little boys would like to pick them; anyhow, some sort of an inducement had to be held out.

Outside his window was a duck-pond, thin sheets of ice still floating in broken pieces on its surface; behind the duck-pond was the dairy; and on either side of the yard were cow-sheds and pig-styes. The farm carts stood in a peaceful Sunday row down one side, and at the other end of the yard, shutting out the same view of the sea and island that Anna saw from her bedroom window, was a mountainous range of manure. When Trudi came, she never entered the rooms on this side of the house, because, as she explained, it was one of her peculiarities not to like manure; and she slept and ate and aired her opinions on the west side, where the garden lay between the house and the road. She never would have come to Lohm at all, not being burdened with any undue sentiment in regard to ties of blood, if it had not been necessary to go somewhere in the summer, and if the other places had not been beyond the resources of the family purse, always at its emptiest when the racing season was over and the card-playing at an end. As it was, this was a cheap and convenient haven, and her brother Axel was kind to the little boys, and not too angry when they plundered his apple-trees, damaged the knees of his ponies, and did their best to twist off the tails of his disconcerted sucking-pigs.

He was the eldest of three brothers, and she came last. She was twenty-six, and he was ten years older. When the father died, the land ought properly to have been divided between the four children, but such a proceeding would have been extremely inconvenient, and the two younger brothers, and the sister just married, agreed to accept their share in money, and to leave the estate entirely to Axel. It was the best course to take, but it threw Axel into difficulties that continued for years. His father, with four times the money, had lived very comfortably at Lohm, and the children had been brought up in prosperity. For eight years his eldest son had farmed the estate with a quarter the means, and had found it so far from simple that his hair had turned grey in the process. It needed considerable skill and vigilance to enable a man to extract a decent living from the soil of Lohm. Part of it was too boggy, and part of it too sandy, and the trees had all been cut down thirty years before by a bland grandfather, serenely indifferent to the opinion of posterity. Axel's first work had been to make plantations of young firs and pines wherever the soil was poorest, and when he rode through the beautiful Kleinwalde forest he endeavoured to extract what pleasure he could from the thought that in a hundred years Lohm too would have a forest. But the pleasure to be extracted from this thought was of a surprisingly subdued quality. All his pleasures were of a subdued quality. His days were made up of hard work, of that effort to induce both ends to meet which knocks the savour out of life with such a singular completeness. He was born with an uncomfortably exact conception of duty; and now at the end of the best half of his life, after years of struggling on that poor soil against the odds of that stern climate, this conception had shaped itself into a fixed belief that the one thing entirely beautiful, the one thing wholly worthy of a man's ambition, is the right doing of his duty. So, he thought, shall a man have peace at the last.

It is a way of thinking common to the educated dwellers in solitary places, who have not been very successful. Trudi scorned it. "Peace," she said, "at the last, is no good at all. What one wants is peace at the beginning and in the middle. But you only think stuff like that because you haven't got enough money. Poor people always talk about the beauty of duty and peace at the last. If somebody left you a fortune you'd never mention either of them again. Or if you married a girl with money, now. I wish, I do wish, that that duty would strike you as the one thing wholly worth doing."

But a man who is all day and every day in his fields, who farms not for pleasure but for his bare existence, has no time to set out in search of girls with money, and none came up his way. Besides, he had been engaged a few years before, and the girl had died, and he had not since had the least inclination towards matrimony. After that he had worked harder than ever; and the years flew by, filled with monotonous labour. Sometimes they were good years, and the ends not only met but lapped over a little; but generally the bare meeting of the ends was all that he achieved. His wish was that his brother Gustav who came after him should find the place in good order; if possible in better order than before. But the working up of an estate for a brother Gustav, with whatever determination it may be carried on, is not a labour that evokes an unflagging enthusiasm in the labourer; and Axel, however beautiful a life of duty might be to him in theory, found it, in practice, of an altogether remarkable greyness. Two-thirds of his house were shut up. In the evenings his servants stole out to court and be courted, and left the place to himself and echoes and memories. It was a house built for a large family, for troops of children, and frequent friends. Axel sat in it alone when the dusk drove him indoors, defending himself against his remembrances by prolonged interviews with his head inspector, or a zealous study of the latest work on potato diseases.

"I see that Bibi Bornstedt is staying with your Regierungspräsident," Trudi had written a little while before. "Now, then, is your chance. She is a true gold-fish. You cannot continue to howl over Hildegard's memory for ever. Bibi will have two hundred thousand marks a year when the old ones die, and is quite a decent girl. Her nose is a fiasco, but when you have been married a week you will not so much as see that she has a nose. And the two hundred thousand marks will still be there. Ach, Axel, what comfort, what consolation, in two hundred thousand marks! You could put the most glorious wreaths on Hildegard's tomb, besides keeping racehorses."

Lohm suddenly remembered this letter as he sat, having finished his own, looking out of the window at two girls in Sunday splendour kissing one of the stable boys behind a farm cart. They were all three apparently enjoying themselves very much, the girls laughing, the boy with an expression at once imbecile and beatific. They thought the master's eye could not see them there, but the master's eye saw most things. He took up his pen again and added a postscript. "If you come soon you will be able to enjoy the society of your friend Bibi. She came on Wednesday, I believe." Then, feeling slightly ashamed of using the innocent Miss Bibi as a bait to catch his sister, he wrote the advertisement for Anna, and put both letters in the post-bag.

The effect of his postscript was precisely the one he had expected. Trudi was drinking her morning coffee in her bedroom at twelve o'clock, when the letter came. Her hair was being done by a Friseur, an artist in hairdressing, who rode about Hanover every day on a bicycle, his pockets bulging out with curling-tongs, and for three marks decorated the heads of Trudi and her friends with innumerable waves. Trudi was devoted to him, with the devotion naturally felt for the person on whom one's beauty depends, for he was a true artist, and really did work amazing transformations. "What! You have never had Herr Jungbluth?" Trudi cried, on the last occasion on which she met Bibi, the daughter of a Hanover banker, and quite outside her set but for the riches that ensured her an enthusiastic welcome wherever she went, "aber Bibi!" There was so much genuine surprise and compassion in this "aber Bibi" that the young person addressed felt as though she had been for years missing a possibility of happiness. Trudi added, as a special recommendation, that Jungbluth smelt of soap. He had carefully studied the nature of women, and if he had to do with a pretty one would find an early opportunity of going into respectful raptures over what he described as her klassisches Profil; and if it was a woman whose face was not all she could have wished, he would tell her, in a tone of subdued enthusiasm, that her profile, as to which she had long been in doubt, was höchst interessant. The popularity of this young man in Trudi's set was enormous; and as all the less aristocratic Hanoverian ladies hastened to imitate, Jungbluth lived in great contentment and prosperity with a young wife whose hair was reposefully straight, and a baby whose godmother was Trudi.

"Blue woods! Anemones!" read Trudi with immense contempt. "Is the boy in his senses? The idea of expecting me to go to that dreary place now. Ah, now I understand," she added, turning the page, "it is Bibi—he is really after her, and of course can get along quicker if I am there to help. Excellent Axel! And why did he go to the pains of trotting out the anemones? What is the use of not being frank with me? I can see through him, whatever he does. He is so good-natured that I am sure he will lend us heaps of Bibi's money once he has got it. So, lieber Jungbluth," she said aloud, "that will do to-day. Beautiful—beautiful— better than ever. I am in a hurry. I travel to Berlin this very afternoon."

And the next day she arrived at Stralsund, and was met by her brother at the station.

She greeted him with enthusiasm. "As we are here," she said, when they were driving through the town, "let us pay our respects to the Regierungspräsidentin. It will save our coming in again to-morrow."

"No, I cannot to-day. I must get back as quickly as possible. The hands had their Easter ball yesterday, and when I left Lohm this morning half of them were still in bed."

"Well, then, the horses will have to do the journey again to-morrow, for no time should be lost."

"Yes, you can come in to-morrow, if you long so much to see your friend."

"And you?" asked Trudi, in a tone of astonishment.

"And I? I am up to my ears now in work. Last week was the first week for four months that we could plough. Now we have lost these three days at Easter. I cannot spare a single hour."

"But, my dear Axel, Bibi is of far greater importance for the future of Lohm than any amount of ploughing."

"I confess I do not see how."

"I don't understand you."

"Why didn't you bring the little boys?"

"What have you asked me to come here for?"

"Come, Trudi, you've not been near me for eight months. Isn't it natural that you should pay me a little visit?"

"No, it isn't natural at all to come to such a place in winter, and leave all the fun at home. I came because of Bibi."

"What! You'll come for Bibi, but not for your own brother?"

"Now, Axel, you know very well that I have come for you both."

"For us both? What would Miss Bibi say if she heard you talking of herself and of me as 'you both'?"

"I wish you would not bother to go on like this. It's a great waste of time."

"So it is, my dear. Any talk about Bibi Bornstedt, as far as I am concerned, is a hopeless waste of time."

"Axel!"

"Trudi?"

"You don't mean to say that you are not thinking of her?"

"Thinking of her? I never let my thoughts linger round strange young ladies."

"Then what in heaven's name have you got me here for?"

"The anemones are coming out———"

"Ach——"

"They really are."

"Suppose instead of teasing me as though I were still ten and you a great bully, you talked sensibly. The Hohensteins give a bal masqué to-night, and I gave it up to come to you."

"Oh, my dear, that was really kind," said Lohm, touched by the tremendousness of this sacrifice.

"Then be a good boy," said Trudi caressingly, edging herself closer to him, "and tell me you are going to be wise about Bibi. Don't throw such a chance away—it's positively wicked."

"My dear Trudi, you'll have us in the ditch. It is very nice when you lean against me, but I can't drive. By the way, you remember my old Kleinwalde neighbour? The old man who spoilt you so atrociously?"

"Bibi will make a most excellent wife," said Trudi, ungratefully indifferent to the memory of old Joachim. "Oh, what a cold wind there is to-day. Do drive faster, Axel. What a taste, to live here and to like it into the bargain!"

"You know that I must live here."

"But you needn't like it."

"You've heard that old Joachim left Kleinwalde to his English niece?"

"You have only seen Bibi once, and she grows on one tremendously."

"I want to talk about old Joachim."

"And I want to talk about Bibi."

"Well, Bibi can wait. She is the younger. You know about the old man's will?"

"I should think I did. One of his unfortunate sons has just joined our regiment. You should hear him on the subject."

"A most disagreeable, grasping lot," said Lohm decidedly. "They received every bit of their dues, and are all well off. Surely the old man could do as he liked with the one place that was not entailed?"

"It isn't the usual thing to leave one's land to a foreigner. Is she coming to live in it?"

"She came last week."

"Oh?" This in a tone of sudden interest.

There was a pause. Then Trudi said, "Is she young?"

"Quite young."

"Pretty?"

"Exceedingly pretty."

Trudi looked up at him and smiled.

"Well?" said Axel, smiling back at her.

"Well?" said Trudi, continuing to smile.

Axel laughed outright. "My dear Trudi, your astuteness terrifies me. You not only know already why I wrote to you, but you know more reasons for the letter than I myself dream of. I want to be able to help this extremely helpless young lady, and I can hardly be of any use to her because I have no woman in the house. If I had a wife I could be of the greatest assistance."

"Only then you wouldn't want to be."

"Certainly I should."

"Pray, why?"

"Because I have a greater debt of obligations to her uncle than I can ever repay to his niece."

"Oh, nonsense—nobody pays their debts of obligations. The natural thing to do is to hate the person who has forced you to be grateful, and to get out of his way."

"My dear Trudi, this shrewdness——" murmured her brother. Then he added, "I know perfectly well that your thoughts have already flown to a wedding. Mine don't reach farther than an elderly companion."

"Who for? For you?"

"Miss Estcourt is looking for an elderly companion, and I would be grateful to you if you would help her."

"But the elderly companion does not exclude the wedding."

"When you see Miss Estcourt you will understand how completely such a possibility is outside her calculations. You won't of course believe that it is outside mine. Why should you want to marry me to every girl within reach? Five minutes ago it was Bibi, and now it is Miss Estcourt. You do not in the least consider what views the girls themselves might have. Miss Estcourt is absorbed at this moment in a search for twelve old ladies."

"Twelve——?"

"Her ambition is to spend herself and her money on twelve old ladies. She thinks happiness and money are as good for them as for herself, and wants to share her own with persons who have neither."

"My dear Axel—is she mad?"

"She did not give me that impression."

"And you say she is young?"

"Yes."

"And really pretty?"

"Yes."

"And could be so well off in that flourishing place!"

"Of course she could."

"I'll go and call on her to-morrow," said Trudi decidedly.

"It will be kind of you," said Lohm.

"Kind! It isn't kindness, it's curiosity," said Trudi with a laugh. "Let us be frank, and call things by their right names."

Anna was in the garden, admiring the first crocus, when Trudi appeared. She drove Axel's cobs up to the door in what she felt was excellent style, and hoped Miss Estcourt was watching her from a window and would see that Englishwomen were not the only sportswomen in the world. But Anna saw nothing but the crocus.

The wilderness down to the marsh that did duty as a garden was so sheltered and sunny that spring stopped there first each year before going on into the forest; and Anna loved to walk straight out of the drawing-room window into it, bare-headed and coatless, whenever she had time. Trudi saw her coming towards the house upon the servant's telling her that a lady had called. "Nothing on, on a cold day like this!" she thought. She herself wore a particularly sporting driving-coat, with an immense collar turned up over her ears. "I wonder," mused Trudi, watching the approaching figure, "how it is that English girls, so tidy in the clothes, so trim in the shoes, so neat in the tie and collar, never apparently brush their hair. A German Miss Estcourt vegetating in this quiet place would probably wear grotesque and disconnected garments, doubtful boots and striking stockings, her figure would rapidly give way before the insidiousness of Schweinebraten, but her hair would always be beautifully done, each plait smooth and in its proper place, each little curl exactly where it ought to be, the parting a model of straightness, and the whole well deserving to be dignified by the name Frisur. English girls have hair, but they do not have Frisurs."

Anna came in through the open window, and Trudi's face
expanded into the most genial smiles. "How glad I am to
make your acquaintance!" she cried enthusiastically. She
spoke English quite as correctly as her brother, and much
more glibly. "I hope you will let me help you if I can be of
any use. My brother says your uncle was so good to him.
When I lived here he was very kind to me too. How brave
of you to stay here! And what wonderful plans you have
made! My brother has told me about your twelve ladies.
What courage to undertake to make twelve women happy. I
find it hard enough work making one person happy."

"One person? Oh, Graf Hasdorf."

"Oh no, myself. You see, if each person devoted his
energies to making himself happy, everybody would be
happy."

"No, they wouldn't," said Anna, "because they do, but
they're not."

They looked at each other and laughed. "She only needs
Jungbluth to be perfect," thought Trudi; and with her usual
impulsiveness began immediately to love her.

Anna was delighted to meet someone of her own class and
age after the severe though short course she had had of
Dellwigs and Manskes; and Trudi was so much interested
in her plans, and so pressing in her offers of help, that she
very soon found herself telling her all her difficulties about
servants, sheets, wall-papers, and whitewash. "Look at this
paper," she said, "could you live in the same room with it?
No one will ever be able to feel cheerful as long as it is
here. And the one in the dining-room is worse."

"It isn't beautiful," said Trudi, examining it, "but it is what we call praktisch."

"Then I don't like what you call praktisch."

"Neither do I. All the hideous things are praktisch—oil-cloth, black wall-papers, handkerchiefs a yard square, thick boots, ugly women—if ever you hear a woman praised as a praktische Frau, be sure she's frightful in every way—ugly and dull. The uglier she is the praktischer she is. Oh," said Trudi, casting up her eyes, "how terrible, how tragic, to be an ugly woman!" Then, bringing her gaze down again to Anna's face, she added, "My flat in Hanover is all pinks and blues—the most becoming rooms you can imagine. I look so nice in them."

"Pinks and blues? That is just what I want here. Can't I get any in Stralsund?"

Trudi was doubtful. She could not think it possible that anybody should ever get anything in Stralsund.

"But I must do my shopping there. I am in such a hurry. It would be dreadful to have to keep anyone waiting only because my house isn't ready."

"Well, we can try," said Trudi. "You will let me go with you, won't you?"

"I shall be more than grateful if you will come."

"What do you think if we went now?" suggested Trudi, always for prompt action, and quickly tired of sitting still. "My brother said I might drive into Stralsund to-day if I

liked, and I have the cobs here now. Don't you think it
would be a good thing, as you are in such a hurry?"

"Oh, a very good thing," exclaimed Anna. "How kind you
are! You are sure it won't bore you frightfully?"

"Oh, not a bit. It will be rather amusing to go into those
shops for once, and I shall like to feel that I have helped the
good work on a little."

Anna thought Trudi delightful. Trudi's new friends always
did think her delightful; and she never had any old ones.

She drove recklessly, and they lurched and heaved through
the sand between Kleinwalde and Lohm at an alarming
rate. They passed Letty and Miss Leech, going for their
afternoon walk, who stood on one side and stared.

"Who's that?" asked Trudi.

"My brother's little girl and her governess."

"Oh yes, I heard about them. They are to stay and take care
of you till you have a companion. Your sister-in-law didn't
like Kleinwalde?"

"No."

Trudi laughed.

They passed Dellwig, riding, who swept off his hat with his
customary deference, and stared.

"Do you like him?" asked Trudi.

"Who?"

"Dellwig. I know him from the days before I married."

"I don't know him very well yet," said Anna, "but he seems to be very—very polite."

Trudi laughed again, and cracked her whip.

"My uncle had great faith in him," said Anna, slightly aggrieved by the laugh.

"Your uncle was one of the best farmers in Germany, I have always heard. He was so experienced, and so clever, that he could have led a hundred Dellwigs round by the nose. Dellwig was naturally quite small, as we say, in the presence of your uncle. He knew very well it would be useless to be anything but immaculate under such a master. Perhaps your uncle thought he would go on being immaculate from sheer habit, with nobody to look after him."

"I suppose he did," said Anna doubtfully. "He told me to keep him. It's quite certain that I can't look after him."

They passed Axel Lohm, also riding. He was on Trudi's side of the road. He looked pleased when he saw Anna with his sister. Trudi whipped up the cobs, regardless of his feelings, and tore past him, scattering the sand right and left. When she was abreast of him, she winked her eye at him with perfect solemnity.

Axel looked stony.

CHAPTER XI

Neither Trudi nor Anna had ever worked so hard as they did during the few days that ended March and began April. Everything seemed to happen at once. The house was in a sudden uproar. There were people whitewashing, people painting, people putting up papers, people bringing things in carts from Stralsund, people trimming up the garden, people coming out to offer themselves as servants, Dellwig coming in and shouting, Manske coming round and glorifying—Anna would have been completely bewildered if it had not been for Trudi, who was with her all day long, going about with a square of lace and muslin tucked under her waist-ribbon which she felt was becoming and said was an apron.

Trudi was enjoying herself hugely. She saw Jungbluth's waves slowly straightening themselves out of her hair, and for the first time in her life remained calm as she watched them go. She even began to have aspirations towards Uncle Joachim's better life herself, and more than once entered into a serious consideration of the advantages that might result from getting rid at one stroke of Bill her husband, and Billy and Tommy her two sons, and from making a fresh start as one of Anna's twelve.

Frau Manske and Frau Dellwig could not face her infinite superciliousness more than once, and kept out of the way in spite of their burning curiosity. When Dellwig's shouts became intolerable, she did not hesitate to wince conspicuously and to put up her hand to her head. When Manske forgot that it was not Sunday, and began to preach, she would interrupt him with a brisk "Ja, ja, sehr schön, sehr schön, aber lieber Herr Pastor, you must tell us all this next Sunday in church when we have time to listen—my friend has not a minute now in which to appreciate the opinions of the Apostel Paulus."

"I believe you are being unkind to my parson," said Anna, who could not always understand Trudi's rapid German, but saw that Manske went away dejected.

"My dear, he must be kept in his place if he tries to come out of it. You don't know what a set these pastors are. They are not like your clergymen. If you are too kind to that man you'll have no peace. I remember in my father's time he came to dinner every Sunday, sat at the bottom of the table, and when the pudding appeared made a bow and went away."

"He didn't like pudding?"

"I don't know if he liked it or not, but he never got any. It was a good old custom that the pastor should withdraw before the pudding, and Axel has not kept it up. My father never had any bother with him."

"But what has the pudding that he didn't get ten years ago to do with your being unkind to him now?"

"I wanted to explain the proper footing for him to be on."

"And the proper footing is a puddingless one? Well, in my house neither pudding nor kindness in suitable quantities shall be withheld from him, so don't ill-use him more than you feel is absolutely necessary for his good."

"Oh, you are a dear little thing!" said Trudi, putting her hands on Anna's shoulders and looking into her eyes—they were both tall young women, and their eyes were on a level—"I wonder what the end of you will be. When you know all these people better you'll see that my way of treating them, which you think unkind, is the only way. You must turn up your nose as high as it will go at them, and they will burst with respect. Don't be too friendly and confiding—they won't understand it, and will be sure to think that something must be wrong about you, and will begin to backbite you, and invent all sorts of horrid stories about you. And as for the pastor, why should he be allowed to treat your rooms as though they were so many pulpits, and you as though you had never heard of the Apostel Paulus?"

Anna admitted that she was not always in the proper frame of mind for these unprovoked sermons, but refused to believe in the necessity for turning up her nose. She ostentatiously pressed Manske, the very next time he came, to stay to the evening meal, which was rather of the nature of a picnic in those unsettled days, but at which, for Letty's sake, there was always a pudding; and she invited him to eat pudding three times running, and each time he accepted the offer; and each time, when she had helped him, she fixed her eyes with a defiant gravity on Trudi's face.

Axel came in sometimes when he had business at the farm, and was shown what progress had been made. Trudi was as interested as though it had been her own house, and took him about, demanding his approval and admiration with an enthusiasm that spread to Anna, and she and Axel soon became good friends. The Stralsund wall-papers were so dreadful that Anna had declared she would have most of the rooms whitewashed; the hall had been done, exchanging its pea-green coat for one of virgin purity, and she had thought it so fresh and clean, and so appropriate to the simplicity of the better life, that to the amazement of the workmen she insisted on the substitution of whitewash in both dining and drawing-room for the handsome chocolate-coloured papers already in those rooms.

"The twelve will think it frightful," said Trudi.

"But why?" asked Anna, who had fallen in love with whitewash. "It is purity itself. It will be symbolical of the innocence and cleanliness that will be in our hearts when we have got used to each other, and are happy."

Trudi looked again at the hall, into which the afternoon sun was streaming. It did look very clean, certainly, and exceedingly cheerful; she was sure, however, that it would never be symbolical of any heart that came into it. But then Trudi was sceptical about hearts.

At the end of Easter week, when Trudi was beginning to feel slightly tired of whitewash and scrambled meals, and to have doubts as to the permanent becomingness of aprons, and misgivings as to the effect on her complexion of running about a cold house all day long, answers to the advertisements began to arrive, and soon arrived in shoals. These letters acted as bellows on the flickering flame of her zeal. She found them extraordinarily entertaining, and would meet Manske in the hall when he brought them round, and take them out of his hands, and run with them to Anna, leaving him standing there uncertain whether he ought to stay and be consulted, or whether it was expected of him that he should go home again without having unburdened himself of all the advice he felt that he contained. He deplored what he called das impulsive Temperament of the Gräfin. Always had she been so, since the days she climbed his cherry-trees and helped the birds to strip them; and when, with every imaginable precaution, he had approached her father on the subject, and carefully excluding the word cherry hinted that the climbing of trees was a perilous pastime for young ladies, old Lohm had burst into a loud laugh, and had sworn that neither he nor anyone else could do anything with Trudi. He actually had seemed proud that she should steal cherries, for he knew very well why she climbed the trees, and predicted a brilliant future for his only daughter; to which Manske had listened respectfully as in duty bound, and had gone home unconvinced.

But Anna did not let him stand long in the hall, and came to fetch him and beg him to help her read the letters and tell her what he thought of them. In spite of Trudi's advice and example she continued to treat the pastor with the deference due to a good and simple man. What did it matter if he talked twice as much as he need have done, and wearied her with his habit of puffing Christianity as though it were a quack medicine of which he was the special patron? He was sincere, he really believed something, and really felt something, and after five days with Trudi Anna turned to Manske's elementary convictions with relief. In five days she had come to be very glad that Trudi stood in no need of a place among the twelve.

Most of the women who wrote in answer to the advertisement sent photographs, and their letters were pitiful enough, either because of what they said or because of what they tried to hide; and Anna's appreciation of Trudi received a great shock when she found that the letters amused her, and that the photographs, especially those of the old ones or the ugly ones, moved her to a mirth little short of unseemly. After all, Trudi was taking a great deal upon herself, Anna thought, reading the letters unasked,

helping her to open them unasked, hurrying down to fetch
them unasked, and deluging her with advice about them
unasked. She saw she had made a mistake in allowing her
to see them at all. She had no right to expose the petitions
of these unhappy creatures to Trudi's inquisitive and
diverted eyes. This fact was made very patent to her when
one of the letters that Trudi opened turned out to be from a
person she had known. "Why," cried Trudi, her face
twinkling with excitement, "here's one from a girl who was
at school with me. And her photo, too—what a shocking
scarecrow she has grown into! She is only two years older
than I am, but might be forty. Just look at her—and she
used to think none of us were good enough for her. Don't
have her, whatever you do—she married one of the officers
in Bill's first regiment, and treated him so shamefully that
he shot himself. Imagine her boldness in writing like this!"
And she began eagerly to read the letter.

Anna got up and took it out of her hands. It was an
unexpected action, or Trudi would have held on tighter.
"She never dreamed you would see what she wrote," said
Anna, "and it would be dishonourable of me to let you. And
the other letters too—I have been thinking it over—they
are only meant for me; and no one else, except perhaps the
parson, ought to see them."

"Except perhaps the parson!" cried Trudi, greatly offended.
"And why except perhaps the parson?"

"I can't always read the German writing," explained Anna.

"But surely a woman of your own age, who isn't such a
simpleton as the parson, is the best adviser you can have."

"But you laugh at the letters, and they are all so unhappy."

Trudi went back to Lohm early that day. "She has taken it into her head that I am not to read the letters," she said to her brother with no little indignation.

"It would be a great breach of confidence if she allowed you to," he replied; which was so unsatisfactory that she drove into Stralsund that very afternoon, and consoled herself with the pliable Bibi.

Bibi's nose seemed more unsuccessful than ever after having had Anna's before her for nearly a week; but then the richness of the girl! And such a good-natured, generous girl, who would adore her sister-in-law and make her presents. Contemplating the good Bibi in her afternoon splendour from Paris, Trudi's heart stirred within her at the thought of all that was within Axel's reach if only he could be induced to put out his hand and take it. Anna would never marry him, Trudi was certain—would never marry anyone, being completely engrossed by her philanthropic follies; but if she did, what was her probable income compared to Bibi's? And Axel would never look at Bibi so long as that other girl lived next door to him; nobody could expect him to. Anna was too pretty; it was not fair. And Bibi was so very plain; which was not fair either.

The Regierungspräsidentin, a cousin by marriage of Bibi's, but a member of an ancient family of the Mark, was delighted to see Trudi and to question her about the new and eccentric arrival. Trudi had offered to take Anna to call on this lady, and had explained that it was her duty to call; but Anna had said there was no hurry, and had talked of some day, and had been manifestly bored by the prospect of making new acquaintances.

"Is she quite—quite in her right senses?" asked the Regierungspräsidentin, when Trudi had described all they had been doing in Anna's house, and all Anna meant to do with her money, and had made her description so smart and diverting that the Regierungspräsidentin, an alert little lady, with ears perpetually pricked up in the hope of catching gossip, felt that she had not enjoyed an afternoon so much for years.

Bibi sat listening with her mouth wide open. It was an artless way of hers when she was much interested in a conversation, and was deplored by those who wished her well.

"Oh, yes, she is quite in her senses. Rather too sure she knows best, always, but quite in her senses."

"Then she is very religious?"

"Not in the ordinary way, I should think. She goes in for nature. Gott in der Natur, and that sort of thing. If the sun shines more than usual she goes and stands in it, and turns up her eyes and gushes. There's a crocus in the garden, and when we came to it yesterday she stopped in front of it and rhapsodised for ten minutes about things that have nothing to do with crocuses—chiefly about the lieben Gott. And all in English, of course, and it sounds worse in English."

"But then, my dear, she is religious?"

"Oh, well, the pastor would not call it religion. It's a sort of huddle-muddle pantheism as far as it is anything at all." From which it will be seen that Trudi was even more frank about her friends behind their backs than she was to their faces.

She drove back to Lohm in a discontented frame of mind. "What's the good of anything?" was the mood she was in. She had over-tired herself helping Anna, and she was afraid that being so much in cold rooms and passages, and washing in hard water, had made her skin coarse. She had caught sight of herself in a glass as she was leaving the Regierungspräsidentin, and had been disconcerted by finding that she did not look as pretty as she felt. Nor was she consoled for this by the consciousness that she had been unusually amusing at Anna's expense; for she was only too certain that the Regierungspräsidentin, when repeating all she had told her to her friends, would add that Trudi Hasdorf had terribly eingepackt—dreadful word, descriptive of the faded state immediately preceding wrinkles, and held in just abhorrence by every self-respecting woman. Of what earthly use was it to be cleverer and more amusing than other people if at the same time you had eingepackt?

"What a stupid world it is," thought Trudi, driving along the chaussée in the early April twilight. A mist lay over the sea, and the pale sickle of the young moon rose ghost-like above the white shroud. Inland the stars were faintly shining, and all the earth beneath was damp and fragrant. It was Saturday evening, and the two bells of Lohm church were plaintively ringing their reminder to the countryside that the week's work was ended and God's day came next. "Oh, the stupid world," thought Trudi. "If I stay here I shall be bored to death—that Estcourt child and her governess have got on to my nerves—horrid fat child with turned-in toes, and flabby, boneless woman, only held together by her hairpins. I am sick of governesses and children—wherever one goes, there they are. If I go home, there are those noisy little boys and Fräulein Schultz worrying all day, and then there's that tiresome Bill coming in to meals.

Anna and Bibi are just in the position I would like to be in—no husbands and children, and lots of money." And staring straight before her, with eyes dark with envy, she fell into gloomy musings on the beauty of Bibi's dress, and the blindness of fate, throwing away a dress like that on a Bibi, when it was so eminently suited to tall, slim women like herself; and it was fortunate for Axel's peace that when she reached Lohm the first thing she saw was a letter from the objectionable Bill telling her to come home, because the foreign prince who was honorary colonel of the regiment was expected immediately in Hanover, and there were to be great doings in his honour.

She left, all smiles, the next morning by the first train.

"Miss Estcourt will miss you," said Axel, "and will wonder why you did not say good-bye. I am afraid your journey will be unpleasant, too, to-day. I wish you had stayed till to-morrow."

"Oh, I don't mind the Sunday people once in a way," said Trudi gaily. "And please tell Anna how it was I had to go so suddenly. I have started her, at least, with the workmen and people she wants. I shall see her in a few weeks again, you know, when Bill is at the man[oe]uvres."

"A few weeks! Six months."

"Well, six months. You must both try to exist without me for that time."

"You seem very pleased to be off," he said, smiling, as she climbed briskly into the dog-cart and took the reins, while her maid, with her arms full of bags, was hoisted up behind.

"Oh, so pleased!" said Trudi, looking down at him with sparkling eyes. "Princes and parties are jollier any day than whitewash and the better life."

"And brothers."

"Oh—brothers. By the way, I never saw Bibi look better than she did yesterday. She has improved so much nobody would know——"

"You will miss your train," said Axel, pulling out his watch.

"Well, good-bye then, alter Junge. Work hard, do your duty, and don't let your thoughts linger too much round strange young ladies. They never do, I think you said? Well, so much the better, for it's no good, no good, no good!" And Trudi, who was in tremendous spirits, put her whip to the brim of her hat by way of a parting salute, touched up the cobs, and rattled off down the drive on the road to Jungbluth and glory. She turned her head before she finally disappeared, to call back her oracular "No good!" once again to Axel, who stood watching her from the steps of his solitary house.

CHAPTER XII

So Anna was left to herself again. She was astonished at
the rapidity of Trudi's movements. Within one week she
had heard of her, met her, liked her, begun to like her less,
and lost her. She had flashed across the Kleinwalde
horizon, and left a trail of workmen and new servants
behind, with whom Anna was now occupied, unaided, from
morning till night. Miss Leech and Letty did all they could,
but their German being restricted to quotations from the
Erl-König and the Lied von der Glocke, it could not be
brought to bear with any profitable results on the workmen.
The servants, too, were a perplexity to Anna. Their
cheapness was extraordinary, but their quality curious. Her
new parlourmaid—for she felt unequal to coping with
German men-servants—wore her arms naked all day long.
Anna thought she had tucked up her sleeves in her zeal for
thoroughness, but when she appeared with the afternoon
coffee—the local tea was undrinkable—she still had bare
arms; and, examining her more closely, Anna saw that it
was her usual state, for her dress was sleeveless. Nor was
her want of sleeves her only peculiarity. Anna began to
wonder whether her house would ever be ready for the
twelve.

The answers to the philanthropic advertisement were in a
proportion of fifty to one answer to the advertisement for a
companion. There were fifty ladies without means willing
to be idle, to one lady without means willing to work. It
worried Anna terribly, being obliged by want of room and
money to limit the number to twelve. She could hardly bear
to read the letters, knowing that nearly all had to be
rejected. "See how many sad lives are being dragged
through while we are so comfortable," she said to Manske,

when he brought round fresh piles of letters to add to those already heaped on her table.

He shook his head in perplexity. He was bewildered by the masses of answers, by the apparent universality of impoverishment and hopelessness among Christian ladies of good family.

He could not come himself more than once a day, and the letters arrived by every post; so in the afternoon he sent Herr Klutz, the young cleric of poetic promptings, who had celebrated Anna on her arrival in a poem which for freshness and spontaneousness equalled, he considered, the best sonnets that had ever been written. What a joy it was to a youth of imagination, to a poet who thought his features not unlike Goethe's, and who regarded it as by no means an improbability that his brain should turn out to be stamped with the same resemblance, to walk daily through the gleaming, whispering forest, swinging his stick and composing snatches not unworthy of her of whom they treated, his face towards the magic Schloss and its enchanted princess, and his pockets full of her letters! Herr Klutz's coat was clerical, but his brown felt hat and the flower in his buttonhole were typical of the worldliness within. "A poet," he assured himself often, "is a citizen of the world, and is not to be narrowed down to any one circle or creed." But he did not expound this view to the good man who was helping him to prepare for the examination that would make him a full-fledged pastor, and received his frequent blessings, and assisted at prayers and intercessions of which he was the subject, with outward decorum.

The first time he brought the letters, Anna received him with her usual kindness; but there was something in his manner that displeased her, whether it was self-assurance, or conceit, or a way he had of looking at her, she could not tell, nor did she waste many seconds trying to decide; but the next day when he came he was not admitted to her presence, nor the next after that, nor for some time to come. This surprised Herr Klutz, who was of Dellwig's opinion that the most superior woman was not equal to the average man; and take away any advantage of birth or position or wealth that she might possess, why, there she was, only a woman, a creature made to be conquered and brought into obedience to man. Being young and poetic he differed from Dellwig on one point: to Dellwig, woman was a servant; to Klutz, an admirable toy. Clearly such a creature could only be gratified by opportunities of seeing and conversing with members of the opposite sex. The Miss's conduct, therefore, in allowing her servant to take the letters from him at the door, puzzled him.

He often met Miss Leech and Letty on his way to or from Kleinwalde, and always stopped to speak to them and to teach them a few German sentences and practise his own small stock of English; and from them he easily discovered all that the young woman he favoured with his admiration was doing. Lohm, riding over to Kleinwalde to settle differences between Dellwig and the labourers, or to try offenders, met these three several times, and supposed that Klutz must be courting the governess.

The day Trudi left, Lohm had gone round to Anna and delivered his sister's message in a slightly embellished form. "You will have everything to do now unassisted," he said. "I do trust that in any difficulty you will let me help you. If the workmen are insolent, for instance, or if your new servants are dishonest or in any way give you trouble. You know it is my duty as Amtsvorsteher to interfere when such things happen."

"You are very kind," said Anna gratefully, looking up at the grave, good face, "but no one is insolent. And look—here is some one who wants to come as companion. It is the first of the answers to that advertisement that pleases me."

Lohm took the letter and photograph and examined them. "She is a Penheim, I see," he said. "It is a very good family, but some of its branches have been reduced to poverty, as so many of our old families have been."

"Don't you think she would do very well?"

"Yes, if she is and does all she says in her letter. You might propose that she should come at first for a few weeks on trial. You may not like her, and she may not appreciate philanthropic housekeeping."

Anna laughed. "I am doubly anxious to get someone soon," she said, "because my sister-in-law wants Letty and Miss Leech."

Letty and Miss Leech heaved tragic sighs at this; they had no desire whatever to go home.

"Will you not feel rather forlorn when they are gone, and you are quite alone among strangers?"

"I shall miss them, but I don't mean to be forlorn," said Anna, smiling.

"The courage of the little thing!" thought Lohm. "Ready to brave anything in pursuit of her ideals. It makes one ashamed of one's own grumblings and discouragements."

Anna arranged with Frau von Penheim that she should
come at once on a three months' trial; and immediately this
was settled she wrote to Susie to ask what day Letty was to
be sent home. She had had no communication with Susie
since that angry lady's departure. To Peter she had written,
explaining her plans and her reasons, and her hopes and
yearnings, and had received a hasty scrawl in reply dated
from Estcourt, conveying his blessing on herself and her
scheme. "Susie came straight down here," he wrote,
"because of the Alderton wedding to which she was not
asked, and went to bed. You know, my dear little sister,
anything that makes you happy contents me. I wish you
could have seen your way to benefiting reduced English
ladies, for you are a long way off; but of course you have
the house free over there. Don't let Miss Leech leave you
till you are perfectly satisfied with your companion.
Yesterday I landed the biggest——" etc. In a word, Peter,
in accordance with his invariable custom, was on her side.

The day before Frau von Penheim was to arrive, Susie's
answer to Anna's letter came. Here it is:—

"Dear Anna,—Your letter surprised me, though I might
have known by now what to expect of you.—Still, I was
surprised that you should not even offer to make the one
return in your power for all I have done for you. As I feel I
have a right to some return I don't hesitate to tell you that I
think you ought to keep Letty for a year or two, or even
longer. Even if you kept her till she is eighteen, and dressed
her and fed her (don't feed her too much), it would only be
four years; and what are four years I should like to know,
compared to the fifteen I had you on my hands? I was
talking to Herr Schumpf about her the other day—his bills
were so absurd that I made him take something off—and he
said by all means let her stay in Germany. Everybody

speaks German nowadays, and Letty will pick it up at once
in that awful place of yours. I was so ill when I got back
that I went to Estcourt, and had to stay in bed for days, the
doctor coming every day, and sometimes twice. He said he
didn't wonder, when I told him all I had gone through.
Peter was quite sorry for me. Send Miss Leech back. Give
her a month's notice for me the day you get this, and see if
you can't find some German who will go to your place—I
can't remember its wretched name without looking in my
address book—and give Letty lessons every day. The rest
of the time she can talk German to your twelve victims. I
believe masters in Germany only charge about 6d. an hour,
so it won't ruin you. Make her take lots of exercise, and let
her ride. She has outgrown her old habit, but German
tailors are so cheap that a new one will cost next to
nothing, and any horse that shakes her up well will do. I
shall be quite happy about her diet, because I know you
don't have anything to eat. I was at the Ennistons' last night.
They seemed very sorry for me being so nearly related to
somebody cracked; but after all, as I tell people, I'm not
responsible for my husband's relations.—Your affectionate,
Susie Estcourt.

"I have never seen Hilton so upset as she was after that
German trip. She cried if anyone looked at her. Poor thing,
no wonder. The doctor says she is all nerves."

The evening meal was in progress at Kleinwalde when this
letter came. The dining-room was finished, and it was the
first meal served there since its transformation. No one who
had seen it on that dark day of Anna's arrival would have
recognised it, so cheerful did it look with its whitewashed
walls. There were no dark corners now where china
shepherds smiled in vain; the western light filled it, and to a
person lately come from Susie's Hill Street house, it was a

refreshment to sit in any place so simple and so clean. Reforms, too, had been made in the food, and the bread was no longer disfigured by caraway seeds. A great bowl of blue hepaticas, fresh from the forest, stood on the table; and the hepaticas were the exact colour of Anna's eyes. When Letty saw her mother's handwriting she turned cold. It was the warrant that was to banish her from Eden, casting her back into the outer darkness of the Popular Concerts and the literature lectures. She was in the act of raising a spoonful of pudding to her already opened mouth, when she caught sight of the well-known writing. She hesitated, her hand shook, and finally she laid her spoon down again and pushed her plate back. At the great crises of life who can go on eating pudding? What then was her relief and joy to see her aunt get up, come round to where she was sitting braced to hear the worst, put her arms round her neck, and to feel herself being kissed. "You are going to stay with me after all!" cried Anna delightedly. "Dear little Letty—I should have missed you horribly. Aren't you glad? Your mother says I'm to keep you for ever so long."

"Oh, I say—how ripping!" exclaimed Letty; and being a practical person at once resumed and finished her pudding.

Miss Leech, too, looked exceedingly pleased. How could she be anything but pleased at the prospect of staying with a person who was always so kind and thoughtful as Anna? Her feelings, somehow, were never hurt by Anna; Lady Estcourt seemed to have a special knack of jumping on them every time she spoke to her. She knew she ought not to have such sensitive feelings, and felt that it was more her fault than anyone else's if they were hurt; yet there they were, and being hurt was painful, and living with someone so even tempered as Anna was very peaceful and pleasant. Mr. Jessup would have liked Anna. She wished he could have known her. A higher compliment it was not in Miss Leech's power to pay.

And when Anna saw the pleasure on Miss Leech's face, and saw that she thought she was to stay too, she felt that for no sister-in-law in the world would she wipe it out with that month's notice. She decided to say nothing, but simply to keep her as well as Letty. Her two thousand a year was in her eyes of infinite elasticity. Never having had any money, she had no notion of how far it would go; and she did not hesitate to come to a decision which would probably ultimately oblige her to reduce the number of those persons Susie described as victims.

The next day the companion arrived. Anna went out into the hall to meet her when she heard the approaching wheels of the shepherd-plaid chariot. She felt rather nervous as she watched her emerging from beneath the hood, for she knew how much of the comfort and peace of the twelve would depend on this lady. She felt exceedingly nervous when the lady, immediately upon shaking hands, asked if she could speak to her alone.

"Natürlich," said Anna, a vague fear lest Fritz, the coachman, should have insulted her on the way coming over her, though she only knew Fritz as the mildest of men.

She led the way into the drawing-room. "Now what is she going to tell me dreadful?" she thought, as she invited her to sit on the sofa, having been instructed by Trudi that that was the place where strangers expected to sit. "Suppose she isn't going to stay, and I shall have to look for someone all over again? Perhaps the lining of the carriage has been too much for her. Bitte" she said aloud, with an uneasy smile, motioning Frau von Penheim towards the sofa.

The new companion was a big, elderly lady with a sensible face. Her boots were thick, and she wore a mackintosh. She sat down, and looking more attentively at Anna, smiled. Most people who saw her for the first time did that. It was such a change and a pleasure after seeing plain faces, and dull faces, and vain, pretty faces for an indefinite period, to rest one's eyes on a person so charming yet manifestly preoccupied by other matters than her charms.

"I feel it my duty," said the lady in German, "before we go any further to tell you the truth."

This was alarming. The lady's manner was solemn. Anna inclined her head, and felt scared. She wished that Axel Lohm were somewhere near.

"I see you are young," continued the lady, "and I presume that you are inexperienced."

"Not so young," murmured Anna, who felt particularly young and uncomfortable at that moment, and very unlike the mistress of a house interviewing a companion. "Not so young—twenty-five."

"Twenty-five? You do not look it. But what is twenty-five?"

Anna did not know, so said nothing.

"My position here would be a responsible one," continued the lady, scrutinising Anna's face, and smiling again at what she saw there. "Taking charge of a motherless girl always is. And the circumstances in this case are peculiar."

"Yes," said Anna, "they are even more peculiar than you imagine——" And she was about to explain the approaching advent of the victims, when the lady held up her hand in a masterful way, as though enjoining silence, and said, "First hear me. Through a series of misfortunes I have been reduced to poverty since my husband's death. But I do not choose to live on the charity of relatives, which is the most unbearable form of charity calling itself by that holy name, and I am determined to work for my bread."

She paused. Anna could find nothing better to say than "Oh."

"Out of consideration for my relatives, who are enraged at my resolution, and think I ought to starve quietly on what they choose to give me sooner than make myself conspicuous by working, I have called myself Frau von Penheim. I will not come here under false pretences, and to you, privately, I will confess that my proper title is the Princess Ludwig, of that house."

She stopped to observe the effect of this announcement. Anna was confounded. A princess was not at all what she wanted. She felt that she had no use whatever for princesses. How could she ever expect one to get up early and see that the twelve received their meat in due season? "Oh," she said again, and then was silent.

The princess watched her closely. She was very poor, and very anxious to have the place. "'Oh' is so English," she said, smiling to hide her anxiety. "We say 'ach!'"

Anna laughed.

"And do not think that all German princesses are like your English ones," she went on eagerly. "My father-in-law was raised to the rank of Fürst for services rendered to the state. He had a large family, and my husband was a younger son."

Still Anna was silent. Then she said "I—I wish——" and then stopped.

"What do you wish, my dear child?"

"I wish—that I—that you——"

"That you had known it beforehand? Then you would never have taken me, even on trial," was the prompt reply.

Anna's eyes said plainly, "No, I would not."

"And it is so important that I should find something to do. At first I answered advertisements in my real name, and received my photograph back by the next post. This, and the anger of my family, decided me to drop the title altogether. But I had always resolved that if I did find a place I would confess to my employer. It is a terrible thing to be very poor," she added, staring straight before her with eyes growing dim at her remembrances.

"Yes," said Anna, under her breath.

"To have nothing, nothing at all, and to be burdened at the same time by one's birth."

"Oh," murmured Anna, with a little catch in her voice.

"And to be dependent on people who only wish that you were safely out of the way—dead."

"Married," whispered Anna.

"Why, what do you know about it?" said the princess, turning quickly to her; for she had been thinking aloud rather than addressing anyone.

"I know everything about it," said Anna; and in a rush of bad but eager German she told her of those old days when even the sweeping of crossings had seemed better than living on relations, and how since then all her heart had been filled with pity for the type of poverty called genteel, and how now that she was well off she was going to help women who were in the same sad situation in which she had been. Her eyes were wet when she finished. She had spoken with extraordinary enthusiasm, a fresh wave of passionate sympathy with such lives passing over her; and not until she had done did she remember that she had never before seen this lady, and that she was saying things to her that she had not as yet said to the most intimate of her friends.

She felt suddenly uncomfortable; her eyelashes quivered and drooped, and she blushed.

The princess contemplated her curiously. "I congratulate you," she said, laying her hand lightly for a moment on Anna's. "The idea and the good intentions will have been yours, whatever the result may be."

This was not very encouraging as a response to an outburst. "I have told you more than I tell most people," Anna said, looking up shamefacedly, "because you have had much the same experiences that I have."

"Except the uncle at the end. He makes such a difference. May I ask if many of the ladies answered both advertisements?"

"No, they did not."

"Not one?"

"Not one."

The princess thought that working for one's bread was distinctly preferable to taking Anna's charity; but then she was of an unusually sturdy and independent nature. "I can assure you," she said after a short silence, "that I would do my best to look after your house and your—your friends and yourself."

"But I want someone who will do everything—order the meals, train the servants—everything. And get up early besides," said Anna, her voice full of doubt. The princess really belonged, she felt, to the category of sad, sick, and sorry; and if she had asked for a place among the twelve there would have been little difficulty in giving her one. But the companion she had imagined was to be a real help, someone she could order about as she chose, certainly not a person unused to being ordered about. Even the parson's sister-in-law Helena would have been better than this.

"I would do all that, naturally. Do you think if I am not too proud to take wages that I shall be too proud to do the work for which they are paid?"

"Would you not prefer——" began Anna, and hesitated.

"Would I not prefer what, my child?"

"Prefer to—would it not be more agreeable for you to come and live here without working? I could find another companion, and I would be happy if you will stay here as— as one of the others."

The princess laughed; a hearty, big laugh in keeping with her big person.

"No," she said. "I would not like that at all. But thank you, dear child, for making the offer. Let me stay here and do what work you want done, and then you pay me for it, and we are quits. I assure you there is a solid satisfaction in being quits. I shall certainly not expect any more consideration than you would give to a Frau Schultz. And I will be able to take care of you; and I think, if you will not be angry with me for saying so, that you greatly need taking care of."

"Well, then," said Anna, with an effort, "let us try it for three months."

An immense load was lifted off the princess's heart by these words. "You will not regret it," she said emphatically.

But Anna was not so sure. Though she did her best to put a cheerful face on her new bargain, she could not help fearing that her enterprise had begun badly. She was unusually pensive throughout the evening.

CHAPTER XIII

What the Princess Ludwig thought of her new place it
would be difficult to say. She accepted her position as
minister to the comforts of the hitherto comfortless without
remark and entirely as a matter of course. She got up at
hours exemplary in their earliness, and was about the house
rattling a bunch of keys all day long. She was wholly
practical, and as destitute of illusions as she was of
education in the ordinary sense. Her knowledge of German
literature was hardly more extensive than Letty's, and of
other tongues and other literatures she knew and cared
nothing. As for illusions, she saw things as they are, and
had never at any period of her life possessed enthusiasms.
Nor had she the least taste for hidden meanings and
symbols. Maeterlinck, if she had heard of him, would have
been dismissed by her with an easy smile. Anna's
whitewash to her was whitewash; a disagreeable but
economical wall-covering. She knew and approved of it as
cheap; how could she dream that it was also symbolic? She
never dreamed at all, either sleeping or waking. If by some
chance she had fallen into musings, she would have mused
blood and iron, the superiority of the German nation,
cookery in its three forms feine, bürgerliche, and
Hausmannskost, in all which forms she was preëminent in
skill—she would have mused, that is, on facts, plain and
undisputed. If she had had children she would have made
an excellent mother; as it was she made excellent cakes—
also a form of activity to be commended. She was a
Dettingen before her marriage, and the Dettingens are one
of the oldest Prussian families, and have produced more
first-rate soldiers and statesmen and a larger number of
mothers of great men than any other family in that part. The
Penheims and Dettingens had intermarried continually, and

it was to his mother's Dettingen blood that the first
[German: Fürst] Penheim owed the energy that procured
him his elevation. Princess Ludwig was a good example of
the best type of female Dettingen. Like many other
illiterates, she prided herself particularly on her sturdy
common sense. Regarding this quality, which she
possessed, as more precious than others which she did not
possess, she was not likely to sympathise much either with
Anna's plan for making people happy, or with those who
were willing to be made happy in such a way. A sensible
woman, she thought, will always find work, and need not
look far for a home. She herself had been handicapped in
the search by her unfortunate title, yet with patience even
she had found a haven. Only the lazy and lackadaisical, the
morally worthless, that is, would, she was convinced,
accept such an offer as Anna's. It was not, however, her
business. Her business was to look after Anna's house; and
she did it with a zeal and thoroughness that struck terror
into the hearts of the maid-servants. Trudi's fitful energy
was nothing to it. Trudi had introduced workmen and
chaos; the princess, with a rapidity and skill little short of
amazing to anyone unacquainted with the capabilities of
the well-trained German Hausfrau, cleared out the
workmen and reduced the chaos to order. Within three
weeks the house was ready, and Anna, palpitating, saw the
moment approaching when the first batch of unhappy ones
might be received.

Manske's time was entirely taken up writing letters of
inquiry concerning the applicants, and it was surprising in
what huge batches they had to be weeded out. Of fifty
applications received in one day, three or four, after due
inquiry, would alone remain for further consideration; and
of these three or four, after yet closer inquiry, sometimes
not one would be left.

At first Anna asked the princess's advice as well as
Manske's, and it was when she was present at the
consultations that the heap into which the letters of the
unworthy were gathered was biggest. All those ladies
belonging to the bürgerliche or middle classes were in her
eyes wholly unworthy. If Anna had proposed to take
washerwomen into her home, and required the princess's
help in brightening their lives, it would have been given in
the full measure, pressed down and running over, that befits
a Christian gentlewoman; but for the Bürgerlichen, those
belonging to the class more immediately below her own,
the princess's feeling was only Christian so long as they
kept a great way off. There was so much good sense in the
objections she made that Anna, who did her best to keep an
open mind and listen attentively to advice, was forced to
agree with her, and added letters to the ever-increasing
heap of the rejected which she might otherwise have
reserved for riper consideration. After two or three days,
however, it became clear to her that if she continued to
consult the princess, no one would be accepted at all, for
Manske's respect for that lady was so profound that he was
invariably of her opinion. She did not, therefore, invite her
again to assist at the interviews. Still, all she had said, and
the knowledge that she must know her own countrywomen
fairly thoroughly, made Anna prudent; and so it came about
that the first arrivals were to be only three in number,
chosen without reference to the princess, and one of them
was bürgerlich.

"We can meanwhile proceed with our inquiries about the
remaining nine," said Manske, "and the gracious Miss will
be always gaining experience."

She trod on air during the days preceding the arrival of the
chosen. To say that she was blissful would be but an

inadequate description of her state of mind. The weather
was beautiful, and it increased her happiness tenfold to
know that their new life was to begin in sunshine. She had
never a doubt as to their delight in the sun-chequered
forest, in the freshness of the glittering sea, in the
peacefulness of the quiet country life, so quiet that the
week seemed to be all Sundays. Were not these things
sufficient for herself? Did she ever tire of those long pine
vistas, with the narrow strip of clearest blue between the
gently waving tree-tops? The dreamy murmur of the forest
gave her an exquisite pleasure. To see the bloom on the
pink and grey trunks of the pines, and the sun on the moss
and lichen beneath, was so deep a satisfaction to her soul
that the thought that others who had been knocked about by
life would not feel it too, would not enter with profoundest
thankfulness into this other world of peace, never struck
her at all. When these poor tired women, freed at last from
every care and every anxiety, had refreshed themselves
with the music and fragrance of the forest, there was the
garden across the road to enjoy, with the marsh already
strewn with kingcups on the other side of the hedge already
turning green; and the sea with the fishing-smacks passing
up and down, and the silver gleam of gulls' wings circling
round the orange sails, and eagles floating high up aloft,
specks in the infinite blue; and then there were drives along
the coast towards the north, where the wholesome wind
blew fresher than in the woods; and quiet evenings in the
roomy house, where all that was asked of them was that
they should be happy.

"It's a lovely plan, isn't it, Letty?" she said joyously, the
evening before they were to arrive, as she stood with her
arm round Letty's shoulder at the bottom of the garden,
where they had both been watching the sails of the fishing-
smacks during those short sunset moments when they

looked like the bright wings of spirits moving over the face of the placid waters.

"I should rather think it was," replied Letty, who was profoundly interested.

They got up at sunrise the next morning, and went out into the forest in search of hepaticas and windflowers with which to decorate the three bedrooms. These bedrooms were the largest and pleasantest in the house. Anna had given up her own because she thought the windows particularly pleasing, and had gone into a little one in the fervour of her desire to lavish all that was best on her new friends. The rooms were furnished with special care, an immense amount of thought having been bestowed on the colour of the curtains, the pattern of the porcelain, and the books filling the shelves above each writing-table. The colours and patterns were the nearest approach Berlin could produce to Anna's own favourite colours and patterns. She wasted half her time, when the rooms were ready, sitting in them and picturing what her own delight would have been if she, like the poor ladies for whom they were intended, had come straight out of a cold, unkind world into such pretty havens.

The choice of books had been a great difficulty, and there had been much correspondence on the subject with Berlin before a selection had been made. Books there must be, for no room, she thought, was habitable without them; and she had tried to imagine what manner of literature would most appeal to her unhappy ones. It was to be presumed that their ages were such as to exclude frivolity; therefore she bought very few novels. She thought Dickens translated into German would be a safe choice; also Schlegel's Shakespeare for loftier moments. The German classics were represented by Goethe in one room, Schiller in another, and Heine in the third. In each room also there was a German-English dictionary, for the facilitation of intercourse. Finally, she asked the princess to recommend something they would be sure to like, and she recommended cookery books.

"But they are not going to cook," said Anna, surprised.

"Es ist egal—it is always interesting to read good recipes. No other reading affords me the same pleasure."

"But only when you want something new cooked."

"No, no, at all times," insisted the princess.

Anna could not quite believe that such a taste was general; but in case one of the three should share it, she put a cookery book in one bookcase. In the other two severally to balance it, she slipt at the last moment a volume of Maeterlinck, to which at that period she was greatly attached; and Matthew Arnold's poems, to which also at that period she was greatly attached.

The princess went about with pursed lips while these preparations were in progress; and when, at sunrise on the last morning, she was awakened by stealthy footsteps and smothered laughter on the landing outside her room, and, opening her door an inch and peering out as in duty bound in case the sounds should be emanating from some unaccountably mirthful maid-servant, she saw Anna and Letty creeping downstairs with their hats on and baskets in their hands, she guessed what they were going to do, and got back into bed with lips more pursed than ever. Did she

not know who had been chosen, and that one of the three
was a Bürgerliche?

About eight o'clock, when the two girls were coming out of
the forest with their baskets full and their faces happy, Axel
Lohm was riding thoughtfully past, having just settled an
unpleasant business at Kleinwalde. Dellwig had sent him
an urgent message in the small hours; there had been a
brawl among the labourers about a woman, and a man had
been stabbed. Axel had ordered the aggressor to be locked
up in the little room that served as a temporary prison till
he could be handed over to the Stralsund authorities. His
wife, a girl of twenty, was ill, and she and her three small
children depended entirely on the man's earnings. The
victim appeared to be dying, and the man would certainly
be punished. What, then, thought Axel, was to become of
the wife and the children? Frau Dellwig had told him that
she sent soup every day at dinner-time, but soup once a day
would neither comfort them nor make them fat. Besides, he
had a notion that the soup of Frau Dellwig's charity was
very thin. He was riding dejectedly enough down the road
on his way home, looking straight before him, his mouth a
mere grim line, thinking how grievous it was that the
consequences of sin should fall with their most terrific
weight nearly always on the innocent, on the helpless
women-folk and the weak little children, when Anna and
Letty appeared, talking and laughing, on the edge of the
forest.

Letty, we know, had not been kindly treated by nature, but
even she was a pleasing object in her harmless morning
cheerfulness after the faces he had just seen; and Anna's
beauty, made radiant by happiness and contentment,
startled him. He had a momentary twinge, gone almost
before he had realised it, a sudden clear conception of his

great loneliness. The satisfaction he strove to extract from improving his estate for the benefit of his brother Gustav appeared to him at that moment to bear a singular resemblance, in its thinness, to Frau Dellwig's charitable soup. He got off his horse to speak to her, and rested his eyes, tired by looking at the hideous passions on the brawler's face, on hers. "To-day is the important day, is it not?" he asked, glancing from her flower-like face to the flowers.

"The first three come this afternoon."

"So Manske told me. You are very happy, I can see," he said, smiling.

"I never was so happy before."

"Your uncle was a wise man. He told me he was going to leave you Kleinwalde because he felt sure you would be happy leading the simple life here."

"Did he talk about me to you?"

"After his last visit to England he talked about you all the time."

"Oh?" said Anna, looking at him thoughtfully. Uncle Joachim, she remembered perfectly, had urged two things—the leading of the better life, and the marrying of a good German gentleman. A faint flush came into her face and faded again. She had suddenly become aware that Axel was the good German gentleman he had meant. Well, the wisest uncle was subject to errors of judgment.

"I trust those women will not worry you too much," he said, thinking how immense would be the pity if those happy eyes ever lost their joyousness.

"Worry me? Poor things, they won't have any energy of any sort left after all they have gone through. I never read such pitiful letters."

"Well, I don't know," said Axel doubtfully. "Manske says one of them is a Treumann. It is a family distinguished by its size and its disagreeableness."

"Oh, but she only married a Treumann, and isn't one herself."

"But a woman generally adopts the peculiarities of the family she marries into, especially if they are unpleasant."

"But she has been a widow for years. And is so poor. And is so crushed."

"I never yet heard of a permanently crushed Treumann," said Axel, shaking his head.

"You are trying to make me uneasy," said Anna, a slight touch of impatience in her voice. She was singularly sensitive about her chosen ones; sensitive in the way mothers are about a child that is deformed.

"No, no," he said quickly, "I only wish to warn you. You maybe disappointed—it is just possible." He could not bear to think of her as disappointed.

"Pray, do you know anything against the other two?" she asked with some defiance. "One of them is a Baroness Elmreich, and the other is a Fräulein Kuhräuber."

Axel looked amused. "I never heard of Fräulein Kuhräuber," he said. "What does Princess Ludwig say to her coming?"

"Nothing at all. What should she say?"

It was Fräulein Kuhräuber's coming that had more particularly occasioned the pursing of the princess's lips.

"I know some Elmreichs," said Axel. "A few of them are respectable; but one branch at least of the family is completely demoralised. A Baron Elmreich shot himself last year because he had been caught cheating at cards. And one of his sisters—oh, well, some of them are harmless, I believe."

"Thank you."

"You are angry with me?"

"Very."

"And why?"

"You want to prejudice me against these poor things. They can't help what distant relations do. They will get away from them in my house, at least, and have peace."

"Miss Letty, is your aunt often—what is the word—so fractious?"

"Oh, I don't know," said Letty, who found it dull waiting in silence while other people talked. "It's breakfast time, you know, and people can't stand much just about then."

"Oh, youthful philosopher!" exclaimed Axel. "So young, and of the female sex, and yet to have pierced to the very root of human weakness!"

"Stuff," said Letty, offended.

"What, are you going to be angry too? Then let me get on my horse and go."

"It's the best thing you can do," said Letty, always frank, but doubly so when she was hungry.

"Shall you come and see us soon?" Anna asked, gathering up her skirts in her one free hand, preparatory to crossing the muddy road.

"But you are angry with me."

She looked up and laughed. "Not now," she said; "I've finished. Do you think I'm going to be angry long this pleasant April morning?"

"I smell the coffee," observed Letty, sniffing.

"Then I will come to-morrow if I may," said Axel, "and make the acquaintance of Frau von Treumann and Baroness Elmreich."

"And Fräulein Kuhräuber," said Anna, with emphasis. She thought she saw the same tendency in him that was so

manifest in the princess, a tendency to ignore the very
existence of any one called Kuhräuber.

"And Fräulein Kuhräuber," repeated Axel gravely.

"They've burnt the toast again," said Letty; "I can hear them
scraping off the black."

"I wish you good luck, then," said Axel, taking off his hat;
"with all my heart I wish you good luck, and that these
ladies may very soon be as happy as you are yourself."

"That's nice," said Anna, approvingly; "so much, much
nicer than the other things you have been saying." And she
nodded to him, all smiles, as she crossed over to the house
and he rode away.

CHAPTER XIV

Long before the carriage bringing the three chosen ones
from the station could possibly arrive, Anna and Letty
began to wait in the hall, standing at the windows, going
out on to the steps, looking into the different rooms every
few minutes to make sure that everything was ready. The
bedrooms were full of the hepaticas of the morning; the
coffee had been set out with infinite care and an eye to
effect by Anna herself on a little table in the drawing-room
by the open window, through which the mild April air

came in and gently fanned the curtains to and fro; and the princess had baked her best cakes for the occasion, inwardly deploring, as she did so, that such cakes should be offered to such people. When she had seen that all was as it should be, she withdrew into her own room, where she remained darning sheets, for she had asked Anna to excuse her from being present at the arrival. "It is better that you should make their acquaintance by yourself," she said. "The presence of too many strangers at first might disconcert them under the circumstances."

Miss Leech profited by this remark, made in her hearing, and did not appear either; so that when the carriage drove in at the gate only Anna and Letty were standing at the door in the sunshine.

Anna's heart bumped so as the three slowly disentangled themselves and got out, that she could hardly speak. Her face flushed and grew pale by turns, and her eyes were shining with something suspiciously like tears. What she wanted to do was to put her arms right round the three poor ladies, and kiss them, and comfort them, and make up for all their griefs. What she did was to put out a very cold, shaking hand, and say in a voice that trembled, "Guten Tag."

"Guten Tag," said the first lady to descend; evidently, from her mourning, the widowed Frau von Treumann.

Anna took her extended hand in both hers, and clasping it tight looked at its owner with all her heart in her eyes. "Es freut mich so—es freut mich so," she murmured incoherently.

"Ach—you are Miss Estcourt?" asked the lady in German.

"Yes, yes," said Anna, still clinging to her hand, "and so
happy, so very happy to see you."

Frau von Treumann hereupon made some remarks which
Anna supposed were of a grateful nature, but she spoke so
rapidly and in such subdued tones, glancing round uneasily
as she did so at the coachman and at the others, and Anna
herself was so much agitated, that what she said was quite
incomprehensible. Again Anna longed to throw her arms
round the poor woman's neck, and interrupt her with kisses,
and tell her that gratitude was not required of her, but only
that she should be happy; but she felt that if she did so she
would begin to cry, and tears were surely out of place on
such a joyful occasion, especially as nobody else looked in
the least like crying.

"You are Frau von Treumann, I know," she said, holding
her hand, and turning to the next one and beaming on her,
"and this is Baroness Elmreich?"

"No, no," said the third lady quickly, "I am Baroness
Elmreich."

Fräulein Kuhräuber, an ample person whose body, swathed
in travelling cloaks, had blotted out the other little woman,
looked frightened and apologetic, and made deep curtseys.

Anna shook their hands one after the other with all the
warmth that was glowing in her heart. Her defective
German forsook her almost completely. She did nothing
but repeat disconnected ejaculations, "so reizend—so
glücklich—so erfreut——" and fill in the gaps with happy,
quivering smiles at each in turn, and timid little pats on any
hand within her reach.

Letty meanwhile stood in the shadow of the doorway, wishing that she were young enough to suck her thumb. It kept on going up to her mouth of its own accord, and she kept on pulling it down again. This was one of the occasions, she felt, when the sucking of thumbs is a relief and a blessing. It gives one's superfluous hands occupation, and oneself a countenance. She shifted from one foot to the other uneasily, and held on tight to the rebellious thumb, for the tall lady who had got out first was fixing her with a stare that chilled her blood. The tall lady, who was very tall and thin, and had round unblinking dark eyes set close together like an owl's, and strongly marked black eyebrows, said nothing, but examined her slowly from the tip of the bow of ribbon trembling on her head to the buckles of the shoes creaking on her feet. Ought she to offer to shake hands with her, or ought she to wait to be shaken hands with, Letty asked herself distractedly. Anyhow it was rather rude to stare like that. She had always been taught that it was rude to stare like that.

Anna had forgotten all about her, and only remembered her when they were in the drawing-room and she had begun to pour out the coffee. "Oh, Letty, where are you? This is my niece," she said; and Letty was at last shaken hands with.

"Ah—she keeps you company," said the baroness. "You found it lonely here, naturally."

"Oh no, I am never lonely," said Anna cheerfully, filling the cups and giving them to Letty to carry round.

"How pleasant the air is to-day," observed Frau von Treumann, edging her chair away from the window. "Damp, but pleasant. You like fresh air, I see."

"Oh, I love it," said Anna; "and it is so beautiful here—so pure, and full of the sea."

"You are not afraid of catching cold, sitting so near an open window?"

"Oh, is it too much for you? Letty, shut the window. It is getting chilly. The days are so fine that one forgets it is only April."

Anna talked German and poured out the coffee with a nervous haste unusual to her. The three women sitting round the little table staring at her made her feel terribly nervous. She was happy beyond words to have got them safely under her own roof at last, but she was nervous. She was determined that there should be no barriers of conventionality from the first between themselves and her; not a minute more of their lives was to be wasted; this was their home, and she was all ready to love them; she had made up her mind that however shy she felt she was going to behave as though they were her dear friends—which indeed, she assured herself, was exactly what they were. Therefore she struggled bravely against her nervousness, addressing them collectively and singly, saying whatever came first into her head in her anxiety to say something, smiling at them, pressing the princess's cakes on them, hardly letting them drink their coffee before she wanted to give them more. But it was no good; she was and remained nervous, and her hand shook so when she lifted it that she was ashamed.

Fräulein Kuhräuber was the one who stared least. If she caught Anna's eye her own drooped, whereas the eyes of the other two never wavered. She sat on the edge of her chair in a way made familiar to Anna by intercourse with

Frau Manske, and whatever anybody said she nodded her
head and murmured "Ja, eben." She was obviously ill at
ease, and dropped the sugar-tongs when she was offered
sugar with a loud clatter on to the varnished floor, nearly
sweeping the cups off the table in her effort to pick them up
again.

"Oh, do not mind," said Anna, "Letty will pick them up.
They are stupid things—much too big for the sugar-basin."

"Ja, eben," said Fräulein Kuhräuber, sitting up and looking
perturbed. The other two removed their eyes from Anna's
face for a moment to stare at the Fräulein. The baroness, a
small, fair person with hair arranged in those little flat curls
called kiss-me-quicks on each cheek, and wide-open pale
blue eyes, and a little mouth with no lips, or lips so thin
that they were hardly visible, sat very still and straight, and
had a way of moving her eyes round from one face to the
other without at the same time moving her head. She was
unmarried, and was probably about thirty-five, Anna
thought, but she had always evaded questions in the
correspondence about her age. Fräulein Kuhräuber was also
thirty-five, and as large and blooming as the baroness was
small and pale. Frau von Treumann was over fifty, and had
had more sorrows, judging from her letters, than the other
two. She sat nearest Anna, who every now and then laid her
hand gently on hers and let it rest there a moment, in her
determination to thaw all frost from the very beginning.
"Oh, I quite forgot," she said cheerfully—the amount of
cheerfulness she put into her voice made her laugh at
herself—"I quite forgot to introduce you to each other."

"We did it at the station," said Frau von Treumann, "when
we found ourselves all entering your carriage."

"The Elmreichs are connected with the Treumanns," observed the baroness.

"We are such a large family," said Frau von Treumann quickly, "that we are connected with nearly everybody."

The tone was cold, and there was a silence. Neither of them, apparently, was connected with Fräulein Kuhräuber, who buried her face in her cup, in which the tea-spoon remained while she drank, and heartily longed for connections.

But she had none. She was absolutely without relations except deceased ones. She had been an orphan since she was two, cared for by her one aunt till she was ten. The aunt died, and she found a refuge in an orphanage till she was sixteen, when she was told that she must earn her bread. She was a lazy girl even in those days, who liked eating her bread better than earning it. No more, however, being forthcoming in the orphanage, she went into a pastor's family as Stütze der Hausfrau. These Stütze, or supports, are common in middle-class German families, where they support the mistress of the house in all her manifold duties, cooking, baking, mending, ironing, teaching or amusing the children—being in short a comfort and blessing to harassed mothers. But Fräulein Kuhräuber had no talent whatever for comforting mothers, and she was quickly requested to leave the busy and populous parsonage; whereupon she entered upon the series of driftings lasting twenty years, which landed her, by a wonderful stroke of fortune, in Anna's arms.

When she saw the advertisement, her future was looking very black. She was, as usual, under notice to quit, and had no other place in view, and had saved nothing. It is true the advertisement only offered a home to women of good family; but she got over that difficulty by reflecting that her family was all in heaven, and that there could be no relations more respectable than angels. She wrote therefore in glowing terms of the paternal Kuhräuber, "gegenwärtig mit Gott," as she put it, expatiating on his intellect and gifts (he was a man of letters, she said), while he yet dwelt upon earth. Manske, with all his inquiries, could find out nothing about her except that she was, as she said, an orphan, poor, friendless, and struggling; and Anna, just then impatient of the objections the princess made to every applicant, quickly decided to accept this one, against whom not a word had been said. So Fräulein Kuhräuber, who had spent her life in shirking work, who was quite thriftless and improvident, who had never felt particularly unhappy, and whose father had been a postman, found herself being welcomed with an enthusiasm that astonished her to Anna's home, being smiled upon and patted, having beautiful things said to her, things the very opposite to those to which she had been used, things to the effect that she was now to rest herself for ever and to be sure and not do anything except just that which made her happiest.

It was very wonderful. It seemed much, much too good to be true. And the delight that filled her as she sat eating excellent cakes, and the discomfort she endured because of the stares of the other two women, and the consciousness that she had never learned how to behave in the society of persons with von before their names, produced such mingled feelings of ecstasy and fright in her bosom that it was quite natural she should drop the sugar-tongs, and upset the cream-jug, and choke over her coffee—all of which things she did, to Anna's distress, who suffered with her in her agitation, while the eyes of the other two watched each successive catastrophe with profoundest attention.

It was an uncomfortable half hour. "I am shy, and they are shy," Anna said to herself, apologising as it were for the undoubted flatness that prevailed. How could it be otherwise, she thought? Did she expect them to gush? Heaven forbid. Yet it was an important crisis in their lives, this passing for ever from neglect and loneliness to love, and she wondered vaguely that the obviously paramount feeling should be interest in the awkwardness of Fräulein Kuhräuber.

Her German faltered, and threatened to give out entirely. The inevitable pause came, and they could hear the sparrows quarrelling in the golden garden, and the creaking of a distant pump.

"How still it is," observed the baroness with a slight shiver.

"You have no farmyard near the house to make it more cheerful," said Frau von Treumann. "My father's house had the garden at the back, and the farmyard in the front, and one did not feel so cut off from everything. There was always something going on in the yard—always life and noises."

"Really?" said Anna; and again the pump and the sparrows became audible.

"The stillness is truly remarkable," observed the baroness again.

"Ja, eben," said Fräulein Kuhräuber.

"But it is beautiful, isn't it," said Anna, gazing out at the light on the water. "It is so restful, so soothing. Look what a lovely sunset there must be this evening. We can't see it from this side of the house, but look at the colour of the grass and the water."

"Ach—you are a friend of nature," said Frau von Treumann, turning her head for a brief moment towards the window, and then examining Anna's face. "I am also. There is nothing I like more than nature. Do you paint?"

"I wish I could."

"Ah, then you sing—or play?"

"I can do neither."

"So? But what have you here, then, in the way of distractions, of pastimes?"

"I don't think I have any," said Anna, smiling. "I have been very busy till now making things ready for you, and after this I shall just enjoy being alive."

Frau von Treumann looked puzzled for a moment. Then she said "Ach so."

There was another silence.

"Have some more coffee," said Anna, laying hold of the pot persuasively. She was feeling foolish, and had blushed stupidly after that Ach so.

"No, no," said Frau von Treumann, putting up a protesting hand, "you are very kind. Two cups are a limit beyond which voracity itself could not go. What do you say? You have had three? Oh, well, you are young, and young people can play tricks with their digestions with less danger than old ones."

At this speech Fräulein Kuhräuber's four cups became plainly written on her guilty face. The thought that she had been voracious at the very first meal was appalling to her. She hastily pushed away her half-empty cup—too hastily, for it upset, and in her effort to save it it fell on to the floor and was broken. "Ach, Herr Je!" she cried in her distress.

The other two looked at each other; the expression is an unusual one on the lips of gentle-women.

"Oh, it does not matter—really it does not," Anna hastened to assure her. "Don't pick it up—Letty will. The table is too small really. There is no room on it for anything."

"Ja, eben," said Fräulein Kuhräuber, greatly discomfited.

"You would like to go upstairs, I am sure," said Anna hurriedly, turning to the others. "You must be very tired," she added, looking at Frau von Treumann.

"I am," replied that lady, closing her eyes for a moment with a little smile expressive of patient endurance.

"Then we will go up. Come," she said, holding out her hand to Fräulein Kuhräuber. "No, no—let Letty pick up the pieces——" for the Fräulein, in her anxiety to repair the disaster, was about to sweep the remaining cups off the table with the sleeve of her cloak.

Anna drew her hand through her arm, and gave it a furtive
and encouraging stroke. "I will go first and show you the
way," she said over her shoulder to the others.

And so it came about that Frau von Treumann and
Baroness Elmreich actually found themselves going
through doors and up stairs behind a person called
Kuhräuber. They exchanged glances again. Whatever
might be their private objections to each other, they had
one point already on which they agreed, for with equal
heartiness they both disapproved of Fräulein Kuhräuber.

CHAPTER XV

As soon as Baroness Elmreich found herself alone in her
bedroom, she proceeded to examine its contents with
minute care. Supper, she had been told, was not till eight
o'clock, and she had not much to unpack; so laying aside
her hat and cloak, and glancing at the reflection of her little
curls in the glass to see whether they were as they should
be, she began her inspection of each separate article in her
room, taking each one up and scrutinising it, holding the
jars of hepaticas high above her head in order to see
whether the price was marked underneath, untidying the
bed to feel the quality of the sheets, poking the mattress to
discover the nature of the stuffing, and investigating with
special attention the embroidery on the pillow-cases. But
everything was as dainty and as perfect as enthusiasm

could make it. Nowhere, with her best endeavours, could she discover the signs she was looking for of cheapness and shabbiness in less noticeable things that would have helped her to understand her hostess. "This embroidery has cost at least two marks the meter," she said to herself, fingering it. "She must roll in money. And the wall-paper—how unpractical! It is so light that every mark will be seen. The flies alone will ruin it in a month."

She shrugged her shoulders, and smiled; strange to say, the thought of Anna's paper being spoiled pleased her.

Never had she been in a room the least like this one. If whitewash prevailed downstairs, and in Anna's special haunts, it had not been permitted to invade the bedrooms of the Chosen. Anna's reflections had led her to the conclusion that the lives of these ladies had till then probably been spent in bare places, and that they would accordingly feel as much pleasure in the contemplation of carpets, papered walls, and stuffed chairs, as she herself did in the severity of her whitewashed rooms after the lavishly upholstered years of her youth. But the daintiness and luxury only filled the baroness with doubts. She stood in the middle of it looking round her when she had finished her tour of inspection and had made guesses at the price of everything, and asked herself who this Miss Estcourt could be. Anna would have been considerably disappointed, and perhaps even moved to tears, if she had known that the room she thought so pretty struck the baroness, whose taste in furniture had not advanced beyond an appreciation for the dark and heavy hangings and walnut-wood tables of her more prosperous years, merely as odd. Odd, and very expensive. Where did the money come from for this reckless furnishing with stuffs and colours that were bound to show each stain? Her eye wandered along the shelves above the writing-table—hers was the Heine and Maeterlinck room—and she wondered what all the books were there for. She did not touch them as she had touched everything else, for except an occasional novel, and, more regularly, a journal beloved of German woman called the Gartenlaube, she never read.

On the writing-table lay a blotter, a pretty, embroidered thing that said as plainly as blotter could say that it had been chosen with immense care; and opening it she found notepaper and envelopes stamped with the Kleinwalde address and her own monogram. This was Anna's little special gift, a childish addition, the making of which had given her an absurd amount of pleasure. The happy idea, as she called it, had come to her one night when she lay awake thinking about her new friends and going through the familiar process of discovering their tastes by imagining herself in their place. "Sonderbar," was the baroness's comment; and she decided that the best thing she could do would be to ring the bell and endeavour to obtain private information about Miss Estcourt by means of a prolonged cross-examination of the housemaid.

She rang it, and then sat very straight and still on the sofa with her hands folded in her lap, and waited. Her soul was full of doubts. Who was this Miss, and where were the proofs that she was, as she had pretended, of good birth? That she was not so very pious was evident; for if she had been, some remark of a religious nature would inevitably have been forthcoming when she first welcomed them to her house. No such word, not the least approach to any such word, had been audible. There had not even been an allusion, a sigh, or an upward glance. Yet the pastor who had opened the correspondence had filled many pages with expatiations on her zeal after righteousness. And then she was so young. The baroness had expected to see an elderly person, or at least a person of the age of everybody else, which was her own age; but this was a mere girl, and a girl, too, who from the way she dressed, clearly thought herself pretty. Surely it was strange that so young a woman should be living here quite unattached, quite independent apparently of all control, with a great deal of money at her disposal, and only one little girl to give her a countenance? Suppose she were not a proper person at all, suppose she were an outcast from society, a being on whom her own countrypeople turned their backs? This desire to share her fortune with respectable ladies could only be explained in two ways: either she had been moved thereto by an enthusiastic piety of which not a trace had as yet appeared, or she was an improper person anxious to rebuild her reputation with the aid and countenance of the ladies of good family she had entrapped into her house.

The baroness stiffened as she sat. It was her brother who had cheated at cards and shot himself, and it was her sister of whom Axel Lohm had heard strange tales; and few people are more savagely proper than the still respectable relations of the demoralised. "The service in this house is very bad," she said aloud and irascibly, getting up to ring again. "No doubt she has trouble with her servants."

But there was a knock at the door while her hand was on the bell, and on her calling "Come in," instead of the servant her hostess appeared, dressed to the baroness's eye in a truly amazing and reprehensible fashion, and looking as cheerful as an innocent infant for whom no such thing as evil-doing exists. Also she seemed quite unconscious of her clothes and bare neck, nor did she offer to explain why she was arrayed as though she were going to a ball; and she stood a moment in the doorway trying to say something in

German and pretending to laugh at her own ineffectual efforts, but really laughing, the baroness felt sure, in order to show that she had dimples; which were not, after all, very wonderful things to have—before she had grown so thin she almost had one herself.

"May I come in?" said Anna at last, giving up the other and more complicated speech.

"Bitte," said the baroness, with the smile the French call pincé.

"Has no one been to unpack your things?"

"I rang."

"And no one came? Oh, I shall scold Marie. It is the only thing I can do well in German. Can you speak English?"

"No."

"Nor understand it?"

"No."

"French?"

"No."

"Oh, well, you must be patient then with my bad German. When I am alone with anyone it goes better, but if there are many people listening I am nervous and can hardly speak at all. How glad I am that you are here!"

Anna's shyness, now that she was by herself with one of
her forlorn ones, had vanished, and she prattled happily for
some time, putting as many mistakes into her sentences as
they would hold, before she became aware that the
baroness's replies were monosyllabic, and that she was
examining her from head to foot with so much attention
that there was obviously none left over for the appreciation
of her remarks.

This made her feel shy again. Clothes to her were such
secondary considerations, things of so little importance.
Susie had provided them, and she had put them on, and
there it had ended; and when she found that it was her dress
and not herself that was interesting the baroness, she
longed to have the courage to say, "Don't waste time over it
now—I'll send it to your room to-night, if you like, and you
can look at it comfortably—only don't waste time now. I
want to talk to you, to you who have suffered so much; I
want to make friends with you quickly, to make you begin
to be happy quickly; so don't let us waste the precious time
thinking of clothes." But she had neither sufficient courage
nor sufficient German.

She put out her hand rather timidly, and making an effort to
bring her companion's thoughts back to the things that
mattered, said, "I hope you will like living with me. I hope
we shall be very happy together. I can't tell you how happy
it makes me to think that you are safely here, and that you
are going to stay with me always."

The baroness's hands were clasped in front of her, and they
did not unclasp to meet Anna's; but at this speech she left
off eyeing the dress, and began to ask questions. "You are
very lonely, I can see," she said with another of the pinched
smiles. "Have you then no relations? No one of your own

family who will live with you? Will not your Frau Mama come to Germany?"

"My mother is dead."

"Ach—mine also. And the Herr Papa?"

"He is dead."

"Ach—mine also."

"I know, I know," said Anna, stroking the unresponsive hands—a trick of hers when she wanted to comfort that had often irritated Susie. "You told me how lonely you were in your letters. I lived with my brother and his wife till I came here. You have no brothers or sisters, I think you wrote."

"None," said the baroness with a rigid look.

"Well, I am going to be your sister, if you will let me."

"You are very good."

"Oh, I am not good, only so happy—I have everything in the world that I have ever wished to have, and now that you have come to share it all there is nothing more I can think of that I want."

"Ach," said the baroness. Then she added, "Have you no aunts, or cousins, who would come and stay with you?"

"Oh, heaps. But they are all well off and quite pleased, and they wouldn't like staying here with me at all."

"They would not like staying with you? How strange."

"Very strange," laughed Anna. "You see they don't know how pleasant I can be in my own house."

"And your friends—they too will not come?"

"I don't know if they would or not. I didn't ask them."

"You have no one, no one at all who would come and live with you so that you should not be so lonely?"

"But I am not lonely," said Anna, looking down at the little woman with a slightly amused expression, "and I don't in the least want to be lived with."

"Then why do you wish to fill your house with strangers?"

"Why?" repeated Anna, a puzzled look coming into her eyes. Had not the correspondence with the ultimately chosen been long? And were not all her reasons duly set forth therein? "Why, because I want you to have some of my nice things too."

"But not your own friends and relations?"

"They have everything they want."

There was a silence. Anna left off stroking the baroness's hands. She was thinking that this was a queer little person—outside, that is. Inside, of course, she was very different, poor little lonely thing; but her outer crust seemed thick; and she wondered how long it would take her to get through it to the soul that she was sure was sweet and lovable. She was also unable to repress a conviction that most people would call these questions rude.

But this train of thought was not one to be encouraged. "I am keeping you here talking," she said, resuming her first cheerfulness, "and your things are not unpacked yet. I shall go and scold Marie for not coming when you rang, and I'll send her to you." And she went out quickly, vexed with herself for feeling chilled, and left the baroness more full of doubts than ever.

When she had rebuked Marie, who looked gloomy, she tapped at Frau von Treumann's door. No one answered. She knocked again. No one answered. Then she opened the door softly and looked in.

These were precious moments, she felt, these first moments of being alone with each of her new friends, precious opportunities for breaking ice. It is true she had not been able to break much of the ice encasing the baroness, but she was determined not to be cast down by any of the little difficulties she was sure to encounter at first, and she looked into Frau von Treumann's room with fresh hope in her heart.

What, then, was her dismay to find that lady walking up and down with the long strides of extreme excitement, her face bathed in tears.

"Oh—what's the matter?" gasped Anna, shutting the door quickly and hurrying in.

Frau von Treumann had not heard the gentle taps, and when she saw her, started, and tried to hide her face in her handkerchief.

"Tell me what is the matter," begged Anna, her voice full of tenderness.

"Nichts, nichts," was the hasty reply. "I did not hear you knock——"

"Tell me what is the matter," begged Anna again, fairly putting her arms round the poor lady. "Our letters have said so much already—surely there is nothing you cannot tell me now? And if I can help you——"

Frau von Treumann freed herself by a hasty movement, and began to walk up and down again. "No, no, you can do nothing—you can do nothing," she said, and wept as she walked.

Anna watched her in consternation.

"See to what I have come—see to what I have come!" said the agitated lady under her breath but with passionate intensity, as she passed and repassed her dismayed hostess; "oh, to have fallen so low! oh, to have fallen so low!"

"So low?" echoed Anna, greatly concerned.

"At my age—I, a Treumann—I, a geborene Gräfin Ilmas-Kadenstein—to live on charity—to be a member of a charitable institution!"

"Institution? Charity? Oh no, no!" cried Anna. "It is a home here, and there is no charity in it from the attic to the cellar." And she went towards her with outstretched hands.

"A home! Yes, that is it," cried Frau von Treumann, waving her back, "it is a home, a charitable home!"

"No, not a home like that—a real home, my home, your home—ein Heim," Anna protested; but vainly, because the

German word Heim and the English word "home" have
little meaning in common.

"Ein Heim, ein Heim," repeated Frau von Treumann with
extraordinary bitterness, "ein Frauenheim—yes, that is
what it is, and everybody knows it."

"Everybody knows it?"

"How could I think," she said, wringing her hands, "how
could I think when I decided to come here that the whole
world was to be made acquainted with your plans? I
thought they were to be kept private, that the world was to
think we were your friends——"

"And so you are."

"—your guests——"

"Oh, more than guests—this is home."

"Home! Home! Always that word——" And she burst into
a fresh torrent of tears.

Anna stood helpless. What she said appeared only to
aggravate Frau von Treumann's sorrow and rage—for
surely there was anger as well as sorrow? She was at a
complete loss for the reason of this outburst. Had not every
detail been discussed in the correspondence? Had not that
correspondence been exhaustive even to boredom?

"You have told your servants——"

"My servants?"

"You have told them that we are objects of charity——"

"I——" began Anna, and then was silent.

"It is not true—I have come here from very different motives—but they think me an object of charity. I rang the bell—I cannot unstrap my trunks—I never have been expected to unstrap trunks." The sobs here interfered for a moment with further speech. "After a long while—your servant came—she was insolent—the trunks are there still unstrapped—you see them—she knows—everything."

"She shall go to-morrow."

"The others think the same thing."

"They shall go to-morrow—that is, have they been rude to you?"

"Not yet, but they will be."

"When they are, they shall go."

"I went into the corridor to seek other assistance, and I met—I met——"

"Who?"

"Oh, to have fallen so low!" cried Frau von Treumann, clasping her hands, and raising her streaming eyes to the ceiling.

"But who did you meet?"

"I met—I met the Penheim."

"The Penheim? Do you mean Princess Ludwig?"

"You never said she was here——"

"I did not know that it would interest you."

"—living on charity—she was always shameless—I was at school with her. Oh, I would not have come for any inducement if I had known she was here! She holds nothing sacred, she will boast of her own degradation, she will write to all her friends that I am here too—I told them I was coming only on a visit to you—they knew I knew your uncle—but the Penheim—the Penheim——" and Frau von Treumann threw herself into a chair and covered her face with her hands to shut out the horrid vision.

The corners of Anna's mouth began to take the upward direction that would end in a smile; and feeling how ill-placed such a contortion would be in the presence of this tumultuous grief, she brought them carefully back to a position of proper solemnity. Besides, why should she smile? The poor lady was clearly desperately unhappy about something, though what it was Anna did not quite know. She had looked forward to this first evening with her new friends as to a thing apart, a thing beyond the ordinary experience of life, profound in its peace, perfect in its harmony, the first taste of rest after war, of port after stormy seas; and here was Frau von Treumann plunged in a very audible grief, and in the next room was the baroness, a disconcerting combination of inquisitiveness and ice, and farther down the passage was Fräulein Kuhräuber—in what state, Anna wondered, would she find Fräulein Kuhräuber? Anyhow she had little reason to smile. But the horror with which Princess Ludwig had been mentioned seemed droll beside her own knowledge of the sterling qualities of that

excellent woman. She went over to the chair in which Frau
von Treumann lay prostrate, and sat down beside her. She
was glad that they had reached the stage of sitting down,
for talking is difficult to a person who will not keep still.

"How sorry I am," she said, in her pretty, hesitating
German, "that you should have been made unhappy the
very first evening. Marie is a little wretch. Don't let her
stupidity make you miserable. You shall not see her again, I
promise you." And she patted Frau von Treumann's arm.
"But about Princess Ludwig, now," she went on cheerfully,
"she has been here some weeks and you soon learn to know
a person you are with every day, and really I have found
her nothing but good and kind."

"Ach, she is shameless—she recoils before no
degradation!" burst out Frau von Treumann, suddenly
removing her hands from her face. "The trouble she has
given her relations! She delights in dragging her name in
the dirt. She has tried to get places in the most impossible
families, and made no attempt to hide what she was doing.
She has broken the old Fürst's heart. And she talks about it
all, and has no shame, no decency——"

"But is it not admirable——" began Anna.

"She will gloat over me, and tell everyone that I am here in
the same way as she is. If she is not ashamed for herself, do
you think she will spare me?"

"But why should you think there is anything to be ashamed
of in coming to live with me and be my dear friend?"

"No, there is nothing, so long as my motives in coming are
known. But people talk so cruelly, and will distort the facts

so gladly, and we have always held our heads so high. And now the Penheim!" She sobbed afresh.

"I shall ask the princess not to write to anyone about your being here."

"Ach, I know her—she will do it all the same."

"No, I don't think so. She does everything I ask. You see, she takes care of my house for me. She is not here in the same way that—that you and Baroness Elmreich are, and her interest is to stay here."

Frau von Treumann's bowed head went up with a jerk. "Ach? She has found a place at last? She is your paid companion? Your housekeeper?"

"Yes, and she is goodness itself, and I don't believe she would be unkind and make mischief for worlds."

"Ach so!" said Frau von Treumann, "ach so-o-o-o!"—a long drawn out so of complete comprehension. Her tears ceased as if by magic. She dried her eyes. Yes, of course the Penheim would hold her tongue if Miss Estcourt ordered her to do so. She had heard all about her efforts to find places, and she would probably be very careful not to lose this one. The poor Penheim. So she was actually working for wages. What a come-down for a Dettingen! And the Dettingens had always treated the Treumanns as though they belonged merely to the kleine Adel. Well, well, each one in turn. She was the dear friend, and the Penheim was the housekeeper. Well, well.

She sat up straight, smoothed her hair, and resumed her first manner of quiet dignity. "I am sorry that you should have witnessed my agitation," she said, with a faint smile. "I am not easily betrayed into exhibitions of feeling, but there are limits to one's endurance, there are certain things the bravest cannot bear."

"Yes," said Anna.

"And for a Treumann, social disgrace, any action that in the least soils our honour and makes us unable to hold up our heads, is worse than death."

"But I don't see any disgrace."

"No, no, there is none so long as facts are not distorted. It is quite simple—you need friends and I am willing to be your friend. That was how my son looked at it. He said 'Liebe Mama, she evidently needs friends and sympathy—why should you hesitate to make yourself of use? You must regard it as a good work.' You would like my son; his brother officers adore him."

"Really?" said Anna.

"He is so sensible, so reasonable; he is beloved and respected by the whole regiment. I will show you his photograph—ach, the trunks are still unstrapped."

"I'll go and send someone—but not Marie," said Anna, getting up quickly. She had no desire to see the photograph, and the son's way of looking at things had considerably astonished her. "It must be nearly supper time. Would you not rather lie down and let me send you something here? Your head must ache after crying so much. You have baptised our new life with tears. I hope it is a good omen."

"Oh, I will come down. You will do as you promised, will you not, and forbid the Penheim to gossip?"

"I shall tell the princess your wishes."

"Or, if she must gossip, let her tell the truth at least. If my son had not pressed me to come here I really do not think——"

Anna went slowly and meditatively down the passage to Fräulein Kuhräuber's room. For a moment she thought of omitting this last visit altogether; she was afraid lest the Fräulein should be in some unlooked-for and perplexing condition of mind. Discouraged? Oh no; she was surely not discouraged already. How had the word come into her head? She quickened her steps. When she reached the door she remembered the cup and the sugar-tongs. Perhaps something in the bedroom was already broken, and the Fräulein would be disclosed sitting in the ruins in tears, for she was unexpectedly large, and the contents of her room were frail. But then woe of that sort was as easily assuaged as broken furniture was mended. It was the more complicated grief of Frau von Treumann that she felt unable to soothe. As to that, she preferred not to think about it at present, and barricaded her thoughts against its image with that consoling sentence, Tout comprendre c'est tout pardonner. It was a sentence she was fond of; but she had not expected that she would need its reassurance so soon.

She opened the door, and the puckers smoothed themselves out of her forehead at once, for here, at last, was peace. There had been no difficulties here with bells, and straps, and Marie. The trunks had been opened and unpacked without assistance; and when Anna came in the contents were all put away and Fräulein Kuhräuber, washed and combed and in her Sunday blouse, was sitting in an easy chair by the window absorbed in a book. Satisfaction was written broadly on her face; content was expressed by every lazy line of her attitude. When she saw Anna, she got up and made a curtsey and beamed. The beams were instantly reflected in Anna's face, and they beamed at each other.

"Well," said Anna, who felt perfectly at her ease with this member of her trio, "are you happy?"

Fräulein Kuhräuber blushed, and beamed more than ever. She was far less shy of Anna than she was of those two terrible adelige Damen, her travelling companions; but at no time had she had much conversation. Hers had been a ruminative existence, for its uncertainty but rarely disturbed her. Had she not an excellent digestion, and a fixed belief that the righteous, of whom she was one, would never be forsaken? And are not these the primary conditions of happiness? Indeed, if everything else is wanting, these two ingredients by themselves are sufficient for the concoction of a very palatable life.

"You have found an interesting book already?" Anna asked, pleased that the literature chosen with such care should have met with instant appreciation. She took it up to see what it was, but put it down again hastily, for it was the cookery book.

"I read much," observed Fräulein Kuhräuber.

"Yes?" said Anna, a flicker of hope reviving in her heart. Perhaps the cookery book was an accident.

"I know by heart more than a hundred recipes for sweet dishes alone."

"Really?" said Anna, the flicker expiring.

"So you can have an idea of the number of books I have read."

"Here are a great many more for you to read."

"Ach ja, ach ja," said Fräulein Kuhräuber, glancing doubtfully at the shelves; "but one must not waste too much time over it—there are other things in life. I read only useful books."

"Well, that is very praiseworthy," said Anna, smiling. "If you like cookery books, I must get you some more."

"How good you are—how very, very good!" said the Fräulein, gazing at the charming figure before her with heartfelt admiration and gratitude. "This beautiful room—I cannot look at it enough. I cannot believe it is really for me—for me to sleep in and be in whenever I choose. What have I done to deserve all this?"

What had she done, indeed? She had not even been unhappy, although of course she had had every opportunity of being so, sent from place to place, from one indignant Hausfrau to another, ever since she left school. But Anna, persuaded that she had rescued her from depths of unspeakable despair, was overjoyed by this speech. "Don't talk about deserving," she said tenderly. "You have had such a life that if you were to be happy now without stopping once for the next fifty years it would only be just and right."

Fräulein Kuhräuber's approval of this sentiment was so
entire that she seized Anna's hand and kissed it fervently.
Anna laughed while this was going on, and her eyes grew
brighter. She had not wanted gratitude, but now that it had
come it was very encouraging after all, and very warming.
She put one arm impulsively round the Fräulein's neck and
kissed her, and this was practically the first kiss that lady
had ever received, for the perfunctory embraces of
reluctantly dutiful aunts can hardly be called by that pretty
name.

"Now," said Anna, with a happy laugh, "we are going to be
friends for ever. Come, let us go down. That was the supper
bell."

And they went downstairs together, appearing in the
doorway of the drawing-room arm in arm, as though they
had loved each other for years.

"As though they were twins," muttered the baroness to Frau
von Treumann, who shrugged one shoulder slightly by way
of reply.

CHAPTER XVI

But in spite of this little outburst of gratitude and appreciation from Fräulein Kuhräuber, the first evening of the new life was a disappointment. The Fräulein, who entered the room so happily under the impression of that recent kiss, became awkward and uncomfortable the moment she caught sight of the others; lapsing, indeed, into a quite pitiful state of nervous flutter on being brought for the first time within the range of the princess's critical and unsympathetic eye. Her experience had not included princesses, and, as she made a series of agitated curtseys, deeming one altogether insufficient for so great a lady, she felt as though that cold eye were piercing her through easily, and had already discovered the inmost recess of her soul, where lay, so carefully hidden, the memory of the postman. Every time the princess looked at her, a sudden vivid consciousness of the postman flamed up within her, utterly refusing to be extinguished by the soothing recollection that he had been angelic for thirty years. That obviously experienced eye and those pursed lips upset her so completely that she made no remark whatever during the meal that followed, but sat next to Anna and ate Leberwurst in a kind of uneasy dream; and she ate it with a degree of emphasis so unusual among the polite and so disastrous to the peace of the ultra-fastidious that Anna felt there really was some slight excuse for the frequent and lengthy stares that came from the other end of the table. "Yet she is an immortal soul—what does it matter how she eats Leberwurst?" said Anna to herself. "What do such trifles, such little mannerisms, really matter? I should indeed be a miserable creature if I let them annoy me." But she turned her head away, nevertheless, and talked assiduously to Letty.

There was no one else for her to talk to. Frau von
Treumann and the baroness had seated themselves at once
one on either side of the princess, and devoted their
conversation entirely to her. In the drawing-room later on,
the same thing happened,—the three German ladies
clustering together near the sofa, and the three English
being left somehow to themselves, except for Fräulein
Kuhräuber, who clung to them. To avoid this division into
what looked like hostile camps Anna pushed her chair to a
place midway between the groups, and tried to join, though
not very successfully, in the talk of each in turn. Outward
calm prevailed in the room, subdued voices, the tranquillity
of fancy-work, and the peace of albums; yet Anna could not
avoid a chilled impression, a feeling as though each person
present were distrustful of the others, and more or less on
the defensive. Frau von Treumann, it is true, was
graciousness itself to the princess, conversing with her
constantly and amiably, and showing herself kind; but, on
the other hand, the princess was hardly gracious to Frau
von Treumann. An unbiassed observer would have said that
she disapproved of Frau von Treumann, but was
endeavouring to conceal her disapproval. She busied
herself with her embroidery and talked as little as she
could, receiving both the advances of Frau von Treumann
and the attentions of the baroness with equal coldness.

As for the baroness, her doubts as to Anna's respectability
were blown away completely and forever when, on opening
the drawing-room door before supper, she had beheld no
less a person than the geborene Dettingen seated on the
sofa. The baroness had spent her life in a remote and tiny
provincial town, but she knew the great Dettingen and
Penheim families well by name, and a princess in her
opinion was a princess, an altogether precious and
admirable creature, whatever she might choose to do. Her

scruples, then, were set at rest, but her ice as far as Anna
was concerned showed no signs of thawing. All her
amiability and her efforts to produce a good impression
were lavished on the princess, who besides being by birth
and marriage the grandest person the baroness had yet met,
spoke her own tongue properly, had no dimples, and did
not try to stroke her hand. She looked on with mingled awe
and irritation at the easy manner in which Frau von
Treumann treated this great lady. It almost seemed as
though she were patronising her. Really these Treumanns
were a brazen-faced race; audacious East Prussian Junkers,
who thought themselves as good as or better than the best.
And this one was not even a true Treumann, but an Ilmas,
and of the inferior Kadenstein branch; and the baroness's
brother—that brother whose end was so abrupt—had been
quartered once during the man[oe]uvres at Kadenstein, and
had told her that it was a wretched place, with a fowl-run
that wanted mending within a few yards of the front door,
and that, the door standing open all day long, he had
frequently met fowls walking about in the hall and
passages. Yet remembering the brother's story, and how
there was no shadow of the sort resting at present on Frau
von Treumann, though as she had a son there was no telling
how long her shadowless state would last, she tried to
ingratiate herself with that lady, who met her advances
coolly, only warming into something like responsiveness
when Fräulein Kuhräuber was in question.

Fräulein Kuhräuber sat behind Letty and Miss Leech, as far
away from the others as she could. She had a stocking in
her hand, but she did not knit. She never knitted if she
could avoid it, and was conscious that from want of
practice her needles moved more slowly than is usual—so
slowly, indeed, as to be conspicuous. Letty showed her
photographs and was very kind to her, instinctively

perceiving that here was someone who was as uneasy under the tall lady's stares as she was herself. She privately thought her by far the best of the new arrivals, and wished she knew enough German to inquire into her views respecting Schiller; there was something in the Fräulein's looks and manner that made her think they would agree about Schiller.

Anna, too, ended by talking exclusively to this group. Her attempts to join in what the others were saying had been unsuccessful; and with a little twinge of disappointment, and a feeling of being for some unexplained reason curiously out of it, she turned to Fräulein Kuhräuber, and devoted herself more and more to her.

"They are inseparables already," remarked the baroness in a low voice to Frau von Treumann. "The Miss finds her congenial, it seems." She could not forgive those doors she had gone through last.

The princess looked up for a moment over the spectacles she wore when she worked, at Anna.

"Fräulein Kuhräuber makes an excellent foil," said Frau von Treumann. "Miss Estcourt looks quite ethereal next to her."

"Do you think her pretty?" asked the baroness.

"She is very distinguished-looking."

A servant came in at that moment and announced Dellwig's usual evening visit, and Anna got up and went out. They watched her as she walked down the long room, and when she had disappeared began to discuss her more at their ease, their rapid German being quite incomprehensible to Letty and Miss Leech.

"Where has she gone?" asked the baroness.

"She has gone to talk to her inspector," said the princess.

"Ach so," said the baroness.

"Ach so," said Frau von Treumann.

"Is the inspector young?" asked the baroness.

"Oh no, quite old," said the princess.

"These English are a strange race," said Frau von Treumann. "What German girl of that age would you find with so much energy and enterprise?"

"Is she so very young?" inquired the baroness, with a look of mild surprise.

"Why, she is plainly little more than a child," said Frau von Treumann.

"She is twenty-five," said the princess.

"Rather an old child," observed the baroness.

"She looks much younger. But twenty-five is surely young enough for this life, away from her own people," said Frau von Treumann.

"Yes—why does she lead it?" asked the baroness eagerly. "Can you tell us, Frau Prinzessin? Has she then quarrelled with all her friends?"

"Miss Estcourt has not told me so."

"But she must have quarrelled. Eccentric as the English are, there are limits to their eccentricity, and no one leaves home and friends and country without some good reason." And Frau von Treumann shook her head.

"She has quarrelled, I am sure," said the baroness.

"I think so too," said Frau von Treumann; "I thought so from the first. My son also thought so. You remember Karlchen, princess?"

"Perfectly."

"I discussed the question thoroughly with him, of course, as to whether I should come here or not. I confess I did not want to come. It was a great wrench, giving up everything, and going so far from my son. But after all one must not be selfish." And Frau von Treumann sighed and paused.

No one said anything, so she continued: "One feels, as one grows older, how great are the claims of others. And a widow with only one son can do so much, can make herself of so much use. That is what Karlchen said. When I hesitated—for I fear one does hesitate before inconvenience—he said, 'Liebste Mama, it would be a charity to go to the poor young lady. You who have always been the first to extend a sympathetic hand to the friendless, how is it that you hesitate now? Depend upon it, she has had differences at home and needs countenance and help. You have no encumbrances. You can go more easily than others. You must regard it as a good work.' And that decided me."

The princess let her work drop for a moment into her lap, and gazed over her spectacles at Frau von Treumann. "Wirklich?" she said in a voice of deep interest. "Those were your reasons? Aber herrlich."

"Yes, those were my reasons," replied Frau von Treumann, returning her gaze with pensive but steady eyes. "Those were my chief reasons. I regard it as a work of charity."

"But this is noble," murmured the princess, resuming her work.

"That is how I have regarded it," put in the baroness. "I agree with you entirely, dear Frau von Treumann."

"I do not pretend to disguise," went on Frau von Treumann, "that it is an economy for me to live here, but poor as I have been since my dear husband's death—you remember Karl, princess?"

"Perfectly."

"Poor as I have been, I always had sufficient for my simple wants, and should not have dreamed of altering my life if Miss Estcourt's letters had not been so appealing."

"Ach—they were appealing?"

"Oh, a heart of stone would have been melted by them. And a widow's heart is not of stone, as you must know yourself. The orphan appealing to the widow—it was irresistible."

"Well, you see she is not by any means alone," said the princess cheerfully. "Here we are, five of us counting the little Letty, surrounding her. So you must not sacrifice yourself unnecessarily."

"Oh, I am not one of those who having put their hand to the plough———"

"But where is the plough, dear Frau von Treumann? You see there is, after all, no plough."

"Dear princess, you always were so literal."

"Ah, you used to reproach me with that in the old days, when you wrote poetry and read it to me and I was rude enough to ask if it meant anything. We did not think then that we should meet here, did we?"

"No, indeed. And I cannot tell you how much I admire your courage."

"My courage? What fine qualities you invest me with!"

"Miss Estcourt has told me how admirably you discharge your duties here. It is wonderful to me. You are an example to us all, and you make me feel ashamed of my own uselessness."

"Oh, you underrate yourself. People who leave everything to go and help others cannot talk of being useless. Yes, I look after her house for her, and I hope to look after her as well."

"After her? Is that one of your duties? Did she stipulate for personal supervision when she engaged you? How times are changed! When my Karl was alive, and we lived at Sommershof, I certainly would not have tolerated that my housekeeper should keep me in order as well as my house."

"The case was surely different, dear Frau von Treumann. Here is an unusually pretty young thing, with money. She will need all the protection I can give her, and it is a satisfaction to me to feel that I am here and able to give it."

"But she may any day turn round and request you to go."

"That of course may happen, but I hope it will not until she is safe."

"But do you think her so pretty?" put in the baroness wonderingly.

"Safe? What special dangers do you then apprehend for her?" asked Frau von Treumann with a look of amusement. "Dear princess, you always did take your duties so seriously. What a treasure you would have been to me in many ways. It is admirable. But do your duties really include watching over Miss Estcourt's heart? For I suppose you are thinking of her heart?"

"I am thinking of adventurers," said the princess. "Any young man with no money would naturally be delighted to secure this young lady and Kleinwalde. And those who instead of money have debts, would naturally be still more delighted." And the princess in her turn gazed pensively but steadily at Frau von Treumann. "No," she said, taking up her work again, "I was not thinking of her heart, but of the annoyance she might be put to. I do not fancy that her heart would easily be touched."

Anna came in at that moment for a paper she wanted, and heard the last words. "What," she said, smiling, as she unlocked the drawer of her writing-table and rummaged among the contents, "you are talking about hearts? You see it is true that women can't be together half an hour without getting on to subjects like that. If you were three men, now, you would talk of pigs." Then, a sudden recollection of Uncle Joachim coming into her mind, she added with conviction, "And pigs are better."

Nor was it till she had closed the door behind her that it struck her that when she came into the room both the princess and Frau von Treumann were looking preternaturally bland.

CHAPTER XVII

Axel Lohm was in the hall, having his coat taken from him by a servant.

"You here?" exclaimed Anna, holding out both hands. She was more than usually pleased to see him.

"Manske had a pile of letters for you, and could not get them to you because he has a pastors' conference at his house. I was there and saw the letters, and thought you might want them."

"Oh, I don't want them—at least, there is no hurry. But the letters are only an excuse. Now isn't it so?"

"An excuse?" he repeated, flushing.

"You want to see the new arrivals."

"Not in the very least."

"Oh, oh! But as you have come one minute too soon, and happened to meet me outside the door, your plan is spoilt. Are those the letters? What a pile!" Her face fell.

"But you are looking for nine more ladies. You want a wide choice. You have still the greater part of your work before you."

"I know. Why do you tell me that?"

"Because you do not seem pleased to get them."

"Oh yes, I am; but I am tired to-night, and the idea of nine more ladies makes me feel—feel sleepy."

She stood under the lamp, holding the packet loosely by its string and smiling up to him. There were shadows in her eyes, he thought, where he was used to seeing two cheerful little lights shining, and a faint ruefulness in the smile.

"Well, if you are tired you must go to bed," he said, in such a matter of fact tone that they both laughed.

"No, I mustn't," said Anna; "I am on my way to Herr Dellwig at this very moment. He's in there," she said, with a motion of her head towards the dining-room door. "Tell me," she added, lowering her voice, "have you got a brick-kiln at Lohm?"

"A brick-kiln? No. Why do you want to know?"

"But why haven't you got a brick-kiln?"

"Because there is nothing to make bricks with. Lohm is almost entirely sand."

"He says there is splendid clay here in one part, and wants to build one."

"Who? Dellwig?"

"Sh—sh."

"Your uncle would have built one long ago if there really had been clay. I must look at the place he means. I cannot remember any such place. And it is unlikely that it should be as he says. Pray do not agree to any propositions of the kind hastily."

"It would cost heaps to set it going, wouldn't it?"

"Yes, and probably bring in nothing at all."

"But he tries to make out that it would be quite cheap. He says the timber could all be got out of the forest. I can't bear the thought of cutting down a lot of trees."

"If you can't bear the thought of anything he proposes, then simply refuse to consider it."

"But he talks and talks till it really seems that he is right. He told me just now that it would double the value of the estate."

"I don't believe it."

"If I made bricks, according to him I could take in twice as many poor ladies."

"I believe you will be happier with fewer ladies and no bricks," said Axel with great positiveness.

Anna stood thinking. Her eyes were fixed on the tip of the finger she had passed through the loop of string that tied the letters together, and she watched it as the packet twisted round and round and pinched it redder and redder. "I suppose you never wanted to be a woman," she said, considering this phenomenon with apparent interest.

Axel laughed.

"The mere question makes you laugh," she said, looking up quickly. "I never heard of a man who did want to. But lots of women would give anything to be men."

"And you are one of them?"

"Yes."

He laughed again.

"You think I would make a queer little man?" she said, laughing too; but her face became sober immediately, and with a glance at the shut dining-room door she continued: "It is so horrid to feel weak. My sister Susie says I am very obstinate. Perhaps I was with her, but different people have different effects on one." She sank her voice to a whisper, and looked at him anxiously. "You can't think what an effort it is to me to say No to that man."

"What, to Dellwig?"

"Sh—sh."

"But if that is how you feel, my dear Miss Estcourt, it is very evident that the man must go."

"How easy it is to say that! Pray, who is to tell him to go?"

"I will, if you wish."

"If you were a woman, do you suppose you would be able to turn out an old servant who has worked here so many years?"

"Yes, I am sure I would, if I felt that he was getting beyond my control."

"No, you wouldn't. All sorts of things would stop you. You would remember that your uncle specially told you to keep him on, that he has been here ages, that he was faithful and devoted——"

"I do not believe there was much devotion."

"Oh yes, there was. The first evening he cried about dear Uncle Joachim."

"He cried?" repeated Axel incredulously.

"He did indeed."

"It was about something else, then."

"No, he really cried about Uncle Joachim. He really loved him."

Axel looked profoundly unconvinced.

"But after all those are not the real reasons," said Anna; "they ought to be, but they're not. The simple truth is that I am a coward, and I am frightened—dreadfully frightened—of possible scenes." And she looked at him and laughed ruefully. "There—you see what it is to be a woman. If I were a man, how easy things would be. Please consider the mortification of knowing that if he persuades long enough I shall give in, against my better judgment. He has the strongest will I think I ever came across."

"But you have not yet given in, I hope, on any point of importance?"

"Up to now I have managed to say No to everything I don't want to do. But you would laugh if you knew what those Nos cost me. Why cannot the place go on as it was? I am perfectly satisfied. But hardly a day passes without some wonderful new plan being laid before me, and he talks—oh, how he talks! I believe he would convince even you."

"The man is quite beyond your control," said Axel in a voice of anger; and voices of anger commonly being loud voices, this one produced the effect of three doors being simultaneously opened: the door leading to the servants' quarters, through which Marie looked and vanished again, retreating to the kitchen to talk prophetically of weddings;

the dining-room door, behind which Dellwig had grown more and more impatient at being kept waiting so long; and the drawing-room door, on the other side of which the baroness had been lingering for some moments, desiring to go upstairs for her scissors, but hesitating to interrupt Anna's business with the inspector, whose voice she thought it was that she heard.

The baroness shut her door again immediately. "Aha—the admirer!" she said to herself; and went back quickly to her seat. "The Miss is talking to a jünge Herr," she announced, her eyes wider open than ever.

"A jünge Herr?" echoed Frau von Treumann. "I thought the inspector was old?"

"It must be Axel Lohm," said the princess, not raising her eyes from her work. "He often comes in."

"He comes courting, evidently," said the baroness with a sub-acid smile.

"It has not been evident to me," said the princess coldly.

"I thought it looked like it," said the baroness, with more meekness.

"Is that the Lohm who was engaged to one of the Kiederfels girls some years ago?" asked Frau von Treumann.

"Yes, and she died."

"But did he not marry soon afterwards? I heard he married."

"That was the second brother. This one is the eldest, and lives next to us, and is single."

Frau von Treumann was silent for a moment. Then she said blandly, "Now confess, princess, that he is the perilous person from whom you think it necessary to defend Miss Estcourt."

"Oh no," said the princess with equal blandness; "I have no fears about him."

"What, is he too possessed of an invulnerable heart?"

"I know nothing of his heart. I said, I believe, adventurers. And no one could call Axel Lohm an adventurer. I was thinking of men who have run through all their own and all their relations' money in betting and gambling, and who want a wife who will pay their debts."

"Ach so," said Frau von Treumann with perfect urbanity. And if this talk about protecting Miss Estcourt from adventurers in a place where there were apparently no human beings of any kind, but only trees and marshes, might seem to a bystander to be foolishness, to the speakers it was luminousness itself, and in no way increased their love for each other.

Meanwhile Dellwig, looking through the door and seeing Lohm, brought his heels together and bowed with his customary exaggeration. "I beg a thousand times pardon," he said; "I thought the gracious Miss was engaged and would not return, and I was about to go home."

"I have found the paper, and am coming," said Anna coldly. "Well, good-night," she added in English, holding out her hand to Axel.

"If you will allow me, I should like to pay my respects to Princess Ludwig before I go," he said, thinking thus to see her later.

"Ah! wasn't I right?" she said, smiling. "You are determined to look at the new arrivals. How can a man be so inquisitive? But I will say good-night all the same. I shall be ages with Herr Dellwig, and shall not see you again." She shook hands with him, and went into the dining-room, Dellwig standing aside with deep respect to let her pass. But she turned to say something to him as he shut the door, and Axel caught the expression of her face, the intense boredom on it, the profound distrust of self; and he went in to the princess with an unusually severe and determined look on his own.

Dellwig went home that night in a savage mood. "That young man," he said to his wife, flinging his hat and coat on to a chair and himself on to a sofa, "is thrusting himself more and more into our affairs."

"That Lohm?" she asked, rolling up her work preparatory to fetching his evening drink.

"I had almost got the Miss to consent to the brick-kiln. She was quite reasonable, and went out to get the plan I had made. Then she met him—he is always hanging about."

"And then?" inquired Frau Dell wig eagerly.

"Pah—this petticoat government—having to beg and pray for the smallest concession—it makes an honest man sick."

"She will not consent?"

"She came back as obstinate as a mule. It all had to be gone into again from the beginning."

"She will not consent?"

"She said Lohm would look at the place and advise her."

"Aber so was!" cried Frau Dellwig, crimson with wrath. "Advise her? Did you not tell her that you were her adviser?"

"You may be sure I did. I told her plainly enough, I fancy, that Lohm had nothing to say here, and that her uncle had always listened to me. She sat without speaking, as she generally does, not even looking at me—I never can be sure that she is even listening."

"And then?"

"I asked her at last if she had lost confidence in me."

"And then?"

"She said oh nein, in her affected foreign way—in the sort of voice that might just as well mean oh ja." And he imitated, with great bitterness, Anna's way of speaking German. "Mark my words, Frau, she is as weak as water for all her obstinacy, and the last person who talks to her can always bring her round."

"Then you must be the last person."

"If it were not for that prig Lohm, that interfering ass, that incomparable rhinoceros——"

"He wants to marry her, of course."

"If he marries her——" Dellwig stopped short, and stared gloomily at his muddy boots.

"If he marries her——" repeated his wife; but she too stopped short. They both knew well enough what would happen to them if he married her.

The building of the brick-kiln had come to be a point of honour with the Dellwigs. Ever since Anna's arrival, their friends the neighbouring farmers and inspectors had been congratulating them on their complete emancipation from all manner of control; for of course a young ignorant lady would leave the administration of her estate entirely in her inspector's hands, confining her activities, as became a lady of birth, to paying the bills. Dellwig had not doubted that this would be so, and had boasted loudly and continually of the different plans he had made and was going to carry out. The estate of which he was now practically master was to become renowned in the province for its enterprise and the extent, in every direction, of its operations. The brick-kiln was a long-cherished scheme. His oldest friend and rival, the head inspector of a place on the other side of Stralsund, had one, and had constantly urged him to have one too; but old Joachim, without illusions as to the quality of the clay, and by no manner of means to be talked into disbelieving the evidence of his own eyes, would not hear of it, and Dellwig felt there was nothing to be done in the face of that curt refusal. The friend, triumphing in his own brick-kiln and his own more pliable master, jeered, dug him in the ribs at the Sunday gatherings, and talked of dependence, obedience, and restricted powers. Such friends are difficult to endure with composure; and Dellwig, and still less his wife, for many months past had hardly been able to bear the word "brick" mentioned in their presence. When Anna appeared on the scene, so young, so foreign, and so obviously foolish, Dellwig, certain now of success, told his friend on the very first Sunday night that the brick-kiln was now a mere matter of weeks. Always a boaster, he could not resist boasting a little too soon. Besides, he felt very sure; and the friend, too, had taken it for granted, when he heard of the impending young mistress, that the thing was as good as built.

That was in March. It was now the end of April, and every Sunday the friend inquired when the building was to be begun, and every Sunday Dellwig said it would begin when the days grew longer. The days had grown longer, would have grown in a few weeks to their longest, as the friend repeatedly pointed out, and still nothing had been done. To the many people who do not care what their neighbours think of them, the torments of the two Dellwigs because of the unbuilt brick-kiln will be incomprehensible. Yet these torments were so acute that in the weaker moments immediately preceding meals they both felt that it would almost be better to leave Kleinwalde than to stay and endure them; indeed, before dinner, or during wakeful nights, Frau Dellwig was convinced that it would be better to die outright. The good opinion of their neighbours— more exactly, the envy of their neighbours—was to them the very breath of their nostrils. In their set they must be the first, the undisputedly luckiest, cleverest, and best off. Any position less mighty would be unbearable. And since Anna came there had been nothing but humiliations. First the

dinner to the Manskes, from which they had been
excluded—Frau Dellwig grew hot all over at the
recollection of the Sunday gathering succeeding it; then the
renovation of the Schloss without the least reference to
them, without the smallest asking for advice or help; then
the frequent communications with the pastor, putting him
quite out of his proper position, the confidence placed in
him, the ridiculous respect shown him, his connection with
the mad charitable scheme; and now, most dreadful of all,
this obstinacy in regard to the brick-kiln. It was becoming
clear that they were fairly on the way to being pitied by the
neighbours. Pitied! Horrid thought. The great thing in life
was to be so situated that you can pity others. But to be
pitied yourself? Oh, thrice-accursed folly of old Joachim, to
leave Kleinwalde to a woman! Frau Dellwig could not
sleep that night for hating Anna. She lay awake staring into
the darkness with hot eyes, and hating her with a heartiness
that would have petrified that unconscious young woman
as she sat about a stone's throw off in her bedroom,
motionless in the chair into which she had dropped on first
coming upstairs, too tired even to undress, after her long
struggle with Frau Dellwig's husband. "The Engländerin
will ruin us!" cried Frau Dellwig suddenly, unable to hate
in silence any longer.

"Wie? Was?" exclaimed Dellwig, who had dozed off, and
was startled.

"She will—she will!" cried his wife.

"Will what? Ruin us? The Engländerin? Ach was—Unsinn.
She can be managed. It is Lohm who is the danger. It is
Lohm who will ruin us. If we could get rid of him——"

"Ach Gott, if he would die!" exclaimed Frau Dellwig, with fervent hands raised heavenwards. "Ach Gott, if he would only die!"

"Ach Gott, ach Gott!" mimicked her husband irritably, for he disliked being suddenly awakened. "People never die when anything depends on it," he grumbled, turning over on his side. And he cursed Axel several times, and went to sleep.

CHAPTER XVIII

The philosopher tells us that, after the healing interval of sleep, we are prepared to meet each other every morning as gods and goddesses; so fresh, so strong, so lusty, so serene, did he consider the newly-risen and the some-time separated must of necessity be. It is a pleasing belief; and Experience, that hopelessly prosaic governess who never gives us any holidays, very quickly disposes of it. For what is to become of the god-like mood if only one in a company possess it? The middle-aged and old, who abound in all companies, are seldom god-like, and are never so at breakfast.

The morning after the arrival of the Chosen, Anna woke up in the true Olympian temper. She had been brought back to the happy world of realities from the happy world of dreams by the sun of an unusually lovely April shining on

her face. She had only to open her window to be convinced
that all which she beheld was full of blessings. Just beneath
her window on the grass was a double cherry tree in flower,
an exquisite thing to look down on with the sunshine and
the bees busy among its blossoms. The unreasoning
joyfulness that invariably took possession of her heart
whenever the weather was fine, filled it now with a rapture
of hope and confidence. This world, this wonderful
morning world that she saw and smelt from her window,
was manifestly a place in which to be happy. Everything
she saw was very good. Even the remembrance of Dellwig
was transfigured in that clear light. And while she dressed
she took herself seriously to task for the depression of the
night before. Depressed she had certainly been; and why?
Simply because she was over-excited and over-tired, and
her spirit was still so mortifyingly unable to rise superior to
the weakness of her tiresome flesh. And to let herself be
made wretched by Dellwig, merely because he talked loud
and had convictions which she did not share! The god-like
morning mood was strong upon her, and she contemplated
her listless self of the previous evening, the self that had sat
so long despondently thinking instead of going to bed, with
contempt. These evening interviews with Dellwig, she
reflected, were a mistake. He came at hours when she was
least able to bear his wordiness and shouting, and it was the
knowledge of his impending visit that made her irritable
beforehand and ruffled the absolute serenity that she felt
was alone appropriate in a house dedicated to love. But it
was not only Dellwig and the brick-kiln that had depressed
her; she had actually had doubts about her three new
friends, doubts as to the receptivity of their souls, as to the
capacity of their souls for returning love. At one awful
moment she had even doubted whether they had souls at
all, but had hastily blown out the candle at this point,
extinguishing the doubt at the same time, smothering it

beneath the bedclothes, and falling asleep at once, after the fashion of healthy young people.

Now, at the beginning of the new day, with all her misgivings healed by sleep, she thought calmly over the interview she had had with Frau von Treumann before supper; for it was that interview that had been the chief cause of her dejection. Frau von Treumann had told her an untruth, a quite obvious and absurd untruth in the face of the correspondence, as to the reason of her coming to Kleinwalde. She had said she had only come at the instigation of her son, who looked upon Anna as a deserving object of help. And Anna had been hurt, had been made miserable, by the paltriness of this fib. Her great desire was to reach her friends' souls quickly, to attain the beautiful intimacy in which the smallest fiction is unnecessary; and so little did Frau von Treumann understand her, that she had begun a friendship that was to be for life with an untruth that would not have misled a child. But see the effect of sleep and a gracious April morning. The very shabbiness and paltriness of the fib made Anna's heart yearn over the poor lady. Surely the pride that tried to hide its wounds with rags of such pitiful flimsiness was profoundly pathetic? With such pride, all false from Anna's point of view, but real and painful enough to its possessor, the necessity that drove her to accept Anna's offer must have been more cruel than necessity, always cruel, generally is. Her heart yearned over her friend as she dressed, and she felt that the weakness that must lie was a weakness greatly requiring love. For nobody, she argued, would ever lie unless driven to it by fear of some suffering. If, then, it made her happy, and made her life easier, let her think that Anna believed she had come for her sake. What did it matter? No one was perfect, and many people were surprisingly pathetic.

Meanwhile the day was glorious, and she went downstairs with the springy step of hope. She was thinking exhilarating thoughts, thinking that there were to be no ripples of misgivings and misunderstandings on the clear surface of this first morning. They would all look into each others' candid eyes at breakfast, and read a mutual consciousness of interests henceforward to be shared, of happiness to be shared, of life to be shared,—the life of devoted and tender sisters.

The hall door stood open, and the house was full of the smell of April; the smell of new leaves budding, of old leaves rotting, of damp earth, pine needles, wet moss, and marshes. "Oh, the lovely, lovely morning!" whispered Anna, running out on to the steps with outstretched arms and upturned face, as though she would have clasped all the beauty round and held it close. She drew in a long breath, and turned back into the house singing in an impassioned but half-suppressed voice the first verse of the Magnificat. The door leading to the kitchen opened, and to her surprise Baroness Elmreich emerged from those dark regions. The Magnificat broke off abruptly. Anna was surprised. Why the kitchen? The baroness saw her hostess's figure motionless against the light of the open door; but the light behind was strong and the hall was dark, and she thought it was Anna's back. Hoping that she had not been noticed she softly closed the door again and waited behind it till she could come out unseen.

Anna supposed that the princess must be showing her the servants' quarters, and went into the breakfast room; but in it sat the princess, making coffee.

"There you are," said the princess heartily. "That is nice. Now we can drink our coffee comfortably together before

the others come down. Have you been out? You smell of
fresh air."

"Only a moment on the doorstep."

"Come, sit next to me. You have slept well, I can see.
Notice the advantage of coming straight in to breakfast, and
not running about the forest—you get here first, and so get
the best cup of coffee."

"But it isn't proper for me to have the best," said Anna,
smiling as she took the cup, "when I have guests here."

"Yes, it is—very proper indeed. Besides, you told me they
were sisters."

"So they are. Has the baroness not been here?"

"No, she is still in bed."

"No, I saw her a moment ago. I thought you were with her."

"Oh, my dear—so early in the morning!" protested the
princess. "When did I see her last? Less than nine hours
ago. She followed me into my bedroom and talked much. I
could not begin again with her the first thing in the
morning, even to please you." And she looked at Anna very
affectionately. "You were tired last night, were you not?"
she continued. "Axel Lohm stayed so late, I think he
wanted to speak to you. But you went straight up to bed."

"I had seen him before he went in to you. He didn't want to
speak to me. He was consumed by curiosity about our new
friends."

"Was he? He did not show much interest in them. He talked to me nearly all the time. He thought for a moment that he knew the baroness—at least, he stared at her at first and seemed surprised. But it turned out that she was only like someone he knew. She had evidently never seen him before. It is a great pleasure to me to talk to that young man," the princess went on, while Anna ate her toast.

"So it is to me," said Anna.

"I have met many people in my life, and have often wondered at the dearth of nice ones—how few there are that one likes to be with and wishes to see again and again. Axel is one of the few, decidedly."

"So he is," agreed Anna.

"There is goodness written on every line of his face."

"Oh, he has the kindest face. And so strong. I feel that if anything happened here, anything dreadful, that he would make it right again at once. He would mend us if we got smashed, and build us up again if we got burned, and protect us, this houseful of lone women, if ever anybody tried to run away with us." And Anna nodded reassuringly at the princess, and took another piece of toast "That is how I feel about him," she said. "So agreeably certain, not only of his willingness to help, but of his power to do it." Talking about Axel she quite forgot the apparition of the baroness that she had just seen. He was so kind, so good, so strong. How much she admired strength of purpose, independence, the character that was determined to find its happiness in doing its best.

"If I had a daughter," said the princess, filling Anna's cup, "she should marry Axel Lohm."

"If I had a daughter," said Anna, "she should marry him, so yours couldn't. I wouldn't even ask her if she liked it. I'd be so sure that it was a good thing for her that I'd just say: 'My dear, I have chosen my son-in-law. Get your hat, and come to church and marry him.' And there'd be an end of that."

The princess felt that it was an unprofitable employment, trying to help on Axel's cause. She could not but see what he thought of Anna; and after the touching manner of widows, was convinced of the superiority of marriage, as a means of real happiness for a woman, over any and every other form of occupation. Yet whenever she talked of him she was met by the same hearty agreement and frank enthusiasm, the very words being taken out of her mouth and her own praises of him doubled and trebled. It was a promising friendship, but it was a singularly unpromising prelude to love.

"Please make some fresh coffee," begged Anna; "the others will be coming down soon, and must not have cold stuff." Her voice grew tender at the mere mention of "the others." For the princess and Axel, both of whom she liked so much, it never took on those tender tones, as the princess had already noted. There was nothing in either of them to appeal to that side of her nature, the tender, mother side, which is in all good women and most bad ones. They were her friends, staunch friends, she felt, and of course she liked and respected them; but they were sturdy, capable people, firmly planted on their own feet, able to battle successfully with life—as different as possible from these helpless ones who needed her, whom she had saved, to whom she was everything, between whom and want and sorrow she was fixed as a shield.

Two of the helpless ones came in at that moment, with frosty, early-morning faces. Anna put the vision she had seen at the kitchen door from her mind, and went to meet them with happy smiles and greetings. Frau von Treumann did her best to respond warmly, but it was very early to be enthusiastic, and at that hour of the day she was accustomed to being a little cross. Besides, she had had no coffee yet, and her hostess evidently had, and that made a great difference to one's sentiments. The baroness looked pinched and bloodless; she was as frigid as ever to Anna, said nothing about having seen her before, and seemed to want to be left alone. So that the mutual gazing into each other's eyes did not, after all, take place.

The princess waited to see that they had all they wanted, and then went out rattling her keys; and after an interval, during which Anna chattered cheerful and ungrammatical German, and the window was shut, and warming food eaten, Frau von Treumann became amiable and began to talk.

She drew from her pocket a letter and a photograph. "This is my son," she said. "I brought it down to show you. And I have had a long letter from him already. He never neglects his mother. Truly a good son is a source of joy."

"I suppose so," said Anna.

The baroness turned her eyes slowly round and fixed them on the photograph. "Aha," she thought, "the son again. Last night the son, this morning the son—always the son. The excellent Treumann loses no time."

"He is good-looking, my Karlchen, is he not?"

"Yes," said Anna. "It is a becoming uniform."

"Oh—becoming! He looks adorable in it. Especially on his
horse. I would not let him be anything but a hussar because
of the charming uniform. And he suits it exactly—such a
lightly built, graceful figure. He never stumbles over
people's feet. Herr von Lohm nearly crushed my poor foot
last night. It was difficult not to scream. I never did admire
those long men made by the meter, who seem as though
they would go on for ever if there were no ceilings."

"He is rather long," agreed Anna, smiling.

"Heartwhole," thought Frau von Treumann. "Tell me, dear
Miss Estcourt——" she said, laying her hand on Anna's.

"Oh, don't call me Miss Estcourt."

"But what, then?"

"Oh, you must call me Anna. We are to be like sisters
here—and you, too, please, call me Anna," she said,
turning to the baroness.

"You are very good," said the baroness.

"Well, my little sister," said Frau von Treumann, smiling,
"my baby sister——"

"Baby sister!" thought the baroness. "Excellent Treumann."

"—you know an old woman of my age could not really
have a sister of yours."

"Yes, she could—not a whole sister, perhaps, but a half one."

"Well, as you please. The idea is sweet to me. I was going to ask you—but Karlchen's letter is too touching, really—such thoughts in it—such high ideals——" And she turned over the sheets, of which there were three, and began to blow her nose.

"He has written you a very long letter," said Anna pleasantly; the extent to which the nose blowing was being carried made her uneasy. Was there to be crying?

"You have a cold, dear Frau von Treumann?" inquired the baroness with solicitude.

"Ach nein—doch nein," murmured Frau von Treumann, turning the sheets over, and blowing her nose harder than ever.

"It will come off," thought Letty, who had slipped in unnoticed, and was eating bread and butter alone at the further end of the table.

"Poor thing," thought Anna, "she adores that Karlchen."

There was a pause, during which the nose continued to be blown.

"His letter is beautiful, but sad—very sad," said Frau von Treumann, shaking her head despondingly. "Poor boy—poor dear boy—he misses his mother, of course. I knew he would, but I did not dream it would be as bad as this. Oh, my dear Miss Estcourt—well, Anna then"—smiling faintly—"I could never describe to you the wrench it was, the terrible, terrible wrench, leaving him who for five years—I am a widow five years—has been my all."

"It must have been dreadful," murmured Anna sympathetically.

The baroness sat straight and motionless, staring fixedly at Frau von Treumann.

"'When shall I see you again, my dearest mamma?' were his last words. And I could give him no hope—no answer." The handkerchief went up to her eyes.

"What is she gassing about?" wondered Letty.

"I can see him now, fading away on the platform as my train bore me off to an unknown life. An only son—the only son of a widow—is everything, everything to his mother."

"He must be," said Anna.

There was another silence. Then Frau von Treumann wiped her eyes and took up the letter again. "Now he writes that though I have only been away two days from Rislar, the town he is stationed at, it seems already like years. Poor boy! He is quite desperate—listen to this—poor boy——" And she smiled a little, and read aloud, "'I must see you, liebste, beste Mama, from time to time. I had no idea the separation would be like this, or I could never have let you go. Pray beg Miss Estcourt——'"

"Aha," thought the baroness.

"'—to allow me to visit my mother occasionally. There must be an inn in the village. If not, I could stay at Stralsund, and would in no way intrude on her. But I must see my dearest mother, the being I have watched over and cared for ever since my father's death.' Poor, dear, foolish boy—he is desperate——" And she folded up the letter, shook her head, smiled, and suddenly buried her face in her handkerchief.

"Excellent Treumann," thought the unblinking baroness.

Anna sat in some perplexity. Sons had not entered into her calculations. In the correspondence, she remembered, the son had been lightly passed over as an officer living on his pay and without a superfluous penny for the support of his parent. Not a word had been said of any unusual affection existing between them. Now it appeared that the mother and son were all in all to each other. If so, of course the separation was dreadful. A mother's love was a sentiment that inspired Anna with profound respect. Before its unknown depths and heights she stood in awe and silence. How could she, a spinster, even faintly comprehend that sacred feeling? It was a mysterious and beautiful emotion that she could only reverence from afar. Clearly she must not come between parent and child; but yet—yet she wished she had had more time to think it over.

She looked rather helplessly at Frau von Treumann, and gave her hand a little squeeze. The hand did not return the squeeze, and the face remained buried in the handkerchief. Well, it would be absurd to want to cut off the son entirely from his mother. If he came occasionally to see her it could not matter much. She gave the hand a firmer squeeze, and said with an effort that she did her best to conceal, "But he

must come then, when he can. It is rather a long way—
didn't you say you had to stay a night in Berlin?"

"Oh, my dear Miss Estcourt—my dear Anna!" cried Frau
von Treumann, snatching the handkerchief from her face
and seizing Anna's hand in both hers, "what a weight from
my heart—what a heavy, heavy weight! All night I was
thinking how shall I bear this? I may write to him, then,
and tell him what you say? A long journey? You are afraid
it will tire him? Oh, it will be nothing, nothing at all to
Karlchen if only he can see his mother. How can I thank
you! You will say my gratitude is excessive for such a little
thing, and truly only a mother could understand it——"

In short, Karlchen's appearance at Kleinwalde was now
only a matter of days.

"Unverschämt," was the baroness's mental comment.

CHAPTER XIX

Anna put on her hat and went out to think it over. Fräulein
Kuhräuber was apparently still asleep. Letty, accompanied
by Miss Leech, had to go to Lohm parsonage for her first
lesson with Herr Klutz, who had undertaken to teach her
German. Frau von Treumann said she must write at once to
Karlchen, and shut herself up to do it. The baroness was
vague as to her intentions, and disappeared. So Anna

started off by herself, crossed the road, and walked quickly away into the forest. "If it makes her so happy, then I am glad," she said to herself. "She is here to be happy; and if she wants Karlchen so badly, why then she must have him from time to time. I wonder why I don't like Karlchen."

She walked quickly, with her eyes on the ground. The mood in which she sang magnificats had left her, nor did she look to see what the April morning was doing. Frau von Treumann had not been under her roof twenty-four hours, and already her son had been added—if only occasionally, still undoubtedly added—to the party. Suppose the baroness and Fräulein Kuhräuber should severally disclose an inability to live without being visited by some cherished relative? Suppose the other nine, the still Unchosen, should each turn out to have a relative waiting tragically in the background for permission to make repeated calls? And suppose these relatives should all be male?

These were grave questions; so grave that she was quite at a loss how to answer them. And then she felt that somebody was looking at her; and raising her eyes, she saw Axel on the mossy path quite close to her.

"So deep in thought?" he asked, smiling at her start.

Anna wondered how it was that he so often went through the forest. Was it a short cut from Lohm to anywhere? She had met him three or four times lately, in quite out of the way parts. He seemed to ride through it and walk through it at all hours of the day.

"How is your potato-planting getting on?" she asked involuntarily. She knew what a rush there was just then putting the potatoes in, for she did not drive every day about her fields in a cart without springs with Dellwig for nothing. Axel must have potatoes to plant too; why didn't he stay at home, then, and do it?

"What a truly proper question for a country lady to ask," he said, looking amused. "You waste no time in conventional good mornings or asking how I do, but begin at once with potatoes. Well, I do not believe that you are really interested in mine, so I shall tell you nothing about them. You only want to remind me that I ought to be seeing them planted instead of walking about your woods."

Anna smiled. "I believe I did mean something like that," she said.

"Well, I am not so aimless as you suppose," he returned, walking by her side. "I have been looking at that place."

"What place?"

"Where Dellwig wants to build the brick-kiln."

"Oh! What do you think of it?"

"What I knew I would think of it. It is a fool's plan. The clay is the most wretched stuff. It has puzzled me, seeing how very poor it is, that he should be so eager to have the thing. I should have credited him with more sense."

"He is quite absurdly keen on it. Last night I thought he would never stop persuading."

"But you did not give in?"

"Not an inch. I said I would ask you to look at it, and then he was simply rude. I do believe he will have to go. I don't really think we shall ever get on together. Certainly, as you say the clay is bad, I shall refuse to build a brick-kiln."

Axel smiled at her energy. In the morning she was always determined about Dellwig. "You are very brave to-day," he said. "Last night you seemed afraid of him."

"He comes when I am tired. I am not going to see him in the evening any more. It is too dreadful as a finish to a happy day."

"It was a happy day, then, yesterday?" he asked quickly.

"Yes—that is, it ought to have been, and probably would have been if—if I hadn't been tired."

"But the others—the new arrivals—they must have been happy?"

"Yes—oh yes—" said Anna, hesitating, "I think so. Fräulein Kuhräuber was, I am sure, at intervals. I think the other two would have been if they hadn't had a journey."

"By the way, do you remember what I said yesterday about the Elmreichs?"

"Yes, I do. You said horrid things." Her voice changed.

"About a Baron Elmreich. But he had a sister who made a hash of her life. I saw her once or twice in Berlin. She was dancing at the Wintergarten, and under her own name."

"Poor thing. But it doesn't interest me."

"Don't get angry yet."

"But it doesn't interest me. And why shouldn't she dance? I knew several people who ended by dancing at London Wintergartens."

"You admit, then, that it is an end?"

"It is hardly a beginning," conceded Anna.

"She was so amazingly like your baroness would be if she painted and wore a wig——"

"That you are convinced they must be sisters. Thank you. Now what do you suppose is the good of telling me that?" And she stood still and faced him, her eyes flashing.

Do what he would, Axel could not help smiling at her wrath. It was the wrath of a mother whose child has been hurt by someone on purpose, "I wish," he said, "that you would not be so angry when I tell you things that might be important for you to know. If your baroness is really the sister of the dancing baroness——"

"But she is not. She told me last night that she has no brothers and sisters. And she wrote it in the letters before she came. Do you think it is a praiseworthy occupation for a man, doing his best to find out disgraceful things about a very poor and very helpless woman?"

"No, I do not," said Axel decidedly. "Under any other circumstances I would leave the poor lady to take her chance. But do consider," he said, following her, for she had begun to walk on quickly again, "do consider your unusual position. You are so young to be living away from your friends, and so young and inexperienced to be at the head of a home for homeless women—you ought to be quite extraordinarily particular about the antecedents of the people you take in. It would be most unpleasant if it got about that they were not respectable."

"But they are respectable," said Anna, looking straight before her.

"A sister who dances at the Wintergarten——"

"Did I not tell you that she has no sister?"

Axel shrugged his shoulders. "The resemblance is so striking that they might be twins," he said.

"Then you think she says what is not true?"

"How can I tell?"

Anna stopped again and faced him. "Well, suppose it were true—suppose it is her sister, and she has tried to hide it— do you know how I should feel about it?"

"Properly scandalised, I hope."

"I should love her all the more. Oh, I should love her twice as much! Why, think of the misery and the shame—poor, poor little woman—trying to hide it all, bearing it all by herself—she must have loved her sister, she must have loved her brother. It isn't true, of course, but supposing it were, could you tell me any reason why I should turn my back on her?"

She stood looking at him, her eyes full of angry tears.

He did not answer. If that was the way she felt, what could he do?

"I never understood," she went on passionately, "why the innocent should be punished. Do you suppose a woman would like her brother to cheat and then shoot himself? Or like her sister to go and dance? But if they do do these things, besides her own grief and horror, she is to be shunned by everybody as though she were infectious. Is that fair? Is that right? Is it in the least Christian?"

"No, of course it is not. It is very hard and very ugly, but it is quite natural. An old woman in a strong position might take such a person up, perhaps, and comfort her and love her as you propose to do, but a young girl ought not to do anything of the sort."

Anna turned away with a quick movement of impatience and walked on. "If you argue on the young girl basis," she said, "we shall never be able to talk about a single thing. When will you leave off about my young girlishness? In five years I shall be thirty—will you go on till I have reached that blessed age?"

"I have no right to go on to you about anything," said Axel.

"Precisely," said Anna.

"But please remember that I owe an enormous debt of gratitude to your uncle, and make allowances for me if I am over-zealous in my anxiety to shield his niece from possible unpleasantness."

"Then don't keep telling me I am too young to do good. It is ludicrous, considering my age, besides being dreadful. You will say that, I believe, till I am thirty or forty, and then when you can't decently say it any more, and I still want to do things, you'll say I'm old enough to know better."

Axel laughed. Anna's dimples appeared for an instant, but vanished again.

"Now," she said, "I am not going to talk about poor little Else any more. Let her distant relations dance till they are tired—it concerns nobody here at all."

"Little Else?"

"The baroness. Of course we shall call each other by our Christian names. We are sisters."

"I see."

"You don't see at all," she said, with a swift sideward glance at him.

"My dear Miss Estcourt——"

"If my plan succeeds it will certainly not be because I have been encouraged."

"I think," he said with sudden warmth, "that the plan is beautiful, and could only have been made by a beautiful nature."

"Oh?" ejaculated Anna, surprised. A flush of gratification came into her face. The heartiness of the tone surprised her even more than the words. She stood still to look at him. "It is a pity," she said softly, "that nearly always when we are together we get angry, for you can be so kind when you choose. Say nice things to me. Let us be happy. I love being happy."

She held out her hand, smiling. He took it and gave it a hearty, matter of fact shake, and dropped it. It was very awkward, but he was struggling with an overpowering desire to take her in his arms and kiss her, and not let her go again till she had said she would marry him. It was exceedingly awkward, for he knew quite well that if he did so it would be the end of all things.

He turned rather white, and thrust his hands deep into his pockets. "Yes, the plan is beautiful," he said cheerfully, "but very unpractical. And the nature that made it is, I am sure, beautiful, but of course quite as unpractical as the plan." And he smiled down at her, a broad, genial smile.

"I know I don't set about things the right way," she said. "If only you wouldn't worry about the pasts of my poor friends and what their relations may have done in pre-historic times, you could help me so much."

To his relief she began to walk on again. "Princess Ludwig is a sensible and experienced woman," he said, "and can help you in many ways that I cannot."

"But she only looks at the praktische side of a question, and that is really only one side. I am too unpractical, I know, but she isn't unpractical enough. But I don't want to talk about her. What I wanted to say was, that once these poor ladies have been chosen and are here, the time for making inquiries is over, isn't it? As far as I am concerned, anyhow, it is. I shall never forsake them, never, never. So please don't try to tell me things about them—it doesn't change my feelings towards them, and only makes me angry with you. Which is a pity. I want to live at peace with my neighbour."

"Well?" he said, as she paused. "That, I take it, is a prelude to something else."

"Yes, it is. It's a prelude to Karlchen."

"To Karlchen?"

She looked at him, and laughed rather nervously. "I am afraid," she said, "that Karlchen is coming to stay with me."

"And who, pray, is Karlchen?"

"The only son of his mother, and she is a widow."

He came to a standstill again. "What," he said, "Frau von Treumann has asked you to invite her son to Kleinwalde?"

"She didn't actually ask, but she got a sad letter from him, and seemed to feel the separation so much, and cried about it, and so—and so I did."

Axel was silent.

"I don't yearn to see Karlchen," said Anna in rather a small voice. She could not help feeling that the invitation had been wrung from her.

Axel bored a hole in the moss with his stick, and did not answer.

"But naturally his poor mother clings to him, and he to her."

Axel was intent on his hole and did not answer.

"They are all the world to each other."

Axel filled up his hole again, and pressed the moss
carefully over it with his foot. Then he said, "I never yet
heard of two Treumanns being all the world to each other."

"You appear to have a down on the Treumanns."

"Not in the least. I do not think they interest me enough. It
is an East Prussian Junker family that has spread beyond its
natural limits, and one meets them everywhere, and knows
their characteristics. What is this young man? I do not
remember having heard of him."

"He is an officer at Rislar."

"At Rislar? Those are the red hussars. Do you wish me to
make inquiries about him?"

"Oh, no. It's no use. His mother can't be happy without him,
so he must come."

"Then may I ask why, if I am not to help you in the matter,
we are talking about him at all?"

"I wanted to ask you whether—whether you think he will
come often."

"I should think," said Axel positively, "that he will come
very often indeed."

"Oh!" said Anna.

They walked on in silence.

"Have you considered," he said presently, "what you would do if your other—sisters want their relations asked down to stay with them? Christmas, for instance, is a time of general rejoicing, when the coldest hearts grow warm. Relations who have quarrelled all the year, seek each other out at Christmas and talk tearfully of ties of blood. And birthdays—will your twelve sisters be content to spend their twelve birthdays remote from all members of their family? Birthdays here are important days. There will be one a month now for you to celebrate at Kleinwalde."

"I have not got farther than considering Karlchen," said Anna with some impatience.

"A male Kuhräuber," said Axel musingly, swinging his stick and gazing up at the fleecy clouds floating over the pine tops, "a male Kuhräuber would be quite unlike anything you have yet seen."

"There are no male Kuhräubers," said Anna. "At least," she added, correcting herself, "Fräulein Kuhräuber said so. She said she had no relations at all, but perhaps—perhaps she has forgotten some, and will remember them by and by. Oh, I wish they would tell me exactly how they stand, and not try to hide anything! I thought we had left nothing unexplained in the letters, but now Karlchen—it seems——" She stopped and bit her lip. She was actually on the verge of criticising, to Axel, the behaviour of her sisters. "Look," she said, catching sight of red roofs through the thinning trees, "isn't that Lohm? I have seen you home without knowing it."

She held out her hand. "It isn't much good talking, is it?" she said, moved by a sudden impulse, and looking up at him with a slightly wistful smile. "How we talk and talk and never get any nearer anything or each other. Such an amount of explaining oneself, and all no use. I don't mean you and me especially—it is always so, with everyone and everywhere. It is very weird. Good-bye."

But he held her hand and would not let her go. "No," he said, in a voice she did not know, "wait one moment. Why will you not let me really help you? Do you think you will ever achieve anything by shutting your eyes to what is true? Is it not better to face it, and then to do one's best—after that, knowing the truth? Why are you angry whenever I try to tell you the truth, or what I believe to be the truth about these ladies? You are certain to find it out for yourself one day. You force me to look on and see you being disappointed, and grieved, and perhaps cheated—anyhow your confidence abused—and you reduce our talks together to a sort of sparring match unworthy, quite unworthy of either of us——" He broke off abruptly and released her hand. The passion in his voice was unmistakable, and she was listening with astonished eyes. "I am lecturing you," he said in his usual even tones, "Forgive me for thinking that you are setting about your plan in a way that can never be successful. As you say, we talk and talk, and the more we talk the less do we understand each other. It is a foolish world, and a pre-eminently lonely one."

He lifted his hat and turned away. Anna opened her lips to say something, but he was gone.

She went home and meditated on volcanoes.

CHAPTER XX

The May that year in Northern Germany was the May of a
poet's dream. The days were like a chain of pearls,
increasing in beauty and preciousness as the chain
lengthened. The lilacs flowered a fortnight earlier than in
other years. The winds, so restless usually on those flat
shores, seemed all asleep, and hardly stirred. About the
middle of the month the moon was at the full, and the forest
became enchanted ground. It was a time for love and
lovers, for vows and kisses, for all pretty, happy, hopeful
things. Only those farmers who were too old to love and
vow, looked at their rye fields and grumbled because there
was no rain.

Karlchen, arriving on the first Saturday of that blessed
month, felt all disposed to love, if the Engländerin should
turn out to be in the least degree lovable. He did not ask
much of a young woman with a fortune, but he inwardly
prayed that she might not be quite so ugly as wives with
money sometimes are. He was a man used to having what
he wanted, and had spent his own and his mother's money
in getting it. There was a little bald patch on the top of his
head, and there were many debts on his mind, and he was
nearing the critical point in an officer's career, the turning
of which is reserved exclusively for the efficient; and so he
had three excellent reasons for desiring to marry. He had
desired it, indeed, for some time, had attempted it often,
and had not achieved it. The fathers of wealthy German
girls knew the state of his finances with an exactitude that
was unworthy; and they knew, besides, every one of his
little weaknesses. As a result, they gave their daughters to
other suitors. But here was a girl without a father, who
knew nothing about him at all. There was, of course, some

story in the background to account for her living in this way; but that was precisely what would make her glad of a husband who would relieve her of the necessity of building up the weaker parts of her reputation on a foundation of what Karlchen, when he saw the inmates of the house, rudely stigmatised as alte Schachteln. Reputations, he reflected, staring at Fräulein Kuhräuber, may be too dearly bought. Naturally she would prefer an easy-going husband, who would let her see life with all its fun, to this dreary and aimless existence.

The Treumanns, he thought, were in luck. What a burden his mother had been on him for the last five years! Miss Estcourt had relieved him of it. Now there were his debts, and she would relieve him of those; and the little entanglement she must have had at home would not matter in Germany, where no one knew anything about her, except that she was the highly respectable Joachim's niece. Anyway, he was perfectly willing to let bygones be bygones. He left his bag at the inn at Kleinwalde, an impossible place as he noted with pleasure, sent away his Droschke, and walked round to the house; but he did not see Anna. She kept out of the way till the evening, and he had ample time to be happy with his mother. When he did see her, he fell in love with her at once. He had quite a simple nature, composed wholly of instincts, and fell in love with an ease acquired by long practice. Anna's face and figure were far prettier than he had dared to hope. She was a beauty, he told himself with much satisfaction. Truly the Treumanns were in luck. He entirely forgot the rôle he was to play of loving son, and devoted himself, with his habitual artlessness, to her. Indeed, if he had not forgotten it, he and his mother were so little accustomed to displays of affection that they would have been but clumsy actors. There is a great difference between affectionate letters

written quietly in one's room, and affectionate conversation
that has to sound as though it welled up from one's heart.
Nothing of the kind ever welled up from Karlchen's heart;
and Anna noticed at once that there were no signs of
unusual attachment between mother and son. Karlchen was
not even commonly polite to his mother, nor did she seem
to expect him to be. When she dropped her scissors, she
had to pick them up for herself. When she lost her thimble,
she hunted for it alone. When she wanted a footstool, she
got up and fetched one from under his very nose. When she
came into the room and looked about for a chair, it was
Letty who offered her hers. Karlchen sat comfortably with
his legs crossed, playing with the paper-knife he had taken
out of the book Anna had been reading, and making
himself pleasant. He had his mother's large black eyes, and
very long thick black eyelashes of which he was proud,
conscious that they rested becomingly on his cheeks when
he looked down at the paper-knife. Letty was greatly struck
by them, and inquired of Miss Leech in a whisper whether
she had ever seen their like.

"Mr. Jessup had silken eyelashes too," replied Miss Leech
dreamily.

"These aren't silk—they're cotton eyelashes," said Letty
scornfully.

"My dear Letty," murmured Miss Leech.

Anna was at a disadvantage because of her imperfect
German. She could not repress Karlchen when he was
unduly kind as she would have done in English, and with
his mother presiding, as it were, at their opening friendship,
she did not like to begin by looking lofty. Luckily the
princess was unusually chatty that evening. She sat next to

Karlchen, and continually joined in the talk. She was cheerful amiability itself, and insisted upon being told all about those sons of her acquaintances who were in his regiment. When he half turned his back on her and dropped his voice to a rapid undertone, thereby making himself completely incomprehensible to Anna, the princess pleasantly advised him to speak very slowly and distinctly, for unless he did Miss Estcourt would certainly not understand. In a word, she took him under her wing whether he would or no, and persisted in her friendliness in spite of his mother's increasingly desperate efforts to draw her into conversation.

"Why do we not go out, dear Anna?" cried Frau von Treumann at last, unable to endure Princess Ludwig's behaviour any longer. "Look what a fine evening it is—and quite warm." And she who till then had gone about shutting windows, and had been unable to bear the least breath of air, herself opened the glass doors leading into the garden and went out.

But although they all followed her, nothing was gained by it. She could have stamped her foot with rage at the princess's conduct. Here was everything needful for the beginning of a successful courtship—starlight, a murmuring sea, warm air, fragrant bushes, a girl who looked like Love itself in the dusk in her pale beauty, a young man desiring nothing better than to be allowed to love her, and a mother only waiting to bless. But here too, unfortunately, was the princess.

She was quite appallingly sociable—"The spite of the woman!" thought Frau von Treumann, for what could it matter to her?—and remained fixed at Anna's side as they paced slowly up and down the grass, monopolising

Karlchen's attention with her absurd questions about his brother officers. Anna walked between them, thinking of other things, holding up her trailing white dress with one hand, and with the other the edges of her blue cloak together at her neck. She was half a head taller than Karlchen, and so was his mother, who walked on his other side. Karlchen, becoming more and more enamoured the longer he walked, looked up at her through his eyelashes and told himself that the Treumanns were certainly in luck, for he had stumbled on a goddess.

"The grass is damp," cried Frau von Treumann, interrupting the endless questions. "My dear princess—your rheumatism—and I who so easily get colds. Come, we will go off the grass—we are not young enough to risk wet feet."

"I do not feel it," said the princess, "I have thick shoes. But you, dear Frau von Treumann, do not stay if you have fears."

"It is damp," said Anna, turning up the sole of her shoe. "Shall we go on to the path?"

On the path it was obvious that they must walk in couples. Arrived at its edge, the princess stopped and looked round with an urbane smile. "My dear child," she said to Anna, taking her arm, "we have been keeping Herr von Treumann from his mother regardless of his feelings. I beg you to pardon my thoughtlessness," she added, turning to him, "but my interest in hearing of my old friends' sons has made me quite forget that you took this long journey to be with your dear mother. We will not interrupt you further. Come, my dear, I wanted to ask you——" And she led

Anna away, dropping her voice to a confidential
questioning concerning the engaging of a new cook.

There was nothing to be done. The only crumb of comfort
Karlchen obtained—but it was a big one—was a reluctantly
given invitation, on his mother's vividly describing at the
hour of parting the place where he was to spend the night,
to remove his luggage from the inn to Anna's house, and to
sleep there.

"You are too good, meine Gnädigste," he said, consoled by
this for the tête-à-tête he had just had with his mother; "but
if it in any way inconveniences you—we soldiers are used
to roughing it——"

"But not like that, not like that, lieber Junge," interrupted
his mother anxiously. "It is not fit for a dog, that inn, and I
heard this very evening from the housemaid that one of the
children there has the measles."

That quite settled it. Anna could not expose Karlchen to
measles. Why did he not stay, as he had written he would,
at Stralsund? As he was here, however, she could not let
him fall a prey to measles, and she asked the princess to
order a room to be got ready.

It is a proof of her solemnity on that first evening with
Karlchen that when his mother, praising her beauty,
mentioned her dimples as specially bewitching, he should
have said, surprised, "What dimples?"

It is a proof, too, of the duplicity of mothers, that the very
next day in church the princess, sitting opposite the
innkeeper's rosy family, and counting its members between

the verses of the hymn, should have found that not one was missing.

Karlchen left on Sunday evening after a not very successful visit. He had been to church, believing that it was expected of him, and had found to his disgust that Anna had gone for a walk. So there he sat, between his mother and Princess Ludwig, and extracted what consolation he could from a studied neglect of the outer forms of worship and an elaborate slumber during the sermon.

The morning, then, was wasted. At luncheon Anna was unapproachable. Karlchen was invited to sit next to his mother, and Anna was protected by Letty on the one hand and Fräulein Kuhräuber on the other, and she talked the whole time to Fräulein Kuhräuber.

"Who is Fräulein Kuhräuber?" he inquired irritably of his mother, when they found themselves alone together again in the afternoon.

"Well, you can see who she is, I should think," replied his mother equally irritably. "She is just Fräulein Kuhräuber, and nothing more."

"Anna talks to her more than to anyone," he said; she was already "Anna" to him, tout court.

"Yes. It is disgusting."

"It is very disgusting. It is not right that Treumanns should be forced to associate on equal terms with such a person."

"It is scandalous. But you will change all that."

Karlchen twisted up the ends of his moustache and looked down his nose. He often looked down his nose because of his eyelashes. He began to hum a tune, and felt happy again. Axel Lohm was right when he doubted whether there had ever been a permanently crushed Treumann.

"She has a strange assortment of alte Schachteln here," he said, after a pause during which his thoughts were rosy. "That Elmreich, now. What relation does she say she is to Arthur Elmreich?"

"The man who shot himself? Oh, she is no relation at all. At most a distant cousin."

"Na, na," was Karlchen's reply; a reply whose English equivalent would be a profoundly sceptical wink.

His mother looked at him, waiting for more.

"What do you really think——?" she began, and then stopped.

He stood before the glass readjusting his moustache into the regulation truculent upward twist. "Think?" he said. "You know Arthur's sister Lolli was engaged at the Wintergarten this winter. She was not much of a success. Too old. But she was down on the bills as Baroness Elmreich, and people went to see her because of that, and because of her brother."

"Oh—terrible," murmured Frau von Treumann.

"Well, I know her; and I shall ask her next time I see her if she has a sister."

"But this one has no relations living at all," said his mother, horrified at the bare suggestion that Lolli was the sister of a person with whom she ate her dinner every day.

"Na, na," said Karlchen.

"But my dear Karlchen, it is so unlikely—the baroness is the veriest pattern of primness. She has such very strict views about all such things—quite absurdly strict. She even had doubts, she told me, when first she came here, as to whether Anna were a fit companion for her."

Karlchen stopped twisting his moustache, and stared at his mother. Then he threw back his head and shrieked with laughter. He laughed so much that for some moments he could not speak. His mother's face, as she watched him without a smile, made him laugh still more. "Liebste Mama," he said at last, wiping his eyes, "it may of course not be true. It is just possible that it is not. But I feel sure it is true, for this Elmreich and the little Lolli are as alike as two peas. Anna not a fit companion for Lolli's sister! Ach Gott, ach Gott!" And he shrieked again.

"If it is true," said Frau von Treumann, drawing herself up to her full height, "it is my duty to tell Anna. I cannot stay under the same roof with such a woman. She must go."

"Take care," said her son, illumined by an unaccustomed ray of sapience, "take care, Mutti. It is not certain that Anna would send her away."

"What! if she knew about this—this Lolli, as you call her?"

Karlchen shook his head. "It is better not to begin with ultimatums," he said sagely. "If you say you cannot stay under the same roof with the Elmreich, and she does not after that go, why then you must. And that," he added, looking alarmed, "would be disastrous. No, no, leave it alone. In any case leave it alone till I have seen Lolli. I shall come down soon again, you may be sure. I wish we could get rid of the Penheim. Now that really would be a good thing. Think it over."

But Frau von Treumann felt that by no amount of thinking it over would they ever get rid of the Penheim.

"You do not like my Karlchen?" she said plaintively to Anna that evening, coming out into the dusky garden where she stood looking at the stars. Karlchen was well on his way to Berlin by that time.

"I am sure I should like him very much if I knew him," replied Anna, putting all the heartiness she could muster into her voice.

Frau von Treumann shook her head sadly. "But now? I see you do not like him now. You hardly spoke to him. He was hurt. A mother"—"Oh," thought Anna, "I am tired of mothers,"—"a mother always knows."

Her handkerchief came out. She had put one hand through Anna's arm, and with the other began to wipe her eyes. Anna watched her in silence.

"What? What? Tears? Do I see tears? Are we then missing our son so much?" exclaimed a cheery voice behind them. And there was the princess again.

"Serpent," thought Frau von Treumann; but what is the use of thinking serpent? She had to submit to being consoled all the same, while Anna walked away.

CHAPTER XXI

Anna seemed always to be walking away during the days that separated Karlchen's first visit from his second. Frau von Treumann noticed it with some uneasiness, and hoped that it was only her fancy. The girl had shown herself possessed of such an abnormally large and warm heart at first, had been so eager in her offers of affection, so enthusiastic, so sympathetic, so—well, absurd; was it possible that there was no warmth and no affection left over from those vast stores for such a good-looking, agreeable man as Karlchen? But she set such thoughts aside as ridiculous. Her son's simple doctrine from his fourteenth year on had been that all girls like all men. It had often been laid down by him in their talks together, and her own experience of girls had sufficiently proved its soundness. "The Penheim must have poisoned her mind against him," she decided at last, unable otherwise to explain the apathy with which Anna received any news of Karlchen. Was there ever such sheer spite? For what could it matter to a woman with no son of her own, who married Anna? Somebody would marry her, for certain, and the Penheim would lose her place; then why should it not be Karlchen?

The princess, however, most innocent of excellent women, had never spoken privately to Anna of Karlchen except once, when she inquired whether he were to have the best sheets on his bed, or the second best sheets; and Anna had replied, "The worst."

But if Frau von Treumann was uneasy about Anna, Anna was still more uneasy about Frau von Treumann. Whenever she could, she went away into the forest and tried to think things out. She objected very much to the feeling that life seemed somehow to be thickening round her—yet, after Karlchen's visit there it was. Each day there were fewer and fewer quiet pauses in the trivial bustle of existence; clear moments, like windows through which she caught glimpses of the serene tranquillity with which the real day, nature's day, the day she ought to have had, was passing. Frau von Treumann followed her about and talked to her of Karlchen. Fräulein Kuhräuber followed her about, with a humble, dog-like affection, and seemed to want to tell her something, and never got further than dark utterances that perplexed her. Baroness Elmreich repulsed all her advances, carefully called her Miss Estcourt, and made acid comments on everything that was said and done. "I believe she dislikes me," thought Anna, puzzled. "I wonder why?" The baroness did; and the reason was simplicity itself. She disliked her because she was younger, prettier, richer, healthier than herself. For this she disliked her heartily; but with far greater heartiness did she dislike her because she knew she ought to be grateful to her. The baroness detested having to feel grateful—it is a detestation not confined to baronesses—and in this case the burden of the obligations she was under was so great that it was almost past endurance. And there was no escape. She had been starving when Anna took her in, and she would starve again if Anna turned her out. She owed her everything; and what more

natural, then, than to dislike her? The rarest of loves is the
love of a debtor for his creditor.

At night, alone in her room, Anna would wonder at the day
lived through, at the unsatisfactoriness of it, and the
emptiness. When were they going to begin the better life,
the soul to soul life she was waiting for? How busy they
had all been, and what had they done? Why, nothing. A
little aimless talking, a little aimless sewing, a little aimless
walking about, a few letters to write that need not have
been written, a newspaper to glance into that did not really
interest anybody, meals in rapid succession, night, and
oblivion. That was what was on the surface. What was
beneath the surface she could only guess at; for after a
whole fortnight with the Chosen she was still confronted
solely by surfaces. In the hot forest, drowsy and aromatic,
where the white butterflies, like points of light among the
shadows of the pine-trunks, fluttered up and down the
unending avenues all day long, she wandered, during the
afternoon hour when the Chosen napped, to the most out-
of-the-way nooks she could find; and sitting on the moss
where she could see some special bit of loveliness, some
distant radiant meadow in the sunlight beyond the trees,
some bush with its delicate green shower of budding leaves
at the foot of a giant pine, some exquisite effect of blue and
white between the branches so far above her head, she
would ponder and ponder till she was weary.

There was no mistaking Karlchen's looks; she had not been
a pretty girl for several seasons at home in vain. Karlchen
meant to marry her. She, of course, did not mean to marry
Karlchen, but that did not smooth any of the ruggedness out
of the path she saw opening before her. She would have to
endure the preliminary blandishments of the wooing, and
when the wooing itself had reached the state of ripeness

which would enable her to let him know plainly her own intentions, there would be a grievous number of scenes to be gone through with his mother. And then his mother would shake the Kleinwalde dust from her offended feet and go, and failure number one would be upon her. In the innermost recesses of her heart, offensive as Karlchen's wooing would certainly be, she thought that once it was over it would not have been a bad thing; for, since his visit, it was clear that Frau von Treumann was not the sort of inmate she had dreamed of for her home for the unhappy. Unhappy she had undoubtedly been, poor thing, but happy with Anna she would never be. She had forgiven the first fibs the poor lady had told her, but she could not go on forgiving fibs for ever. All those elaborate untruths, written and spoken, about Karlchen's visit, how dreadful they were. Surely, thought Anna, truthfulness was not only a lovely and a pleasant thing but it was absolutely indispensable as the basis to a real friendship. How could any soul approach another soul through a network of lies? And then more painful still—she confessed with shame that it was more painful to her even than the lies—Frau von Treumann evidently took her for a fool. Not merely for a person wanting in intelligence, or slow-witted, but for a downright fool. She must think so, or she would have taken more pains, at least some pains, to make her schemes a little less transparent. Anna hated herself for feeling mortified by this; but mortified she certainly was. Even a philosopher does not like to be honestly mistaken during an entire fortnight for a fool. Though he may smile, he will almost surely wince. Not being a philosopher, Anna winced and did not smile.

"I think," she said to Manske, when he came in one morning with a list of selected applications, "I think we will wait a little before choosing the other nine."

"The gracious one is not weary of well-doing?" he asked quickly.

"Oh no, not at all; I like well-doing," Anna said rather lamely, "but it is not quite—not quite as simple as it looks."

"I have found nine most deserving cases," he urged, "and later there may not be——"

"No, no," interrupted Anna, "we will wait. In the autumn, perhaps—not now. First I must make the ones who are here happy. You know," she said, smiling, "they came here to be made happy."

"Yes, truly I know it. And happy indeed must they be in this home, surrounded by all that makes life fair and desirable."

"One would think so," said Anna, musing. "It is pretty here, isn't it—it should be easy to be happy here,—yet I am not sure that they are."

"Not sure——?" Manske looked at her, startled.

"What do people—most people, ordinary people, need, to make them happy?" she asked wistfully. She was speaking to herself more than to him, and did not expect any very illuminating answer.

"The fear of the Lord," he replied promptly; which put an end to the conversation.

But besides her perplexities about the Chosen, Anna had other worries. Dellwig had received the refusal to let him build the brick-kiln with such insolence, and had, in his

anger, said such extraordinary things about Axel Lohm,
that Anna had blazed out too, and had told him he must go.
It had been an unpleasant scene, and she had come out
from it white and trembling. She had intended to ask Axel
to do the dismissing for her if she should ever definitely
decide to send him away; but she had been overwhelmed
by a sudden passion of wrath at the man's intolerable
insinuations—only half understood, but sounding for that
reason worse than they were—and had done it herself.
Since then she had not seen him. By the agreement her
uncle had made with him, he was entitled to six months'
notice, and would not leave until the winter, and she knew
she could not continue to refuse to see him; but how she
dreaded the next interview! And how uneasy she felt at the
thought that the management of her estate was entirely in
the hands of a man who must now be her enemy. Axel was
equally anxious, when he heard what she had done. It had
to be done, of course; but he did not like Dellwig's looks
when he met him. He asked Anna to allow him to ride
round her place as often as he could, and she was grateful
to him, for she knew that not only her own existence, but
the existence of her poor friends, depended on the right
cultivation of Kleinwalde. And she was so helpless. What
creature on earth could be more helpless than an English
girl in her position? She left off reading Maeterlinck,
borrowed books on farming from Axel, and eagerly studied
them, learning by heart before breakfast long pages
concerning the peculiarities of her two chief products,
potatoes and pigs.

"He cannot do much harm," Axel assured her; "the
potatoes, I see, are all in, and what can he do to the pigs?
His own vanity would prevent his leaving the place in a bad
state. I have heard of a good man—shall I have him down
and interview him for you?"

"How kind you are," said Anna gratefully; indeed, he seemed to her to be a tower of strength.

"Anyone would do what they could to help a forlorn young lady in the straits you are in," he said, smiling at her.

"I don't feel like a forlorn young lady with you next door to help me out of the difficulties."

"People in these lonely country places learn to be neighbourly," he replied in his most measured tones.

He had not again spoken of the Chosen since his walk with her through the forest; and though he knew that Karlchen had been and gone he did not mention his name. Nor did Anna. The longer she lived with her sisters the less did she care to talk about them, especially to Axel. As for Frau von Treumann's plans, how could she ever tell him of those?

And just then Letty, the only being who was really satisfactory, became a cause to her of fresh perplexity. Letty had been strangely content with her German lessons from Herr Klutz. Every day she and Miss Leech set out without a murmur, and came back looking placid. They brought back little offerings from the parsonage, a bunch of narcissus, the first lilac, cakes baked by Frau Manske, always something. Anna took the flowers, and ate the cakes, and sent pleased messages in return. If she had been less preoccupied by Dellwig and the eccentricities of her three new friends, she would certainly have been struck by Letty's silence about her lessons, and would have questioned her. There was no grumbling after the first day, and no abuse of Schiller and the muses. Once Anna met Klutz walking through Kleinwalde, and asked him how the studies were progressing. "Colossal," was the reply, "the progress made is colossal." And he crushed her rings into her fingers when she gave him her hand to shake, and blushed, and looked at her with eyes that he felt must burn into her soul. But Anna noticed neither his eyes nor his blush; for his eyes, whatever he might feel them to be doing, were not the kind that burn into souls, and he was a pale young man who, when he blushed, did it only in his ears. They certainly turned crimson as he crushed Anna's fingers, but she was not thinking of his ears.

"Frau Manske is too kind," she said, as the nosegays, at first intermittent, became things of daily occurrence. They grew bigger, too, every day, attaining such a girth at last that Letty could hardly carry them. "She must not plunder her garden like this."

"It is very full of flowers," said Miss Leech. "Really a wonderful display. The bunch is always ready, tied together and lying on the table when we arrive. I tried to tell her yesterday that you were afraid she was spoiling her garden, sending so much, but she did not seem to understand. She is showing me how to make those cakes you said you liked."

"I wish I had some of these in my garden," said Anna, laying her cheek against the posy of wallflowers Letty had just given her. There was nothing in her garden except grass and trees; Uncle Joachim had not been a man of flowers.

She took them up to her room, kissing them on the way, and put them in a jar on the window-sill; and it was not until two or three days later, when they began to fade, that she saw the corner of an envelope peeping out from among them. She pulled it out and opened it. It was addressed to

Ihr Hochwohlgeboren Fräulein Anna Estcourt; and inside was a sheet of notepaper with a large red heart painted on it, mangled, and pierced by an arrow; and below it the following poem in a cramped, hardly readable writing:—

The earth am I, and thou the heaven,

The mass am I, and thou the leaven,

No other heaven do I want but thee,

Oh Anna, Anna, Anna, pity me!

August Klutz, Kandidat.

In an instant Letty's unnatural cheerfulness about her lessons flashed across her. What had they been doing, and where was Miss Leech, that such things could happen?

It was a very terrible, stern-browed aunt who met Letty that day on the stairs when she came home.

"Hullo, Aunt Anna, seen a ghost?" Letty inquired pleasantly; but her heart sank into her boots all the same as she followed her into her room.

"Look," said Anna, showing her the paper, "how could you do it? For of course you did it. Herr Klutz doesn't speak English."

"Doesn't he though—he gets on like anything. He sits up all night——"

"How is it that this was possible?" interrupted Anna, striking the paper with her hand.

"It's pretty, isn't it," said Letty, faintly grinning. "The last line had to be changed a little. It isn't original, you know, except the Annas. I put in those. That footman mother got cheap because he had one finger too few sent it to Hilton on her birthday last year—she liked it awfully. The last line was 'Oh Hilton, Hilton, Hilton——'"

"How came you to talk such hideous nonsense with Herr Klutz, and about me?"

"I didn't. He began. He talked about you the whole time, and started doing it the very first day Leechy cooked."

"Cooked?"

"She is always in the kitchen with Frau Manske. We brought you some of the cakes one day, and you seemed as pleased as anything."

"And instead of learning German you and he have been making up this sort of thing?"

Anna's voice and eyes frightened Letty. She shifted from one foot to the other and looked down sullenly. "What's the good of being angry?" she said, addressing the carpet; "it's only Mr. Jessup over again. Leechy wasn't angry with Mr. Jessup. She was frightfully pleased. She says it's the greatest compliment a person can pay anybody, going on about them like Herr Klutz does, and talking rot."

Anna stared at her, bewildered. "Mr. Jessup?" she repeated. "And do you mean to tell me that Miss Leech knows of this—this disgusting nonsense?" She held the mangled heart at arm's length, crushing it in her hand.

"I say, you'll spoil it. He worked at it for days. There weren't any paints red enough for the wound, and he had to go to Stralsund on purpose. He thought no end of it." And Letty, scared though she was, could not resist giggling a little.

"Do you mean to tell me that Miss Leech knows about this?" insisted Anna.

"Rather not. It's a secret. He made me promise faithfully never to tell a soul. Of course it doesn't matter talking to you, because you're one of the persons concerned. You can't be married, you know, without knowing about it, so I'm not breaking my promise talking to you——"

"Married? What unutterable rubbish have you got into your head?"

"That's what I said—or something like it. I said it was jolly rot. He said, 'What's rot?' I said 'That.'"

"But what?" asked Anna angrily. She longed to shake her.

"Why, that about marrying you. I told him it was rot, and I was sure you wouldn't, but as he didn't know what rot was, it wasn't much good. He hunted it out in the dictionary, and still he didn't know."

Anna stood looking at her with indignant eyes. "You don't know what you have done," she said, "evidently you don't. It is a dreadful thing that the moment Miss Leech leaves you you should begin to talk of such things—such horrid things—with a stranger. A little girl of your age——"

"I didn't begin," whimpered Letty, overcome by the wrath in Anna's voice.

"But all this time you have been going on with it, instead of at once telling Miss Leech or me."

"I never met a—a lover before—I thought it—great fun."

"Then all those flowers were from him?"

"Ye—es." Letty was in tears.

"He thought I knew they were from him?"

No answer.

"Did he?" insisted Anna.

"Ye—es."

"You are a very wicked little girl," said Anna, with awful sternness. "You have been acting untruths every day for ages, which is just as bad as telling them. I don't believe you have an idea of the horridness of what you have done—I hope you have not. Of course your lessons at Lohm have come to an end. You will not go there again. Probably I shall send you home to your mother. I am nearly sure that I shall. Go away." And she pointed to the door.

That night neither Letty nor Miss Leech appeared at supper; both were shut up in their rooms in tears. Miss Leech was quite unable to forgive herself. It was all her

fault, she felt. She had been appalled when Anna showed
her the heart and told her what had been going on while she
was learning to cook in Frau Manske's kitchen. "Such a
quiet, respectable-looking young man!" she exclaimed,
horror-stricken. "And about to take holy orders!"

"Well, you see he isn't quiet and respectable at all," said
Anna. "He is unusually enterprising, and quite without
morals. Only a demoralised person would take advantage
of a poor little pupil in that way."

She lit a candle, and burnt the heart. "There," she said,
when it was in ashes, "that's the end of that. Heaven knows
what Letty has been led into saying, or what ideas he has
put into her head. I can't bear to think of it. I hadn't the
courage to cross-question her much—I was afraid I should
hear something that would make me too angry, and I'd have
to tell the parson. Anyhow, dear Miss Leech, we will not
leave her alone again, ever, will we? I don't suppose a thing
like this will happen twice, but we won't let it have a
chance, will we? Now don't be too unhappy. Tell me about
Mr. Jessup."

It was Miss Leech's fault, Anna knew; but she so evidently
knew it herself, and was so deeply distressed, that rebukes
were out of the question. She spent the evening and most of
the night in useless laments, while, in the room adjoining,
Letty lay face downwards on her bed, bathed in tears. For
Letty's conscience was in a grievous state of tumult. She
had meant well, and she had done badly. She had not
thought her aunt would be angry—was she not in full
possession of the facts concerning Mr. Jessup's courtship?
And had not Miss Leech said that no higher honour could
be paid to a woman than to fall in love with her and make
her an offer of marriage? Herr Klutz, it is true, was not the

sort of person her aunt could marry, for her aunt was stricken in years, and he looked about the same age as her brother Peter; besides, he was clearly, thought Letty, of the guttersnipe class, a class that bit its nails and never married people's aunts. But, after all, her aunt could always say No when the supreme moment arrived, and nobody ought to be offended because they had been fallen in love with, and he was frightfully in love, and talked the most awful rot. Nor had she encouraged him. On the contrary, she had discouraged him; but it was precisely this discouragement, so virtuously administered, that lay so heavily on her conscience as she lay so heavily on her bed. She had been proud of it till this interview with her aunt; since then it had taken on a different complexion, and she was sure, dreadfully sure, that if her aunt knew of it she would be very angry indeed—much, much angrier than she was before. Letty rolled on her bed in torments; for the discouragement administered to Klutz had been in the form of poetry, and poetry written on her aunt's notepaper, and purporting to come from her. She had meant so well, and what had she done? When no answer came by return to his poem hidden in the wallflowers, he had refused to believe that the bouquet had reached its destination. "There has been treachery," he cried; "you have played me false." And he seemed to fold up with affliction.

"I gave it to her all right. She hasn't found the letter yet," said Letty, trying to comfort, and astonished by the loudness of his grief. "It's all right—you wait a bit. She liked the flowers awfully, and kissed them."

"Poor young lover," she thought romantically, "his heart must not bleed too much. Aunt Anna, if she ever does find the letter, will only send him a rude answer. I will answer it for her, and gently discourage him." For if the words that proceeded from Letty's mouth were inelegant, her thoughts, whenever they dwelt on either Mr. Jessup or Herr Klutz, were invariably clothed in the tender language of sentiment.

And she had sat up till very late, composing a poem whose mission was both to discourage and console. It cost her infinite pains, but when it was finished she felt that it had been worth them all. She copied it out in capital letters on Anna's notepaper, folded it up carefully, and tied it with one of her own hair-ribbons to a little bunch of lilies-of-the-valley she had gathered for the purpose in the forest.

This was the poem:—

It is a matter of regret

That circumstances won't

Allow me to call thee my pet,

But as it is they don't.

For why? My many years forbid,

And likewise thy position.

So take advice, and strive amid

Thy tears for meek submission.

Anna.

And this poem was, at that very moment, as she well knew, in Herr Klutz's waistcoat pocket.

CHAPTER XXII

The ordinary young man, German or otherwise, hungrily emerging from boyhood into a toothsome world made to be eaten, cures himself of his appetite by indulging it till he is ill, and then on a firm foundation of his own foolish corpse, or, as the poet puts it, of his dead self, begins to build up the better things of his later years.

Klutz was an ordinary young man, and arrived at early manhood as hungry as his fellows; but his father was a parson, his grandfather had been a parson, his uncles were all parsons, and Fate, coming cruelly to him in the gloomy robes of the Lutheran Church, his natural follies had had no opportunity of getting out, developing, and dissolving, but remained shut up in his heart, where they amused themselves by seething uninterruptedly, to his great discomfort, while the good parson, in whose care he was, talked to him of the world to come.

"The world to come," thought Klutz, hungering and thirsting for a taste of the world in which he was, "may or may not be very well in its way; but its way is not my way." And he listened in a silence that might be taken either for awed or bored to Manske's expatiations. Manske, of course,

interpreted it as awed. "Our young vicar," he said to his
wife, "thinks much. He is serious and contemplative
beyond his years. He is not a man of many and vain
words." To which his wife replied only by a sniff of
scepticism.

She had no direct proofs that Klutz was not serious and
contemplative, but during his first winter in their house he
had fallen into her bad graces because of a certain
indelicately appreciative attitude he displayed towards her
apple jelly. Not that she grudged him apple jelly in just
quantities; both she and her husband were fond of it, and
the eating of it was luckily one of those pleasures whose
indulgence is innocent. But there are limits beyond which
even jelly becomes vicious, and these limits Herr Klutz
continually overstepped. Every autumn she made a
sufficient number of pots of it to last discreet appetites a
whole year. There had always been vicars in their house,
and there had never been a dearth of jelly. But this year, so
early as Easter, there were only two pots left. She could not
conveniently lock it up and refuse to produce any, for then
she and her husband would not have it themselves; so all
through the winter she had watched the pots being emptied
one after the other, and the thinner the rows in her
storeroom grew, the more pronounced became her
conviction that Klutz's piety was but skin deep. A young
man who could behave in so unbridled a fashion could not
be really serious; there was something, she thought, that
smacked suspiciously of the flesh and the devil about such
conduct. Great, then, was her astonishment when, the
penultimate pot being placed at Easter on the table, Klutz
turned from it with loathing. Nor did he ever look at apple
jelly again; nor did he, of other viands, eat enough to keep
him in health. He who had been so voracious forgot his
meals, and had to be coaxed before he would eat at all. He

spent his spare time writing, sitting up sometimes all night, and consuming candles at the same head-long rate with which he had previously consumed the jelly; and when towards May her husband once more commented on his seriousness, Frau Manske's conscience no longer permitted her to sniff.

"You must be ill," she said to him at last, on a day when he had sat through the meals in silence and had refused to eat at all.

"Ill!" burst out Klutz, whose body and soul seemed both to be in one fierce blaze of fever, "I am sick—sick even unto death."

And he did feel sick. Only two days had elapsed since he had received Anna's poem and had been thrown by it into a tumult of delight and triumph; for the discouragement it contained had but encouraged him the more, appearing to be merely the becoming self-depreciation of a woman before him who has been by nature appointed lord. He was perfectly ready to overlook the obstacles to their union to which she alluded. She could not help her years; there were, truly, more of them than he would have wished, but luckily they were not visible on that still lovely face. As to position, he supposed she meant that he was not adelig; but a man, he reflected, compared to a woman, is always adelig, whatever his name may be, by virtue of his higher and nobler nature. He had been for rushing at once to Kleinwalde; but his pupil and confidant had said "Don't," and had said it with such energy that for that day at least he had resisted. And now, the very morning of the day on which the Frau Pastor was asking him whether he were ill, he had received a curt note from Miss Leech, informing him that Miss Letty Estcourt would for the present discontinue her German studies. What had happened? Even the poem, lying warm on his heart, was not able to dispel his fears. He had flown at once to Kleinwalde, feeling that it was absurd not to follow the dictates of his heart and cast himself in person at Anna's no doubt expectant feet, and the door had been shut in his face—rudely shut, by a coarse servant, whose manner had so much enraged him that he had almost shown her the precious verses then and there, to convince her of his importance in that house; indeed, the only consideration that restrained him was a conviction of her ignorance of the English tongue.

"Would you like to see the doctor?" inquired Frau Manske, startled by his looks and words; perhaps he had caught something infectious; an infectious vicar in the house would be horrible.

"The doctor!" cried Klutz; and forthwith quoted the German rendering of the six lines beginning, Canst thou not minister to a mind diseased.

Frau Manske was seriously alarmed. Not aware that he was quoting, she was horrified to hear him calling her Du, a privilege confined to lovers, husbands, and near relations, and asking her questions that she was sure no decent vicar would ever ask the respectable mother of a family. "I am sure you ought to see the doctor," she said nervously, getting up hastily and going to the door.

"No, no," said Klutz; "the doctor does not exist who can help me."

His hand went to the breast-pocket containing the poem, and he fingered it feverishly. He longed to show it to Frau Manske, to translate it for her, to let her see what the young

Kleinwalde lady, joint patron with Herr von Lohm of her husband's living, thought of him.

"I will ask my husband about the doctor," persisted Frau Manske, disappearing with unusual haste. If she had stayed one minute longer he would have shown her the poem.

Klutz did not wait to hear what the pastor said, but crushed his felt hat on to his head and started for a violent walk. He would go through Kleinwalde, past the house; he would haunt the woods; he would wait about. It was a hot, gusty May afternoon, and the wind that had been quiet so long was blowing up the dust in clouds; but he hurried along regardless of heat and wind and dust, with an energy surprising in one who had eaten nothing all day. Love had come to him very turbulently. He had been looking for it ever since he left school; but his watchful parents had kept him in solitary places, empty, uninhabited places like Lohm, places where the parson's daughters were either married or were still tied on the cushions of infancy. Sometimes he had been invited, as a great condescension, to the Dellwigs' Sunday parties; and there too he had looked around for Love. But the company consisted solely of stout farmers' wives, ladies of thirty, forty, fifty—of a dizzy antiquity, that is, and their talk was of butter-making and sausages, and they cared not at all for Love. "Oh, Love, Love, Love, where shall I find thee?" he would cry to the stars on his way home through the forest after these evenings; but the stars twinkled coldly on, obviously profoundly indifferent as to whether he found it or not. His chest of drawers was full of the poems into which he had poured the emotions of twenty, the emotions and longings that well-fed, unoccupied twenty mistakes for soul. And then the English Miss had burst upon his gaze, sitting in her carriage on that stormy March day, smiling at him from the very first, piercing his heart through and through with eyes that many persons besides Klutz saw were lovely, and so had he found Love, and for ever lost his interest in apple jelly.

It was a confident, bold Love, with more hopes than fears, more assurance than misgivings. The poem seemed to burn his pocket, so violently did he long to show it round, to tell everyone of his good fortune. The lilies-of-the-valley to which it had been tied and that he wore since all day long in his coat, were hardly brown, and yet he was tired already of having such a secret to himself. What advantage was there in being told by the lady of Kleinwalde that she regretted not being able to call him Lämmchen or Schätzchen (the alternative renderings his dictionary gave of "pet") if no one knew it?

When he reached the house he walked past it at a snail's pace, staring up at the blank, repellent windows. Not a soul was to be seen. He went on discontentedly. What should he do? The door had been shut in his face once already that day, why he could not imagine. He hesitated, and turned back. He would try again. Why not? The Miss would have scolded the servant roundly when she heard that the person who dwelt in her thoughts as a Lämmchen had been turned away. He went boldly round the grass plot in front of the house and knocked.

The same servant appeared. Instantly on seeing him she slammed the door, and called out "Nicht zu Haus!"

"Ekelhaftes Benehmen!" cried Klutz aloud, flaming into sudden passion. His mind, never very strong, had grown weaker along with his body during these exciting days of love and fasting. A wave of fury swept over him as he stood before the shut door and heard the servant going away; and hardly knowing what he did, he seized the knocker, and knocked and knocked till the woods rang.

There was a sound of hurried footsteps on the path behind him, and turning his head, his hand still knocking, he saw Dellwig running towards him.

"Nanu!" cried Dellwig breathlessly, staring in blankest astonishment. "What in the devil's name are you making this noise for? Is the parson on fire?"

Klutz stared back in a dazed sort of way, his fury dying out at once in the presence of the stronger nature; then, because he was twenty, and because he was half-starved, and because he felt he was being cruelly used, there on Anna's doorstep, in the full light of the evening sun, with Dellwig's eyes upon him, he burst into a torrent of tears.

"Well of all—what's wrong at Lohm, you great sheep?" asked Dellwig, seizing his arm and giving him a shake.

Klutz signified by a movement of his head that nothing was wrong at Lohm. He was crying like a baby, into a red pocket-handkerchief, and could not speak.

Dellwig, still gripping his arm, stared at him a moment in silence; then he turned him round, pushed him down the steps, and walked him off. "Come along, young man," he said, "I want some explanation of this. If you are mad you'll be locked up. We don't fancy madmen about our place. And if you're not mad you'll be fined by the Amtsvorsteher for disorderly conduct. Knocking like that at a lady's door! I wonder you didn't kick it in, while you were about it. It's a good thing the Herrschaften are out."

Klutz really felt ill. He leaned on Dellwig's arm and let himself be helped along, the energy gone out of him with the fury. "You have never loved," was all he said, wiping his eyes.

"Oh that's it, is it? It is love that made you want to break the knocker? Why didn't you go round to the back? Which of them is it? The cook, of course. You look hungry. A Kandidat crying after a cook!" And Dellwig laughed loud and long.

"The cook!" cried Klutz, galvanised by the word into life. "The cook!" He thrust a shaking hand into his breast-pocket and dragged it out, the precious paper, unfolding it with trembling fingers, and holding it before Dellwig's eyes. "So much for your cooks," he said, tremulously triumphant. They were in the road, out of sight of the house. Dellwig took the paper and held it close to his eyes. "What's this?" he asked, scrutinising it. "It is not German."

"It is English," said Klutz.

"What, the governess——?"

Klutz merely pointed to the name at the end. Oh, the sweetness of that moment!

"Anna?" read out Dellwig, "Anna? That is Miss Estcourt's name."

"It is," said Klutz, his tears all dried up.

"It seems to be poetry," said Dellwig slowly.

"It is," said Klutz.

"Why have you got it?"

"Why indeed! It's mine. She sent it to me. She wrote it for me. These flowers——"

"Miss Estcourt? Sent it to you? Poetry? To you?" Dellwig looked up from the paper at Klutz, and examined him slowly from head to foot as if he had never seen him before. His expression while he did it was not flattering, but Klutz rarely noticed expressions. "What's it all about?" he asked, when he had reached Klutz's boots, by which he seemed struck, for he looked at them twice.

"Love," said Klutz proudly.

"Love?"

"Let me come home with you," said Klutz eagerly, "I'll translate it there. I can't here where we might be disturbed."

"Come on, then," said Dellwig, walking off at a great pace with the paper in his hand.

Just as they were turning into the farmyard the rattle of a carriage was heard coming down the road. "Stop," said Dellwig, laying his hand on Klutz's arm, "the Herrschaften have been drinking coffee in the woods—here they are, coming home. You can get a greeting if you wait."

They both stood on the edge of the road, and the carriage with Anna and a selection from her house-party drove by. Dellwig and Klutz swept off their hats. When Anna saw Klutz she turned scarlet—undeniably, unmistakably scarlet—and looked away quickly. Dellwig's lips shaped themselves into a whistle. "Come in, then," he said, glancing at Klutz, "come in and translate your poem."

Seldom had Klutz passed more delicious moments than those in which he rendered Letty's verses into German, with both the Dellwigs drinking in his words. The proud and exclusive Dellwigs! A month ago such a thing would have been too wild a flight of fancy for the most ambitious dream. In the very room in which he had been thrust aside at parties, forgotten in corners, left behind when the others went in to supper, he was now sitting the centre of interest, with his former supercilious hosts hanging on his words. When he had done, had all too soon come to the end of his delightful task, he looked round at them triumphantly; and his triumph was immediately dashed out of him by Dellwig, who said with his harshest laugh, "Put aside all your hopes, young man—Miss Estcourt is engaged to Herr von Lohm."

"Engaged? To Herr von Lohm?" Klutz echoed stupidly, his mouth open and the hand holding the verses dropping limply to his side.

"Engaged, engaged, engaged," Dellwig repeated in a loud sing-song, "not openly, but all the same engaged."

"It is truly scandalous!" cried his wife, greatly excited, and firmly believing that the verses were indeed Anna's. Was she not herself of the race of Weiber, and did she not therefore well know what they were capable of?

"Silence, Frau!" commanded Dellwig.

"And she takes my flowers—my daily offerings, floral and poetical, and she sends me these verses—and all the time she is betrothed to someone else?"

"She is," said Dellwig with another burst of laughter, for Klutz's face amused him intensely. He got up and slapped him on the shoulder. "This is your first experience of Weiber, eh? Don't waste your heartaches over her. She is a young lady who likes to have her little joke and means no harm——"

"She is a person without shame!" cried his wife.

"Silence, Frau!" snapped Dellwig. "Look here, young man—why, what does he look like, sitting there with all the wind knocked out of him? Get him a glass of brandy, Frau, or we shall have him crying again. Sit up, and be a man. Miss Estcourt is not for you, and never will be. Only a vicar could ever have dreamed she was, and have been imposed upon by this poetry stuff. But though you're a vicar you're a man, eh? Here, drink this, and tell us if you are not a man."

Klutz feebly tried to push the glass away, but Dellwig insisted. Klutz was pale to ghastliness, and his eyes were brimming again with tears.

"Oh, this person! Oh, this Englishwoman! Oh, the shameful treatment of an estimable young man!" cried Frau Dellwig, staring at the havoc Anna had wrought.

"Silence, Frau!" shouted Dellwig, stamping his foot. "You can't be treated like this," he went on to Klutz, who, used to drinking much milk at the abstemious parsonage, already felt the brandy running along his veins like liquid fire, "you can't be made ridiculous and do nothing. A vicar can't fight, but you must have some revenge."

Klutz started. "Revenge! Yes, but what revenge?" he asked.

"Nothing to do with Miss Estcourt, of course. Leave her alone——"

"Leave her alone?" cried his wife, "what, when she it is——"

"Silence, Frau!" roared Dellwig. "Leave her alone, I say. You won't gain anything there, young man. But go to her Bräutigam Lohm and tell him about it, and show him the stuff. He'll be interested."

Dellwig laughed boisterously, and took two or three rapid turns up and down the room. He had not lived with old Joachim and seen much of old Lohm and the surrounding landowners without having learned something of their views on questions of honour. Axel Lohm he knew to be specially strict and strait-laced, to possess in quite an unusual degree the ideals that Dellwig thought so absurd and so unpractical, the ideals, that is, of a Christian gentleman. Had he not known him since he was a child? And he had always been a prig. How would he like Miss Estcourt to be talked about, as of course she would be talked about? Klutz's mouth could not be stopped, and the whole district would know what had been going on. Axel Lohm could not and would not marry a young lady who wrote verses to vicars; and if all relations between Lohm and Kleinwalde ceased, why then life would resume its former pleasant course, he, Dellwig, staying on at his post, becoming, as was natural, his mistress's sole adviser, and certainly after due persuasion achieving all he wanted, including the brick-kiln. The plainness and clearness of the future was beautiful. He walked up and down the room making odd sounds of satisfaction, and silencing his wife with vigour every time she opened her lips. Even his wife, so quick as a rule of comprehension, had not grasped how this poem had changed their situation, and how it behoved them now not to abuse their mistress before a mischief-making young man. She was blinded, he knew, by her hatred of Miss Estcourt. Women were always the slaves, in defiance of their own interests, to some emotion or other; if it was not love, then it was hatred. Never could they wait for anything whatever. The passing passion must out and be indulged, however fatal the consequences might be. What a set they were! And the best of them, what fools. He glanced angrily at his wife as he passed her, but his glance, travelling from her to Klutz, who sat quite still with head sunk on his chest, legs straight out before him, the hand with the paper loosely held in it hanging down out of the cuffless sleeve nearly to the floor, and vacant eyes staring into space, his good humour returned, and he gave another harsh laugh. "Well?" he said, standing in front of this dejected figure. "How long will you sit there? If I were you I'd lose no time. You don't want those two to be making love and enjoying themselves an hour longer than is necessary, do you? With you out in the cold? With you so cruelly deceived? And made to look so ridiculous? I'd spoil that if I were you, at once."

"Yes, you are right. I'll go to Herr von Lohm and see if I can have an interview."

Klutz got up with a great show of determination, put the paper in his pocket, and buttoned his coat over it for greater security. Then he hesitated.

"It is a shameful thing, isn't it?" he said, his eyes on Dellwig's face.

"Shameful? It's downright cruel."

"Shameful?" began his wife.

"Silence, I tell thee! Young ladies' jokes are sometimes cruel, you see. I believe it was a joke, but a very heartless one, and one that has made you look more foolish even than half-fledged pastors of your age generally do look. It is only fair in return to spoil her game for her. Take another glass of brandy, and go and do it."

Klutz stared hard for a moment at Dellwig. Then he seized the brandy, gulped it down, snatched up his hat, and taking no farewell notice of either husband or wife, hurried out of the room. They saw him pass beneath the window, his hat over his eyes, his face white, his ears aflame.

"There goes a fool," said Dellwig, rubbing his hands, "and as useful a one as ever I saw. But here's another fool," he added, turning sharply to his wife, "and I don't want them in my own house."

And he proceeded to tell her, in the vigorous and convincing language of a justly irritated husband, what he thought of her.

CHAPTER XXIII

Klutz sped, as fast as his shaking limbs allowed, to Lohm. When he passed Anna's house he flung it a look of burning contempt, which he hoped she saw and felt from behind some curtain; and then, trying to put her from his mind, he made desperate efforts to arrange his thoughts a little for the coming interview. He supposed that it must be the brandy that made it so difficult for him to discern exactly why he was to go to Herr von Lohm instead of to the person principally concerned, the person who had treated him so scandalously; but Herr Dellwig knew best, of course, and judged the matter quite dispassionately. Certainly Herr von Lohm, as an insolently happy rival, ought in mere justice to be annoyed a little; and if the annoyance reached such a pitch of effectiveness as to make him break off the engagement, why then—there was no knowing—perhaps after all——? The ordinary Christian was bound to forgive his erring brother; how much more, then, was it incumbent on a pastor to forgive his erring sister? But Klutz did wish that someone else could have done the annoying for him, leaving him to deal solely with Anna, a woman, a member of the sex in whose presence he was always at his ease. The brandy prevented him from feeling it as acutely as he would otherwise have done, but the plain truth, the truth undisguised by brandy, was that he looked up to Axel Lohm with a respect bordering on fear, had never in his life been alone with him, or so much as spoken to him beyond ordinary civilities when they met, and he was frightened.

By the time he reached Axel's stables, which stood by the roadside about five minutes' walk from Axel's gate, he found himself obliged to go over his sufferings once again

one by one, to count the dinners he had missed, to
remember the feverish nights and the restless days, to
rehearse what Dellwig had just told him of his present
ridiculousness, or he would have turned back and gone
home. But these thoughts gave him the courage necessary
to get him through the gate; and by the time he had rounded
the bend in the avenue escape had become impossible, for
Axel was standing on the steps of the house. Axel had a
cigar in his mouth; his hands were in his pockets, and he
was watching the paces of a young mare which was being
led up and down. Two pointers were sitting at his feet, and
when Klutz appeared they rushed down at him barking.
Klutz did not as a rule object to being barked at by dogs,
but he was in a highly nervous state, and shrank aside
involuntarily. The groom leading the mare grinned; Axel
whistled the dogs off; and Klutz, with hot ears, walked up
and took off his hat.

"What can I do for you, Herr Klutz?" asked Axel, his hands
still in his pockets and his eyes on the mare's legs.

"I wish to speak with you privately," said Klutz.

"Gut. Just wait a moment." And Klutz waited, while Axel,
with great deliberation, continued his scrutiny of the mare,
and followed it up by a lengthy technical discussion of her
faults and her merits with the groom.

This was intolerable. Klutz had come on business of vital
importance, and he was left standing there for what seemed
to him at least half an hour, as though he were rather less
than a dog or a beggar. As time passed, and he still was
kept waiting, the fury that had possessed him as he stood
helpless before Anna's shut door in the afternoon, returned.
All his doubts and fears and respect melted away. What a

day he had had of suffering, of every kind of agitation! The ground alone that he had covered, going backwards and forwards between Lohm and Kleinwalde, was enough to tire out a man in health; and he was not in health, he was ill, fasting, shaking in every limb. While he had been suffering (leidend und schwitzend, he said to himself, grinding his teeth), this comfortable man in the gaiters and the aggressively clean cuffs had no doubt passed very pleasant and easy hours, had had three meals at least where he had had none, had smoked cigars and examined horses' legs, had ridden a little, driven a little, and would presently go round, now that the cool of the evening had come, to Kleinwalde, and sit in the twilight while Miss Estcourt called him Schatz. Oh, it was not to be borne! Dellwig was right—he must be annoyed, punished, at all costs shaken out of his lofty indifference. "Let me remind you," Klutz burst out in a voice that trembled with passion, "that I am still here, and still waiting, and that I have only two legs. Your horse, I see, has four, and is better able to stand and wait than I am."

Axel turned and stared at him. "Why, what is the matter?" he asked, astonished. "You are Manske's vicar? Yes, of course you are. I did not know you had anything very pressing to tell me. I am sorry I have kept you—come in."

He sent the mare to the stables, and led the way into his study. "Sit down," he said, pushing a chair forward, and sitting down himself by his writing-table. "Have a cigar?"

"No."

"No?" Axel stared again. "'No thank you' is the form prejudice prefers," he said.

"I care nothing for that."

"What is the matter, my dear Herr Klutz? You are very angry about something."

"I have been shamefully treated by a woman."

"It is what sometimes happens to young men," said Axel, smiling.

"I do not want cheap wisdom like that," cried Klutz, his eyes ablaze.

Axel's brows went up. "You are rude, my good Herr Klutz," he said. "Try to be polite if you wish me to help you. If you cannot, I shall ask you to go."

"I will not go."

"My dear Herr Klutz."

"I say I will not go till I have told you what I came to tell you. The woman is Miss Estcourt."

"Miss Estcourt?" repeated Axel, amazed. Then he added, "Call her a lady."

"She is a woman to all intents and purposes——"

"Call her a lady. It sounds better from a young man of your station."

"Of my station! What, a man with the brains of a man, the mind of a man, the sinews of a man, is not equal, is not superior, whatever his station may be, to a mere woman?"

"I will not discuss your internal arrangements. Has there, then, been some mistake about the salary you are to receive?"

"What salary?"

"For teaching Miss Letty Estcourt?"

"Pah—the salary. Love does not look at salaries."

"That sounds magnificent. Did you say love?"

"For weeks past, all the time that I have taught the niece, she has taken my flowers, my messages, at first verbal and at last written——"

"One moment. Of whom are we talking? I have met you with Miss Leech——"

"The governess? Ich danke. It is Miss Estcourt who has encouraged me and led me on, and now, after calling me her Lämmchen, takes away her niece and shuts her door in my face——"

"You have been drinking?"

"Certainly not," cried Klutz, the more indignantly because of his consciousness of the brandy.

"Then you have no excuse at all for talking in this manner of my neighbour?"

"Excuse! To hear you, one would think she must be a queen," said Klutz, laughing derisively. "If she were, I should still talk as I pleased. A cat may look at a king, I suppose?" And he laughed again, very bitterly, disliking even for one moment to imagine himself in the rôle of the cat.

"A cat may look as long and as often as it likes," said Axel, "but it must not get in the king's way. I am sure you can guess why."

"I have not come here to guess why about anything."

"Oh, it is not very abstruse—the cat would be kicked by somebody, of course."

"Oh, ho! Not if it could bite, and had what I have in its pocket."

"Cats do not have pockets, my dear Herr Klutz. You must have noticed that yourself. Pray, what is it that you have in yours?"

"A little poem she sent me in answer to one of mine. A little, sweet poem. I thought you might like to see how your future wife writes to another man."

"Ah—that is why you have called so kindly on me? Out of pure thoughtfulness. My future wife, then, is Miss Estcourt?"

"It is an open secret."

"It is, most unfortunately, not true."

"Ach—I knew you would deny it," cried Klutz, slapping his leg and grinning horribly. "I knew you would deny it when you heard she had been behaving badly. But denials do not alter anything—no one will believe them——"

Axel shrugged his shoulders. "Am I to see the poem?" he asked.

Klutz took it out and handed it to him. The twilight had come into the room, and Axel put the paper down a moment while he lit the candles on his table. Then he smoothed out its creases, and holding it close to the light read it attentively. Klutz leaned forward and watched his face. Not a muscle moved. It had been calm before, and it remained calm. Klutz could hardly keep himself from leaping up and striking that impassive face, striking some sort of feeling into it. He had played his big card, and Axel was quite unmoved. What could he do, what could he say, to hurt him?

"Shall we burn it?" inquired Axel, looking up from the paper.

"Burn it? Burn my poem?"

"It is such very great nonsense. It is written by a child. We know what child. Only one in this part can write English."

"Miss Estcourt wrote it, I tell you!" cried Klutz, jumping to his feet and snatching the paper away.

"Your telling me so does not in the very least convince me. Miss Estcourt knows nothing about it."

"She does—she did——" screamed Klutz, beside himself. "Your Miss Estcourt—your Braut—you try to brazen it out because you are ashamed of such a Braut. It is no use—

everyone shall see this, and be told about it—the whole
province shall ring with it—I will not be the laughing-
stock, but you will be. Not a labourer, not a peasant, but
shall hear of it——"

"It strikes me," said Axel, rising, "that you badly want
kicking. I do not like to do it in my house—it hardly seems
hospitable. If you will suggest a convenient place, neutral
ground, I shall be pleased to come and do it."

He looked at Klutz with an encouraging smile. Then
something in the young man's twitching face arrested his
attention. "Do you know what I think?" he said quickly, in
a different voice. "It is less a kicking that you want than a
good meal. You really look as though you had had nothing
to eat for a week. The difference a beefsteak would make to
your views would surprise you. Come, come," he said,
patting him on the shoulder, "I have been taking you too
seriously. You are evidently not in your usual state. When
did you have food last? What has Frau Pastor been about?
And your eyelids are so red that I do believe——" Axel
looked closer—"I do believe you have been crying."

"Sir," began Klutz, struggling hard with a dreadful
inclination to cry again, for self-pity is a very tender and
tearful sentiment, "Sir——"

"Let me order that beefsteak," said Axel kindly. "My cook
will have it ready in ten minutes."

"Sir," said Klutz, with the tremendous dignity that
immediately precedes tears, "Sir, I am not to be bribed."

"Well, take a cigar at least," said Axel, opening his case.
"That will not corrupt you as much as the beefsteak, and

will soothe you a little on your way home. For you must go home and get to bed. You are as near an illness as any man I ever saw."

The tears were so near, so terribly near, that, hardly knowing what he did, and sooner than trust himself to speak, Klutz took a cigar and lit it at the match Axel held for him. His hand shook pitifully.

"Now go home, my dear Klutz," said Axel very kindly. "Tell Frau Pastor to give you some food, and then get to bed. I wish you would have taken the beefsteak—here is your hat. If you like, we will talk about this nonsense later on. Believe me, it is nonsense. You will be the first to say so next week."

And he ushered him out to the steps, and watched him go down them, uneasy lest he should stumble and fall, so weak did he seem to be. "What a hot wind!" he exclaimed. "You will have a dusty walk home. Go slowly. Good-night."

"Poor devil," he thought, as Klutz without speaking went down the avenue into the darkness with unsteady steps, "poor young devil—the highest possible opinion of himself, and the smallest possible quantity of brains; a weak will and strong instincts; much unwholesome study of the Old Testament in Hebrew with Manske; a body twenty years old, and the finest spring I can remember filling it with all sorts of anti-parsonic longings. I believe I ought to have taken him home. He looked as though he would faint."

This last thought disturbed Axel. The image of Klutz fainting into a ditch and remaining in it prostrate all night, refused to be set aside; and at last he got his hat and went down the avenue after him.

But Klutz, who had shuffled along quickly, was nowhere to be seen. Axel opened the avenue gate and looked down the road that led past the stables to the village and parsonage, and then across the fields to Kleinwalde; he even went a little way along it, with an uneasy eye on the ditches, but he did not see Klutz, either upright or prostrate. Well, if he were in a ditch, he said to himself, he would not drown; the ditches were all as empty, dry, and burnt-up as four weeks' incessant drought and heat could make them. He turned back repeating that eminently consolatory proverb, Unkraut vergeht nicht, and walked quickly to his own gate; for it was late, and he had work to do, and he had wasted more time than he could afford with Klutz. A man on a horse coming from the opposite direction passed him. It was Dellwig, and each recognised the other; but in these days of mutual and profound distrust both were glad of the excuse the darkness gave for omitting the usual greetings. Dellwig rode on towards Kleinwalde in silence, and Axel turned in at his gate.

But the poor young devil, as Axel called him, had not fainted. Hurrying down the dark avenue, beyond Axel's influence, far from fainting, it was all Klutz could do not to shout with passion at his own insufferable weakness, his miserable want of self-control in the presence of the man he now regarded as his enemy. The tears in his eyes had given Lohm an opportunity for pretending he was sorry for him, and for making insulting and derisive offers of food. What could equal in humiliation the treatment to which he had been subjected? First he had been treated as a dog, and then, far worse, far, far worse and more difficult to bear with dignity, as a child. A beefsteak? Oh, the shame that seared his soul as he thought of it! This revolting specimen of the upper class had declared, with a hateful smile of indulgent superiority, that all his love, all his sufferings, all his just indignation, depended solely for their existence on whether he did or did not eat a beefsteak. Could coarse-mindedness and gross insensibility go further? "Thrice miserable nation!" he cried aloud, shaking his fist at the unconcerned stars, "thrice miserable nation, whose ruling class is composed of men so vile!" And, having removed his cigar in order to make this utterance, he remembered, with a great start, that it was Axel's.

He was in the road, just passing Axel's stables. The gate to the stableyard stood open, and inside it, heaped against one of the buildings, was a waggon-load of straw. Instantly Klutz became aware of what he was going to do. A lightning flash of clear purpose illumined the disorder of his brain. It was supper time, and no one was about. He ran inside the gate and threw the lighted cigar on to the straw; and because there was not an instantaneous blaze fumbled for his matchbox, and lit one match after the other, pushing them in a kind of frenzy under the loose ends of straw.

There was a puff of smoke, and then a bright tongue of flame; and immediately he had achieved his purpose he was terrified, and fled away from the dreadful light, and hid himself, shuddering, in the darkness of the country road.

CHAPTER XXIV

"It's in Stralsund," cried the princess, hurrying out into the Kleinwalde garden when first the alarm was given.

"It's in Lohm," cried someone else.

Anna watched the light in silence, her face paler than ordinary, her hair blown about by the hot wind. The trees in the dark garden swayed and creaked, the air was parching and full of dust, the light glared brighter each moment. Surely it was very near? Surely it was nearer than Stralsund? "It's in Lohm," cried someone with conviction; and Anna turned and began to run.

"Where are you running to, Aunt Anna?" asked Letty, breathlessly following her; for since the affair with Klutz she followed her aunt about like a conscience-stricken dog.

"The fire-engine—there is one at the farm—it must go——"

They took each other's hands and ran in silence. Between the gusts of wind they could hear the Lohm church-bells ringing; and almost immediately the single Kleinwalde bell began to toll, to toll with a forlorn, blood-curdling sound altogether different from its unmeaning Sunday tinkle.

In front of her house Frau Dellwig stood, watching the sky. "It is Lohm," she said to Anna as she came up panting.

"Yes—the fire-engine—is it ordered? Has it gone? No? Then at once—at once——"

"Jawohl, jawohl," said Frau Dellwig with great calm, the philosophic calm of him who contemplates calamities other than his own. She said something to one of the maids, who were standing about in pleased and excited groups laughing and whispering, and the girl shuffled off in her clattering wooden shoes. "My husband is not here," she explained, "and the men are at supper."

"Then they must leave their supper," cried Anna. "Go, go, you girls, and tell them so—look how terrible it is getting——"

"Yes, it is a big fire. The girl I sent will tell them. They say it is the Schloss."

"Oh, go yourself and tell the men—see, there is no sign of them—every minute is priceless——"

"It is always a business with the engine. It has not been required, thank God, for years. Mietze, go and hurry them."

The girl called Mietze went off at a trot. The others put their heads together, looked at their young mistress, and whispered. A stable-boy came to the pump and filled his pail. Everyone seemed composed, and yet there was that bloody sky, and there was that insistent cry for help from the anxious bell.

Anna could hardly bear it. What was happening down there to her kind friend?

"It is the Schloss," said the stable-boy in answer to a question from Frau Dellwig as he passed with his full pail, spilling the water at every step.

"Ach, I thought so," she said, glancing at Anna.

Anna made a passionate movement, and ran down the steps after the girl Mietze. Frau Dellwig could not but follow, which she did slowly, at a disapproving distance.

But Dellwig galloped into the yard at that moment, his horse covered with sweat, and his loud and peremptory orders extracted the ancient engine from its shed, got the horses harnessed to it, and after what Anna thought an eternity it rattled away. When it started, the whole sky to the south was like one dreadful sheet of blood.

"It is the stables," he said to Anna.

"Herr von Lohm's?"

"Yes. They cannot be saved."

"And the house?"

He shrugged his shoulders. "It's a windy night," he said, "and the wind is blowing that way. There are pine-trees between. Everything is as dry as cinders."

"The stables—are they insured?"

But Dellwig was off again, after the engine.

"What can we do, Letty? What can we do?" cried Anna, turning to Letty when the sound of the wheels had died away and only the hurried bell was heard above the whistling and banging of the wind. "It's horrible here, listening to that bell tolling, and looking at the sky. If I could throw one single bucketful of water on the fire I should not feel so useless, so utterly, utterly of no use or good for anything."

Neither of them had ever seen a fire, and horror had seized them both. The night seemed so dark, the world all round so black, except in that one dreadful spot. Anna knew Axel could not afford to lose money. From things Trudi had said, from things the princess had said, she knew it. There was at Lohm, she felt rather than knew, an abundance of everything necessary to ordinary comfortable living, as there generally is in the country on farms; but money was scarce, and a series of bad seasons, perhaps even one bad season, or anything out of the way happening, might make it very scarce, might make the further proper farming of the place impossible. Suppose the stables were not insured, where would the money come from to rebuild them? And the horses—she had heard that horses went mad with fright in a fire, and refused to leave their stables. And the house—suppose this cruel wind made the checking of the fire impossible, and it licked its way across the trees to Axel's house? "Oh, what can we do?" she cried to the frightened Letty.

"Let's go there," said Letty.

"Yes!" cried Anna, striking her hands together. "Yes! The carriage—Frau Dellwig, order the carriage—order Fritz to bring the carriage out at once. Tell him to be quick—quick!"

"The gracious Miss will go to Lohm?"

"Yes—call him, send for him—Fritz! Fritz!" She herself began to call.

"But——"

"Fritz! Fritz! Run, Letty, and see if you can find him."

"If I may be permitted to advise——"

"Fritz! Fritz! Fritz!"

"Call the herrschaftliche Kutscher Fritz," Frau Dellwig then commanded a passing boy in a loud and stern voice. "Not only mad, but improper," was her private comment. "She goes by night to her Bräutigam—to her unacknowledged Bräutigam." Even a possible burning Bräutigam did not, in her opinion, excuse such a step.

The darkness concealed the anger on her face, and Anna neither noticed nor cared for the anger in her voice, but began herself to run in the direction of the stables, leaving Frau Dellwig to her reflections.

"Princess Ludwig is looking for you everywhere, Aunt Anna," said Letty, coming towards her, having found Fritz and succeeded in making him understand what she wanted.

"Where is she? Is the carriage coming?"

"He said five minutes. She was at the house, asking the servants if they had seen you."

"Come along then, we'll go to her."

"I was afraid I should not find you here," said the princess as Anna came up the steps of the house into the light of the entry, "and that you had run off to Lohm to put the fire out.

My dear child, what do you look like? Come and look at yourself in the glass."

She led her to the glass that hung above the Dellwig hat-stand.

"I am just going there," said Anna, looking at her reflection without seeing it. "The carriage is being got ready now."

"Then I am coming too. What has the wind been doing to your hair? See, I knew you were running about bare-headed, and have brought you a scarf. Come, let me tie it over all these excited little curls, and turn you into a sober and circumspect young woman."

Anna bent her head and let the princess do as she pleased. "Herr Dellwig is afraid the fire will spread to the house," she said breathlessly. "Our engine has only just gone——"

"I heard it."

"It is such a lumbering thing, it will be hours getting there——"

"Oh, not hours. Half a one, perhaps."

"Are they insured?"

"The buildings? They are sure to be. But there is always a loss that cannot be covered—ach, Frau Dellwig, good-evening—you see we have taken possession of your house. To have no stables and probably no horses just when the busy time is beginning is terrible. Poor Axel. There—now you are tidy. Wait, let me fasten your cloak and cover up your pretty dress. Is Letty to come too?"

"Oh—if she likes. Why doesn't the carriage come?"

"It will be much better if Letty goes to bed," said the princess.

"Oh!" said Letty.

"It is long past her bedtime, and she has no hat, and nothing round her. Shall we not ask Frau Dellwig to send a servant with her home?"

"Aber gewiss——" began Frau Dellwig.

But Anna was out again on the steps, was shutting out the flaming sky with one hand while she strained her eyes into the darkness of the corner where the coach-house was. She could hear Fritz's voice, and the horses' hoofs on the cobbles, and she could see the light of a lantern jogging up and down as the stable-boy who held it hurried to and fro. "Quick, quick, Fritz," she cried.

"Jawohl, gnädiges Fräulein," came back the answer in the old man's cheery, reassuring tones. But it was like a nightmare, standing there waiting, waiting, the precious minutes slipping by, terrible things happening to Axel, and she herself unable to stir a step towards him.

"Take me with you—let me come too," pleaded Letty from behind her, slipping her hand into Anna's.

"Then tie a handkerchief or something round your head," said Anna, her eyes on the lantern moving about before the coach-house. Then the carriage lamps flashed out, and in another moment the carriage rattled up.

It was a ghostly drive. As the tops of the pine-trees swayed aside they caught glimpses of the red horror of the sky; and when they got out into the open Anna cried out involuntarily, for it seemed as if the whole world were on fire. The spire of Lohm church and the roofs of the cottages stood out clear and sharp in the fierce light. The horses, more and more frightened the nearer they drew, plunged and reared, and old Fritz could hardly hold them in. On turning the corner by the parsonage they were not to be induced to advance another yard, but swerved aside, kicking and terrified, and threatening every moment to upset the carriage into the ditch.

Anna jumped out and ran on. The princess, slower and more bulky, was helped out by Letty and followed after as quickly as she could. In the road and in the field opposite the stables the whole population was gathered, illuminated figures in eager, chattering groups. From the pump on the green in front of the schoolhouse, a chain of helpers had been formed, and buckets of water were being passed along from hand to hand to the engines; and there was no other water. The engines were working farther down the road, keeping the hose turned on to the trees between the stables and the house. There were clumps of pine-trees among them, and these were the trees that would carry the fire across to Axel's house. Men in the garden were hacking at them, the blows of their axes indistinguishable in the uproar, but every now and then one of the victims fell with a crash among its fellows still standing behind it.

"Oh, poor Axel, poor Axel!" murmured Anna, drawing her scarf across her face as she passed along to protect it from the intolerable heat. But she was an unmistakable figure in her blue cloak and white dress, stumbling on to where the engines were; and the groups of onlookers nudged each other and turned to stare after her as she passed.

"How did it happen?" she asked, suddenly stopping before a knot of women. They were in the act of discussing her, and started and looked foolish.

"No one knows," said the eldest, when Anna repeated her question. "They say it was done on purpose."

"Done on purpose!" echoed Anna, staring at the speaker. "Why, who would set fire to a place on purpose?"

But to this question no reply at all was forthcoming. They fidgeted and looked at each other, and one of the younger ones tittered and then put her hand before her mouth.

In the potato field across the road, two storks, whose nest for many springs had been on one of the roofs now burning, had placed their young ones in safety and were watching over them. The young storks were only a few days old, and had been thrown out of the nest by the parents, and then dragged away out of danger into the field, the parents mounting guard over their bruised and dislocated offspring, and the whole group transformed in the glow into a beautiful, rosy, dazzling white, into a family of spiritualised, glorified storks, as they huddled ruefully together in their place of refuge. Anna saw them without knowing that she saw them; there were three little ones, and one was dead. The princess and Letty found her standing beside them, watching the roaring furnace of the stableyard with parted lips and wide-open, horror-stricken eyes.

"Most of the horses were got out in time," said the princess, taking Anna's arm, determined that she should not again slip away, "and they say the buildings are fully insured, and he will be able to have much better ones."

"But the time lost—they can't be built in a day——"

"The man I spoke to said they were such old buildings and in such a bad state that Axel can congratulate himself that they have been burned. But of course there will always be the time lost. Have you seen him? Let us go on a little—we shall be scorched to cinders here."

Both Axel and Dellwig were superintending the working of the hose. "I do not want my trees destroyed," he said to Dellwig, with whom in the stress of the moment he had resumed his earlier manner; "they are not insured." He had watched the stables go with an impassiveness that struck several of the bystanders as odd. Dellwig and many others of the dwellers in that district were used to making a great noise on all occasions great and small, and they could by no means believe that it was natural to Axel to remain so calm at such a moment. "It is a great nuisance," Axel said more than once; but that also was hardly an adequate expression of feelings.

"They are well insured, I believe?" said Dellwig.

"Oh yes. I shall be able to have nice tight buildings in their place."

"They were certainly rather—rather dilapidated," said Dellwig, eyeing him.

"They were very dilapidated," said Axel.

Anna and the princess stood a little way from the engines watching the efforts to check the spread of the fire for some time before Axel noticed them. Manske, who had been the first to volunteer as a link in the human chain to the pump, bowed and smiled from his place at them, and was stared at in return by both women, who wondered who the begrimed and friendly individual could be. "It is the pastor," then said the princess, smiling back at him; on which Manske's smiles and bows redoubled, and he spilt half the contents of the bucket passing through his hands.

"So it is," said Anna.

"Take care there, No. 3!" roared Dellwig, affecting not to know who No. 3 was, and glad of an opportunity of calling the parson to order. Dellwig was making so much noise flinging orders and reprimands about, that a stranger would certainly have taken him for the frantic owner of the burning property.

"You see the pastor looks anything but alarmed," said the princess. "If Axel were losing much by this, Manske would be weeping into his bucket instead of smiling so kindly at us."

"So he would," said Anna, a little reassured by that cheerful and grimy countenance. Her eyes wandered to Axel, so cool and so vigilant, giving the necessary orders so quietly, losing no precious moments in trying to save what was past saving, and without any noise or any abuse getting what he wanted done. "It can't be a good thing, a fire like this," she said to herself. "Whatever they say, it can't be a good thing."

A huge pine-tree was dragged down at that moment, dragged in a direction away from its fellows, against a beech, whose branches it tore down in its fall, ruining the beech for ever, but smothering a few of its own twigs that had begun to burn among the fresh young leaves. Anna watched the havoc going on among poor Axel's trees in silence. "He can't not care," she said to herself. He turned round quickly at that moment, as though he heard her thinking of him, and looked straight into her eyes. "You here!" he exclaimed, striding across the road to her at once.

"Yes, we are here," replied the princess. "We cannot let our neighbour burn without coming to see if we can do anything. But seriously, I hear that it is a good thing for you."

"I prefer the less good thing that I had before, just now. But it is gone. I shall not waste time fretting over it."

He ran back again to stop something that was being done wrong, but returned immediately to tell them to go into his house and not stand there in the heat. "You look so tired—and anxious," he said, his eyes searching Anna's face. "Why are you anxious? The fire has frightened you? It is all insured, I assure you, and there is only the bother of having to build just now."

He could not stay, and hurried back to his men.

"We can go indoors a moment," said the princess, "and see what is going on in his house. It will be standing empty and open, and it is not necessary that he should suffer losses from thieves as well as from fire. His Mamsell is like all bachelors' Mamsells—losing, I am sure, no opportunity of feathering her nest at his expense."

Anna thought this a practical way of helping Axel, since the throwing of water on the flames was not required of her. She turned to call Letty, and found that no Letty was to be seen. "Why, where is Letty?" she asked, looking round.

"I thought she was behind us," said the princess.

"So did I," said Anna anxiously.

They went back a few steps, looking for her among the bystanders. They saw her at last a long way off, her handkerchief still round her head and her long thick hair blowing round her shoulders, rapt in contemplation of the fiery furnace. Then a shout went up from the people in the road, and they all ran back into the potato field. Anna and the princess stood rooted to the spot, clutching each other's hands. Letty looked round when she heard the shout, and began to run too. The flaming outer wall of the yard swayed and tottered and then fell outwards with a terrific crash and crackling, filling the road with a smoking heap of rubbish, and sending a shower of sparks on a puff of wind after the flying spectators.

The princess had certainly not run so fast since her girlhood as she did with Anna towards the spot in the field where they had last seen Letty. A crowd had gathered round it, they could see, an excited, gesticulating crowd. But they found her apparently unhurt, sitting on the ground, surrounded by sympathisers, and with someone's coat over her head. She looked up, very pale, but smiling apologetically at her aunt. "It's all gone," she said, pointing to her head.

"What is gone?" cried Anna, dropping on her knees beside her.

"Ach Gott, die Haare—die herrlichen Haare!" lamented a woman in the crowd. The smell of burnt hair explained what had happened.

Anna seized her in her arms. "You might have been killed—you might have been killed," she panted, rocking her to and fro. "Oh, Letty—who saved you?"

"Somebody put this beastly thing over my head—it smells of herrings. Sparks got into my hair, and it all frizzled up. Can't I take this off? It's out now—and off too."

The princess felt all over her head through the coat, patting and pressing it carefully; then she took the coat off, and restored it with effusive thanks to its sheepish owner. There was a murmur of sympathy from the women as Letty emerged, shorn of those flowing curls that were her only glory. "Oh Weh, die herrlichen Haare!" sighed the women to one another, "Oh Weh, oh Weh!" But the handkerchief tied so tightly round her head had saved her from a worse fate; she had been an ugly little girl before—all that had happened was that she looked now like an ugly little boy.

"I say, Aunt Anna, don't mind," said Letty; for her aunt was crying, and kissing her, and tying and untying the handkerchief, and arranging and rearranging it, and stroking and smoothing the singed irregular wisps of hair that were left as though she loved them. "I'm frightfully sorry—I didn't know you were so fond of my hair."

"Come, we'll go to the house," was all Anna said, stumbling on to her feet and putting her arm round Letty. And they clung to each other so close that they could hardly walk.

"We are going indoors a moment," called the princess, who was very pale, to Axel as they passed the engines.

He smiled across at her, and lifted his hat.

"I never saw anyone quite so composed," she observed to Anna, trying to turn her attention to other things. "Your man Dellwig, who has nothing to do with it all, is displaying the kind of behaviour the people expect on these occasions. I am sure that Axel has puzzled a great many people to-night."

Anna did not answer. She was thinking only of Letty. What a slender thread of chance had saved her from death, from a dreadful death, the little Letty who was under her care, for whom she was responsible, and whom she had quite forgotten in her stupid interest in Axel Lohm's affairs. Woman-like, she felt very angry with Axel. What did it matter to her whether his place burnt to ashes or not? But Letty mattered to her, her own little niece, poor solitary Letty, practically motherless, so ugly, and so full of good intentions. She had scolded her so much about Klutz; wretched Klutz, it was entirely his fault that Letty had been so silly, and yet only Letty had had the scoldings. Anna held her closer. In the light of that narrow escape how trivial, how indifferent, all this folly of love-talk and messages and anger seemed. For a short space she touched the realities, she saw life and death in their true proportion; and even while she was looking at them with clear and startled vision they were blurred again into indistinctness, they faded away and were gone—rubbed out by the inevitable details of the passing hour.

"I thought as much," said the princess, as they drew near the house. "All the doors wide open and the place deserted." And Anna came back with a start from the reality to the well-known dream of daily life, and immediately felt as though that other flash had been the dream and only this were real.

The hall was in darkness, but there was light shining through the chinks of a door, and they groped their way towards it. The house was as quiet as death. They could hear the distant shouts of the men cutting down the trees in the garden, and the blows of the axes. The princess pushed open the door behind which the light was, and they found themselves in Axel's study, where the candles he had lit in order to read Letty's poem were still guttering and flaring in the draught from the open window. A clock on the writing-table showed that it was past midnight. The room looked very untidy and ill-cared for.

"A man without a wife," said the princess, gazing round at the litter, composed chiefly of cigar-ashes and old envelopes, "is a truly miserable being. What condition can be more wretched than to be at the mercy of a Mamsell? I shall go and inquire into the whereabouts of this one. Axel will want some food when he comes in."

She took up one of the candles and went out. Letty had sat down at once on the nearest chair, and was looking very pale. Anna untied the handkerchief, and tried to arrange what was left of her hair. "I must cut off these uneven ends," she said, "but there won't be any scissors here."

"I say," began Letty, staring very hard at her.

"I believe you were terribly scared, you poor little creature," said Anna, struck by her pale face, and passing her hand tenderly over the singed head.

"Oh, not much. A bit, of course. But it was soon over. Don't worry. What will mamma say to my head?" And Letty's mouth widened into a grin at this thought. "I say," she began again, relapsing into solemnity.

"Well, what?" smiled Anna, sitting down on the same chair and putting her arm round her.

"You don't know the whole of that poetry business."

"That silly business with Herr Klutz? Oh, was there more of it? Oh, Letty, what did you do more? I am so tired of it, and of him, and of everything. Tell me, and then we'll forget it for ever."

"I'm afraid you won't forget it. I'm afraid I'm a bigger beast than you think, Aunt Anna," said Letty, with a conviction that frightened Anna.

"Oh, Letty," she said faintly, "what did you do?"

"Why, I—I will get it out—I—he was so miserable, and went on so when you didn't answer that poetry—that he sent with the heart, you know——"

"Oh yes, I know."

"Well, he was in such a state about it that I—that I made up a poem, just to comfort him, you know, and keep him quiet, and—and pretended it came from you." She threw back her head and looked up at her aunt. "There now, it's out," she said defiantly.

Anna was silent for a moment. "Was it—was it very affectionate?" she asked under her breath. Then she slipped down on to the floor, and put both her arms round Letty. "Don't tell me," she cried, laying her face on Letty's knees, "I don't want to know. Suppose you had been dreadfully hurt just now, burnt, or—or dead, what would it have mattered? Oh, we will forget all that ridiculous nonsense, and only never, never be so silly again. Let us be happy together, and finish with Herr Klutz for ever—it was all so stupid, and so little worth while." And she put up her face, and they both began to cry and kiss each other through their tears. And so it came about that Letty was in the same hour relieved of the burden on her conscience, of most of her hair, and was taken once again, and with redoubled enthusiasm, into Anna's heart. Logic had never been Anna's strong point.

CHAPTER XXV

When Axel came in two hours later, bringing Dellwig and Manske and two or three other helpers, farmers, who had driven across the plain to do what they could, he found his house lit up and food and drink set out ready in the dining-room.

Letty and Anna had had time to recover from their tears and vows, sundry small blisters on the back of Letty's neck had been treated with cotton wool, and they had emerged from their agitation to a calmer state in which the helping of the princess in the middle of the night to make somebody else's house comfortable was not without its joys. The Mamsell, no more able than the Kleinwalde servants to withstand the authority of the princess's name and eye, had collected the maids and worked with a will; and when, all danger of the fire spreading being over, Axel came in dirty and smoky and scorched, prepared to have to hunt himself in the dark house for the refreshment he could not but offer his helpers, he was agreeably surprised to find the lamp in the hall alight, and to be met by a wide-awake Mamsell in a clean apron who proposed to provide the gentlemen with hot water. This was very attentive. Axel had never known her so thoughtful. The gentlemen, however, with one accord refused the hot water; they would drink a glass of wine, perhaps, as Herr von Lohm so kindly suggested, and then go to their homes and beds as quickly as possible. Manske, by far the grimiest, was also the most decided in his refusal; he was a godly man, but he did not love supererogatory washings, under which heading surely a washing at two o'clock in the morning came. Axel left them in the hall a moment, and went into his study to fetch cigars; and there he found Letty, hiding behind the door.

"You here, young lady?" he exclaimed surprised, stopping short.

"Don't let anyone see me," she whispered. "Princess Ludwig and Aunt Anna are in the dining-room. I ran in here when I heard people with you. My hair is all burnt off."

"What, you went too near?"

"Sparks came after me. Don't let them come in——"

"You were not hurt?"

"No. A little—on the back of my neck, but it's hardly anything."

"I am very glad your hair was burnt off," said Axel with great severity.

"So am I," was the hearty reply. "The tangles at night were something awful."

He stood silent for a moment, the cigar-boxes under his arm, uncertain whether he ought not to enlighten her as to the reprehensibility of her late conduct in regard to her aunt and Klutz. Evidently her conscience was cloudless, and yet she had done more harm than was quite calculable. Axel was fairly certain that Klutz had set fire to the stables. Absolutely certain he could not be, but the first blaze had occurred so nearly at the moment when Klutz must have reached them on his way home, that he had hardly a doubt about it. It was his duty as Amtsvorsteher to institute inquiries. If these inquiries ended in the arrest of Klutz, the whole silly story about Anna would come out, for Klutz would be only too eager to explain the reasons that had driven him to the act; and what an unspeakable joy for the province, and what a delicious excitement for Stralsund! He could only hope that Klutz was not the culprit, he could only hope it fervently with all his heart; for if he was, the child peeping out at him so cheerfully from behind the door had managed to make an amount of mischief and bring an amount of trouble on Anna that staggered him. Such a little nonsense, and such far-reaching consequences! He could not speak when he thought of it, and strode past her indignantly, and left the room without a word.

"Now what's the row with him?" Letty asked herself, her finger in her mouth; for Axel had looked at her as he passed with very grave and angry eyes.

The men waiting in the hall were slightly disconcerted, on being taken into the dining-room, to find the Kleinwalde ladies there. None of them, except Manske, liked ladies; and ladies in the small hours of the morning were a special weariness to the flesh. Dellwig, having made his two deep bows to them, looked meaningly at his friends the other farmers; Miss Estcourt's private engagement to Lohm seemed to be placed beyond a doubt by her presence in his house on this occasion.

"How delightful of you," said Axel to her in English.

"I am glad to hear," she replied stiffly in German, for she was still angry with him because of Letty's hair, "I am glad to hear that you will have no losses from this."

"Losses!" cried Manske. "On the contrary, it is the best thing that could happen—the very best thing. Those stables have long been almost unfit for use, Herr von Lohm, and I can say from my heart that I was glad to see them go. They were all to pieces even in your father's time."

"Yes, they ought to have been rebuilt long ago, but one has not always the money in one's pocket. Help yourself, my dear pastor."

"Who is the enemy?" broke in Dellwig's harsh voice.

"Ah, who indeed?" said Manske, looking sad. "That is the melancholy side of the affair—that someone, presumably of my parish, should commit such a crime."

"He has done me a great service, anyhow," said Axel, filling the glasses.

"He has imperilled his immortal soul," said Manske.

"Have you such an enemy?" asked Anna, surprised.

"I did not know it. Most likely it was some poor, half-witted devil, or perhaps—perhaps a child."

"But I saw the blaze immediately after I passed you," said Dellwig. "You were within a stone's throw of the stables, going home. I had hardly reached them when the fire broke out. Did you then see no one on the road?"

"No, I did not," said Axel shortly. There was an aggressive note in Dellwig's voice that made him fear he was going to be very zealous in helping to bring the delinquent to justice.

"It was the supper hour," said Dellwig, musing, "and the men would all be indoors. Had you been to the stables, gnädiger Herr?"

"No, I had not. Take another glass of wine. A cigar? Whoever it was, he has done me a good turn."

"Beyond all doubt he has," said Dellwig, his eyes fixed on Axel with an odd expression.

"Some of us would have no objection to the same thing happening at our places," remarked one of the farmers jocosely.

"No objection whatever," agreed another with a laugh.

"If the man could be trusted to display the same discrimination everywhere," said the third.

"Joke not about crime," said Manske, rebuking them.

"The discrimination was certainly remarkable," said Dellwig.

"That is why I think it must have been done by some person more or less imbecile," said Axel; "otherwise one of the good buildings, whose destruction would really have harmed me, would have been chosen."

"He must be hunted down, imbecile or not," said Dellwig.

"I shall do my duty," said Axel stiffly.

"You may rely on my help," said Dellwig.

"You are very good," said Axel.

Dellwig's voice had something ominous about it that made Anna shiver. What a detestable man he was, always and at all times. His whole manner to-night struck her as specially offensive. "What will be done to the poor wretch when he is caught?" she asked Axel.

"He will be imprisoned," Dellwig answered promptly.

She turned her back on him. "Even though he is half-witted?" she said to Axel. "Are you obliged to look for him? Can't you leave him alone? He has done you a service, after all."

"I must look for him," said Axel; "it is my duty as Amtsvorsteher."

"And the gracious Miss should consider——" shouted Dellwig from behind.

"I'll consider nothing," said Anna, turning to him quickly.

"——should consider the demands of justice——"

"First the demands of humanity," said Anna, her back to him.

"Noble," murmured Manske.

"The gracious Miss's sentiments invariably do credit to her heart," said Dellwig, bowing profoundly.

"But not to her head, he thinks," said Anna to Axel in English, faintly smiling.

"Don't talk to him," Axel replied in a low voice; "the man so palpably hates us both. You must go home. Where is your carriage? Princess, take her home."

"Ach, Herr Dellwig, seien Sie so freundlich——" began the princess mellifluously; and despatched him in search of Fritz.

When they reached Kleinwalde, silent, wornout, and only desiring to creep upstairs and into their beds, they were met by Frau von Treumann and the baroness, who both wore injured and disapproving faces. Letty slipped up to her room at once, afraid of criticisms of her hairlessness.

"We have waited for you all night, Anna," said Frau von Treumann in an aggrieved voice.

"You oughtn't to have," said Anna wearily.

"We could not suppose that you were really looking at the fire all this time," said the baroness.

"And we were anxious," said Frau von Treumann. "My dear, you should not make us anxious."

"You might have left word, or taken us with you," said the baroness.

"We are quite as much interested in Herr von Lohm as Letty or Princess Ludwig can be," said Frau von Treumann.

"Nobody could tell us here for certain whether you had really gone there or not."

"Nor could anybody give us any information as to the extent of the disaster."

"We presumed the princess was with you, but even that was not certain."

"My dear baroness," murmured the princess, untying her shawl, "only you would have had a doubt of it."

"The reflection in the sky faded hours ago," said Frau vein Treumann.

"And yet you did not return," said the baroness. "Where did you go afterwards?"

"Oh, I'll tell you everything to-morrow. Good-night," said Anna, candle in hand.

"What! Now that we have waited, and in such anxiety, you will tell us nothing?"

"There really is nothing to tell. And I am so tired—good-night."

"We have kept the servants up and the kettle boiling in case you should want coffee."

"That was very kind, but I only want bed. Good-night."

"We too were weary, but you see we have waited in spite of it."

"Oh, you shouldn't have. You will be so tired. Good-night."

She went upstairs, pulling herself up each step by the baluster. The clock on the landing struck half-past three. Was it not Napoleon, she thought, who said something to the point about three-o'clock-in-the-morning courage? Had no one ever said anything to the point about three-o'clock-in-the-morning love for one's fellow-creatures? "Good-night," she said once more, turning her head and nodding wearily to them as they watched her from below with indignant faces.

She glanced at the clock, and went into her room dejectedly; for she had made a startling discovery: at three o'clock in the morning her feeling towards the Chosen was one of indifference verging on dislike.

CHAPTER XXVI

Looking up from her breakfast the morning after the fire to
see who it was riding down the street, Frau Manske beheld
Dellwig coming towards her garden gate. Her husband was
in his dressing-gown and slippers, a costume he affected
early in the day, and they were taking their coffee this fine
weather at a table in their roomy porch. There was,
therefore, no possibility of hiding the dressing-gown, nor
yet the fact that her cap was not as fresh as a cap on which
the great Dellwig's eyes were to rest, should be. She knew
that Dellwig was not a star of the first magnitude like Herr
von Lohm, but he was a very magnificent specimen of
those of the second order, and she thought him much more
imposing than Axel, whose quiet ways she had never
understood. Dellwig snubbed her so systematically and so
brutally that she could not but respect and admire him: she
was one of those women who enjoy kissing the rod. In a
great flutter she hurried to the gate to open it for him,
receiving in return neither thanks nor greeting. "Good-
morning, good-morning," she said, bowing repeatedly. "A
fine morning, Herr Dellwig."

"Where's Klutz?" he asked curtly, neither getting off his
horse nor taking off his hat.

"Oh, the poor young man, Herr Dellwig!" she began with
uplifted hands. "He has had a letter from home, and is
much upset. His father——"

"Where is he?"

"His father? In bed, and not expected to——"

"Where's Klutz, I say—young Klutz? Herr Manske, just step down here a minute—good-morning. I want to see your vicar."

"My vicar has had bad news from home, and is gone."

"Gone?"

"This very morning. Poor fellow, his aged father——"

"I don't care a curse for his aged father. What train?"

"The half-past nine train. He went in the post-cart at seven."

Dellwig jerked his horse round, and without a word rode away in the direction of Stralsund. "I'll catch him yet," he thought, and rode as hard as he could.

"What can he want with the vicar?" wondered Frau Manske.

"A rough manner, but I doubt not a good heart," said her husband, sighing; and he folded his flapping dressing-gown pensively about his legs.

Klutz was on the platform waiting for the Berlin train, due in five minutes, when Dellwig came up behind and laid a hand on his shoulder.

"What! Are you going to jump out of your skin?" Dellwig inquired with a burst of laughter.

Klutz stared at him speechlessly after that first start, waiting for what would follow. His face was ghastly.

"Father so bad, eh?" said Dellwig heartily. "Nerves all gone, what? Well, it's enough to make a boy look pale to have his father on his last——"

"What do you want?" whispered Klutz with pale lips. Several persons who knew Dellwig were on the platform, and were staring.

"Why," said Dellwig, sinking his voice a little, "you have heard of the fire—I did not see you helping, by the way? You were with Herr von Lohm last night—don't look so frightened, man—if I did not know about your father I'd think there was something on your mind. I only want to ask you—there is a strange rumour going about——"

"I am going home—home, do you hear?" said Klutz wildly.

"Certainly you are. No one wants to stop you. Who do you think they say set fire to the stables?"

Klutz looked as though he would faint.

"They say Lohm did it himself," said Dellwig in a low voice, his eyes fixed on the young man's face.

Klutz's ears burnt suddenly bright red. He looked down, looked up, looked over his shoulder in the direction from whence the train would come. Small cold beads of agitation stood out on his narrow forehead.

"The point is," said Dellwig, who had not missed a movement of that twitching face, "that you must have been with Lohm nearly till the time when—you went straight to him after leaving us?"

Klutz bowed his head.

"Then you couldn't have left him long before it broke out. I met him myself between the stables and his gate five minutes, two minutes, before the fire. He went past without a word, in a great hurry, as though he hoped I had not recognised him. Now tell me what you know about it. Just tell me if you saw anything. It is to both our interests to cut his claws."

Klutz pressed his hands together, and looked round again for the train.

"Do you know what will certainly happen if you try to be generous and shield him? He'll say you did it, and so get rid of you and hush up the affair with Miss Estcourt. I can see by your face you know who did it. Everyone is saying it is Lohm."

"But why? Why should he? Why should he burn his own——" stammered Klutz, in dreadful agitation.

"Why? Because they were in ruins, and well insured. Because he had no money for new ones; and because now the insurance company will give him the money. The thing is so plain—I am so convinced that he did it——"

They heard the train coming. Klutz stooped down quickly and clutched his bag. "No, no," said Dellwig, catching his arm and gripping it tight, "I shall not let you go till you say what you know. You or Lohm to be punished—which do you prefer?"

Klutz gave Dellwig a despairing, hunted look. "He—he——" he began, struggling to get the words over his dry lips.

"He did it? You know it? You saw it?"

"Yes, yes, I saw it—I saw him——"

Klutz burst into a wild fit of sobbing.

"Armer Junge," cried Dellwig very loud, patting his back very hard. "It is indeed terrible—one's father so ill—on his death-bed—and such a long journey of suspense before you——"

And sympathising at the top of his voice he looked for an empty compartment, hustled him into it, pushing him up the high steps and throwing his bag in after him, and then stood talking loudly of sick fathers till the last moment. "I trust you will find the Herr Papa better than you expect," he shouted after the moving train. "Don't give way—don't give way. That is our vicar," he exclaimed to an acquaintance who was standing near; "an only son, and he has just heard that his father is dying. He is overwhelmed, poor devil, with grief."

To his wife on his arrival home he said, "My dear Theresa,"—a mode of address only used on the rare occasions of supremest satisfaction—"my dear Theresa, you may set your mind at rest about our friend Lohm. The Miss will never marry him, and he himself will not trouble us much longer." And they had a short conversation in private, and later on at dinner they opened a bottle of champagne, and explaining to the servant that it was an aunt's birthday, drank the aunt's health over and over again, and were merrier than they had been for years.

CHAPTER XXVII

It was an odd and a nearly invariable consequence of Anna's cold morning bath that she made resolutions in great numbers. The morning after the fire there were more of them than ever. In a glow she assured herself that she was not going to allow dejection and discouragement to take possession of her so easily, that she would not, in future, be so much the slave of her bodily condition, growing selfish, indifferent, unkind, in proportion as she grew tired. What, she asked, tying her waist-ribbon with great vigour, was the use of having a soul and its longings after perfection if it was so absolutely the slave of its encasing body, if it only received permission from the body to flutter its wings a little in those rare moments when its master was completely comfortable and completely satisfied? She was ashamed of herself for being so easily affected by the heat and stress of the days with the Chosen. How was it that her ideals were crushed out of sight continually by the mere weight of the details of everyday existence? She would keep them more carefully in view, pursue them with a more unfaltering patience—in a word, she was going to be wise. Life was such a little thing, she reflected, so very quickly done; how foolish, then, to forget so constantly that everything that vexed her and made her sorry was flying past and away even while it grieved her, dwindling in the distance with every hour, and never coming back. What she had done and suffered last year, how indifferent, of what infinitely little importance it was, now; and yet she had been very strenuous about it at the time, inclined to resist and struggle, taking it over-much to heart, acting as though it were always going to be there. Oh, she would be wise in future, enjoying all there was to enjoy, loving all there was to love, and shutting her eyes to the rest. She would not, for instance, expect more from her Chosen than they, being as they were, could give. Obviously they could not give her more than they possessed, either of love, or comprehension, or charitableness, or anything else that was precious; and it was because she looked for more that she was for ever feeling disappointed. She would take them as they were, being happy in what they did give her, and ignoring what was less excellent. She herself was irritating, she was sure, and often she saw did produce an irritating effect on the Chosen. Of sundry minor failings, so minor that she was ashamed of having noticed them, but which had yet done much towards making the days difficult, she tried not to think. Indeed, they could hardly be made the subject of resolutions at all, they were so very trivial. They included a habit Frau von Treumann had of shutting every window and door that stood open, whatever the weather was, and however pointedly the others gasped for air; the exceedingly odd behaviour, forced upon her notice four times a day, of Fräulein Kuhräuber at table; and an insatiable curiosity displayed by the baroness in regard to other people's correspondence and servants—every postcard she read, every envelope she examined, every telegram, for some always plausible reason, she thought it her duty to open: and her interest in the doings of the maids was unquenchable. "These are little ways," thought Anna, "that don't matter." And she thought it impatiently, for the little ways persisted in obtruding themselves on her remembrance in the middle of her fine plans of future wisdom. "If we could all get outside our bodies, even for one day, and simply go about in our souls, how nice it would be!" she sighed; but meanwhile the souls of the Chosen were still enveloped in aggressive bodies that continued to shut windows, open telegrams, and convey food into their mouths on knives.

The one belonging to Frau von Treumann was at that moment engaged in writing with feverish haste to Karlchen, bidding him lose no time in coming, for mischief was afoot, and Anna was showing an alarming interest in the affairs of that specious hypocrite Lohm. "Come unexpectedly," she wrote; "it will be better to take her by surprise; and above all things come at once."

She gave the letter herself to the postman, and then, having nothing to do but needlework that need not be done, and feeling out of sorts after the long night's watch, and uneasy about Axel Lohm's evident attraction for Anna, she went into the drawing-room and spent the morning elaborately differing from the baroness.

They differed often; it could hardly be called quarrelling, but there was a continual fire kept up between them of remarks that did not make for peace. Over their needlework they addressed those observations to each other that were most calculated to annoy. Frau von Treumann would boast of her ancestral home at Kadenstein, its magnificence, and the style in which, with a superb disregard for expense, her brother kept it up, well knowing that the baroness had had no home more ancestral than a flat in a provincial town; and the baroness would retort by relating, as an instance of the grievous slanderousness of so-called friends, a palpably malicious story she had heard of manure heaps before the ancestral door, and of unprevented poultry in the Schloss itself. Once, stirred beyond the bounds of prudence enjoined by Karlchen, Frau von Treumann had begun to sympathise with the Elmreich family's misfortune in including a member like Lolli; but had been so much frightened by her victim's immediate and dreadful pallor that she had turned it off, deciding to leave the revelation of her full knowledge of Lolli to Karlchen.

The only occasions on which they agreed were when together they attacked Fräulein Kuhräuber; and more than once already that hapless young woman had gone away to cry. Anna's thoughts had been filled lately by other things, and she had not paid much attention to what was being talked about; but yet it seemed to her that Frau von Treumann and the baroness had discovered a subject on which Fräulein Kuhräuber was abnormally sensitive and secretive, and that again and again when they were tired of sparring together they returned to this subject, always in amiable tones and with pleasant looks, and always reducing the poor Fräulein to a pitiable state of confusion; which state being reached, and she gone out to hide her misery in her bedroom, they would look at each other and smile.

In all that concerned Fräulein Kuhräuber they were in perfect accord, and absolutely pitiless. It troubled Anna, for the Fräulein was the one member of the trio who was really happy—so long, that is, as the others left her alone. Invigorated by her cold tub into a belief in the possibility of peace-making, she made one more resolution: to establish without delay concord between the three. It was so clearly to their own advantage to live together in harmony; surely a calm talking-to would make them see that, and desire it. They were not children, neither were they, presumably, more unreasonable than other people; nor could they, she thought, having suffered so much themselves, be intentionally unkind. That very day she would make things straight.

She could not of course dream that the periodical putting to confusion of Fräulein Kuhräuber was the one thing that kept the other two alive. They found life at Kleinwalde terribly dull. There were no neighbours, and they did not like forests. The princess hardly showed herself; Anna was

English, besides being more or less of a lunatic—the combination, when you came to think of it, was alarming,—and they soon wearied of pouring into each other's highly sceptical ears descriptions of the splendours of their prosperous days. The visits of the parson had at first been a welcome change, for they were both religious women who loved to impress a new listener with the amount of their faith and resignation; but when they knew him a little better, and had said the same things several times, and found that as soon as they paused he began to expatiate on the advantages and joys of their present mode of life with Miss Estcourt, of which no one had been talking, they were bored, and left off being pleased to see him, and fell back for amusement on their own bickerings, and the probing of Fräulein Kuhräuber's tender places.

About midday Anna, who had been writing German letters all the morning helped by the princess, letters of inquiry concerning a new teacher for Letty, came round by the path outside the drawing-room window looking for the Chosen, and prepared to talk to them of concord. The window was shut, and she knocked on the pane, trying to see into the shady room. It was a broiling day, and she had no hat; therefore she knocked again, and held her hands above her head, for the sun was intolerable. She wore one of her last summer's dresses, a lilac muslin that in spite of its age seemed in Kleinwalde to be quite absurdly pretty. She herself looked prettier than ever out there in the light, the sun beating down on her burnished hair.

"Anna wants to come in," said Frau von Treumann, looking up from her embroidery at the figure in the sun.

"I suppose she does," said the baroness tranquilly.

Neither of them moved.

Anna knocked again.

"She will be sunstruck," observed Frau von Treumann.

"I think she will," agreed the baroness.

Neither of them moved.

Anna stooped down, and tried to look into the room, but could see nothing. She knocked again; waited a moment; and then went away.

The two ladies embroidered in silence.

"Absurd old maid," Frau von Treumann thought, glancing at the baroness. "As though a married woman of my age and standing could get up and open windows when she is in the room."

"Ridiculous old Treumann," thought the baroness, outwardly engrossed by her work. "What does she think, I wonder? I shall teach her that I am as good as herself, and am not here to open windows any more than she is."

"Why, you are here," said Anna, surprised, coming in at the door.

"Where have you been all the morning?" inquired Frau von Treumann amiably. "We hardly ever see you, dear Anna. I hope you have come now to sit with us a little while. Come, sit next to me, and let us have a nice chat."

She made room for her on the sofa.

"Where is Emilie?" Anna asked; Emilie was Fräulein Kuhräuber, and Anna was the only person in the house who called her so.

"She came in some time ago, but went away at once. She does not, I fear, feel at ease with us."

"That is exactly what I want to talk about," said Anna.

"Is it? Why, how strange. Last night, while we were waiting for you, the baroness and I had a serious conversation about Fräulein Kuhräuber, and we decided to tell you what conclusions we came to on the first opportunity."

"Certainly," said the baroness.

"It is surprising that Princess Ludwig should not have opened your eyes."

"It is truly surprising," said the baroness.

"But they are open. And they have seen that you are not very—not quite—well, not very kind to poor Emilie. Don't you like her?"

"My dear Anna, we have found it quite impossible to like Fräulein Kuhräuber."

"Or even endure her," amended the baroness.

"And yet I never saw a kinder, more absolutely amiable creature," said Anna.

"You are deceived in her," said Frau von Treumann.

"We have found out that she is here under false pretences," said the baroness.

"Which," said Frau von Treumann, unable to forbear glancing at the baroness, "is a very dreadful thing."

"Certainly," agreed the baroness.

Anna looked from one to the other. "Well?" she said, as they did not go on. Then the thought of her peace-making errand came into her mind, and her certainty that she only needed to talk quietly to these two in order to convince. "What do you think I came in to say to you?" she said, with a low laugh in which there was no mirth. "I was going to propose that you should both begin now to love Emilie. You have made her cry so often—I have seen her coming out of this room so often with red eyes—that I was sure you must be tired of that now, and would like to begin to live happily with her, loving her for all that is so good in her, and not minding the rest."

"My dear Anna," said Frau von Treumann testily, "it is out of the question that ladies of birth and breeding should tolerate her."

"Certainly it is," emphatically agreed the baroness.

"And why? Isn't she a woman like ourselves? Wasn't she poor and miserable too? And won't she go to heaven by and by, just as we, I hope, shall?"

They thought this profane.

"We shall all, I trust, meet in heaven," said Frau von Treumann gently. Then she went on, clearing her throat,

"But meanwhile we think it our duty to ask you if you know what her father was."

"He was a man of letters," said Anna, remembering the very words of Fräulein Kuhräuber's reply to her inquiries.

"Exactly. But of what letters?"

"She tried to give us that same answer," said the baroness.

"Of what letters?" repeated Anna, looking puzzled.

"He carried all the letters he ever had in a bag," said Frau von Treumann.

"In a bag?"

"In a word, dear child, he was a postman, and she has told you untruths."

There was a silence. Anna pushed at a neighbouring footstool with the toe of her shoe. "It is not pretty," she said after a while, her eyes on the footstool, "to tell untruths."

"Certainly it is not," agreed the baroness.

"Especially in this case," said Frau von Treumann.

"Yes, especially in this case," said Anna, looking up.

"We thought you could not know the truth, and felt certain you would be shocked. Now you will understand how impossible it is for ladies of family to associate with such a person, and we are sure that you will not ask us to do so, but will send her away."

"No," said Anna, in a low voice.

"No what, dear child?" inquired Frau von Treumann sweetly.

"I cannot send her away."

"You cannot send her away?" they cried together. Both let their work drop into their laps, and both stared blankly at Anna, who looked at the footstool.

"Have you made a lifelong contract with her?" asked Frau von Treumann, with great heat, no such contract having been made in her own case.

"I did not quite say what I mean," said Anna, looking up again. "I do not mean that I cannot really send her away, for of course I can if I choose. Exactly what I mean is that I will not."

There was a pause. Neither of the ladies had expected such an attitude.

"This is very serious," then observed Frau von Treumann helplessly. She took up her work again and pulled at the stitches, making knots in the thread. Both she and the baroness had felt so certain that Anna would be properly incensed when she heard the truth. Her manner without doubt suggested displeasure, but the displeasure, strangely enough, seemed to be directed against themselves instead of Fräulein Kuhräuber. What could they, with dignity, do next? Frau von Treumann felt angry and perplexed. She remembered Karlchen's advice in regard to ultimatums, and wished she had remembered it sooner; but who could have imagined the extent of Anna's folly? Never, she reflected, had she met anyone quite so foolish.

"It is a case for the police," burst out the baroness passionately, all the pride of all the Elmreichs surging up in revolt against a fate threatening to condemn her to spend the rest of her days with the progeny of a postman. "Your advertisement specially mentioned good birth as essential, and she is here under false pretences. You have the proofs in her letters. She is within reach of the arm of the law."

Anna could not help smiling. "Don't denounce her," she said. "I should be appalled if anything approaching the arm of the law got into my house. I'll burn the proofs after dinner." Then she turned to Frau von Treumann. "If you think it over," she said, "I know you will not wish me to be so merciless, so pitiless, as to send Emilie back to misery only because her father, who has been dead thirty years, was a postman."

"But, Anna, you must be reasonable—you must look at the other side. No Treumann has ever yet been required to associate——"

"But if he was a good man? If he did his work honestly, and said his prayers, and behaved himself? We have no reason for doubting that he was a most excellent postman," she went on, a twinkle in her eye; "punctual, diligent, and altogether praiseworthy."

"Then you object to nothing?" cried the baroness with extraordinary bitterness. "You draw the line nowhere? All the traditions and prejudices of gentlefolk are supremely indifferent to you?"

"Oh, I object to a great many things. I would have liked it better if the postman had really been the literary luminary poor Emilie said he was—for her sake, and my sake, and your sakes. And I don't like untruths, and never shall. But I do like Emilie, and I forgive it all."

"Then she is to remain here?"

"Yes, as long as she wants to. And do, do try to see how good she is, and how much there is to love in her. You have done her a real service," Anna added, smiling, "for now she won't have it on her mind any more, and will be able to be really happy."

The baroness gathered up her work and rose. Frau von Treumann looked at her nervously, and rose too.

"Then——" began the baroness, pale with outraged pride and propriety.

"Then really——" began Frau von Treumann more faintly, but feeling bound in this matter to follow her example. After all, they could always allow themselves to be persuaded to change their minds again.

Anna got up too, and they stood facing each other. Something awful was going to happen, she felt, but what? Were they, she wondered, both going to give her notice?

The baroness, drawn up to her full height, looked at her, opened her lips to complete her sentence, and shut them again. She was exceedingly agitated, and held her little thin, claw-like hands tightly together to hide how they were shaking. All she had left in the world was the pride of being an Elmreich and a baroness; and as, with the relentless years, she had grown poorer, plainer, more insignificant, so had this pride increased and strengthened, until, together with her passionate propriety and horror of everything in the least doubtful in the way of reputations, it had come to be the very mainspring of her being. "Then——" she began again, with a great effort; for she remembered how there had actually been no food sometimes when she was hungry, and no fire when she was cold, and no doctor when she was sick, and how severe weather had seemed to set in invariably at those times when she had least money, making her first so much hungrier than usual, and afterwards so much more sick, as though nature itself owed her a grudge.

"Oh, these ultimatums!" inwardly deplored Frau von Treumann; the baroness was very absurd, she thought, to take the thing so tragically.

And at that instant the door was thrown open, and without waiting to be announced, Karlchen, resplendent in his hussar uniform, and beaming from ear to ear, hastened, clanking, into the room.

"Karlchen! Du engelsgute Junge!" shrieked his mother, in accents of supremest relief and joy.

"I could not stay away longer," cried Karlchen, returning her embrace with vigour, "I felt impelled to come. I obtained leave after many prayers. It is for a few hours only. I return to-night. You forgive me?" he added, turning to Anna and bowing over her hand.

"Yes," she said, smiling; Karlchen had come this time, she felt, exactly at the right moment.

"I wrote this very morning——" began his mother in her excitement; but she stopped in time, and covered her confusion by once again folding him in her arms.

Karlchen was so much delighted by this unexpectedly cordial reception that he lost his head a little. Anna stood smiling at him as she had not done once last time. Yes, there were the dimples—oh, sweet vision!—they were, indeed, glorious dimples. He seized her hand a second time and kissed it. The pretty hand—so delicate and slender. And the dress—Karlchen had an eye for dress—how dainty it was! "Your kind welcome quite overcomes me," he said enthusiastically; and he looked so gay, and so intensely satisfied with himself and the whole world, that Anna laughed again. Besides, the uniform was really surprisingly becoming; his civilian clothes on his first visit had been melancholy examples of what a military tailor cannot do.

"Ah, baroness," said Karlchen, catching sight of the small, silent figure. He brought his heels together, bowed, and crossing over to her shook hands. "I have come laden with greetings for you," he said.

"Greetings?" repeated the baroness, surprised. Then an odd look of fear came into her eyes.

He had not meant to do it then; he had not been certain whether he would do it this time at all; but he was feeling so exhilarated, so buoyant, that he could not resist. "I was at the Wintergarten last night," he said, "and had a talk with your sister, Baroness Lolli. She dances better than ever. She sends you her love, and says she is coming down to see you."

The baroness made a queer little sound, shut her eyes, spread out her hands, and dropped on to the carpet as though she had been shot.

CHAPTER XXVIII

"Is Herr von Treumann gone?"

It was late the same afternoon, and Princess Ludwig had come into the bedroom where the Stralsund doctor was still vainly endeavouring to bring the baroness back to life, to ask Anna whether she would see Axel Lohm, who was waiting downstairs and hoped to be allowed to speak to her. "But is Herr von Treumann gone?" inquired Anna; and would not move till she was sure of that.

"Yes, and his mother has gone with him to the station."

Anna had not left the baroness's side since the catastrophe. She could not see the unconscious face on the pillow for tears. Was there ever such barbarous, such gratuitous cruelty as young Treumann's? His mother had been in once or twice on tiptoe, the last time to tell Anna that he was leaving, and would she not come down so that he might explain how sorry he was for having unwittingly done so much mischief? But Anna had merely shaken her head and turned again to the piteous little figure on the bed. Never again, she told herself, would she see or speak to Karlchen.

The movement with which she turned away was
expressive; and Frau von Treumann went out and heaped
bitter reproaches on Karlchen, driving with him to
Stralsund in order to have ample time to heap all that were
in her mind, and doing it the more thoroughly that he was
in a crushed condition and altogether incapable of
defending himself. For what had he really cared about the
baroness's relationship to Lolli? He had thought it a huge
joke, and had looked forward with enjoyment to seeing
Anna promptly order her out of the house. How could he,
thick of skin and slow of brain, have foreseen such a crisis?
He was very much in love with Anna, and shivered when
he thought of the look she had given him as she followed
the people who were carrying the baroness out of the room.
Certainly he was exceedingly wretched, and his mother
could not reproach him more bitterly than he reproached
himself. While she was vehemently pointing out the
obvious, he meditated sadly on the length of the journey he
had taken for worse than nothing. All the morning he had
been roasted in trains, and he was about to be roasted again
for a dreary succession of hours. His hot uniform, put on
solely for Anna's bedazzlement, added enormously to his
torments; and the distance between Rislar and Stralsund
was great, and the journey proportionately expensive—
much too expensive, if all you got for it was one
intoxicating glimpse of dimples, followed by a flashing
look of wrath that made you feel cold with the thermometer
at ninety. He had not felt so dejected since the eighties, he
reflected, in which dark ages he had been forced to fight a
duel. Karlchen had a prejudice against duelling; he thought
it foolish. But, being an officer—he was at that time a
conspicuously gay lieutenant—whatever he might think
about it, if anyone wanted to fight him fight he must, or
drop into the awful ranks of Unknowables. He had made a
joke of a personal nature, and the other man turned out to

have no sense of humour, and took it seriously, and expressed a desire for Karlchen's blood. Driving with his justly incensed mother through the dust and heat to the station, he remembered the dismal night he had passed before the duel, and thought how much his dejection then had resembled in its profundity his dejection now; for he had been afraid he was going to be hurt, and whatever people may say about courage nobody really likes being hurt. Well, perhaps after all, this business with Anna would turn out all right, just as that business had turned out all right; for he had killed his man, and, instead of wounds, had been covered with glory. Thus Karlchen endeavoured to snatch comfort as he drove, but yet his heart was very heavy.

"I hope," said his mother bitingly when he was in the train, patiently waiting to be taken beyond the sound of her voice, "I do hope that you are ashamed of yourself. It is a bitter feeling, I can tell you, the feeling that one is the mother of a fool."

To which Karlchen, still dazed, replied by unhooking his collar, wiping his face, and appealing with a heart-rending plaintiveness to a passing beer-boy to give him, um Gottes Willen, beer.

Axel was in the drawing-room, where the remains of Karlchen's valedictory coffee and cakes were littered on a table, when Anna came down. "I am so sorry for you," he said. "Princess Ludwig has been telling me what has happened."

"Don't be sorry for me. Nothing is the matter with me. Be sorry for that most unfortunate little soul upstairs."

Axel kissed Anna's right hand, which was, she knew, the custom; and immediately proceeded to kiss her other hand, which was not the custom at all. She was looking woebegone, with red eyelids and white cheeks; but a faint colour came into her face at this, for he did it with such unmistakable devotion that for the first time she wondered uneasily whether their pleasant friendship were not about to come to an end.

"Don't be too kind," she said, drawing her hands away and trying to smile. "I—I feel so stupid to-day, and want to cry dreadfully."

"Well then, I should do it, and get it over."

"I did do it, but I haven't got it over."

"Well, don't think of it. How is the baroness?"

"Just the same. The doctor thinks it serious. And she has no constitution. She has not had enough of anything for years—not enough food, or clothes, or—or anything."

She went quickly across to the coffee table to hide how much she wanted to cry. "Have some coffee," she said with her back to him, moving the cups aimlessly about.

"Don't forget," said Axel, "that the poor lady's past misery is over now and done with. Think what luck has come in her way at last. When she gets over this, here she is, safe with you, surrounded by love and care and tenderness—blessings not given to all of us."

"But she doesn't like love and care and tenderness. At least, if it comes from me. She dislikes me."

Axel could not exclaim in surprise, for he was not surprised. The baroness had appeared to him to be so hopelessly sour; and how, he thought, shall the hopelessly sour love the preternaturally sweet? He looked therefore at Anna arranging the cups with restless, nervous fingers, and waited for more.

"Why do you say that?" she asked, still with her back to him.

"Say what?"

"That when she gets over this she will have all those nice things surrounding her. You told me when first she came, that if she really were the poor dancing woman's sister I ought on no account to keep her here. Don't you remember?"

"Quite well. But am I not right in supposing that you will keep her? You see, I know you better now than I did then."

"If she liked being here—if it made her happy—I would keep her in defiance of the whole world."

"But as it is——?"

She came to him with a cup of cold coffee in her hands. He took it, and stirred it mechanically.

"As it is," she said, "she is very ill, and has to get well again before we begin to decide things. Perhaps," she added, looking up at him wistfully, "this illness will change her?"

He shook his head. "I am afraid it won't," he said. "For a little while, perhaps—for a few weeks at first while she still remembers your nursing, and then—why, the old self over again."

He put the untasted coffee down on the nearest table. "There is no getting away," he said, coming back to her, "from one's old self. That is why this work you have undertaken is so hopeless."

"Hopeless?" she exclaimed in a startled voice. He was saying aloud what she had more than once almost—never quite—whispered in her heart of hearts.

"You ought to have begun with the baroness thirty years ago, to have had a chance of success."

"Why, she was five years old then, and I am sure quite cheerful. And I wasn't there at all."

"Five ought really to be the average age of the Chosen. What is the use of picking out unhappy persons well on in life, and thinking you are going to make them happy? How can you make them be happy? If it had been possible to their natures they would have been so long ago, however poor they were. And they would not have been so poor or so unhappy if they had been willing to work. Work is such an admirable tonic. The princess works, and finds life very tolerable. You will never succeed with people like Frau von Treumann and the baroness. They belong to a class of persons that will grumble even in heaven. You could easily make those who are happy already still happier, for it is in them—the gratitude and appreciation for life and its blessings; but those of course are not the people you want to get at. You think I am preaching?" he asked abruptly.

"But are you not?"

"It is because I cannot stand by and watch you bruising yourself."

"Oh," said Anna, "you are a man, and can fight your way well enough through life. You are quite comfortable and prosperous. How can you sympathise with women like Else? Because she is not young you haven't a feeling for her—only indifference. You talk of my bruising myself—you don't mind her bruises. And if I were forty, how sure I am that you wouldn't mind mine."

"Yes, I would," said Axel, with such conviction that she added quickly, "Well—I don't want to talk about bruises."

"I hope the baroness will soon get over the cruel ones that singularly brutal young man has inflicted. You agree with me that he is a singularly brutal young man?"

"Absolutely."

"And I hope that when she is well again you will make her as happy as she is capable of being."

"If I knew how!"

"Why, by letting her go away, and giving her enough to live on decently by herself. It would be quite the best course to take, both for you and for her."

Anna looked down. "I have been thinking the same thing," she said in a low voice; she felt as though she were hauling down her flag.

"Perhaps you will let me help."

"Help?"

"Let me contribute. Why may I not be charitable too? If we join together it will be to her advantage. She need not know. And you are not a millionaire."

"Nor are you," said Anna, smiling up at him.

"We unfortunates who live by our potatoes are never millionaires. But still we can be charitable."

"But why should you help the baroness? I found her out, and brought her here, and I am the only person responsible for her."

"It will be much more costly than just having her here."

"I don't mind, if only she is happy. And I will not have you pay the cost of my experiments in philanthropy."

"Is Frau von Treumann happy?" he asked abruptly.

"No," said Anna, with a faint smile.

"Is Fräulein Kuhräuber happy?"

"No."

"Tell me one thing more," he said; "are you happy?"

Anna blushed. "That is a queer question," she said. "Why should I not be happy?"

"But are you?"

She looked at him, hesitating. Then she said, in a very small voice, "No."

Axel took two or three turns up and down the room. "I knew it," he said; and added something in German under his breath about Weiber. "After this, you will not, I suppose, receive young Treumann again?" he asked, coming to a halt in front of her.

"Never again."

"You have a difficult time before you, then, with his mother."

Anna blushed. "I am afraid I have," she admitted.

"You have a very difficult few weeks before you," he said. "The baroness probably dangerously ill, and Frau von Treumann very angry with you. I know Princess Ludwig does all she can, but still you are alone—against odds."

The odds, too, were greater than she knew. All day he had been officially engaged in making inquiries into the origin of the fire the night before, and every circumstance pointed to Klutz as the culprit. He had sent for Klutz, and Klutz, they said, had gone home. Then he sent a telegram after him, and his father replied that he was neither expecting his son nor was he ill. Klutz, then, had disappeared in order to avoid the consequences of what he had done; but it was only a question of days before the police brought him back again, and then he would tell the whole absurd story, and Pomerania would chuckle at Anna's expense. The thought of this chuckling made Axel cold with rage.

He stood looking out of the window at the parched garden, the drooping lilac-bushes, the hazy island across the water. The wind had dropped, and a gray film had drawn across the sky. At the bottom of the garden, under a chestnut-tree, Miss Leech was sewing, while Letty read aloud to her. The monotonous drone of Letty's reading, interrupted by her loud complaints each time a mosquito stung her, reached Axel's ears as he stood there in silence. A grim struggle was going on within him. He loved Anna with a passion that would no longer be hidden; and he knew that he must somehow hide it. He was so certain that she did not care about him. He was so certain that she would never dream of marrying him. And yet if ever a woman needed the protection of an all-enfolding love it was Anna at that moment "That child down there has made a pretty fair amount of mischief for a person of her age," he burst out with a vehemence that startled Anna.

"What child?" she said, coming up behind him and looking over his shoulder.

He turned round quickly. The feeling that she was so close to him tore away the last shred of his self-control. "You know that I love you," he said, his voice shaking with passion.

Her face in an instant was colourless. She stood quite still, almost touching him, as though she did not dare move. Her eyes were fixed on his with a frightened, fascinated look.

"You know it. You have known it a long time. Now what are you going to say to me?"

She looked at him without speaking or moving.

"Anna, what are you going to say to me?" he cried; and he caught up her hands and kissed them one after the other, hardly knowing what he did, beside himself with love of her.

She watched him helplessly. She felt faint and sick. She had had a miserable day, and was completely overwhelmed by this last misfortune. Her good friend Axel was gone, gone for ever. The pleasant friendship was done. In place of the friend she so much needed, of the friendship she had found so comforting, there was—this.

"Won't you—won't you let my hands go?" she said faintly. She did not know him again. Was it possible that this agony of love was for her? She knew herself so well, she knew so well what it was for which he was evidently going to break his heart. How wonderful, how pitiful beyond expression, that a good man like Axel should suffer anything because of her. And even in the midst of her fright and misery the thought would not be put from her that if she had happened to look like the baroness or Fräulein Kuhräuber, while inwardly remaining exactly as she was, he would not have broken his heart for her. "Oh, let me go——" she whispered; and turned her head aside, and shut her eyes, unable to look any longer at the love and despair in his.

"But what are you going to say to me?"

"Oh, you know—you know——"

"But you are so sorry always for people who suffer——"

"Oh, stop—oh, stop!"

"No, I won't stop; here have I been condemned to look on at you lavishing love on people who don't want it, don't like it, are wearied by it—who don't know how precious it is, how priceless it is, and how I am hungering and thirsting—oh, starving, starving, for one drop of it——" His voice shook, and he fell once more to covering her hands with kisses that seemed to scorch her soul.

This was very dreadful. Her soul had never been scorched before. Something must be done to stop him. She could not stand there with her eyes shut and her hands being kissed for ever. "Please let me go," she entreated faintly; and in her helplessness began to cry.

He instantly released her, and she stood before him crying. What a horrible thing it was to lose her friend, to be forced to hurt him. "I never dreamt that you—that you——" she wept.

"What, that I loved you?" he asked incredulously; but more gently, subdued by her deep distress. His face grew very hopeless. She was crying because she was sorry for him.

"I don't know—I think I did dream that—lately—once or twice—but I never dreamt that it was so bad—that you were such a—such a—such a volcano. Oh, Axel, why are you a volcano?" she cried, looking up at him, the tears rolling down her cheeks. "Why have you spoilt everything? It was so nice before. We were such friends. And now—how can I be friends with a volcano?"

"Anna, if you make fun of me——"

"Oh no, no—as though I would—as though I could do anything so unutterable. But don't let us be tragic. Oh, don't let us be tragic. You know my plans—you know my plans inside out, from beginning to end—how can I, how can I marry anybody?"

"Good God, those women—those women who are not happy, who have spoilt your happiness, they are to spoil mine now—ours, Anna?" He seized her arm as though he would wake her at all costs from a fatal sleep. "Do you mean to say that if it were not for those women you would be my wife?"

"Oh, if only you wouldn't be tragic——"

"Do you mean to say that is the reason?"

"Oh, isn't it sufficient——"

"No. If you cared for me it would be no reason at all."

She cried bitterly. "But I don't," she sobbed. "Not like that—not in that way. It is atrocious of me not to—I know how good you are, how kind, how—how everything. And still I don't. I don't know why I don't, but I don't. Oh, Axel, I am so sorry—don't look so wretched—I can't bear it."

"But what can it matter to you how I look if you don't care about me?"

"Oh, oh," sobbed Anna, wringing her hands.

He caught hold of her wrist. "See here, Anna. Look at me."

But she would not look at him.

"Look at me. I don't believe you know your own mind. I want to see into your eyes. They were always honest—look at me."

But she would not look at him.

"Surely you will do that—only that—for me."

"There isn't anything to see," she wept, "there really isn't. It is dreadful of me, but I can't help it."

"Well, but look at me."

"Oh, Axel, what is the use of looking at you?" she cried in despair; and pulled her handkerchief away and did it.

He searched her face for a moment in silence, as though he thought that if only he could read her soul he might understand it better than she did herself. Those dear eyes— they were full of pity, full of distress; but search as he might he could find nothing else.

He turned away without a word.

"Don't, don't be tragic," she begged, anxiously following him a few steps. "If only you are not tragic we shall still be able to be friends——"

But he did not look round.

A servant with a tray was outside coming in to take the coffee away. "Oh," exclaimed Anna, seeing that it was impossible to hide her tear-stained face from the girl's calm scrutiny, "oh, Johanna, the poor baroness—she is so ill—it is so dreadful——" And she dropped into a chair and hid herself in the cushions, weeping hysterically with an abandonment of woe that betokened a quite extraordinary affection for the baroness.

"Gott, die arme Baronesse," sympathised Johanna perfunctorily. To herself she remarked, "This very moment has the Miss refused to marry gnädiger Herr."

CHAPTER XXIX

What Anna most longed for in the days that followed was a mother. "If I had a mother," she thought, not once, but again and again, and her eyes had a wistful, starved look when she thought it, "if I only had a mother, a sweet mother all to myself, of my very own, I'd put my head on her dear shoulder and cry myself happy again. First I'd tell her everything, and she wouldn't mind however silly it was, and she wouldn't be tired however long it was, and she'd say 'Little darling child, you are only a baby after all,' and would scold me a little, and kiss me a great deal, and then I'd listen so comfortably, all the time with my face against her nice soft dress, and I would feel so safe and sure and wrapped round while she told me what to do next. It is lonely and cold and difficult without a mother."

The house was in confusion. The baroness had come out of her unconsciousness to delirium, and the doctors, knowing that she was not related to anyone there, talked openly of

death. There were two doctors, now, and two nurses; and
Anna insisted on nursing too, wearing herself out with all
the more passion because she felt that it was of so little
importance really to anyone whether the baroness lived or
died.

They were all strangers, the people watching this frail
fighter for life, and they watched with the indifference
natural to strangers. Here was a middle-aged person who
would probably die; if she died no one lost anything, and if
she lived it did not matter either. The doctors and nurses,
accustomed to these things, could not be expected to be
interested in so profoundly uninteresting a case; Frau von
Treumann observed once at least every day that it was
schrecklich, and went on with her embroidery; Fräulein
Kuhräuber cried a little when, on her way to her bedroom,
she heard the baroness raving, but she cried easily, and the
raving frightened her; the princess felt that death in this
case would be a blessing; and Letty and Miss Leech
avoided the house, and spent the burning days rambling in
woods that teemed with prodigal, joyous life.

As for Anna, to see her in the sick-room was to suppose her
the nearest and tenderest relative of the baroness; and yet
the passion that possessed her was not love, but only an
endless, unfathomable pity. "If she gets well, she shall
never be unhappy again," vowed Anna in those days when
she thought she could hear Death's footsteps on the stairs.
"Here or somewhere else—anywhere she likes—she shall
live and be happy. She will see that her poor sister has
made no difference, except that there will be no shadow
between us now."

But what is the use of vowing? When June was in its
second week the baroness slowly and hesitatingly turned

the corner of her illness; and immediately the corner was
turned and the exhaustion of turning it got over, she
became fractious. "You will have a difficult time," Axel
had said on the day he spoilt their friendship; and it was
true. The difficult time began after that corner was turned,
and the farther the baroness drew away from it, the nearer
she got to complete convalescence, the more difficult did
life for Anna become. For it resumed the old course, and
they all resumed their old selves, the same old selves, even
to the shadow of an unmentioned Lolli between them, that
Axel had said they would by no means get away from; but
with this difference, that the peculiarities of both Frau von
Treumann and the baroness were more pronounced than
before, and that not one of the trio would speak to either of
the other two.

Frau von Treumann was still firmly fixed in the house,
without the least intention apparently of leaving it, and she
spent her time lying in wait for Anna, watching for an
opportunity of beginning again about Karlchen. Anna had
avoided the inevitable day when she would be caught, but it
came at last, and she was caught in the garden, whither she
had retired to consider how best to approach the baroness,
hitherto quite unapproachable, on the burning question of
Lolli.

Frau von Treumann appeared suddenly, coming softly
across the grass, so that there was no time to run away.
"Anna," she called out reproachfully, seeing Anna make a
movement as though she wanted to run, which was exactly
what she did want to do, "Anna, have I the plague?"

"I hope not," said Anna.

"You treat me as if I had it."

Anna said nothing. "Why does she stay here? How can she stay here, after what has happened?" she had wondered often. Perhaps she had come now to announce her departure. She prepared herself therefore to listen with a willing ear.

She was sitting in the shade of a copper beech facing the oily sea and the coast of Rügen quivering opposite in the heat-haze. She was not doing anything; she never did seem to do anything, as these ladies of the busy fingers often noticed.

"Blue and white," said Anna, looking up at the gulls and the sky to give Frau von Treumann time, "the Pomeranian colours. I see now where they come from."

But Frau von Treumann had not come out to talk about the Pomeranian colours. "My Karlchen has been ill," she said, her eyes on Anna's face.

Anna watched the gulls overhead in the deep blue. "So has Else," she remarked.

"Dear me," thought Frau von Treumann, "what rancour."

She laid her hand on Anna's knee, and it was taken no notice of. "You cannot forgive him?" she said gently. "You cannot pardon a momentary indiscretion?"

"I have nothing to forgive," said Anna, watching the gulls; one dropped down suddenly, and rose again with a fish in its beak, the sun for an instant catching the silver of the scales. "It is no affair of mine. It is for Else to forgive him."

Frau von Treumann began to weep; this way of looking at it was so hopelessly unreasonable. She pulled out her handkerchief. "What a heap she must use," thought Anna; never had she met people who cried so much and so easily as the Chosen; she was quite used now to red eyes; one or other of her sisters had them almost daily, for the farther their old bodily discomforts and real anxieties lay behind them the more tender and easily lacerated did their feelings become.

"He could not bear to see you being imposed upon," said Frau von Treumann. "As soon as he knew about this terrible sister he felt he must hasten down to save you. 'Mother,' he said to me when first he suspected it, 'if it is true, she must not be contaminated.'"

"Who mustn't?"

"Oh, Anna, you know he thinks only of you!"

"Well, you see," said Anna, "I don't mind being contaminated."

"Oh, dear child, a young pretty girl ought to mind very much."

"Well, I don't. But what about yourself? Are you not afraid of—of contamination?" She was frightened by her own daring when she had said it, and would not have looked at Frau von Treumann for worlds.

"No, dear child," replied that lady in tones of tearful sweetness, "I am too old to suffer in any way from associating with queer people."

"But I thought a Treumann——" murmured Anna, more and more frightened at herself, but impelled to go on.

"Dear Anna, a Treumann has never yet flinched before duty."

Anna was silenced. After that she could only continue to watch the gulls.

"You are going to keep the baroness?"

"If she cares to stay, yes."

"I thought you would. It is for you to decide who you will have in your house. But what would you do if this—this Lolli came down to see her sister?"

"I really cannot tell."

"Well, be sure of one thing," burst out Frau von Treumann enthusiastically, "I will not forsake you, dear Anna. Your position now is exceedingly delicate, and I will not forsake you."

So she was not going. Anna got up with a faint sigh. "It is frightfully hot here," she said; "I think I will go to Else."

"Ah—and I wanted to tell you about my poor Karlchen—and you avoid me—you do not want to hear. If I am in the house, the house is too hot. If I come into the garden, the garden is too hot. You no longer like being with me."

Anna did not contradict her. She was wondering painfully what she ought to do. Ought she meekly to allow Frau von Treumann to stay on at Kleinwalde, to the exclusion, perhaps, of someone really deserving? Or ought she to brace herself to the terrible task of asking her to go? She thought, "I will ask Axel"—and then remembered that there was no Axel to ask. He never came near her. He had dropped out of her life as completely as though he had left Lohm. Since that unhappy day, she had neither seen him nor heard of him. Many times did she say to herself, "I will ask Axel," and always the remembrance that she could not came with a shock of loneliness; and then she would drop into the train of thought that ended with "if I had a mother," and her eyes growing wistful.

"Perhaps it is the hot weather," she said suddenly, an evening or two later, after a long silence, to the princess. They had been speaking of servants before that.

"You think it is the hot weather that makes Johanna break the cups?"

"That makes me think so much of mothers."

The princess turned her head quickly, and examined Anna's face. It was Sunday evening, and the others were at church. The baroness, whose recovery was slow, was up in her room.

"What mothers?" naturally inquired the princess.

"I think this everlasting heat is dreadful," said Anna plaintively. "I have no backbone left. I am all limp, and soft, and silly. In cold weather I believe I wouldn't want a mother half so badly."

"So you want a mother?" said the princess, taking Anna's hand in hers and patting it kindly. She thought she knew why. Everyone in the house saw that something must have been said to Axel Lohm to make him keep away so long. Perhaps Anna was repenting, and wanted a mother's help to set things right again.

"I always thought it would be so glorious to be independent," said Anna, "and now somehow it isn't. It is tiring. I want someone to tell me what I ought to do, and to see that I do it. Besides petting me. I long and long sometimes to be petted."

The princess looked wise. "My dear," she said, shaking her head, "it is not a mother that you want. Do you know the couplet:—

Man bedarf der Leitung

Und der männlichen Begleitung?

A truly excellent couplet."

Anna smiled. "That is the German idea of female bliss— always to be led round by the nose by some husband."

"Not some husband, my dear—one's own husband. You may call it leading by the nose if you like. I can only say that I enjoyed being led by mine, and have missed it grievously ever since."

"But you had found the right man."

"It is not very difficult to find the right man."

"Yes it is—very difficult indeed."

"I think not," said the princess. "He is never far off. Sometimes, even, he is next door." And she gazed over Anna's head at the ceiling with elaborate unconsciousness.

"And besides," said Anna, "why does a woman everlastingly want to be led and propped? Why can't she go about the business of life on her own feet? Why must she always lean on someone?"

"You said just now it is because it is hot."

"The fact is," said Anna, "that I am not clever enough to see my way through puzzles. And that depresses me."

"I well know that you must be puzzled."

"Yes, it is puzzling, isn't it? I can talk to you about it, for of course you see it all. It seems so absurd that the only result of my trying to make people happy is to make everyone, including myself, wretched. That is waste, isn't it. Waste, I mean, of happiness. For I, at least, was happy before."

"And, my dear, you will be happy again."

Anna knit her brows in painful thought. "If by being wretched I had managed to make the others happy it wouldn't have been so bad. At least it wouldn't have been so completely silly. The only thing I can think of is that I must have hit upon the wrong people."

"I Gott bewahre!" cried the princess with energy. "They are all alike. Send these away, you get them back in a different shape. Faces and names would be different, never the women. They would all be Treumanns and Elmreichs, and not a single one worth anything in the whole heap."

"Well, I shall not desert them—Else and Emilie, I mean. They need help, both of them. And after all, it is simple selfishness for ever wanting to be happy oneself. I have begun to see that the chief thing in life is not to be as happy as one can, but to be very brave."

The princess sighed. "Poor Axel," she said.

Anna started, and blushed violently. "Pray what has my being brave to do with Herr von Lohm?" she inquired severely.

"Why, you are going to be brave at his expense, poor man. You must not expect anything from me, my dear, but common sense. You give up all hope of being happy because you think it your duty to go on sacrificing him and yourself to a set of thankless, worthless women, and you call it being brave. I call it being unnatural and silly."

"It has never been a question of Herr von Lohm," said Anna coldly, indeed freezingly. "What claims has he on me? My plans were all made before I knew that he existed."

"Oh, my dear, your plans are very irritating things. The only plan a sensible young woman ought to make is to get as good a husband as possible as quickly as she can."

"Why," said Anna, rising in her indignation, and preparing to leave a princess suddenly become objectionable, "why, you are as bad as Susie!"

"Susie?" said the princess, who had not heard of her by that name. "Was Susie also one who told you the truth?"

But Anna walked out of the room without answering, in a very dignified manner; went into the loneliest part of the garden; sat down behind some bushes; and cried.

She looked back on those childish tears afterwards, and on all that had gone before, as the last part of a long sleep; a sleep disturbed by troubling and foolish dreams, but still only a sleep and only dreams. She woke up the very next day, and remained wide awake after that for the rest of her life.

CHAPTER XXX

Anna drove into Stralsund the next morning to her banker, accompanied by Miss Leech. When they passed Axel's house she saw that his gate-posts were festooned with wreaths, and that garlands of flowers were strung across the gateway, swaying to and fro softly in the light breeze. "Why, how festive it looks," she exclaimed, wondering.

"Yesterday was Herr von Lohm's birthday," said Miss Leech. "I heard Princess Ludwig say so."

"Oh," said Anna. Her tone was piqued. She turned her head away, and looked at the hay-fields on the opposite side of the road. Axel must have birthdays, of course, and why should he not put things round his gate-posts if he wanted to? Yet she would not look again, and was silent the rest of

the way; nor was it of any use for Miss Leech to attempt to
while away the long drive with pleasant conversation. Anna
would not talk; she said it was too hot to talk. What she
was thinking was that men were exceedingly horrid, all of
them, and that life was a snare.

Far from being festive, however, Axel's latest birthday was
quite the most solitary he had yet spent. The cheerful
garlands had been put up by an officious gardener on his
own initiative. No one, except Axel's own dependents, had
passed beneath them to wish him luck. Trudi had
telegraphed her blessings, administering them thus in their
easiest form. His Stralsund friends had apparently forgotten
him; in other years they had been glad of the excuse the
birthday gave for driving out into the country in June, but
this year the astonished Mamsell saw her birthday cake
remain untouched and her baked meats waiting vainly for
somebody to come and eat them.

Axel neither noticed nor cared. The haymaking season had
just begun, and besides his own affairs he was preoccupied
by Anna's. If she had not been shut up so long in the
baroness's sick-room she would have met him often
enough. She thought he never intended to come near her
again, and all the time, whenever he could spare a moment
and often when he could not, he was on her property,
watching Dellwig's farming operations. She should not
suffer, he told himself, because he loved her; she should
not be punished because she was not able to love him. He
would go on doing what he could for her, and was
certainly, at his age, not going to sulk and leave her to face
her difficulties alone.

The first time he met Dellwig on these incursions into
Anna's domain, he expected to be received with a scowl;

but Dellwig did not scowl at all; was on the contrary quite affable, even volunteering information about the work he had in hand. Nor had he been after all offensively zealous in searching for the person who had set the stables on fire; and luckily the Stralsund police had not been very zealous either. Klutz was looked for for a little while after Axel had denounced him as the probable culprit, but the matter had been dropped, apparently, and for the last ten days nothing more had been said or done. Axel was beginning to hope that the whole thing had blown over, that there was to be no unpleasantness after all for Anna. Hearing that the baroness was nearly well, he decided to go and call at Kleinwalde as though nothing had happened. Some time or other he must meet Anna. They could not live on adjoining estates and never see each other. The day after his birthday he arranged to go round in the afternoon and take up the threads of ordinary intercourse again, however much it made him suffer.

Meanwhile Anna did her business in Stralsund, discovered on interviewing her banker that she had already spent more than two-thirds of a whole year's income, lunched pensively after that on ices with Miss Leech, walked down to the quay and watched the unloading of the fishing-smacks while Fritz and the horses had their dinner, was very much stared at by the inhabitants, who seldom saw anything so pretty, and finally, about two o'clock, started again for home.

As they drew near Axel's gate, and she was preparing to turn her face away from its ostentatious gaiety, a closed Droschke came through it towards them, followed at a short distance by a second.

Miss Leech said nothing, strange though this spectacle was
on that quiet road, for she felt that these were the departing
guests, and, like Anna, she wondered how a man who loved
in vain could have the heart to give parties. Anna said
nothing either, but watched the approaching Droschkes
curiously. Axel was sitting in the first one, on the side near
her. He wore his ordinary farming clothes, the Norfolk
jacket, and the soft green hat. There were three men with
him, seedy-looking individuals in black coats. She bowed
instinctively, for he was looking out of the window full at
her, but he took no notice. She turned very white.

The second Droschke contained four more queer-looking
persons in black clothes. When they had passed, Fritz
pulled up his horses of his own accord, and twisting
himself round stared after the receding cloud of dust.

Anna had been cut by Axel; but it was not that that made
her turn so white—it was something in his face. He had
looked straight at her, and he had not seen her.

"Who are those people?" she asked Fritz in a voice that
faltered, she did not know why.

Fritz did not answer. He stared down the road after the
Droschkes, shook his head, began to scratch it, jerked
himself round again to his horses, drove on a few yards,
pulled them up a second time, looked back, shook his head,
and was silent.

"Fritz, do you know them?" Anna asked more
authoritatively.

But Fritz only mumbled something soothing and drove on.

Anna had not failed to notice the old man's face as he watched the departing Droschkes; it wore an oddly amazed and scared expression. Her heart seemed to sink within her like a stone, yet she could give herself no reason for it. She tried to order him to turn up the avenue to Axel's house, but her lips were dry, and the words would not come; and while she was struggling to speak the gate was passed. Then she was relieved that it was passed, for how could she, only because she had a presentiment of trouble, go to Axel's house? What did she think of doing there? Miss Leech glanced at her, and asked if anything was the matter.

"No," said Anna in a whisper, looking straight before her. Nor was there anything the matter; only that blind look on Axel's face, and the strange feeling in her heart.

A knot of people stood outside the post office talking eagerly. They all stopped talking to stare at Anna when the carriage came round the corner. Fritz whipped up his horses and drove past them at a gallop.

"Wait—I want to get out," cried Anna as they came to the parsonage. "Do you mind waiting?" she asked Miss Leech. "I want to speak to Herr Pastor. I will not be a moment."

She went up the little trim path to the porch. The maid-of-all-work was clearing away the coffee from the table. Frau Manske came bustling out when she heard Anna's voice asking for her husband. She looked extraordinarily excited. "He has not come back yet," she cried before Anna could speak, "he is still at the Schloss. Gott Du Allmächtiger, did one ever hear of anything so terrible?"

Anna looked at her, her face as white as her dress. "Tell me," she tried to say; but no sound passed her lips. She made a great effort, and the words came in a whisper: "Tell me," she said.

"What, the gracious Miss has not heard? Herr von Lohm has been arrested."

It was impossible not to enjoy imparting so tremendous a piece of news, however genuinely shocked one might be. Frau Manske brought it out with a ring of pride. It would not be easy to beat, she felt, in the way of news. Then she remembered the gossip about Anna and Axel, and observed her with increased interest. Was she going to faint? It would be the only becoming course for her to take if it were true that there had been courting.

But Anna, whose voice had failed her before, when once she had heard what it was that had happened, seemed curiously cold and composed.

"What was he accused of?" was all she asked; so calmly, Frau Manske afterwards told her friends, that it was not even womanly in the face of so great a misfortune.

"He set fire to the stables," said Frau Manske.

"It is a lie," said Anna; also, as Frau Manske afterwards pointed out to her friends, an unwomanly remark.

"He did it himself to get the insurance money."

"It is a lie," repeated Anna, in that cold voice.

"Eye-witnesses will swear to it."

"They will lie," said Anna again; and turned and walked away. "Go on," she said to Fritz, taking her place beside Miss Leech.

She sat quite silent till they were near the house. Then she called to the coachman to stop. "I am going into the forest for a little while," she said, jumping out "You drive on home." And she crossed the road quickly, her white dress fluttering for a moment between the pine-trunks, and then disappearing in the soft green shadow.

Miss Leech drove on alone, sighing gently. Something was troubling her dear Miss Estcourt. Something out of the ordinary had happened. She wished she could help her. She drove on, sighing.

Directly the road was out of sight, Anna struck back again to the left, across the moss and lichen, towards the place where she knew there was a path that led to Lohm. She walked very straight and very quickly. She did not miss her way, but found the path and hastened her steps to a run. What were they doing to Axel? She was going to his house, alone. People would talk. Who cared? And when she had heard all that could be told her there, she was going to Axel himself. People would talk. Who cared? The laughable indifference of slander, when big issues of life and death were at stake! All the tongues of all the world should not frighten her away from Axel. Her eyes had a new look in them. For the first time she was wide awake, was facing life as it is without dreams, facing its absolute cruelty and pitilessness. This was life, these were the realities— suffering, injustice, and shame; not to be avoided apparently by the most honourable and innocent of men; but at least to be fought with all the weapons in one's power, with unflinching courage to the end, whatever that end might be. That was what one needed most, of all the gifts of the gods—not happiness—oh, foolish, childish dream! how could there be happiness so long as men were wicked?—but courage. That blind look on Axel's face—no, she would not think of that; it tore her heart. She stumbled a little as she ran—no, she would not think of that.

Out in the open, between the forest and Lohm, she met Manske. "I was coming to you," he said.

"I am going to him," said Anna.

"Oh, my dear young lady!" cried Manske; and two big tears rolled down his face.

"Don't cry," she said, "it does not help him."

"How can I not do so after seeing what I have this day seen?"

She hurried on. "Come," she said, "we must not waste time. He needs help. I am going to his house to see what I can do. Where did they take him?"

"They took him to prison."

"Where?"

"Stralsund."

"Will he be there long?"

"Till after the trial."

"And that will be?"

"God knows."

"I am going to him. Come with me. We will take his horses."

"Oh, dear Miss, dear Miss," cried Manske, wringing his hands, "they will not let us see him—you they will not let in under any circumstances, and me only across mountains of obstacles. The official who conducted the arrest, when I prayed for permission to visit my dear patron, was brutality itself. 'Why should you visit him?' he asked, sneering. 'The prison chaplain will do all that is needful for his soul.' 'Let it be, Manske,' said my dear patron, but still I prayed. 'I cannot give you permission,' said the man at last, weary of my importunity, 'it rests with my chief. You must go to him.'"

"Who is the chief?"

"I know not. I know nothing. My head is in a whirl."

"He must be somewhere in Stralsund. We will find him, if we have to ask from door to door. And I'll get permission for myself."

"Oh, dearest Miss, none will be given you. The man said only his nearest relatives, and those only very seldom—for I asked all I could, I felt the moments were priceless—my dear patron spoke not a word. 'His wife, if he has one,' said the man, making hideous pleasantries—he well knew there is no wife—or his Braut, if there is one, or a brother or a sister, but no one else."

"Do his brothers and Trudi know?"

"I at once telegraphed to them."

"Then they will be here to-night."

The women and children in the village ran out to look at
Anna as she passed. She did not see them. Axel's house
stood open. The Mamsell, overcome by the shame of
having been in such a service, was in hysterics in the
kitchen, and the inspector, a devoted servant who loved his
master, was upbraiding her with bitterest indignation for
daring to say such things of such a master. The Mamsell's
laments and the inspector's furious reproaches echoed
through the empty house. The door, like the gate, was
garlanded with flowers. Little more than an hour had gone
by since Axel passed out beneath them to ruin.

Anna went straight to the study. His papers were lying
about in disorder; the drawer of the writing-table was
unlocked, and his keys hung in it He had been writing
letters, evidently, for an unfinished one lay on the table.
She stood a moment quite still in the silent room. Manske
had gone to find the coachman, and she could hear his steps
on the stones beneath the open windows. The desolation of
the deserted room, the terrible sense of misfortune worse
than death that brooded over it, struck her like a blow that
for ever destroyed her cheerful youth. She never forgot the
look and the feeling of that room. She went to the writing-
table, dropped on her knees, and laid her cheek, with an
abandonment of tenderness, on the open, unfinished letter.
"How are such things possible—how are they possible——
" she murmured passionately, shutting her eyes to press
back the useless tears. "So useless to cry, so useless," she
repeated piteously, as she felt the scalding tears, in spite of
all her efforts to keep them back, stealing through her
eyelashes. And everything else that she did or could do—

how useless. What could she do for him, who had no claim
on him at all? How could she reach him across this gulf of
misery? Yes, it was good to be brave in this world, it was
good to have courage, but courage without weapons, of
what use was it? She was a woman, a stranger in a strange
land, she had no friends, no influence—she was useless.
Manske found her kneeling there, holding the writing-table
tightly in her outstretched arms, pressing her bosom against
it as though it were something that could feel, her eyes
shut, her face a desolation. "Do not cry," he begged in his
turn, "dearest Miss, do not cry—it cannot help him."

They locked up his papers and everything that they thought
might be of value before they left. Manske took the keys.
Anna half put out her hand for them, then dropped it at her
side. She had less claim than Manske: he was Axel's pastor;
she was nothing to him at all.

They left the dog-cart at the entrance to the town and went
in search of a Droschke. Manske's weather-beaten face
flushed a dull red when he gave the order to drive to the
prison. The prison was in a by-street of shabby houses.
Heads appeared at the windows of the houses as the
Droschke rattled up over the rough stones, and the children
playing about the doors and gutters stopped their games
and crowded round to stare.

They went up the dirty steps and rang the bell. The door
was immediately opened a few inches by an official who
shouted "The visiting hour is past," and shut it again.

Manske rang a second time.

"Well, what do you want?" asked the man angrily, thrusting
out his head.

Manske stated, in the mildest, most conciliatory tones, that he would be infinitely obliged if he would tell him what steps he ought to take to obtain permission to visit one of the inmates.

"You must have a written order," snapped the man, preparing to shut the door again. The street children were clustering at the bottom of the steps, listening eagerly.

"To whom should I apply?" asked Manske.

"To the judge who has conducted the preliminary inquiries."

The door was slammed, and locked from within with a great noise of rattling keys. The sound of the keys made Anna feel faint; Axel was on the other side of that ostentation of brute force. She leaned against the wall shivering. The children tittered; she was a very fine lady, they thought, to have friends in there.

"The judge who conducted the preliminary inquiries," repeated Manske, looking dazed. "Who may he be? Where shall we find him? I fear I am sadly inexperienced in these matters."

There was nothing to be done but to face the official's wrath once more. He timidly rang the bell again. This time he was kept waiting. There was a little round window in the door, and he could see the man on the other side leaning against a table trimming his nails. The man also could see him. Manske began to knock on the glass in his desperation. The man remained absorbed by his nails.

Anna was suffering a martyrdom. Her head drooped lower and lower. The children laughed loud. Just then heavy steps were heard approaching on the pavement, and the children fled with one accord. Immediately afterwards an official, apparently of a higher grade than the man within, came up. He glanced curiously at the two suppliants as he thrust his hand into his pocket and pulled out a key. Before he could fit it in the lock the man on the other side had seen him, had sprung to the door, flung it open, and stood at attention.

Manske saw that here was his opportunity. He snatched off his hat. "Sir," he cried, "one moment, for God's sake."

"Well?" inquired the official sharply.

"Where can I obtain an order of admission?"

"To see——?"

"My dear patron, Herr von Lohm, who by some incomprehensible and appalling mistake——"

"You must go to the judge who conducted the preliminary inquiries."

"But who is he, and where is he to be found?"

The official looked at his watch. "If you hurry you may still find him at the Law Courts. In the next street. Examining Judge Schultz."

And the door was shut.

So they went to the Law Courts, and hurried up and down staircases and along endless corridors, vainly looking for someone to direct them to Examining Judge Schultz. The building was empty; they did not meet a soul, and they went down one passage after the other, anguish in Anna's heart, and misery hardly less acute in Manske's. At last they heard distant voices echoing through the emptiness. They followed the sound, and found two women cleaning.

"Can you direct me to the room of the Examining Judge Schultz?" asked Manske, bowing politely.

"The gentlemen have all gone home. Business hours are over," was the answer. Could they perhaps give his private address? No, they could not; perhaps the porter knew. Where was the porter? Somewhere about.

They hurried downstairs again in search of the porter. Another ten minutes was wasted looking for him. They saw him at last through the glass of the entrance door, airing himself on the steps.

The porter gave them the address, and they lost some more minutes trying to find their Droschke, for they had come out at a different entrance to the one they had gone in by. By this time Manske was speechless, and Anna was half dead.

They climbed three flights of stairs to the Examining Judge's flat, and after being kept waiting a long while— "Der Herr Untersuchungsrichter ist bei Tisch," the slovenly girl had announced—were told by him very curtly that they must go to the Public Prosecutor for the order. Anna went out without a word. Manske bowed and apologised profusely for having disturbed the Herr Untersuchungsrichter at his repast; he felt the necessity of grovelling before these persons whose power was so almighty. The Examining Judge made no reply whatever to these piteous amiabilities, but turned on his heel, leaving them to find the door as best they could.

The Public Prosecutor lived at the other end of the town. They neither of them spoke a word on the way there. In answer to their anxious inquiry whether they could speak to him, the woman who opened the door said that her master was asleep; it was his hour for repose, having just supped, and he could not possibly be disturbed.

Anna began to cry. Manske gripped hold of her hand and held it fast, patting it while he continued to question the servant. "He will see no one so late," she said. "He will sleep now till nine, and then go out. You must come to-morrow."

"At what time?"

"At ten he goes to the Law Courts. You must come before then."

"Thank you," said Manske, and drew Anna away. "Do not cry, liebes Kind," he implored, his own eyes brimming with miserable tears. "Do not let the coachman see you like this. We must go home now. There is nothing to be done. We will come early to-morrow, and have more success."

They stopped a moment in the dark entrance below, trying to compose their faces before going out. They did not dare look at each other. Then they went out and drove away.

The stars were shining as they passed along the quiet country road, and all the way was drenched with the fragrance of clover and freshly-cut hay. The sky above the rye fields on the left was still rosy. Not a leaf stirred. Once, when the coachman stopped to take a stone out of a horse's shoe, they could hear the crickets, and the cheerful humming of a column of gnats high above their heads.

CHAPTER XXXI

Gustav von Lohm found Manske's telegram on his table when he came in with his wife from his afternoon ride in the Thiergarten.

"What is it?" she inquired, seeing him turn pale; and she took it out of his hand and read it. "Disgraceful," she murmured.

"I must go at once," he said, looking round helplessly.

"Go?"

When a wife says "Go?" in that voice, if she is a person of determination and her husband is a person of peace, he does not go; he stays. Gustav stayed. It is true that at first he decided to leave Berlin by the early train next morning; but his wife employed the hours of darkness addressing him, as he lay sleepless, in the language of wisdom; and the wisdom being of that robust type known as worldly, it inevitably produced its effect on a mind naturally receptive.

"Relations," she said, "are at all times bad enough. They do less for you and expect more from you than anyone else. They are the last to congratulate if you succeed, and the first to abandon if you fail. They are at one and the same time abnormally truthful, and abnormally sensitive. They regard it as infinitely more blessed to administer home-truths than to receive them back again. But, so long as they do not actually break the laws, prejudice demands that they shall be borne with. In my family, no one ever broke the laws. It has been reserved for my married life, this connection with criminals."

She was a woman of ready and frequent speech, and she continued in this strain for some time. Towards morning, nature refusing to endure more, Gustav fell asleep; and when he woke the early train was gone.

In the same manner did his wife prevent his writing to his unhappy brother. "It is sad that such things should be," she said, "sad that a man of birth should commit so vulgar a crime; but he has done it, he has disgraced us, he has struck a blow at our social position which may easily, if we are not careful, prove fatal. Take my advice—have nothing to do with him. Leave him to be dealt with as the law shall demand. We who abide by the laws are surely justified in shunning, in abhorring, those who deliberately break them. Leave him alone."

And Gustav left him alone.

Trudi was at a picnic when the telegram reached her flat. With several of her female friends and a great many lieutenants she was playing at being frisky among the haycocks beyond the town. Her two little boys, Billy and Tommy, who would really have enjoyed haycocks, were left sternly at home. She invited the whole party to supper at her flat, and drove home in the dog-cart of the richest of the young men, making immense efforts to please him, and feeling that she must be looking very picturesque and sweet in her flower-trimmed straw hat and muslin dress, silhouetted against the pale gold of the evening sky.

Her eye fell on the telegram as the picnic party came crowding in.

"Bill coming home?" inquired somebody.

"I'm afraid he is," she said, opening it.

She read it, and could not prevent a change of expression. There was a burst of laughter. The young men declared they would never marry. The young women, prone at all times to pity other women's husbands, criticised Trudi's pale face, and secretly pitied Bill. She lit a cigarette, flung herself into a chair, and became very cheerful. She had never been so amusing. She kept them in a state of uproarious mirth till the small hours. The richest lieutenant, who had found her distinctly a bore during the drive home, went away feeling quite affectionate. When they had all gone, she dropped on to her bed, and cried, and cried.

It was in the papers next morning, and at breakfast Trudi and her family were in every mouth. Bibi came running round, genuinely distressed. She had not been invited to the picnic, but she forgot that in her sympathy. "I wanted to catch you before you start," she said, vigorously embracing her poor friend.

"Where should I start for?" asked Trudi, offering a cold cheek to Bibi's kisses.

"Are you not going to Herr von Lohm?" exclaimed Bibi, open-mouthed.

"What, when he tries to cheat insurance companies?"

"But he never, never set fire to those buildings himself."

"Didn't he, though?" Trudi turned her head, and looked straight into Bibi's eyes. "I know him better than you do," she said slowly.

She had decided that that was the only way—to cast him off altogether; and it must be done at once and thoroughly. Indeed, how was it possible not to hate him? It was the most dreadful thing to happen to her. She would suffer by it in every way. If he were guilty or not guilty, he was anyhow a fool to let himself get into such a position, and how she hated such fools! She registered a solemn vow that she had done with Axel for ever.

At Kleinwalde the effect of the news was to make Frau Dellwig slay a pig and send out invitations for an unusually large Sunday party. She and her husband could hardly veil their beaming satisfaction with a decent appearance of dismay. "What would his poor father, our gracious master's oldest friend, have said!" ejaculated Dellwig at dinner, when the servant was in the room.

"It is truly merciful that he did not live to see it," said his wife, with pious head-shakings.

What Anna was doing at Stralsund, no one knew. She said she was having some bother with her bank. Miss Leech related how they had been to the bank on the Monday. "I must go again," Anna said on the evening of the fruitless

Tuesday, when she had been the whole day again with Manske, vainly trying to obtain permission to visit Axel; and she added, her head drooping, her voice faint, that it was a great bore. Certainly she looked profoundly unhappy.

"One cannot be too careful in money matters," remarked Frau von Treumann, alarmed by Anna's white looks, and afraid lest by some foolish neglect on her part supplies should cease. She enthusiastically encouraged these visits to the bank. "Take care of your bank," she said, "and your bank will take care of you. That is what we say in Germany."

But Anna did not hear. There was but one thought in her mind, one cry in her heart—how could she reach, how could she help, Axel?

He was in a cell about five yards long by three wide. There was just room to pass between the camp bedstead and the small deal table standing against the opposite wall. Besides this furniture, there was one chair, an empty wooden box turned up on end, with a tin basin on it—that was his washstand—a little shelf fixed on the wall, and on the little shelf a tin mug, a tin plate, a pot of salt, a small loaf of black bread, and a Bible. The walls were painted brown, and the window, fitted with ground glass, was high up near the ceiling; it was barred on the outside, and could only be opened a few inches at the top. On the door a neat printed card was fastened, giving, besides information for the guidance of the habitually dirty as to the cleansing properties of water, the quantity of oakum the occupant of the cell would be expected to pick every day. The cell was used sometimes for condemned criminals, hence the mention of the oakum; but the card caught Axel's eye whenever he reached that end of the room in his pacings up and down, and without knowing it he learnt its rules by heart.

At first he had been completely dazed, absolutely unable to understand the meaning and extent of the misfortune that had overtaken him; but there was a grim, uncompromising reality about the prison, about the heavy doors he passed through, each one barred and locked behind him, each one cutting him off more utterly from the common free life outside, about the look of the miserable beings he met being taken to or from their work by armed warders, about the warders themselves with their great keys, polished by frequent use—there was about these things an inexorable reality that shook him out of the blind apathy into which he had fallen after his arrest. Some extraordinary mistake had been made; and, knowing that he had done nothing, when first he began to think connectedly he was certain that it could only be a matter of hours before he was released. But the horror of his position was there. Released or not released, who would make good to him what he was suffering and what he would have lost? He had been searched on his arrival—his money, watch, and a ring he wore of his mother's taken from him. The young official who arrested him—he was the Junior Public Prosecutor—presided at these operations with immense zeal. Being young and obscure, he thirsted to make a name for himself, and opportunities were few in that little town. To be put in charge, therefore, of this sensational case, was to behold opening out before him the rosiest prospects for the future. His name, which was Meyer, would flare up in flames of glory from the ashes of Axel's honour. Stralsund, ringing with the ancient name of Lohm, would be forced to ring simultaneously with the less ancient and not in itself interesting name of Meyer. He had arrested Lohm, he had special charge of the case, he could not but be talked about at last. His zeal and satisfaction accordingly were great, carrying him far beyond the limits usual on such occasions. Axel stood amazed at the trick of fortune that had so suddenly flung him into the power of a young man called Meyer.

Soon after he was locked in his cell, a warder came in with a great pot of liquid food, a sort of thick soup made chiefly of beans, with other bodies, unknown to Axel, floating about among them.

"Your plate," said the warder, jerking his head in the direction of the little shelf on which stood Axel's dining facilities; and he raised the pot preparatory to pouring out some of its contents.

"Thank you," said Axel, "I don't want any."

"You'll be hungry then," said the man, going away. "There is no more food to-day."

Axel said nothing, and he went out. The smell of the soup, which was apparently of great potency, filled the little room. Axel tried to open the window wider, but though he was tall and he stood on his table, he could not reach it.

It began to get dark. The lamps in the street below were lit, and the shouts of the children at play came up to him. He guessed that it must be past nine, and wondered how long he was to be left there without a light. As it grew darker, his thoughts grew very dark. He paced up and down more and more restlessly, trying to force them into clearness. In the hurry and dismay he had left his keys at Lohm, he remembered, and all his money and papers were at the mercy of the first-comer. And he was poor; he could not

afford to lose any money, or any time. Supposing he were
to be kept here more than a few hours, what would become
of his farming, just now at its busiest season, his people
used to his constant direction and control, his inspector
accustomed to do nothing without the master's orders? And
what would be the moral effect on them of his arrest? If he
had a pencil and paper he would write some hasty messages
to keep them all at their posts till his return; but he had no
writing materials, he was quite helpless. He had sent urgent
word to his lawyer in Stralsund, telegraphing to him
through Manske before leaving home, and he had expected
to find him waiting for him at the prison. But he had not
come. Why did he not come? Why did he leave him
helpless at such a moment? Axel was determined to face
his misfortune quietly; yet the feeling of absolute
impotence, of being as it were bound hand and foot when
there was such dire necessity for immediate action, almost
broke down his resolution.

But it was only for a few hours, he assured himself,
walking faster, thrusting his hands deeper into his pockets,
and he could bear anything for a few hours. His brothers
would come to him—to-morrow the first thing his lawyer
would certainly come. It was all so extremely absurd; yet it
was amazing the amount of suffering one such absurd
mistake could inflict. "Thank God," he exclaimed aloud,
stopping in his walk, struck by a new thought, "thank God
that I have neither wife nor children." And he paced up and
down again more slowly, his shoulders bent, his head sunk,
a dull flush on his face; he was thinking of Anna.

The door was unlocked, and a warder with a bull's-eye
lantern came in quickly. "The Public Prosecutor is coming
up," he said breathlessly. "When he comes in, you stand at

attention and recite your name and the crime of which you are accused."

He had hardly finished when the Public Prosecutor appeared. The warder sprang to attention. Axel slowly and unwillingly did the same.

"Well?" snarled the great man, as Axel did not speak. He was an old man, with a face grown sly and hard during years of association with criminals, of experiences confined solely to the ugly sides of life.

"My name is Lohm," said Axel, feeling the folly of attempting to defy anyone so absolutely powerful in the place where he was; and he proceeded to explain the crime of which he was suspected.

The Public Prosecutor, who knew perfectly well everything about him, having himself arranged every detail of the arrest, said something incomprehensible and was going away.

"May I have a light of some sort?" asked Axel, "and writing materials? I absolutely must be able to——"

"You cannot expect the luxuries of a Schloss here," said the Public Prosecutor with a scowl, turning on his heel and signing to the warder to lock the door again. And he continued his rounds, congratulating himself on having demonstrated that in his independent eye the bearer of the most ancient name and the offscourings of the street, tried or untried, were equal—sinners, that is, all of them—and would receive exactly the same treatment at his hands. Indeed, he was so anxious to impress this laudable impartiality on the members of the little prison-world, which was the only world he knew, that he overshot the mark, refusing Axel small conveniences that he would have unhesitatingly granted a suppliant called Schmidt, Schultz, or Meyer.

It was now quite dark, except for the faint light from the lamps in the street below. Weary to death, Axel flung himself down on the little bed. He had brought a few necessaries, hastily thrown into a bag by his servant, necessaries that had first been carefully handled and inspected with every symptom of distrust by the Junior Public Prosecutor Meyer; but he did not unpack them. Judging from the shortness of the bed, he concluded that criminals must be a stunted race. Sleeping was not made easy by this bed, and he lay awake staring at the shadows cast by the iron bars outside his window on to the ceiling. These shadows affected him oddly. He shut his eyes, but still he saw them; he turned his head to the wall and tried not to think of them, but still he saw them. They expressed the whole misery of his situation.

He had dozed off, worn out, when a bright light on his face woke him. He started up in bed, confused, hardly remembering where he was. A feeling very nearly resembling horror came over him. A bull's-eye lantern was being held close to his face. He could see nothing but the bright light. The man holding it did not speak, and presently backed out again, bolting the door behind him. Axel lay down, reflecting that such surprises, added to anxiety and bad food, must wear out a suspected culprit's nerves with extraordinary rapidity and thoroughness. There could not, he thought, be much left of a man in the way of brains and calmness by the time he was taken before the judge to clear himself. The incident completely banished all tendency to sleep. He remained wide awake after that, tormented by anxious thoughts.

Towards dawn, for which he thanked God when it came, the silence of the prison was broken by screams. He started up again and listened, his blood frozen by the sound of them. They were terrible to hear, echoing through that place. Again a feeling of sheer horror came over him. How long would he be able to endure these things? The screams grew more and more appalling. He sprang up and went to the door, and listened there. He thought he heard steps outside, and knocked. "What is that screaming?" he cried out. But no one answered. The shrieks reached a climax of anguish, and suddenly stopped. Death-like stillness fell again upon the prison. Axel spent what was left of the night pacing up and down.

The prison day did not begin till six. Axel, used to his busy country life that got him out of his bed and on to his horse at four these fine summer mornings, heard sounds of life below in the street—early carts and voices—long before life stirred within the walls. He understood afterwards why the inmates were allowed to lie in bed so long: it was convenient for the warders. The prisoners rose at six, and went to bed again at six, in the full sunshine of those June afternoons. Thus disposed of, the warders could relax their vigilance and enjoy some hours of rest. The effect, moralising or the reverse, on the prisoners, who could by no means get themselves off to sleep at six o'clock, was of the supremest indifference to everyone concerned. Axel, not yet having been tried, and not yet therefore having been placed in the common dormitory, was not forced into bed at any particular time. He might enjoy evenings as long as those of the warders if he chose, and he might get up as early as though his horse were waiting below to take him to his hay-fields if he liked; but this privilege, without the means of employing the extra hours, was valueless. He watched anxiously for the broad daylight that would bring his lawyer and put an end to this first martyrdom of helpless waiting. Towards seven, one of the prisoners, whose good conduct had procured him promotion to cleaning the passages and doing other work of the kind, brought him another loaf of bread and a pot of coffee. From this young man, a white-faced, artful-looking youth, with closely-cropped hair and wearing the coarse, brown prison dress, Axel heard that the ghastly screams in the night came from a prisoner who had delirium tremens; he had been put in the cellar to get over the attack; he could scream as loud as he liked there, and no one would hear him; they always put him in the cellar when the attacks came on. The young man grinned. Evidently he thought the arrangement both good and funny.

"Poor wretch," said Axel, profoundly pitying those other wretched human beings, his fellow-prisoners.

"Oh, he is very happy there. He plays all day long at catching the rats."

"The rats?"

"They say there are no rats—that he only thinks he sees them. But whether the rats are real or not it amuses him trying to catch them. When he is quiet again, he is brought back to us."

A warder appeared and said there was too much talking. The young man slid away swiftly and silently. He was a thief by profession, of superior skill and intelligence.

Axel ate part of the bread, and succeeded in swallowing some of the coffee, and then began his walk again, up and down, up and down, listening intently at the door each time he came to it for sounds of his lawyer's approach. The morning must be halfway through, he thought; why did he not come? How could he let him wait at such a crisis? How could any of them—Gustav, Trudi, Manske—let him wait at such a crisis? He grew terribly anxious. He had expected Gustav by the first train from Berlin; he might have been with him by nine o'clock. The other brother, he knew, would be less easily reached by the telegram—he was attached to the person of a prince whose movements were uncertain; but Gustav? Well, he must be patient; he may not have been at home; the next train arrived in the afternoon; he would come by that.

The door opened, and he turned eagerly; but it was the Public Prosecutor again.

"Name, name, and crime!" frantically whispered the accompanying warder, as Axel stood silent. Axel repeated the formula of the night before. Every time these visits were made he had to go through this performance, his heels together, his body rigid.

"Bed not made," said the Public Prosecutor.

"Bed not made," repeated the warder, glaring at Axel.

"Make it," ordered the chief; and went out.

"Make it," hissed the warder; and followed him.

His lawyer came in simultaneously with his dinner.

"Plate," said the warder with the pot.

"This is a sad sight, Herr von Lohm," said the lawyer.

"It is," agreed Axel, reaching down his plate. He allowed some of the mess to be poured into it; he was not going to starve only because the soup was potent.

"I expected you yesterday," he said to the lawyer.

"Ah—I was engaged yesterday."

The lawyer's manner was so peculiar that Axel stared at him, doubtful if he really were the right man. He was a native of Stralsund, and Axel had employed him ever since he came into his estate, and had found his work satisfactory, and his manners exceedingly polite—so polite, indeed, as to verge on cringing; but then, as Manske would have pointed out, he was a Jew. Now the whole man was changed. The ingratiating smiles, the bows, the rubbed hands, where were they? The lawyer sat at his ease on the one chair, his hands in his pockets, a toothpick in his mouth, and scrutinised Axel while he told him his case, with an insolent look of incredulity.

"He actually believes I set the place on fire," thought Axel, struck by the look.

He did actually believe it. He always believed the worst, for his experience had been that the worst is what comes most often nearest the truth; but then, as Manske would have explained, he was a Jew.

The interview was extremely unsatisfactory. "I have an appointment," said the lawyer, pulling out his watch before they had half discussed the situation.

"You appear to forget that this is a matter of enormous importance to me," said Axel, wrath in his eyes and voice.

"That is what each of my clients invariably says," replied the lawyer, stretching across the table for his gloves.

"How can we arrange anything in a ten minutes' conversation?" inquired Axel indignantly.

The lawyer shrugged his shoulders. "I cannot neglect all my other business."

"I do not remember your having been so pressed for time formerly. I shall expect you again this afternoon."

"An impossibility."

"Then to-morrow the first thing. That is, if I am still here."

The lawyer grinned. "It is not so easy to get out of these places as it is to get in," he said, drawing on his gloves. "By the way, my fees in such cases are payable beforehand."

Axel flushed. He could hardly believe the evidence of his senses that this was the obsequious person who had for so long managed his affairs. "My brother Gustav will arrange all that," he said stiffly. "You know I can do nothing here. He is coming this afternoon."

"Oh, is he?" said the lawyer sceptically. "Is he indeed, now? That will be a remarkable instance of brotherly devotion. I am truly glad to hear that. Good-afternoon," he nodded; and went out, leaving Axel in a fury.

The one good result of his visit was that some time later Axel was provided with writing materials. He immediately fell to writing letters and telegrams; urgent letters and telegrams, of a desperate importance to himself. When his coffee was brought he gave them to the warder, and begged him to see that they were despatched at once; then he paced up and down again, relieved at least by feeling that he could now communicate with the outer world.

"They have gone?" he asked anxiously, next time he saw the warder. "Jawohl," was the reply. And gone they had, but only by slow stages to the office of the Examining Judge Schultz, where they lay in a heap waiting till he should have leisure and inclination to read them, and, if he approved of their contents, order them to be posted. There they lay for three days, and most of them were not passed after all, because the Examining Judge disliked the tone of the assurances in them that the writer was innocent. He knew that trick; every prisoner invariably protested the same thing. But these protestations were unusually strong. They were of such strength that they actually produced in his own hardened and experienced mind a passing doubt, absurd of course, and not for one moment to be considered, whether the Stralsund authorities might not have blundered. It was a dangerous notion to put into people's heads, that the Stralsund authorities, of whom he was one, could blunder. Blunders meant a reproof from headquarters and a retarded career; their possibility, therefore, was not to be entertained for a moment. Even should they have been made, it must not get about that they had been made. He accordingly suppressed nearly all the letters.

Gustav must have missed the second train as well, for when the sky grew rosy, and Axel knew that the sun was setting, he was still alone.

The few hours he had thought to stay in that place were lengthening out into days, he reflected. If Gustav did not come soon, what should he do? Someone he must have to look after his affairs, to arrange with the lawyer, to be a link connecting him with outside. And who but his brother and heir? Still, he would certainly come soon, and Trudi too. Poor little Trudi—he was afraid she would be terribly upset.

But the hours passed, and no one came.

That evening he was given a lamp. It burnt badly and smelt atrociously. He asked if the window might be opened a little wider. The request had to be made in writing, said the warder, and submitted through the usual channels to the Public Prosecutor, without whose permission no window might be touched. Axel wrote the request, and the warder took it away. It came back two days later with an intimation scrawled across it that if the prisoner von Lohm were not satisfied with his cell he would be given a worse one.

The night came, and had to be gone through somehow. Axel sat for hours on the side of his bed, his head supported in his hands, struggling with despair. A profound gloom was settling down on him. The knowledge that he had done nothing had ceased to reassure him. The lawyer was right when he said that it was easier to get into such a place than to get out again. Klutz had denounced him, to save himself; of that he had not a doubt. And Dellwig, well known and greatly respected, had supported Klutz. This explained Dellwig's conduct lately completely. Axel's courage was perilously near giving way as he recognised the difficulty he would have in proving that he was innocent. If no one helped him from outside, his case was indeed desperate. He did not remember ever to have turned his back on a friend in distress; how was it, then, that not a friend was to be found to come to him in his extremity? Where were they all, those jovial companions who shot over his estate with him so often, driving any distance for the pleasure of killing his game? What was keeping Gustav back? Why did he not even send a message? How was it that Manske, who professed so much attachment to his house, besides such stores of Christian charity, did not make an effort to reach him? He had never asked or wanted anything of anyone in his life; but this was so terrible, his need was so extreme. What a failure his whole life was. He had been alone, always. During all the years when other men have wives and children he had been working hard, alone. He had had no happy days, as the old Romans would have said. And now total ruin was upon him. Sitting there through the night, he began to understand the despair that impels unhappy beings in a like situation, forsaken of God and men, to make wild efforts to get out of such places, conscious that they avail nothing, but at least bruising and crushing themselves into the blessed indifference of exhaustion.

The hours dragged by, each one a lifetime, each one so packed with opportunities for going mad, he thought, as he counted how many of them separated him already from his free, honourable past life. By the time morning came, added to his other torturing anxieties, was the fear lest he should fall ill in there before any steps had been taken for his release. He sat leaning his head against the wall, indifferent to what went on around him, hardly listening any more for Gustav's footsteps. He had ceased to expect him. He had ceased to expect anyone. He sat motionless, suffering bodily now, a strange feeling in his head, his thoughts dwelling dully on his physical discomforts, on the closeness of the cell, on the horrible nights. He made a great effort to eat some dinner, but could not. What would become of him if he could neither eat nor sleep? On what stores of energy would he be able to draw when the time came for defending himself? He was sitting by the table, leaning his head against the wall, his eyes closed, when the prisoner-attendant came to take away his dinner. "Ill?" inquired the young man cheerfully. Axel did not move or answer. It was too much trouble to speak.

The warder, upon the attendant's remarking that No. 32 seemed unwell, examined him through the peep-hole in the door, but decided that he was not ill yet; not ill enough, that is. In another week he would be ready for the prison doctor, but not yet. These things must take their course. It was always the same course; he had been a warder twenty years, and knew almost to an hour the date on which, after the arrest, the doctor would be required.

Axel was sitting in the same position when, about three o'clock, the door was unlocked again. He did not move or open his eyes.

"Ihr Fräulein Braut ist hier," said the warder.

The word Braut, betrothed, sent Axel's thoughts back across the years to Hildegard. His betrothed? Had he heard the mocking words, or had he been dreaming? He turned his head and looked vaguely towards the door. All the sunlight was out there in the wide corridor, and in it, on the threshold, stood Anna.

What had she meant to say? She never could remember. It had been something deeply apologetic, ashamed. But her fears and her shame fell from her like a garment when she saw him. "Oh, poor Axel—oh, poor Axel——" she murmured with a quick sob.

He tried to get up to come to her. In an instant she was at his side, and, stumbling, he fell on his knees, holding her by the dress, clinging to her as to his salvation. "It is not pity, Anna?" he asked in a voice sharp with an intolerable fear.

And Anna, half blinded by her tears, deliberately put her arms round his neck, relinquishing by that one action herself and her future entirely to him, hauling down for ever her flag of independent womanhood, and bending down her face to that upturned face of agonised questioning laid her lips on his. "No," she whispered, and she kissed him with a passionate tenderness between the words, "it is only love—only love——"

CHAPTER XXXII

There was a grave beauty, an austerity almost, about this betrothal in the prison. Here was no room for the archnesses and coynesses of ordinary lovemaking. All that was not simple truth fell away from them both like tawdry ornaments, for which there was no use in that sad place. Soul to soul, unseparated by even the flimsiest veil of conventionality, of custom; soul to soul, clear-visioned, steadfast, as those may be who are quietly watching the approach of death, they looked into each other's eyes and knew that they were alone, he and she, against the world. To cleave to one another, to stand together, he and she, against the whole world,—that was what their betrothal meant. Axel, cut off for ever from his kind if he should not be able to clear himself, Anna, cutting herself off for ever to follow him. Her feet had found the right path at last. Her eyes were open. As two friends on the eve of a battle in which both must fight and whose end may be death, or as two friends starting on a long journey, whose end too, after tortuous ways of suffering, may well be death, they quietly made their plans, talked over what was best to be done, gravely encouraging each other, always with the light of perfect trustfulness in their eyes. How strong they felt together! How able to go fearlessly towards the future to meet any pain, any sorrow, together! The warder standing by, the miserable little room, the wretched details of the situation, no longer existed for either of them. Nothing could harm them, nothing could hurt them any more, if only they might be together. They were safe within a circle drawn round them by love—safe, and warm, and blest. So long as he had her and she him, though they saw how great their misery would be if they came to be less brave, they could not but believe in the benevolence of the future, they could not but have hope. If he were sentenced, she said, what, at the worst, would it mean? Two years', three years', waiting, and then together for the rest of their life. Was not that worth looking forward to? Would not that take away every sting? she asked, her hands on his shoulders, her face beautiful with confidence and courage. When he told her that she ought not now to cast in her lot with his, she only smiled, and laid her cheek against his sleeve. All her childish follies, and incertitudes, and false starts were done with now. Life had grown suddenly simple. It was to be a cleaving to him till death. Yet they both knew that when that golden hour was over, and she must go, the suffering would begin again. She was only to come twice a week; and the days between would be days of torture. And when the moment had come, and they had said good-bye with brave eyes, each telling the other that so short a separation was nothing, that they did not mind it, that it would be over before they had had time to feel it, and the door was shut, and he was left behind, she went out to find misery again, waiting for her there where she had left it, taking entire possession of her, brooding heavily, immovably over her, a desolation of misery that threatened by its dreadful weight to break her heart.

A sense of physical cold crept over her as she drove home with Letty—the bodily expression of the unutterable forlornness within. Away from him, how weak she was, how unable to be brave. Would Letty understand? Would she say some kind word, some little word, something, anything, that might make her feel less terribly alone? With many pauses and falterings she told her the story, looking at her with eyes tortured by the thought of him waiting so patiently there till she should come again. Letty was awestruck, as much by the profound grief of Anna's face as by the revelation. She knew of course that Axel had been arrested—did anyone at Kleinwalde talk of anything else all day long?—but she had not dreamt of this. She could find nothing to say, and put out her hand timidly and laid it on Anna's. "I am so cold," was all Anna said, her head drooping; and she did not speak again.

As they passed between his fields, by his open gate, through the village that belonged, all of it, to him, she shut her eyes. She could not look at the happy summer fields, at the placid faces, knowing him where he was. Not the poorest of his servants, not a ragged child rolling in the dust, not a wretched, half-starved dog sunning itself in a doorway, whose lot was not blessed compared to his. The haymakers were piling up his hay on the waggons. Girls in white sun-bonnets, with bare arms and legs, stood on the top of the loads catching the fragrant stuff as the men tossed it up. Their figures were sharply outlined against the serene sky; their shouts and laughter floated across the fields. Freedom to come and go at will in God's liberal sunlight—just that—how precious it was, how unspeakably precious it was. Of all God's gifts, surely the most precious. And how ordinary, how universal. Only for Axel there was none.

When they reached the house, the hall seemed to be full of people. The supper bell had lately rung, and the inmates, talking and laughing, were going into the dining-room. Dellwig, his hands full of papers, not having found Anna at home, was in the act of making elaborate farewell bows to the assembled ladies. After the two silent hours of suffering that lay between herself and Axel, how strange it was, this noisy bustle of daily life. She caught fragments of what they were saying, fragments of the usual prattle, the same nothings that they said every day, accompanied by the same vague laughs. How strange it was, and how awful, the tremendousness of life, the nearness of death, the absolute relentlessness of suffering, and all the prattle.

"Um Gottes Willen!" shrieked Frau von Treumann, when she caught sight of this white image of grief set suddenly in their midst. "It has smashed up, then, your bank?" And she made a hasty movement towards the hall table, on which lay a letter for Anna from Karlchen, containing, as she knew, an offer of marriage.

Anna turned with a blind sort of movement, and stretched out her hand for Letty, drawing her to her side, instinctively seeking any comfort, any support; and she stood a moment clinging to her, gazing at the little crowd with sombre, unseeing eyes.

"What has happened, Anna?" asked the princess uneasily.

"You must congratulate me," said Anna slowly in German, her head held very high, her face of a deathly whiteness.

A lightening look of comprehension flashed into Dellwig's eyes; he scarcely needed to hear the words that came next.

"Herr von Lohm and I were to-day," she said. Then she looked round at them with a vague, piteous look, and put her hand up to her throat. "We shall be married—we shall be married—when—when it pleases God."

CONCLUSION

The moral of this story, as Manske, wise after the event, pointed out when relating those parts of it that he knew on winter evenings to a dear friend, plainly is that all females—alle Weiber—are best married. "Their aspirations," he said, "may be high enough to do credit to the noblest male spirit; indeed, our gracious lady's aspirations were nobility itself. But the flesh of females is very weak. It cannot stand alone. It cannot realise the aspirations formed by its own spirit. It requires constant guidance. It is an excellent material, but it is only material in the raw."

"What?" cried his wife.

"Peace, woman. I say it is only material in the raw. And it is never of any practical use till the hand of the master has moulded it into shape."

"Sehr richtig," agreed the friend; with the more heartiness that he was conscious of a wife at home who had successfully withstood moulding during a married life of twenty years.

"That," said Manske, "is the most obvious moral. But there is yet another."

"The story is full of them," said the friend, who had had them all pointed out to him, different ones each time, during those evenings of howling tempests and indoor peace—the perfect peace of pipes, hot stoves, and Glühwein.

"The other," said Manske, "is, that it is very sinful for little girls to write love-poetry in the name of their aunts."

"To write love-poetry is at no time the function of little girls," said the friend.

"Such conduct cannot be too strongly censured," said Manske. "But to do it in the name of someone else is not only not mädchenhaft, it is sinful."

"These English little girls appear to know no shame," said his wife.

"Truly they might learn much from our own female youth," said the friend.

Letty's poems had undoubtedly been the indirect cause of the fire, of Axel's arrest, and of his marriage with Anna. But if they had brought about Anna's happiness, a happiness more complete and perfect than any of which she had dreamed, they had also brought about Klutz's ruin. For Klutz, shattered in nerves, weak of will, overcome by the state of his conscience and the possible terrors of the next world, with the blood of three generations of pastors in his veins, every drop of which cried out to him day and night to save his soul at least, whatever became of his body, Klutz had confessed. He was only twenty, he knew himself to be really harmless, he had never had any intentions worse than foolish, and here he was, ruined. The act had been an act of temporary madness; and influenced by Dellwig, he had saved his skin afterwards as best he could. Now there was the price to pay, the heavy price, so tremendous when compared to the smallness of the follies that had led him on step by step. His bad genius, Dellwig, went free; and later on lived sufficiently far away from

Kleinwalde to be greatly respected to the end of his days. Manske's eyes filled with tears when he came to the action of Providence in this matter—the mysteriousness of it, the utter inscrutableness of it, letting the morally responsible go unpunished, and allowing the poor young vicar, handicapped from his very entrance into the world by his weakness of character, to be overtaken on the threshold of life by so terrific a fate. "Truly the ways of Providence are past finding out," said Manske, sorrowfully shaking his head.

"I never did believe in Klutz," said his wife, thinking of her apple jelly.

"Woman, kick not him who is down," said her husband, turning on her with reproachful sternness.

"Kick!" echoed his wife, tossing her head at this rebuke, administered in the presence of the friend; "I am not, I hope, so unwomanly as to kick."

"It is a figure of speech," mildly explained the friend.

"I like it not," said Frau Manske gloomily.

"Peace," said her husband.

Made in the USA
Coppell, TX
01 November 2020

40637894R00236